BE MY
December

the crawford brothers, book #1

Becky
Will you be
Ky's december?
♡ Rachel Brookes xoxo

RACHEL BROOKES

Final editing: Jennifer Sell
First round editing: Jenny Sims from Editing4Indies
Proofreading: Ellie from LoveNBooks and Emma from Tink's Typos
Cover photography: Perrywinkle Photography
Cover Design: Wicked By Design
EBook and Paperback Formatting: Champagne Formats

ISBN-13: 978-1502310101
ISBN-10: 1502310104

Other Books

The Breathe Series
Just Breathe
Breathless
Breathe Again

DEDICATED *to those who thought they'd lost it all.*

Life will give you the greatest gift when you least expect it.

Always believe.

Prologue

Four Years Earlier

"I SAID NO, JEREMY!"

The sound of my weak, pleading voice didn't offer my shivering body one piece of desperately-craved strength. The skin on my arm seared under his dominant grip, and I could barely keep up with his broad stride through the empty college grounds. At one point, I swear my feet weren't even touching the graveled ground below.

"Man, where are you going?"

A savior's voice rang out through the freezing air, and we stopped moving. Safety was close. A glimmer of hope hit me as my eyes darted around the darkness, trying to make out who was coming to my rescue.

"Help," I choked out, my voice lost in the severe coldness around me.

"Shut the fuck up," Jeremy Davis snarled at me, and his threatening grip tightened on my arm. "Just heading to the dorm to grab some more booze, will be back at the party soon," he said loudly, his voice calm and way too convincing.

We remained still, waiting for my savior's next move. I prayed to every god there was that he would offer to help and that he would move closer and be able to make me out, but he remained in the shadows, simply a distant voice.

"Please, let me go," I begged, and my heart sunk as my

savior disappeared into the pitch black night sky.

The dwindling temperature of December in New York was the least of my worries as the wind swirled around my naked shoulders, fiercely biting my flesh. Every word I sputtered out between clenched teeth was laced with pure fear. Where was the stubborn, strong, and highly-resilient Eden Rivers who had stepped through the doors of her first keg party only hours ago?

I stumbled on the heel of my boot when possessive hands thrust sharply into my back as we began to move. I was pushed up the stairs to the dorm rooms with such intensity that my long, dark hair whipped sharply around my face. The moment I was pushed through the door, my eyes, desperate to adjust to the darkness of the room, bounced around the four walls surrounding me. The glow from the street light illuminated the space, but I wished there was no light at all. My shallow breathing and the grunts of the man who stalked toward me like a possessed animal broke the silence. A petrified shiver cascaded down my back as reality slammed me squarely in the chest, and I was soon backed up against the far wall with no escape. His face was brutal, stone cold, and evil. My eyes slammed shut as he manhandled me, running his hands over my breasts, down my sides, and soon fumbling in the confines of my panties. I pushed against his broad chest with every ounce of strength I could muster, but it was useless, and he barely moved.

"No! No! No!" I repeatedly screamed, so loudly that my voice went hoarse and was barely audible. Survival instincts kicked in, and my nails scratched at his face and my body thrashed in pure fight.

A vicious blow to my left cheek stole the air from my lungs, and my mouth was invaded by the metallic taste of blood. My vision instantly went hazy, and I swayed on my feet.

"That's going to be the biggest fucking mistake of your life, Eden! Big fucking mistake," Jeremy hissed, his spittle hitting my face and bringing me back to reality.

2

In the minutes that followed, as the perfect world I knew was destroyed, I ceased to exist as Eden Rivers. With the ruthless tear of my panties and the pain of a thousand knives digging into the most sacred and untouched part of my body, everything disappeared around me and I vanished into darkness as blow after blow tore within me.

From that moment, I would become a yes girl—as saying no seemed to be the worst decision I ever made.

KY

" **I** AM SOOOOOOOOOOOOOOO GETTING my dick wet tonight."

What the fuck?

I rolled my eyes at the over-exaggeration of my pussy-obsessed brother's admission as he burst into my apartment like he owned the place. Friday afternoon fuck-ups were happening all over the place at work. My assistant had gone home sick earlier in the day, the marketing department fucked up the advertisements for the next issue, and there was an issue mounting in the Los Angeles office. At two o'clock, I had enough and escaped to my apartment to get some much-needed work done in peace. Well, that was until my over-eager brother decided to visit.

"You whip out lines like that, yet you still wonder why Mom asks why you are single?" I shot as I stood from the couch and moved toward the kitchen.

"Dude, you and I both know that single is what we do best."

My laughter ricocheted off the cream walls of my ninth-floor apartment that were lined with black and white abstract photographs of cities around the world, including Paris, Sydney, New York, and London. My job at Anderson Publications allowed me to revel in escapism—traveling and working obscenely long hours. It provided me with the distraction I needed, and allowed my fucked-up head a moment of peace from the regrets that continually haunted me.

My life had been a whirlwind since I started working at

Anderson Publications. Anderson Publications was an internationally-renowned publishing company, founded by my father's best friend, Roger Anderson, a man who had, without a doubt, saved me more times than he would ever know.

During college, as I double majored in Business and Marketing, he took me under his wing and became my mentor, much to my parents' delight. My college years were all about basketball with the guys, banging numerous girls, and partying with my frat brothers. I lived the college dream until my senior year. That was when everything went to shit. When the life I knew, the life I had planned, fell apart around me because of one fucked-up, life-changing mistake. A mistake that haunted me ever since.

That was the moment I changed. Studying became my life; I shied away from my usual crowd, and I stopped partying, which was unheard of for a guy who held my stature. My parents and Josh were in a constant state of worry while I pretended as if life was moving on perfectly well. Thankfully, it was during this time that Roger Anderson saw my quick demise and swooped in. I was not sure if it was Mom and Dad who influenced his decision, but I would be forever thankful for his intrusion into my life at my time of need. His brutal honesty put me on the right track, and it was within a couple of weeks that I started working at his company.

I sure as hell didn't get my job handed to me on a gold platter. If anything, he made me work twice as hard to get where I am. Now, after five and a half years under his watchful eye, I was leading the marketing team at *Bangs and Beats.* I had a high-paying job, which provided me with a very comfortable life. I invested my money wisely when I first started working, and now I am the owner of the building that Josh and I live in, all at the age of twenty-six.

"So tell me big brother, how long has it been since you've been between some sweet thighs?"

The amusement in Josh's tone wasn't lost in his question. I rolled my eyes at his taunt and nodded when he held up a Corona he'd just pulled out of my refrigerator, as I took a seat at the breakfast bar.

He moved around the sparkling white space with chrome appliances and midnight-black accessories like the arrogant prick he was because he knew exactly how long it had been.

After grabbing a fresh lime from the fruit bowl, he sliced it up and shoved a piece down the neck of the Corona. When I finally met his gaze, he looked at me expectedly as I snatched the beer from his hands.

"It's been too fucking long," I growled in response, before taking a long swig of beer.

Why the fuck did we need to talk about this? Immediately, my head and my dick started reacting to the thought of the last woman I'd been with. The feisty and leggy Samantha, a British model who had been hired to be the cover model for last month's issue of the magazine. My best friend, Ashlyn, the assistant stylist for the shoot, had forced me into attending the cover reveal party. After one too many free celebratory beers, I was balls deep in Samantha in the supply closet of one of the ritziest cocktail bars in New York City, fucking like my life depended on it.

"Let's go out for a drink. You, me, the new sports bar, strippers, and pussy?"

I shot him a look of pure outrage. "Strippers and pussy should never be mentioned in the same sentence."

He moved around the kitchen island and pulled out a stool, taking a seat opposite me as a knowing look swept over his smug face. "Are you saying you've never fucked a stripper?" His question dripped with amusement, and I knew he had me by the balls.

"Fuck off! She was a dancer. Big fucking difference."

A muffled groan poured out from deep within my chest, and

I knew I wasn't going to win this battle. Of course, he would suggest going out. It was Friday night, and for the past three weeks I had made every excuse under the sun not to go out for a drink. He had accepted it, but I knew it was only a matter of time before he wore me down. The thing with Josh and me was that we had a relationship that couldn't be matched. Yes, he was my younger brother, but he was also my best friend. We have been through thick and thin together, seen the best and worst of what life could offer, and we have come through the other side—with a few hiccups along the way. There had been plenty of times when he annoyed the shit out of me, to the point of wanting to punch his face in, but I would take a bullet for him without question or a couple of broken bones from bar fights when he tried to pick up the wrong woman. He was my blood. It was as simple as that.

"So, are you and your little guy going to come out tonight or what?" Josh cocked a brow in my direction.

I was tired. I was beyond exhausted, and letting off some steam seemed like an enticing prospect when I thought about it. Honestly, a strip club would just equal trouble, but it could also mean an easy lay. It was a catch twenty-two.

"Just come out. A couple of drinks and a few titties. What's the worst that can happen?"

"You are a persistent little prick. Pick me up at nine."

The stabbing aggression of the headache that had been annoying me for a couple of days sprung back to life the moment Josh and I stepped into Delights. Low lights, soft pulsating music, and an atmosphere thick with sex and greed hit me with full force. Everything about this place exuded excess, temptation, and the whispered promise of sex. Within seconds, two scantily-clad women made a beeline for us. Suddenly, my date for the night seemed to be a tight little blonde named Lyndsey, who was hanging off my every word and looking at me with expectation.

Now don't get me wrong, I was a man, and I fucking loved women. But I certainly didn't have any plans for securing anything long term, much to the disgust of my mom. In her eyes, I should have a house in the 'burbs with at least two kids running around by now. I certainly shouldn't have a ninth-floor bachelor pad and work fifteen-hour days. Of course, I had sexual needs, and I fed those needs when required, but my needs didn't include a relationship. And it certainly didn't include a happily-fucking-ever after. That kind of happiness was foreign to me, and the reasons why have continued to squeeze and taunt me, eating away at my total being in an attempt to destroy me.

It was something that I had to live with. It was something I kept so tightly strapped to my chest that only a few knew. As long as she was still hurting, and as long as I still hated everything I was, I would never give myself a chance of happiness or contentment. I didn't deserve it; it was as simple as that.

"You do realize that I'm a sure bet." Lindsey grabbed my attention and licked her lips, before rubbing herself aggressively against me. Any urge to take this woman to a motel room faded the moment she said those words. I liked the thrill of the chase, the game, the anticipation. This woman in front of me would have allowed me to fuck her in the middle of the room if I'd asked her. I groaned inwardly and shook that thought out of my head.

I was content with doing what I wanted, when I wanted, with whomever I wanted, and that included women. I wasn't a male slut, I didn't jump from bed to bed, from pussy to pussy, from woman to woman, but I knew where to go when I wanted it, and I knew what to do or say to guarantee I wasn't left unsatisfied. I left the slut tag for my brother who was now standing beside me.

"So who's the unlucky girl who is, as you put it, wetting

your dick tonight?" I asked, and then tilted back my head to allow the beer to cascade down my throat, blatantly ignoring the advances of Lindsey, much to her annoyance.

"Ky and Joshua Crawford, about damn time you showed your handsome faces."

Josh didn't get a chance to answer, as the sound of my best friend's sultry voice filled the space behind me. Ashlyn Hart's amused eyes found mine the moment I spun around to face her.

"Who's this?" Ashlyn nodded at Lindsey, who still stood close beside me and had attached herself to my arm.

"Lindsey," I said. "And she was just leaving."

"I can't believe you got him to leave the office." Ashlyn fired a wink in Josh's direction, something I chose to ignore and turned back to me. "It's good to see you out and about, even if you do have *something* hanging off you."

"Are we getting out of here or what?" Lindsey shot me one last pleading look, obviously choosing to ignore my earlier statement and Ashlyn's insult.

I shook my head dismissively. I ran my hands through my thick dark hair and groaned as tightness flooded my pants. It was almost like my dick was telling me what an idiot I was to say no to an easy lay. With a huff, Lindsey spun away from me and stormed through the crowd and out of my sight. I felt like a prick because I was thankful for the peace her leaving offered.

"What the fuck was that?" Ashlyn shot in amusement, as her eyes bounced back to mine. "I know it's been a while between fucks, but shit, that was desperation if I've ever seen it. I am proud of you for keeping your dick in your pants."

"Can we at least have one drink in our systems before we start discussing the lack of action my dick has had lately?" I laughed as I turned to the bar to give the bartender our order.

As I waited for the drinks, I tapped the bar with my fingers and hummed along to some random top-forty song that was thumping through the place.

My patience wavered. Just as I was ready to cancel the order and head home, a flash of red gripped a tight hold of my attention. Through the sea of men and women, my eyes followed the stunning brunette's every step. Instant recognition flashed within me, and I sucked in a sharp unsteady breath the moment she turned around and I saw her face.

It couldn't be.

I spun around and leaned my back against the bar, allowing myself to get lost in the vision before me. My eyes, full of intrigue and lust, ran the length of her body several times. Dressed in skinny jeans that hugged her curves like a second skin, the red jacket she wore opened so subtly, allowing a glimpse of her enticing chest. I was completely captivated as I took in everything about the girl in the red jacket.

As she dodged and weaved her way through the crowd, her wide eyes scoped out the room. Loose curls fell over her shoulder and swayed over the middle of her back. She looked so out of place amongst the lingerie-covered women surrounding me, yet she was the only one holding my attention.

"Eden Rivers."

At the sound of Ashlyn's admission, I tore my gaze from my new obsession for the night and raised an eyebrow in question. "What did you say?"

"The girl you are staring at is Eden Rivers." The smile gracing Ashlyn's face was magnificent, and it took me a moment to realize she was holding out my beer. I grabbed it, and immediately lifted it to my lips, desperate for some calm to sweep over me.

Eden Rivers.

"Fuck."

I knew exactly who she was.

Eden

FOR THE LAST FOUR years, I thought of myself as a walking contradiction, an enigma of society's belief of what a twenty-four-year-old woman should be like. I was Eden Rivers. Daughter, best friend, survivor, and tonight, on a cold November night in New York City, I was putting on my best mask and becoming the party girl everyone should be on their twenty-fourth birthday.

My best friend Tori and I had just spent four days driving cross-country. We had stopped at all the cliché road stops, taking honorary photos in front of inappropriate signs and landmarks, singing off-key to hits of the eighties, and eating way too much junk. But the fun all but dissolved into a smoldering pit of unwanted torment the moment we crossed the New York state line. Now I was back in the city I had promised myself I would never step foot in again.

For the past four years, I had created a safety blanket in San Francisco. My life revolved around taking photos and getting lost in the escapism that it provided me. Most of my conscious hours were spent hidden behind the lens or sitting at my desk overlooking San Francisco Bay editing photos. The thing I loved most about photography was that I could create a different world, a different scene, simply by a few clicks of a button. It was my comfort, and the hundreds of photos I had taken were my therapy. Hiding behind my laptop and a camera allowed me to shut down the fear of being pushed into a situation I had no control over. Control was now everything to me—it was the air in my lungs, the beat of my heart—and I needed it to survive. I controlled my life and the people I allowed to get close to me with such a strong will. I needed that. It was crucial for my ability to function, and it allowed me to create a world that would let me find a purpose. It allowed me to be whoever I wanted to be when I needed to be someone else. The scariest part of my new life was that I had absolutely no clue exactly who I was anymore. Who was Eden Rivers?

Pretending to be someone else was how I survived, and it seemed to be working for now. The best part was that it allowed me to go through life as a blank canvas. Whenever I wanted, I could transform into whoever I wanted to be when the need arose, and tonight I would have to pull out the big guns—tonight I was back in New York City, I was back in nightmare territory, and I had to give the impression that I was having a damn good time.

We stepped through the double doors of Delights, which was described online as a gentlemen's club with high-class strippers and Victoria's Secret-dressed girls at your beck and call. It would be the perfect place to escape for a few hours, because what man would pay attention to me when there were buxom blondes and sultry brunettes wearing expensive lingerie right at their fingertips.

"Aren't you glad we came out tonight?" Tori asked excitedly, bumping her hip against mine in the process. "We have so much to celebrate, Eden! My girl is having a birthday, and there is every chance you will be surrounded by hot rock stars for the next few weeks. I have a feeling someone is going to get laid."

Ahh yes, the very reason I had returned, and no, it had nothing to do with the promise of getting laid, much to Tori's frustration.

It happened three weeks ago when I was on my morning run along Pier 39. The crisp fall air of San Francisco blanketed my body, and my mind was busily planning my day ahead, which included two fashion shoots for a local designer. As I stopped, hunched over and gasping for air, I received an email. An email with the Subject line: Meeting Request. The moment I opened it, the bubble that I had created for myself in San Fran quickly started to deflate around me. I read the email more times than I could possibly count. The words—we want you; amazing talent; rock bands; our magazine—were the ones that stuck out, the words that seized my attention. It was an offer that was so unrealistic that I didn't believe it to be real. This kind of opportunity had the potential to change my life. I still didn't understand how they had come across my work, but I knew that word of mouth was rife in this industry. , So what was the life changing opportunity I was offered, the one reason I went against everything I had promised myself and come back to my nightmare? It was the chance to shoot the cover and editorial for a leading music magazine that would take my photography global.

Anderson Publications was known everywhere. I was a fan of many of their magazines and had spent a lot of time relaxing in the bath with a glass of wine and their latest issue, and the fact that they wanted me was unimaginable. The magazine they wanted me for was *Bangs and Beats,* which—surprise, surprise—was located in New York . . . The one place I said I'd never return to.

So here I was, in the midst of a gentlemen's club in the belly of New York City, with a meeting booked for the following week. I couldn't fucking say no, because I had a best friend who told me I'd be stupid to reject the offer handed to me.

Story of my life.

I stood anxiously beside Tori, enclosed by the safety of women flaunting the bodies they had been blessed with, and men whose hungry eyes were locked on every other woman but us. I sighed in relief. The tension in my shoulders escaped. Two things about this place offered the safety I needed; first, knowing that I was the most overdressed woman in the place; and second, that men with this kind of money were only concerned with the women shaking their goods in their faces. Yep, this was my safety net, and this was the reason Tori and I frequented strip clubs and highly-exclusive clubs when we wanted a night out on the town. These kinds of establishments offered me the chance to fade into the shadows and not allow myself to get into a situation where I couldn't control the outcome. Thank fuck I had a best friend who liked to party, no matter where it was.

"You know what? I think it's time I let my hair down." Even allowing those words to fall from my lips caused me to shudder in shock. It was my damn birthday, and I should be allowed to celebrate. Yep, it was my night. "However, that certainly doesn't mean I am looking to get laid. You know that's not me."

"What!" she shrieked, loud enough to be heard over the loud thump of the bass pounding out of the speakers around us. "Eden Rivers is letting her hair down?"

"Fuck off!" I chuckled deeply, thanking my lucky stars that she didn't mention anything about my, not getting laid comment. I wrapped my arm around the girl who knew every deep dark secret there was in the life of Eden Rivers, and took off in the direction of the main bar.

My eyes scoped out the place, mostly focusing on the patrons around me. Men in suits, with their wealth clearly on display, occupied the mahogany tables and deep tub chairs, while their lips took in the taste of expensive scotch and their eyes darkened with lust. Women surrounded me, dressed in high-class lingerie with immaculate makeup and perfectly-manicured hair, giving the men exactly what they wanted. They were the perfect prey for the lions waiting in the wings. This was definitely the perfect place to celebrate my birthday. Another year, another chance to try and figure out who in the hell I was.

I struggled daily with the idea of being the girl I thought I had to be and the girl I now was. The life I lived would never compare to the life I believed I would have at the age of twenty-four. Shouldn't I have a college degree, be open to a loving relationship, and be living a life without constant panic or restrictions? No. That life was ripped away four years ago. December sixteenth. The night Jeremy Davis decided I didn't deserve a choice, that I was purely a piece of meat that he assumed he could devour in a dimly-lit college dorm room. It was on that night he ripped my innocence away from me without consideration or consent.

Today I lived the life of Eden Rivers, the girl with a smile plastered on her face as her heart died one flashback at a time. The girl who said yes to everything asked of her in fear of the consequences of saying no, and the girl who pretended to be someone else every chance she got. I held no pride in being a yes girl, but there wasn't a damn thing I could do about it. Saying yes kept me safe, it held me in a tight cocoon where I could shut off every emotion that was drowning me. It was a simple word that didn't even mean a thing to me anymore.

"Who are you tonight?" Tori's inquisitive voice asked beside me, raising one of her perfectly groomed brows in my direction. She knew me way too well. This was the one question I knew she'd ask; it was a guaranteed every time we stepped foot out of our apartment for a night out. I took another glance around the bar, allowing my brain to scroll through the many faces of Eden Rivers.

I turned back toward her, a smile the size of the Grand Canyon spreading over my face. Into character, I would go. "I am Kellie, a teacher from Chicago, and I am in town for the weekend with my best friend to celebrate my birthday."

"Kellie it is."

"Now that we have discussed my alter-ego let's go and get the most colorful and stupidly alcoholic drinks we can order and shove dollar bills down the panties of willing women?" I winked suggestively. "Kellie wants to have some fun."

Tori's infectious laughter sounded around us, providing the encouragement I needed and killing the nerves that were swarming inside of me. I could do this. She wrapped an arm around my waist as we weaved our way through the pulsating crowd and headed toward the corner of the bar where the lights were low and the music was soft. I pulled out one of the empty bar stools and took a seat, immediately grabbing the cocktail menu.

The space around me grew thick with sound, the music echoing through the bar as the first show of the night began. The deep thump of the bass pulsated through my body, rattling every bone. I glanced quickly toward the front as a sultry redhead wearing deep purple lingerie strutted onto the stage. *Gorgeous lingerie,* even if I did say so myself. I was a sucker for sexy lingerie; it was almost a shame that no one got to see it. The little baby pink panty and bra set gracing my body tonight would have definitely been good to show someone. I scoffed at my thoughts, knowing full well that the only person who would be seeing it would be Tori when we got back to the hotel. And that would only be because I would be drunk and have a lack of modesty.

My friendship with Tori was so unconventional. It began the moment she opened her townhouse to me when I first arrived in San Francisco and found her roommate wanted ad online. What I believe she failed to realize was that she saved me that day; she became my security blanket and my confidant as I tried to reclaim what little there was left of me.

"Can you order two cosmopolitans, two quick fucks, and two jaeger bombs? That should do us." I winked as I slid off the stool. "I need to go to the ladies' room."

"Do you want me to come with you?"

"I'm good. I'll be back soon."

I took off, weaving my way through the crowd. I averted my eyes from the couple of men who acknowledged my existence and gripped hold of my clutch, increasing my pace. I pushed open the bathroom door with my hip and took a deep breath as the solitude of the glamorous 1800s-inspired bathroom immersed me. Grasping onto the marbled top of the vanity, I looked at my disheveled reflection staring back at me and a grin spread across my face. The heat from the club had caused my eye makeup, which I spent an hour working on, to melt and begin its descent from the outline of my sea blue eyes. My lips no longer had the gloss I entered with, and the pinkness of my cheeks showed the warmth circulating through my body. I was on a quick path to looking like a hot mess and, for some crazy reason, I couldn't be happier.

"Are you okay?"

I spun on my heel at the sound of a throaty yet sultry voice behind me. I inhaled sharply at the stunning woman with platinum blond hair shimmering around her shoulders and wide emerald green eyes that were gazing back at me. I scanned her face—her makeup was impeccable, her hair perfectly styled, and the way she wore the skinny jeans, off-the-shoulder black top, and killer turquoise heels made her look like an absolute bombshell.

"Yep, sorry, I don't mean to hold up the bathroom." I turned back quickly, leaned over the vanity, and painted my lips in blood-red gloss, giving them a quick smack together before I smiled at my reflection and then turned back to face her.

"Eden Rivers?" She gasped as recognition flashed over her face. "I'm Ashlyn Hart."

My jaw hit the ground as I took in the beauty before me. This woman wasn't the Ashlyn Hart I remembered from college. Long gone were the thick glasses, the braces, and the large, oversized shirts that hid her body.

My silence and obvious gawking caused her to chuckle.

"Yeah, I've changed a bit over the years. My annoying big brother likes to say I'm an ugly duckling who transformed into a swan."

"You look beautiful." I finally found my voice and gave her a nervous yet friendly smile. I was not planning on reuniting with anyone from my past while I was here, but now, on my first night back, I was running headfirst into my past, and someone from college at that.

Ashlyn Hart had been in a few of my classes and lived in the same dorm. We spoke in passing, but she was always so shy and kept to herself. She was exactly like I was now. That Ashlyn was entirely different than the Ashlyn standing before me who now had confidence and charisma emanating from her.

Ashlyn's brow furrowed as she moved toward the vanity and began applying her own lip gloss. "I never thought I'd see you again."

Fuck! This wasn't the conversation I wanted to have in the bathroom of a high-end gentlemen's club, especially not on my birthday. I dropped my eyes to the floor and started twisting my hands as the first signs of panic bubbled to the surface.

She caught on to my shift in mood and thankfully changed the subject by saying, "Just so you're aware, you are officially known as the girl in the red jacket to a guy out there."

"Uh, well, that's interesting." I laughed nervously and shook my head.

"You have someone out there who is showing more interest in you than he has in anyone in God only knows how many years." Her emerald eyes sparkled as my cheeks flushed a deep crimson.

"What's his name?"

"K—"

"Eden Rivers, we have a bar full of drinks, and I am ready to celebrate your birthday in style, so put your Kellie Carter hat on and get the fuck out there!" Tori strutted through the bathroom, her hands on her hips, and a look of pure determination cemented on her face. She completely missed that we weren't in the bathroom alone.

"Jesus, don't get your panties in a knot." I laughed, rolling my eyes at my excitable friend. I turned back toward Ashlyn to find her slipping her lip gloss in her clutch, and her gaze met mine. Shit! Tori had mentioned Kellie Carter. "I, uh, use a pretend name when I'm out. It's like a thing I do."

I held my breath as I awaited her response. It sounded so pathetic. I was a grown woman who pretended I was someone else when I went out. God, she was going to think I was a complete idiot.

"Who am I to judge? Kellie it is." Ashlyn's smile was infectious, and I found myself smiling back at her.

"How about you just be Eden tonight?" Tori suggested as she looked anxiously at Ashlyn, a look I didn't miss. "How about you try it? I'll be right by your side."

Was she serious? Where the hell was this coming from?

"Tori, I can't," I whispered, and instantly my defenses shot to life.

"Babe, you can but you won't."

"Tori, this isn't the place to discuss this. Tonight I am Kellie, and that's the only way I will be staying here. Your choice. Am I staying or leaving?"

"Just trust me, Eden. This isn't the nigh—"

"Am I staying or leaving?" I repeated and the look of defeat that flooded her face gave me my answer.

Tori shifted her eyes away from mine, and they landed on Ashlyn.

"Ashlyn, Tori . . . Tori, Ashlyn. I went to college with Ashlyn," I announced and looked between the girls. I couldn't ignore the look in Ashlyn's eye as she watched me. I didn't even want to think about the rumors, the comments, and the snickers about me after I suddenly disappeared from college four years ago.

I shook the thought from my head and moved toward the door. I stopped when I grabbed hold of the handle and turned back to look at Ashlyn.

"How would you feel about coming and having a drink with us for my birthday? As you heard, drinks have arrived, and there are women just waiting to strip for my birthday."

"How could I possibly refuse an offer like that?"

"Ready?" I asked with a fake smile as I shifted my gaze between Tori and Ashlyn while my insides were jittery with nerves.

"Sure," Tori mumbled, and her energetic need to get me back out into the club seemed to have disappeared quicker than I could say boo.

"Babe, please just let me do this. I promise that next time we are out back home I'll just be known as Eden."

Tori crossed the room until she stood beside me and wrapped an arm around my waist, pulling me in close. "What happens if there is someone out there, what if there is a guy out there who may make you believe in guys again?"

"That's very unlikely, babe." I huffed.

"But what if there is?" she continued, pestering. "Will you at least give the guys out there a chance?" Tori's voice dripped with a motherly tone. Seriously, was she really going to act like I was thirteen?

Frustration raged like a wild bull within me. My fists clamped, and my fingernails dug into my palms like sharpened blades. Tori was the one person who knew my inability to say a word as simple as no, but here she was, blatantly rubbing it in my face and pushing me until I was balancing precariously on the edge of completely losing it. Suddenly a feeling of rebellion roared to life, and I lifted my eyes from the floor to meet hers.

"Yes."

I plastered the biggest smile I could muster on my lips and

shifted my gaze back toward the mirror to give myself the once-over while silently wishing for confidence to burst to life within me. My gaze fixated squarely on the girl who reflected back at me. My blue eyes were wide and swam with reluctance, and my red painted lips were drawn tight together in stubbornness. I was very aware of who this girl was, and I knew there was no way in the world that she could be around tonight. I swallowed hard, and it only took a couple of frantic blinks to witness the girl I knew as Eden Rivers disappear right before my eyes as my gaze turned resilient. I was the girl in the red jacket; I was Kellie Carter, and I'd be fucked if I didn't play the part. I had been pretending for four years, what damage could another few hours of soul-destroying lies do?

"Let's go," I shout.

I didn't wait for their response. I pushed the heavy door open and instantly my body was intoxicated by the music coming from the stage. My lingerie-envy resurfaced as I focused on a vivacious blonde strutting around in a lacy black number. Note to self: put a Victoria's Secret visit in my planner. My heels vibrated against the wooden floorboards as I walked with fake confidence toward the bar. I slid onto the barstool I had abandoned and slammed down the first shot I saw.

The stool beside me scraped against the floor, and Ashlyn slid in and joined me at the bar. We sat in a comfortable silence, yet I couldn't help but notice her eyes falling to me on more than one occasion, or the subtle smile regularly gracing her lips. Ashlyn and Tori began flirting up a storm with a handsome bartender, who seemed to be glued to the space in front of us, while I continued to swirl the cosmopolitan around in front of me.

My eyes were drawn across the bar as the feeling of being watched swept through me like a torrent. It wasn't lost on me that Ashlyn not-so-subtly looked over the shoulder of the bartender as he flirted with her, and she seemed to be distracted by something or someone. My eyes locked onto the culprit, whose eyes were fixated on me. I felt my stomach flip-flop at the sight of the man across the bar. He looked to be a few years older than me and was dressed in a black button-down shirt that clung to his broad chest, with the sleeves rolled up to his elbows, revealing strong arms. My curious eyes took him in; thick brown hair, a strong jaw covered in stubble, and intense eyes. And the moment his lips twitched into a smile when he realized he was caught, a dimple appeared.

Oh God.

His eyes bounced quickly from mine, and he turned his body away from the bar, leaning effortlessly with his back toward me. A woman with bleach-blond hair, heavy makeup, and a scrap of red lace covering her surgically-enhanced body sidled up to him and proceeded to put her hands all over him. He stiffened under her touch, and his head shook from side to side as she leaned in to say something to him.

I couldn't tear my eyes away from him.

My instinct to ogle a handsome man took over. No matter what lock I had placed on my body and heart, I was still a woman, he was a beautiful man, and my eyes didn't listen as my head told me to look away.

Suddenly, without warning, he cocked his head to the side and flashed his gaze back to me, and this time I was the one caught staring. A hint of a smile flickered over his lips, giving me the opportunity to relish in the perfectly-placed dimple in his right cheek yet again.

I felt myself nervously return his smile, something that I never did. How strong were these drinks? The smile that hung on his lips suddenly fell, and his eyes narrowed in on something happening behind me.

"I'm going to take you home tonight."

A hot thick breath battered my bare neck as unwanted fingers ran down the length of my back. My throat immediately tightened, squeezing out every last bit of air I could muster, and my eyes shot wide with fear at the sound of those words. *Fuck.* Slowly, on its own accord, my body twisted on the bar stool and I came face to face with the intruder. The moment I looked at him, I felt the cockiness he was portraying smack me hard. The smug look on his face as his beady, imposing eyes roamed over my face and then focused solely on my chest, caused bile to rise from the depths of my stomach. Where the hell was Tori? Ashlyn? When did they disappear? My eyes finally latched on to Ashlyn walking toward the other side of the bar, and Tori was nowhere to be found.

I was on my own.

"Come and have a drink with me?"

No!

My mind completely shut off. I felt myself floating away from reality. My body reacted before I could comprehend what I was doing, before I could stop myself. The threatening tone of his voice and the burning of his fingertips into my flesh made me shift into survival mode, and I knew I had to protect myself by allowing my body to say yes. *Just like I had for the past four years.* I rose to shaky feet and his hand gripped tightly around my arm, causing a shot of pain to roar through my body as he jerked me away from the bar.

We moved away from the main bar, and the dim lights above that were intended to add an ambiance were now providing the perfect cover for me to be taken into the shadows. He pulled me toward a vacant couch and proceeded to push me down until I was practically sitting on his lap. I had to allow my mind to shut off, to take me to a place of solitude and bliss, away from the reality pressing into me in the form of his over-eager hands. My eyes darted through the club, and they fell to the man from across the bar.

"What the fuck are you doing?"

I jumped at the harsh statement that threatened in front of me. The voice was thick, with a velvety tone that oozed confidence and intimidation, and the undertones of a growl weren't missed. If a voice could cause a shiver to run down your spine that would ignite every part of your body, then his voice was exactly that. Safety had arrived, in the form of the man from across the bar.

KY

THE MOMENT EDEN WALKED back into the bar, I took her in without reluctance. She was a perfect example of uniqueness; a vision of nervousness, while desperation to leave radiated from her. I watched with increased interest as she made her way back across the bar with Ashlyn. Fuck me.

I sat at the bar, completely engrossed by this girl. The moment our eyes first connected, I immediately turned into a fucking dog in heat. Josh had disappeared to god-only-knows where and, as beer passed my lips, my gaze never faltered.

My body stiffened, and I watched in complete horror as Chris Edwards slithered up behind Eden, just after she had given me the sweetest of smiles. It felt like it happened in slow motion. Eden stood from the bar stool and allowed Chris Edwards to lead her to the far corner of the club without question, his hand gripping her arm with force. His other hand was all over her, fawning her body like a piece of fucking meat. Her eyes darted furiously around the bar, looking for something or someone to latch on to. Panic filled her face. She didn't want to be there. My legs moved before my brain kicked in. I was sure I heard Ashlyn's voice behind me, yelling for Josh, but I couldn't be sure, and to be honest it was the least of my concerns. I marched across the floor like a possessed caveman or something just as fucked-up. My eyes never moved from her. No one deserved to be in the presence of Chris fucking Edwards.

"Don't!" Ashlyn appeared beside me and grabbed hold of

my arm, desperate to stop me and my manic thoughts. It was no good; I was like a charging bull, with only red in my sight. It was pretty fucking accurate, considering I was storming toward the girl in the red jacket.

"Leave it," I snapped back, and continued moving to the girl who looked frozen stiff with fear.

Her eyes rose from the floor and found mine amongst the crowd and, for a brief moment, hope flashed before me as she locked onto my gaze. I shuddered at the thought that this would be our introduction, but I couldn't let that stop me. I felt bile rise from the pits of my stomach as Chris's hand skimmed up the length of her thigh. When his lips fell to her neck and his fingers brushed over her crotch, I felt a fury pulsate through me that I never knew existed. Fuck this! I increased my pace until I was almost at a jog.

I'd come to believe that your past shaped your present, and your present influenced your future, and right now it was slapping me in the face. My past had molded me into the person I was today. A man whose faults, regrets, and worst mistakes swam through his veins and were so ingrained in his memories that there was no chance of hiding. However, on the flip side, it had also made me a man who refused to stand back; it made me not give a fuck and it made me storm across a crowded room to save a girl who didn't know who the fuck I was.

The moment I stood before them, I exploded.

"What the fuck are you doing?" I roared with such fevered intensity that even the stripper on stage froze for a moment. "I turn my back for two fucking minutes, and it's just enough time for you to disappear and let this guy feel you up? You are mine. Stand up." I glared at her as my teeth gritted shut. Eden's eyes widened, and the color fell from her face as she took in my words. I was yelling in this poor girl's face. I heard Ashlyn inhale sharply behind me, and out of the corner of my eye, I saw Josh standing with the woman I had earlier seen with Eden.

Chris put his filthy hand on Eden's ass as she attempted to stand, and pulled her back into his lap. "Piss off, Crawford. This one is mine. Go back to your preppy little office and leave us the fuck alone."

I saw red. "Get. Your. Fucking. Hands. Off. Her."

"She wants it, and she certainly hasn't said no. Look at this tight little body, the little slut was begging for it." His hands tauntingly ran up and down her thighs, running higher than they should as a smug look took over his face.

I reached out and snatched her hand, pulling her away from his grasp with all of my strength until she crashed into my chest.

"Stay here," I growled into her ear, hauling her close to my body, which allowed me to feel her thudding heart against my chest. I wrapped my arms tightly around her waist, locking her in, and then turned my attention back to Chris. "Get the fuck out of here Edwards, and stay away from my fucking girlfriend."

A cocky laugh boomed from him as he stood. "She isn't your girlfriend." He hissed, glaring at us. "I know what this is. You just want to dive into that sweet pussy yourself, don't you Crawford?"

I unlocked Eden from my embrace and moved her so she was standing behind me. With one step, I was chest to chest with Chris. I didn't hesitate. "I don't just dive into her pussy, Edwards. I fuck it hard, I taste every inch of it, and I savor every time her body shudders against mine. That pussy is mine, so just remember that when you are fucking some three-dollar hooker tonight."

I didn't stick around to hear anything else Chris decided to spit. My hand encased Eden's, entwining our fingers in some protective move that I couldn't put into words. I tugged at our joined hands, and she instantly followed me through the crowd toward the far corner of the bar. I knew we would still be close enough to the action, but we would also be hidden from the fuckwit likes of Chris. My mind raced with what I could possibly say to explain my irrational actions. Since when had I become some knight in shining armor? When we reached a vacant couch, I halted and promptly dropped her hand from mine. Stepping back, I collided with the hard wall of Josh's body, and over my shoulder I found him staring at me with curious eyes. I ran my hands through my unruly hair and groaned in frustration.

"Do something, dickhead. All eyes are on you after that little performance. You don't go caveman and grab your *woman,* and then just stand beside her like she's a stranger," Josh threw at me, and his eyes darted between me and Eden.

He was right. I looked back toward the sleazy corner of the bar and wasn't surprised to find Chris and his crew watching with knowing smirks on their faces. I had two choices. I could walk away and leave the bar knowing that I had done a good deed and hope that Eden could take care of herself, or I could man the fuck up and finish off what I started.

Within a heartbeat, Eden was against my chest, and my arms were wrapped tightly around her waist so her back was to me. Resting my chin on the top of her head, I couldn't help but notice how well her body molded against mine. She still hadn't spoken, but her body roared every unspoken word. She was rigid in my arms, frozen in fear and what I was sure was confusion, and after I heard her inhale sharply, she held her breath.

I leaned down until my mouth was beside her ear and whispered, "You've got to breathe."

She merely nodded, while she trembled like a leaf in a hurricane against me. Her hands clutched onto my forearms that I rested over her stomach and her sharp nails dug into my flesh, sending a shot of pain up through my arms, but I didn't say a thing.

Her body continued to tremble, and my grip tightened, pulling her body closer to mine. She was completely breaking down in my arms, and I didn't know what the fuck to do, so I did what I hoped would calm her down—I attempted to provide her comfort and quiet while the crowds around us continued with their night, completely oblivious to what was happening.

"I need a drink." I barely heard her voice.

"Come again?"

She turned her face until she was looking at me, her eyes filled with panic. "I need a drink," she repeated louder.

"Come on then." I released my grip, and my hand fell to the small of her back as we moved toward the black leather couch.

She haltered and whispered, "I'm sorry."

Two words that no woman should ever say when it came to what I just witnessed. She turned around slowly, only for me to find her eyes brimming with tears ready to spill over her cheeks. She inhaled sharply at the look of sheer outrage that I knew graced my face.

"Look at me," I demanded, and painstakingly waited for her blue eyes to meet mine.

Finally, she looked at me, and I let out a breath. "You have nothing to be sorry about. You hear me? Nothing."

"Who are you?" she asked meekly as her eyes danced over my face.

Who was I? How could I possibly answer that question?

"I am the guy who's going to keep you the fuck away from assholes like Chris. That's who I am."

Eden

IMISSED HIS SECURITY the moment he left.

It confused the hell out of me.

I twisted my hands in my lap, and my eyes shifted around the bar as fear revisited me. I looked at everyone like they were a threat. This was the part that I hated; the paranoia, the never-ending fear, the crazy thoughts that swamped my mind.

"Can someone please tell me what just happened?" I asked, finally finding my voice as I shifted my gaze and watched the man with the super soft hands storm toward the bar. I could feel my body trembling against the black leather of the couch I sat on, and my heart was thumping erratically in my chest. If I didn't get myself under control within the next couple of minutes, I would collapse into a wave of panic, and that was something I didn't want anyone to witness.

"It seems that my brother is playing the knight in shining armor card tonight."

A deep voice rumbled behind the couch, and words laced with amusement and intrigue grabbed hold of my attention. I shifted on the couch and found a guy who held a strong resemblance to the stranger who, just minutes ago, had screamed in my face and then saved me from the evil clutches of who I now knew as Chris.

"This is Josh. Josh, this is, uh . . . Kellie." Tori introduced us, her voice trembling as she spoke.

At the sound of my *name,* Josh's eyes flashed quickly to Ashlyn, who looked on with an entirely unreadable look on her face, before he found my eyes again. "Nice to meet you, *Kellie.*"

I shook the hand he held out, and then he and Ashlyn collapsed on the couch opposite me and fell into a quiet conversation. I leaned back against the plush leather and took the opportunity to take in the guy who had offered me protection in a very confrontational way. He stood rigid at the bar, his shoulders slumped as he looked at his phone. He was a towering figure of strength and intimidation; a vision that deserved respect. Tall, masculine, with sensuality dripping off him, he oozed confidence.

"Are you okay?" Tori asked, grabbing my hand as she took a seat beside me. When I turned toward her, I was greeted with worry etched on her face, which offered me a unique kind of comfort.

"I'm not sure," I admitted.

I was safe. I was away from the threat, but my heart continued to beat furiously in my chest, and I felt myself jump every time someone would come too close to me. I hadn't been in a situation like that since that fateful day. I was usually so careful. I usually had Colby with me. My inability to say a word as simple as no frustrated me. It was a hindrance and an open invitation to the wrong people, just as it had been tonight. But my fear of the consequences was so overwhelming that it overshadowed every other option.

"I am so sorry I wasn't there." Her voice wavered under her words.

"This isn't your fault. Look at it this way, you got your wish. I'm now waiting for a drink that's being bought by a handsome guy." I nodded toward the bar and once again took in my rescuer.

"Do you know who he is?" she asked as her eyes ran over

his body.

"No clue."

"Fuck he is hot though, and he can't keep his eyes off you."

I felt my cheeks flush at her words, and, as if he was magnetic, I found myself drawn to look at him yet again. I inhaled sharply as I found his eyes fixed on me. He stood at the bar, leaning back against it with a beer bottle in his hand. He looked like he was contemplating something. Was he planning to escape? He had no reason to stick around, but I knew I had to thank him, and I had to do it a million times over.

When I couldn't bear being under his gaze any longer, I shifted on the couch and focused everywhere but him. I counted the number of lights that lit up the chandelier above, I scrutinized the lingerie the girls were wearing, and I mentally made a note of what I wanted to look at when I next visited Victoria's Secret. I was in the middle of determining whether the cute blonde was wearing violet or midnight blue panties, when the couch beside me dipped and my senses were overcome by the familiar scent of who I now knew as Crawford.

KY

SITTING IN THE VIP section, I felt like I was dangling between crazy and euphoric, ready to either crash or soar. Beside me sat the girl in the red fucking jacket, the same girl who had just dealt with me screaming in her face. She was frozen stiff against me, her hands clasped tightly in her lap and her eyes fixated on the floor below. I refused to allow her out of my sight. It felt like she was now my responsibility, and I refused to let Chris get anywhere near her. He was the fucking scum of the earth, a minuscule piece of dirt you'd find in the loneliest corners of life. He was a parasite, and no woman deserved to be around the likes of him.

It was official; my Friday night was completely fucked-up, and she was oblivious to exactly who I was.

"What's your name?" I asked her, saying the first thing I could think of to break the tension. I shifted my gaze and concentrated entirely on her.

"Kellie."

Kellie

"Your name is Kellie?" I repeated her answer, all the while trying to cover the confusion tainting my voice.

Why was she lying about her name?

Her eyes darted quickly away from mine, breaking the intense connection we seemed to be locked in. I continued to watch her closely.

"Thank you for what you did earlier. I don't even want to think—" She shook her head as her thoughts hit her. "You don't

33

have to stay with me."

"I'm staying put." I crossed my arms over my chest, and my eyes closed momentarily as exhaustion swept through me. There was nothing about tonight that even the best psychic in the world could have predicted. A few drinks and some inappropriate conversations with Josh was what I expected.

I certainly didn't expect Eden Rivers.

I felt her move beside me, and my eyes shot open as the thoughts of her escaping and going back into the crowd and toward the atrocity of Chris flooded me.

Her body had twisted, and she now faced me in such a way that her knees pressed into the side of my thigh. Instinctively, I moved into a similar pose until our knees were pressed against one another's. I froze under her penetrating gaze. My throat constricted as her inquisitive blue eyes, flickering with intensity, floated over my face, taking me completely in. Every inch of my face was under her scrutiny, and I had never felt so exposed or vulnerable. It was like she was reading every one of my fucked-up thoughts, and that was one thing I didn't want her to do.

"What are you looking for?" I whispered gruffly, my tone coming across too strong.

"I am trying to work you out." Her tone dropped in seriousness as her eyes narrowed, darkening to a shade of midnight blue. "I don't know why you want to sit here babysitting me, when the woman with the blond hair at the bar is waiting to pounce on you the moment I leave. I am pretty sure it's rude to leave your date."

I felt myself shifting closer to her, and I couldn't stop the pull. Her eyes widened the moment my voice dropped so only she could hear. "First off, there is nothing you need to work out about me. Secondly, I am not babysitting you, and thirdly, she is most definitely not my date. If you haven't already worked it out, I prefer the company of a brunette with dangerously inviting eyes who gives me a fake name and pretend attitude, while she shakes like a leaf beside me."

Our eyes latched onto each other's with a fierce intensity that confused the fuck out of me. My protection of the truth was slowly cracking under her watchful gaze. As I sat opposite her, it was now my turn to look at her, to push every strength of my gaze toward her, and ultimately draw her to the surface. Her composure faltered, and the smallest of frowns swept over her red painted lips before she snapped back to throwing her false attitude my way. I didn't buy it. Her weakness was coming to the surface at a rapid pace, swallowing the fake confidence that she was desperately trying to portray.

"My name is Kellie," she muttered, and her voice wavered ever so slightly. Finally, her eyes broke away from mine and focused on Ashlyn, who was making her way back toward us.

Ashlyn glided through the crowd with a tray of drinks balancing precariously in her hands. Eden's friend walked behind her with her hand clasped tightly in Josh's. I shot an exasperated look at Josh, whose eyebrows wiggled as a knowing smirk greeted his lips.

"I brought drinks. Kellie, Vodka Orange for you. I got you a double." Ashlyn's gaze danced questioningly between Eden and me. I felt my frustration level rising at Ashlyn calling her Kellie.

"Uh, thanks." Eden grabbed the tall glass from the tray and immediately drank half of it in one swift gulp. She fell into a vortex of silence while the conversation around us buzzed as drink after drink was downed. The more Eden drank, the more she seemed to relax, and her closeness to me didn't falter.

Tori shifted from Josh's lap, stumbled over to the couch, and plopped herself beside Eden, forcing her to move even closer to me.

"I am going to fuck his brains out tonight." Tori nodded in Josh's direction. "And you should do the same with his brother.

Latch onto him and ride him like a goddamn stallion. Did you see what he did for you out there?" Her attempts at whispering were foiled by her intoxicated state, and I heard every damn word she said.

"Jesus, Tori. Drop your voice," Eden said, groaning. She shot me an apologetic look.

"No one will be riding me," I growled and stood from the couch. Josh's eyes found mine, and I knew he would follow the moment I left. I stormed through the crowd back to the main bar, slammed a fifty down, and ordered another round of drinks for the group, plus ice water for myself. I knew for a fact that Chris was still sniffing around and would pounce the moment I let down my guard, so the beers had to stop.

"So, it's pretty obvious that I'm taking Tori home. Are you alright to take Eden and Ashlyn with you?" Josh spoke from behind me.

I shifted my gaze back to the couches where Eden sat with Ashlyn and Tori. Tori and Ashlyn laughed together while Eden looked absently out onto the dance floor; a stoic expression plastered on her face.

"Why the fuck is she pretending her name is Kellie?"

"Your guess is as good as mine." He shook his head as his eyes focused on her. "She has absolutely no clue that we know who she is."

Tori stumbled toward us, her curls bouncing around her face while her eyes locked tightly on me, ultimately dispersing mine and Josh's conversation. She latched onto my arm for support as her body swayed under the effects of too much alcohol. Just how strong were those vodkas Ashlyn was buying?

"I know your name is Ky," she slurred and poked me in the chest. It wasn't a hidden fact what my name was; it just hadn't been asked, and I didn't just go around saying "by the way, my name is Ky."

"And I know your name is Tori," I shot back.

"She can't say no. My best friend can't say no. She can't even be herself on her birthday," she announced with a heavy sigh, fiercely grabbing my attention in the process. Her voice swam with frustration, hurt, and distress as she glanced back to the table. "That's why she went with that guy. We come to places like this because it's usually safe. We usually have the best time because no one pays any attention to us. But tonight it wasn't. If you hadn't come along, I don't know what would have happened."

"What do you mean?" Josh asked as my ability to speak faded and anger fired within me.

"For as long as I've known her, she always says yes, because she is scared to say no."

"Why is she saying her name is Kellie?" I growled as my blood boiled at hearing Tori's admissions.

"Because she hides behind these masks she puts up. She does it every time we go out. I tried to talk her out of it tonight, but she wouldn't listen to me. She is never Eden."

I needed to get out of here before I said something I'd regret or did something that would lead to me looking like a complete tool. "I've got to go. Josh, take Tori and Ashlyn with you."

"What?"

"Josh, please." I shot my brother a pleading look, and he nodded in agreement. I knew my time here was done. I felt like I was teetering on the edge of completely blowing the fuck up, and I needed to get out—but first I needed to see for myself. I marched back to the table, focused on Eden who looked at me with Bambi-like eyes, before shifting my attention to Ashlyn.

"I'm done for the night. Ash, I'll see you on Monday." I leaned down and kissed her cheek softly, and then returned my attention to a gawking Eden.

"*Kellie,* come with me."

Eden

I SHOULD HAVE BEEN panicked.
  I should have been frightened.
  I should have been alarmed.
But I wasn't.

I stood on the sidewalk, the night air of New York swirling around me in a teasing manner, and I waited for his next move. I chewed my lip and pulled my jacket tightly around my body. What a crazy night. The moment he asked me to leave with him, I was done for. I had no choice but to follow him out of the bar and into the uncertainty of the city. His eyes had widened when I stood from the couch and moved toward him as if he didn't expect me to agree so quickly. What choice did I have? He asked, and I followed. I said yes. At that moment my weakness was on full display, every confidence that I tried to show was squashed by a simple statement, and as usual, I couldn't say no. The mask I tried so desperately to portray quickly fell to the floor in a heap of lies and trepidation.

"What are we doing?" I asked, finding my voice and desperate to put to sleep the awkwardness that was beaming from me.

He shifted slowly, taking purposeful steps until his towering body completely overshadowed mine. He shoved his hands deep into his jean pockets, and his eyes roamed over my face, taking in my features and increasing my insecurity with one enduring look. Hazel eyes beamed into mine, then they dropped and lingered on my lips for a moment too long, a moment that both of us noticed. Ripping his gaze from my mouth, he looked me squarely in the eyes. "I don't know. I didn't think you would follow me."

"I had no choice."

"You always have a choice."

His eyes darkened, and the delicious amber color dissolved into a shade of murky brown, then his jaw tensed as if I had just said the most shocking thing in the world. Why did I even say that? Silence fell between us as we stood on the sidewalk on a cold November night. I shivered in the night air, and thankfully a cab soon pulled up to the curb. He walked over, opening the door for me. I didn't look at him as I ducked under his arm and collapsed onto the leather seat. The warmth in the air comforted me, and I felt my body start to relax.

Still I felt no fear.

The seat dipped when he slid in beside me, and the air immediately thickened.

"To the island," he directed the cab driver, as he shifted in his seat and looked out the window beside him. "Head toward City Towers."

I folded back into the cushioned seat and closed my eyes as scenarios burst into my thoughts. A guy like him obviously always got what he wanted. His confidence alone was earth shattering, let alone the looks that the heavens above had blessed him with.

I sat beside this figure of mystery in silence. The bright lights and an abundance of people crowding the sidewalk faded behind us as we weaved our way out of the city that never slept and headed across the river. A million thoughts went trampling through my head at a frightening rate. I knew I was getting myself into dangerous territory yet again. I was in a cab, with a strange man, on my way to his apartment. This was not how my night was meant to end, but why the fuck wasn't I scared out of my wits?

We pulled up in front of a towering building twinkling in the night sky. He opened the door and slid out, and moments later the door beside me opened, and I stepped out into the crisp air.

"You ready?" he asked in a low tone.

"Yes."

I walked beside him in silence and concentrated on my breathing. The closer we moved to the entrance, the more my heart rate increased. Shock and confusion collided head on as we continued past the entrance. I halted and spun around. I gazed through the double glass doors into the welcoming foyer with what looked like a coffee bar at one end and a pizzeria on the other, both bursting with late night revelers.

"Are we not going in there?" I asked with shock hinted in my words as my eyes locked on the pizzeria.

He stopped and turned back toward me, a look of disbelief cascading over his way-too-perfect face. "Did you think we were going to my apartment?"

"Yes," I whispered honestly, my voice dropping dangerously low. Cautiously, I allowed my eyes to finally find his. He looked at me like I was the most precious commodity in the world, a look that sent a million butterflies loose in my stomach.

A look that finally terrified me.

"Not every guy is a complete asshole. Yes, you are beautiful, and yes, I'd love to have you in my bed. Believe me, I'd take great pleasure in worshiping your body, but I'm not going to touch you or even attempt to touch you when you are clearly petrified to even be here with me. " His honesty was brutal but refreshing.

"I'll have you know that I'm not petrified of you."

His brow rose curiously. "Riiggght." Over exaggeration dripped from his words. "That's why you have barely said two words to me." He took off around the corner and disappeared from sight.

What the hell?

My stubbornness and desire to prove him wrong shot through me like a cannon. I could have a conversation with this guy. Couldn't I? He made it as clear as the night sky above that he wasn't taking me to his apartment tonight, so that was one thing I didn't have to worry about. I mumbled obscenities under my breath and took off with a rush to find where this annoying yet intriguing stranger had run off to.

I turned the corner and inhaled sharply the moment he came into view. He leaned against the red brick wall with his arms crossed across his chest, his eyes focused solely on me and where I would appear. He looked like a freaking poster boy of intimidating good looks and devilish intentions.

My eyes shot up to the neon sign flashing above my head, Joe's Place. I shot him a look, and he nudged his head in the direction of the door leading into the 50's inspired diner. Well, this wasn't how I thought my night would end. I swallowed my frustration and entered through the doors, headed for the far corner, and slid into an empty booth. When I realized I wasn't being followed, my gaze searched the busy room until I found my stranger leaning over the counter, talking closely to a middle-aged woman with black hair and wearing a pink frilly dress. It looked like she had stepped out of *Happy Days*.

I fumbled through my clutch in search of my phone. I was in desperate need of a distraction—something, anything to pull me away from staring like a complete fool at a man who I had no clue about. I pulled out a couple of twenty-dollar bills, tissues, and my lip gloss before I finally grabbed hold of my phone. Three unread message icons flashed before me.

*Tori: I am so proud of you leaving with **Mr. Get in my panties**. Happy Birthday!!!*
Message two.

Tori: I love this city. I love strip clubs. I love the man I am going to fuck tonight. I love yooooooooooooooooooooooooooooooou.

Message three.

Unknown number: I'd say it's great to see you back in town, but then I'd be lying.

I gasped loudly, and my body shuddered as a familiar feeling incapacitated me. My eyes continued to bounce over the words that tormented me from the confines of my phone. With a painful stab, my heart stopped with every letter, with every stomach-churning word laid out before me. I read the message over and over again, like I had a sick and twisted need to allow it to consume me further. I didn't understand this, as my number was private. No one knew I was back in town. I sat back against the leather of the booth. Suddenly, I felt like the world was watching me, scrutinizing me, waiting in the darkness to take me in. My eyes darted and dodged around the busy diner. I couldn't do this. I couldn't shut down. Not here. Not with him walking toward me, looking at me so all consuming.

"What's wrong?" He pulled his wallet and phone from his pocket, placed them on the table between us, and slid in across from me.

"This place seems cool." I darted away from his question, desperate to change the subject and hoping he would follow suit. Exhaustion was hitting me at an alarming rate, and I craved the security my hotel room and bed would provide. The thought of actually having a conversation with this man felt exhausting, yet seemed somewhat necessary. "I didn't know this place existed."

We were interrupted by the arrival of the same lady from

the counter. She shifted her gaze between me and Crawford, *seriously what kind of name was Crawford,* and smiled widely, her cheeks flushing. I swore I even heard her sigh. She placed two plates on the table, containing lush-looking pieces of chocolate cake with mountains of snow white whipped cream towering sky high. My mouth watered at the sight. My head bounced between looking at the amazingness in front of me, a lovely lady whose nametag told me her name was Carole, and the man across from me grinning. Talk about confused. Carole turned on her heel and headed back to the counter, giving us one last look over her shoulder.

"What's this?" I asked breathlessly.

"You need to eat cake on your birthday."

"You bought me cake?" I asked, astonished beyond belief.

"So it seems." He fired a wink at me before digging into the piece of cake that sat on the table in front of him, a moan of delight escaping his lips. I stared at him completely overwhelmed and at a loss for words. His eyes left the cake and met mine, and a perfect smirk flitted over his lips. "You need to pick up the fork, put it in the cake, and then eat it. It's delicious. My aunt knows how to bake a mean cake."

I lifted the fork, sank it into the rich looking cake, and brought it up to my lips. The smell alone caused me to sigh in anticipation. I felt his eyes on me. My eyes closed as the chocolate wonder set off my taste buds, smashing the emptiness of my stomach with pure delight, and a soft moan escaped. This was hands down the best cake I'd ever eaten.

"Why did you do that?" I asked between bites of cake.

"Why did I do what?"

"Um, back at the club. With that, uh, that guy," I stuttered, immediately regretting bringing it up.

He placed his fork down and gave me his full attention. "I have never seen someone look as terrified as you did. I knew you didn't want to be there, and I had to do something. I had to stop that asshole from putting his hands on you."

"But why me?"

"I couldn't take my eyes off you from the moment I saw you, so yeah, I noticed when a fucktard came on to you and took you away, and I refused to sit back and watch that."

He couldn't take his eyes off me? I tried to let his words settle within me, but to be honest, this whole situation was freaking me out. What was I meant to say to that?

"Is that not what you wanted to hear?" He leaned in, and his eyes twinkled in amusement.

I felt my lips curl slightly. "I'm not exactly sure."

"How about we just eat our cake?" he suggested and dropped his eyes to the half-eaten piece sitting in front of me.

I nodded and picked up my fork. Silence fell over the table as I got lost in a world of rich chocolate goodness, and I soon I forgot where I was and who I was with.

"This is so good," I spluttered between mouthfuls of cake, losing all sense of manners. His laughter flooded my ears as my cheeks flushed crimson. *Nice one, Eden. Way to play the sophistication card.* "Thank you so much for bringing me here. What started as a pretty shitty night is turning into being quite awesome."

"The night isn't over yet," he declared with a straight face.

His fork clinked against the plate once he finished his mountain of cake, and he folded his hands together and sat watching me. Every bite I took, his eyes followed the fork to my lips. My hands trembled with nerves under the intensity of his gaze and, what would have usually been massive forkfuls of cake, were now tiny, petite bites as I sat opposite this handsome stranger. My head throbbed with his declaration that the night wasn't over. What the hell did that mean? He said we wouldn't be going to his apartment.

I licked the fork before the icing dripped off, and the sound of his sharp intake of breath grabbed my attention, and my eyes met his.

"I never thought I'd witness someone who could make eating chocolate cake look so sexy." His voice had dropped dangerously low, rumbling with intent and seduction. "Fuck, I am damn jealous of that fork."

Heat rushed to my face, and I knew I was a billboard for how his words were affecting me. I slowly put the fork down because suddenly I felt like I couldn't stomach another bite. I was desperate to finish it, but I didn't want to encourage this guy any further.

"It looks like our night is coming to an abrupt end." His amused expression focused on something over my shoulder at the same time as a loud crash sounded from the doorway. I jumped in my seat and shifted to find out what the commotion was. Deep laughter flooded out from within me. Josh walked in with Tori on one arm and Ashlyn on the other, and both girls looked a little worse for wear. Ashlyn's eyes locked onto where we were sitting, and she slipped out of Josh's grasp and stumbled across the diner.

"We found you!" she cried in an over-exaggerated sing song and slid in the booth opposite me. Her eyes squinted as she tried to gain focus. "You bought her cake. Oh my God, you do have a beating heart in there."

Crawford rolled his eyes at Ashlyn and huffed. "And on that note, it's time for me to leave."

"Let's all go," Josh suggested, gaining an exasperated look from Crawford.

Ashlyn slid out of the booth just as quickly as she slid in. My hand was soon encased by hers, and I was pulled to my feet. She marched out of the diner and hooked her arm through mine. What the hell was happening? Deep voices mumbled behind me, but I couldn't make out what was being said. Within five minutes, we were entering the brightly lit foyer of City Towers that was still abuzz with chatter.

"What are we doing, Tori?" I asked as we all lingered in the foyer. All I wanted to do was go back to the hotel, have a shower until the hot water ran cold and go to sleep.

"I am going to be doing him," she slurred and drunkenly pointed to Josh. "What do you want to do?"

"I'm going to call a cab and go back to the hotel," I announced swiftly.

Tori grabbed my hands. "Are you sure? I can come with you."

"You stay. Have fun. I'll be okay. I just want to go to bed. It's been a crazy night," I admitted.

The sharp ding of the elevator's arrival sounded, and Josh, Ashlyn, and Tori piled in. Crawford still hadn't said another word to me. I finally allowed myself to look at him and surprise, surprise, his entire focus was locked on me. The color of his eyes intrigued me, and tonight I had seen so many different shades. They unnerved me. The longer I spent with him, the more nervous I became, the more fidgety, and the more desperate I was to escape.

"Can I have a word, *Kellie?*"

I nodded, and he stepped toward me. I knew we were under Tori, Ashlyn, and Josh's inquisitive gaze.

It happened so quickly.

With two confident steps, his body, like an impenetrable wall, was in front of me. His warm hands cupped my face, the warmness colliding harshly with the coldness the New York winter had inflicted on my cheeks. His eyes danced with mine. My breath caught.

This couldn't.

I couldn't.

He couldn't.

With a swift movement, he dropped his mouth to my ear, and the soft caress of his breath caused my emotions to roar to life.

"Happy Birthday," he whispered in my ear. "Until we meet again."

His lips peppered a kiss on my cheek and without another word, he turned and disappeared into the elevator, his eyes glued to mine until the closing door broke the intensity of our gaze.

KY

MONDAY MORNING BARRELED INTO my life like a catapulting freight train. My body felt weak, my brain was fried, and my mind compacted so tightly with memories of Friday night. It wasn't a surprise that my weekend had been spent rehashing conversations, looks, and flashbacks—all revolving around the girl in the red jacket.

Saturday had been spent locked away in my apartment working until I couldn't stand to look at my laptop any longer, so I stopped briefly to go and visit my parents for a long over-due visit. The usual conversations happened; how was work? How was Ashlyn? Had I gotten myself a girl? When was I go-ing to give her grandchildren? Just the regular topics of conver-sation Mom decided to start when I visited. Dad chuckled in the corner and let Mom run her course. When I informed her that I was going to remain a bachelor for the rest of my years, I re-ceived a warning glance that would frighten even the hardest of men. On Sunday, I had spent three hours at the gym with Josh, boxing, running and lifting weights until I could barely stand. It was fucking fantastic, and for those three hours I was distracted from thinking about *her.*

But now it was Monday and, once again, she invaded my thoughts. I groaned loudly and yanked the covers from my body. I threw my legs over the edge of the bed and stood, stretching tall until I heard every bone in my stiff body crack to life. Stumbling out of my bedroom and into the guts of my apartment, I made my way into the sprawling kitchen as the promise of coffee made the morning seem a little easier to face. My morning routine was simple: coffee, turning on my iPod, checking my phone, and getting ready to face another day at Anderson Publications. It worked, it was a ritual, and there was no need to change it.

When I arrived at work, I took the elevator to the top floor. The silence of the office was disturbing, and it only served to accentuate the pounding of my headache. I made my way down the dimly-lit halls, illuminated only by the night lights above. As usual, I was the second to arrive for the day. When I stopped by my ever-appeasing executive assistant's desk, she looked up and greeted me with a smile that was way too friendly for six thirty in the morning. Why she stuck with me was anyone's guess.

"How's my day looking, Lauren?" I took a seat on the edge of her desk, handing a steaming hot chocolate to her as I did every morning. Lauren had been with me from my very first day so our friendship was one of trust and understanding, and her fiancé had become a good friend who Josh and I would often go to games with. "And why are you here so early?"

"Meeting at ten a.m. with the production team, lunch with Josh, and this afternoon you should be receiving the final contracts for your meeting on Thursday." She smiled brightly and then took a sip of her hot chocolate before saying, "And I am here because you have a shitload of work coming up so someone has to keep you in line. I don't get paid the big bucks for doing nothing, you know. "

"You are too good to me, Lauren." I laughed at the brutal honesty of my assistant. "I'm going to go and lock myself away for the day. Come and get me if you need anything, and tell me as soon as those contracts arrive."

"Will do."

I left Lauren tapping away at her computer and slipped into my office. Monday morning blues were hitting me at an alarming rate, and my motivation to work was running for the hills and taking my fucked-up brain with it. I collapsed into my chair with an oomph and opened my emails, scanning for anything urgent, but I was drawn to Facebook and, before I could control what I was typing into the search bar, Eden Rivers' profile was glaring back at me.

What I had chosen to omit on Friday night was that I already knew her, and I sure as hell knew her name wasn't Kellie fucking Carter. Fuck that pissed me off. Eden Rivers had been on my radar for longer than most people realized. It had taken everything that I was not to call her out on it, but I also knew that she would possibly freak the fuck out and I didn't want that.

I leaned back in my chair and looked out over the city. How was I going to explain this to her? The fact that she was in the city was partially my doing. However, she wasn't meant to be here yet. As far as I knew, she was arriving on Wednesday. The realization that this was going to get messy set in, but there was no way I could back down now, not after she barreled herself into my life.

I clicked on the glowing X and Facebook disappeared before me.

Before I knew it, morning had turned into afternoon, and afternoon into night. This was my life. Anderson Publications. I spent way too much time in this exact position; sitting in my obnoxiously large chair, behind my way-too-conceited desk, in my expansive office. I was a workaholic, and I would be the first to admit it. The buzz of an incoming text vibrated on my desk, and I smiled as I saw Ashlyn's name flash before me.

Ashlyn: Let's grab dinner. I want to get pizza at Joey's.

I looked at my watch and the thought of digging into a pizza made my stomach roar to life.

Me: I'll meet you there at eight.

Ashlyn: Look at us two leaving work before midnight.

Me: What is becoming of us?

An hour later, I walked through the doors of Joey's and I was greeted with loud chatter and the saliva-inducing smell of fresh pizza and garlic. I scanned the room, finally spotting Ashlyn sitting in a booth in the far corner, tapping away on her phone, no doubt working as she waited. Ashlyn looked up when I reached the table and greeted me with a killer watt smile, which I returned before kissing her on the cheek and sliding into the booth opposite her.

"I didn't think you'd show," she teased, turning over her phone as to not be interrupted.

"What, and leave you desperate and dateless? Please. I am a gentleman."

"Well, that's true, and your gentleman qualities were on full display Friday night," she taunted with a wink.

So, we are getting straight to it.

I rolled my eyes as my back stiffened. This was a conversation I did not wish to have in the middle of the restaurant. I grabbed for the menu, but it was ripped from my fingertips. I looked up and was greeted by Ashlyn smirking across from me. "Seriously Ash, I just got here. Are we really going to do this now?"

She leaned over the table, dropping her voice. "What was Friday night all about?"

I narrowed my eyes and knew this conversation was going to happen right here, right now. We were equally stubborn, like two bulls locking horns, and I knew neither of us would back down. The arguments the two of us had were known to be explosive and unpredictable—they often led to days of no contact—but it was critical to the structure of our relationship. It was what allowed our friendship to work. We refused to accept each other's bullshit and, to be honest, it was a breath of fresh air.

Through clenched teeth, I glared at her, throwing every ounce of my frustration her way. I was hungry, irritated, and tired. Fuck it! I would give in to her banter just this once.

"I had to do something. He is a fucking asshole." The thought of Chris touching Eden made my hands fist on the table. A reaction Ashlyn didn't miss.

"So you had to beat your chest like a caveman and go and save the girl?"

"Ashlyn, you know why I did what I did. I couldn't just stand there and—" I swallowed hard as anger roared to life within me, and I had to take back control. "Can we just order a damn pizza and talk about something else?"

"Don't go back there, Ky. Nothing was ever your fault, and you need to stop living with this whole hero mentality. It's fucking with your head." She grabbed my hand from across the table and squeezed it tightly.

"Pepperoni or mushroom?" I growled, shooting her a warning look. This conversation was over.

With a huff, Ashlyn let go of my hand and crossed her arms over her chest. Our stormy eyes battled each other. The woman sitting opposite me knew me better than I knew myself. She knew everything about me, and that frightened the living shit out of me. She knew every piece of my jagged puzzle, every reason why I was what she lovingly called a "no" guy. More importantly, yet most frightening, was that she knew things that could bring everything unglued. Was I afraid she would divulge the information she had on me? No. Was I afraid that I would do something to fuck everything up? Absolutely.

Once we placed our order, we called a truce and talked about our day. I listened as Ashlyn divulged secrets of the latest up-and-coming pop star she had been hired to style, and she listened as I discussed the upcoming cover shoot and special featuring some of the most exciting bands in the US.

"Shit," Ashlyn suddenly mumbled, her eyes darting toward the door. I shifted in my seat, glanced over my shoulder, and almost choked on my soda. Eden casually walked into the restaurant, her chocolate brown hair falling down her back under a cream beanie. Her laughter was the only thing I heard. Her arm was linked with Tori's as they made their way to the counter. I was totally engrossed. She scanned the restaurant, and the moment our eyes connected, the faintest of smiles filtered over her perfectly pink pout.

"Kellie!" Ashlyn's excited voice broke my thoughts, and I looked at her like she was the craziest woman to grace the earth. "Over here."

"What the fuck are you doing?" I hissed between clenched teeth.

Eden moved through the crowded pizzeria toward Ashlyn and me. What the hell was Ashlyn thinking, and why the fuck did she continue to call her Kellie? I tried my hardest to avoid looking at her, but I couldn't stop myself. I was swimming into dangerous territory, but there was no way in hell that I wanted to get out of this current. Eden walked with grace, elegance, and confidence. This girl making her way toward us was so different from the one I left on Friday night. She confused the hell out of me. Her eyes never left me, and I swallowed hard under her gaze. What the fuck was this?

"Hey Ashlyn." She smiled sweetly at Ashlyn and then turned to me. "Hi."

"Hey." My voice was rough. Both Ashlyn and Eden turned to stare at me. Ky Crawford never got nervous under the gaze of women, but now I felt like I was sweating bullets. "I need to go and make a call."

I slipped out of the booth and headed for the corner of the room, away from the piercing watch of Eden Rivers—or Kellie—fuck this was confusing. I just wanted to grab her by the shoulders, shake her and say, *I know you are Eden Rivers, and I know you'll be sitting in my office in a few days' time.* I collapsed into a vacant seat and pulled out my phone. Scrolling through my emails, I went to my draft folder and saw the exact email that had been playing on my mind all day. I opened the draft email, and my eyes darted over the words as the battle of want against conscious began. If I sent this email, there was no turning back, but if I didn't send this email, then I'd never know who Eden Rivers *was.*

From: ky@andersonpublications.com
To: edenriversphotography@gmail.com
Time: 20:25pm
Subject: Meeting request
Eden,
This is an email to confirm your attendance on Thursday November 16ᵗʰ at three p.m.
Kindest of Regards,
Ky

Eden

"**W**HAT'S GOING THROUGH THAT head of yours?" Tori questioned, giving me the worried look that I had witnessed so many times before.

After five days on the East Coast, Tori was heading back home, ultimately leaving me to my own devices. I knew the time was coming quickly, but I didn't want to believe that it was here. I had become so reliant on her. Tori and I sat on the edge of the pier, our legs dangling over the edge, and our shoulders wrapped in a blanket as the fall air swirled around us. Silence fell, and I knew the moment I spoke my emotions would bubble over.

"I don't want you to go," I finally admitted, my voice cracking.

"Babe, you will see me in a little over five weeks. Honestly, I think this will be great for you. This opportunity is freaking amazing, and you've been working toward this for years. This is your dream, so live it."

Tori's head fell to my shoulder, and we sat in silence as we looked out over the white crested waves of the ocean. The chill in the air shocked me to life; it smacked me in the face and made me awaken to the world that was revolving around me.

The thought of being away from Tori petrified me. She was the glue that kept me together and kept me moving forward, and the thought of her not being around made me fearful that

I would dissolve into pits of despair and take two steps back.

Tori sighed softly beside me. "Remember that Josh guy, Ashlyn's friend? He was hands down the best cock I've ever had. I am still feeling him. That is the sign of a good fucking."

And just like that, Tori lightened my mood.

I'd be lying if I said I didn't often wish that could be me—so carefree, so open, and so honest. The idea of opening myself up to a man who could, as Tori would say, be the best fuck I'd ever have, was something that had crossed my mind, but I squashed the thought immediately. To make love was a myth. To be cherished was the complete opposite of what I allowed in my life. Over the past four years, there had only been one guy who got close, and that was because I had absolute trust in him. He was my best friend and had slipped into the role of being my pretend boyfriend when we went out. Colby Andrews was my protector, my conscience, and the only guy who I had allowed to touch me. In my despair, as I slipped into a state of devastation, he had wrapped me in his arms, rocked me until I settled, and then spent the night showing me exactly how I wasn't completely destroyed.

"Can I tell you something?" I whispered, and immediately Tori's head shot up from my shoulder and she looked at me expectantly. "I wish I could let loose. I don't want to be crippled by fear anymore, and I wish I could stop being scared of the idea of being with a guy."

"There is someone out there who is going to completely knock you on your ass, and he will be everything you need and more. He will treat you like the princess you are, he will treasure every second he is with you, and when he isn't with you, he will be thinking of you. I know he is out there, and when he comes for you, I hope you take a chance."

Outfit after outfit greeted my body. My suitcase lay open on my hotel bed, with every item of clothing I brought spewing out all over the place. Jeans, skirts, dresses, shirts, and shoes covered every surface, and after two hours and numerous Face-Time calls with Tori, I finally settled on a charcoal pencil skirt, a white blouse, and my signature blood red heels. In an hour, I was due at Anderson Publications for my initial meeting with a man I only knew as Ky to discuss my freelance work with them.

I was a walking mass of nerves as I took my first step into the pristine foyer. My eyes darted frantically, desperate for my memories to be swamped by the magnitude of perfection that was on display in front of me. From the marble floors to the pristine white walls displaying the Andy Warhol artwork, I was experiencing what I could only imagine heaven would be like. Tearing my eyes away from an eclectic piece of art showing Central Park in a futuristic setting, I glided toward the reception desk. The sound of my heels clicking on the floor below me grabbed the attention of a very polished-looking young woman who looked up and offered a sweet smile.

"Hi, I have a meeting at three p.m. My name is Eden Rivers." I smiled nervously and watched as she lifted the phone to her ear and announced my arrival.

"Mr. Crawford will be down in a few minutes if you'd like to take a seat."

Nodding in response, I sunk into the leather tub chair and began nervously bouncing my leg. The enormity of the meeting I was about to attend suddenly hit me. This magazine was huge, and the fact that they wanted me, Eden Rivers, to shoot not only the cover but also an editorial feature, was just too much to comprehend. This was the magazine that Tori and I would read on our lazy Sundays. This was the magazine that always had the most beautiful covers. Shit! I was going to be sick. My stomach rolled, and the desire to run and never look back fell upon me, but something out of my control stopped me.

A strong masculine voice greeted me, my name rolled off his tongue with ease and certainty. Familiarity struck me. "Eden, thanks for coming in, how about we move to my office?"

I twisted in my chair, and under the shadow of Josh Crawford I felt my world stop.

Recognition flashed before me, and his eyes narrowed in. The look I was receiving made me feel like my dream and this opportunity was going up in flames before my eyes.

"Shit," I muttered and stood on shaky feet. My mouth hung open in shock and his amused gaze didn't offer me any comfort.

"Ready?" he asked, and I nodded in silent response.

I followed Josh through the open space of the ground floor, cursing myself for wearing my very noisy heels. The walls lining the hall led to the elevators that featured framed copies of previous issues, which I couldn't help but admire. I stepped into the elevator, moved to the back, and watched as the numbers rose with every passing floor. I could feel Josh's inquisitive eyes watching me. I gnawed on my bottom lip, and my foot tapped nervously as I gripped hold of my bag.

"Almost there," Josh announced as I anxiously watched floor seven change to floor eight.

The fifteenth floor finally arrived, and with a swift movement, Josh was out of the elevator. I followed closely behind him as we made our way through an open-plan office space. Cubicle after cubicle was filled with professional-looking people tapping away at computers or talking on the phone, and occasionally someone would look up and give me the once-over.

Josh stopped in front of a closed door and turned toward me. "You look petrified."

"I am. I'm waiting for you to tell me to leave."

His laughter, once again, didn't comfort me.

Josh opened the door to his office and motioned for me to step through. It was not what I expected; it was gleaming white, with a white desk, white shelving, and an oversized white office chair. Art graced the walls, displaying everything from portraits to landscapes—but one common dominator was the abstract and fieriness of colors on display. It grabbed my attention immediately.

I took a seat across from the desk and placed my hands nervously in my lap. The longer he took to speak, the more my anxiety piqued.

"So I won't keep you for long. First, I don't care that you chose not to tell me your real name when we first met. I am sure you have your reasons, and it's not for me to judge, so we will get that off the table. How's that work for you?"

I nodded in silent agreement.

"So this is how it is. My brother, whom you met the other night, first made me aware of you and your work, and we are very interested in having you shoot the cover and editorial spread for the next issue." He folded his hands together, resting them on the immaculate white desk, and looked at me with anticipation of my response.

His *brother!*

Crawford. Chocolate cake. Perfect eyes. Had come to my rescue.

Oh God! I was going to pass out.

"Is this some sort of joke?" My words were short as my defenses shot sky high. Things like this didn't just happen to me. They didn't just land on my lap without consequences. His eyes bore into mine as he gauged my brutal questioning. "Your brother bought me chocolate cake!"

Without a word, Josh rose from behind his desk and effortlessly moved toward me, his eyes never leaving mine. I stood to meet him, desperate for strength to appear while inside I was trembling.

"We want your photography skills, Eden. My brother was extremely surprised to find you right under his nose." He took one step closer me, and I froze. "And yes, he did. He has never bought a girl chocolate cake before, Eden, and I've never seen him go all alpha-fucking-male for a girl before, so you just think about that."

The breath I was unaware I was holding escaped in a loud rush, and I blinked frantically. "I'm only here until January fifth."

"That should be okay. The only thing I can think of is that there may be a launch party on December sixteenth that you will be required to attend, but Ky will have all the details regarding your schedule."

Hearing that date sent fear roaring through my body. I hated that date and everything about it was hell to me. For the past four years, I had spent that day locked in my apartment, buried so deep in the confines of my bed and away from the world. December 16th saw me drowning in a mixture of cheap vodka and Xanax until I passed out and escaped from realism. It was a pathetic way to hide from the truth, but it was the only thing I could do. I could hear Josh talking, but I couldn't understand anything he was saying. I was thrown back to four years prior, to the moment that I was a beaten, broken, and fearful young woman. I felt my heart thump dangerously fast in my chest, my palms began sweating, and my lungs ached as I desperately tried to gain a breath. My eyes snapped back to Josh's worried face.

"Eden—"

"Thank you for the opportunity. I will see myself out."

I hastily grabbed my bag from the floor and rushed for the door, with Josh close on my heels. I felt a familiar panic attack brutally coming to life, and the last thing I wanted was Josh Crawford to witness me unravel into a pit of anxiety and be frozen as my nightmares unleashed their attack. I needed my solitude and the relief that only locking myself away from the world could provide. I punched the button time and time again when I reached the elevator. I could feel the presence of Josh standing beside me, close enough to know he was worried about my reaction, but still far enough away to give me the space I needed. I must have looked utterly ridiculous. I was just given the best opportunity of my life and instead of saying, "Where do I sign?" I was fleeing the building like a raving lunatic.

The moment the elevator door opened, I hurried in, and Josh followed in close pursuit. He hit the ground floor button and stood back against the wall, an awkward silence falling between us. Thankfully we didn't stop until we reached the ground floor.

The moment the elevator door opened, I rushed for the glass doors with the promise of escape within reach. My eager steps halted, and I froze on the spot as a voice wrapped itself around me and caressed my very soul. It floated through the air like the perfect song and was a voice I couldn't forget.

My eyes darted through the foyer as the need to find the owner of the voice hit me. My need to escape fading as my gaze locked onto a man with broad shoulders, a slim waist, and chocolate brown hair. Covered in a crisp white shirt and form-fitting charcoal trousers, he paced in front of the Andy Warhol artwork of Marilyn Monroe that I had been transfixed on earlier.

His phone was glued to his ear, and his velvet smooth voice rose and faded as the conversation obviously grew heated and then resolved. My eyes roamed unashamedly over his body. He was the epitome of confidence and charisma. His stance showed ownership and determination while the slouch of his shoulders indicated frustration and fatigue. As my eyes took him in, I stiffened as something so unusual hit my body, something that I had refused to accept or experience; a want, a need assaulted my senses and terrified yet exhilarated me all in one heartbeat.

Josh laughed beside me, and the man under my watchful gaze spun around quickly.

Shit!

Familiar hazel eyes bounced furiously between Josh and me, and a new desire to run hit me. His jaw flexed and he ceased talking into his phone as he narrowed his eyes at me with a darkened intensity that stole my ability to breathe. As he stared at me, it felt like the world around me failed to exist, and he looked so deep inside me that all of my secrets were being presented to him on a platter. I watched his mouth as he spoke quickly, before ending the call abruptly. With long strides, he crossed the room to where Josh stood beside me with a smirk twisting his lips.

"We were supposed to meet at three thirty," he muttered and tore his gaze from mine. He glared at Josh with a force that transformed his eyes from a beautiful hazel to a darkened chocolate brown that matched Josh's.

"Eden Rivers, I'd like to officially introduce you to Ky Crawford." Josh waved his hand effortlessly between the guy formerly known as Crawford and me. My body stiffened, and I lost the ability to speak. Ky's eyes softened momentarily at my shocked expression while his mouth hardened into a tight line. "Ky is the Marketing Manager of Anderson Publications, the less cool Crawford brother, and as we all know, your knight in shining armor."

Shit! Fuck! Bullshit!

Finding my voice and silently demanding my confidence to return, I held out my hand warily. "I had no idea."

Ky shook my hand firmly, and when he spoke, his words were laced with animosity. "I knew all along."

He dropped my hand dismissively and stormed through the open space of the foyer. It was as if he was desperate to get as far away from me as possible. My eyes were glued to his re-treating figure, and no matter how hard I tried, I couldn't tear my gaze away from him. My head swirled with disbelief. How did I not put two and two together? Who would call their child

Crawford anyway? The look on his face, when I was called out, would be engrained in me for a long time. My heart beat so erratically in my chest that I was sure Josh could hear the thumping.

"I'll text you later, Eden," Josh said softly with a subtle shake of his head. "I'll get your number from Lauren."

I had barely made it out of the building and into the craziness of New York City before my phone's constant buzzing from within my bag grabbed my attention.

Tori's name flashed on the screen, and her excited voice shattered my hearing when I clicked to accept the call. "Eden, tell me everything. What did they offer?"

Leaning against the glass walls of the building, the air of New York City was hastily chilling around me. Late November had hit, and it was only a matter of time before the air you breathed shattered your lungs, and the beautiful spectacular of December in New York City would arrive. I listened as my best friend rattled off a million questions, never allowing me the chance to answer.

I looked back at the vast double doors, and my heartbeat returned to normal, although my sense of unease was sky high. My nerves had disappeared and were replaced by frustration. Confidence I had longed for was now gripping me fiercely. "I feel like I should go back in there and apologize for rushing out and find out if *Ky Crawford* actually wants me to work for them. God, I've probably just completely fucked this up. "

I heard Tori inhale sharply before she responded. "If it were me, I would storm back in there and demand to know what the fuck was going on, but you aren't me Eden. You do what you feel like you should do."

KY

JOSH'S PRESENCE TAUNTED ME as we stood side by side in the foyer. Our receptionist's eyes widened as she watched us nervously. A Crawford showdown was only moments away, and she had been front row for many in the past. I loved my brother to death, but seriously, he annoyed the fuck out of me on occasion. Brutal silence fell around us as we fired unspoken words at each other. This wasn't how it was meant to happen. Josh wasn't meant to meet with Eden, I was. I was the one who was supposed to schmooze her, not my pussy-obsessed brother.

"What the fuck was that?" Josh's bitter words finally broke the silence.

My head swung wildly to the door, hoping to Christ that Eden had left and wasn't witness to this. Thankfully, my eyes found an empty space, and she was nowhere to be found. I turned back to Josh to find him eagerly awaiting my response.

"It's none of your concern." I sighed deeply in frustration.

"This is going to blow up in your fucking face." Frustration fell from his words. He took off toward the elevator. I shot the receptionist a warm smile and followed closely behind my fuming brother.

"Just let me do this, Josh. I know what I am doing," I demanded as we stepped into the elevator and made our way to the fifteenth floor. The space around us filled with heated testosterone and frustration.

The moment the elevator door opened, I stepped out. Curious eyes took me in as I stormed through the open-plan office toward my corner office that looked over the city.

"You need to apologize to her for the way you acted."

Josh stormed through my office door, slamming it loudly behind him. He could be such a bitch at times. I stalked toward him.

"I know," I said, sighing. "I was just shocked to see her. Why was she here anyway? She was on my calendar for three thirty."

"I got a text that I had a meeting at three p.m. today, and then I was called down saying Eden Rivers was here. I guess our appointments got mixed up. It's not a big deal." Josh strode across the room and opened the hidden liquor cabinet beside my private bathroom. He fished out a bottle of vodka and two glasses, then poured the clear liquid. "I told her what I knew, but you will have to inform her of the finer details."

I took a glass from Josh and crossed my office to the window to take in my view of New York City. I loved the enormity of this city. I had disappeared into the nooks and corners when I needed to escape many a time.

The crackle of my desk intercom crushed the silence. "Ky, Miss Rivers would like to speak with you if you have a moment."

I looked at Josh, who shrugged his shoulders in confusion. I thought she had left. "Sure, Lauren, send her in."

Soon enough, a soft knock penetrated the air before the door crept open. She didn't wait to be invited in. Very interesting. Eden's head poked around the door and her eyes connected with mine.

"Come in, Miss Rivers," I instructed. Hesitation greeted her steps as she walked in and stood beside my desk. Josh coughed, and Eden's gaze flew to the bar where Josh looked on amusingly.

"Vodka?" Josh asked, raising his glass in suggestion.

I stared at her like a bloodhound. I didn't hide the fact that my needy eyes were basking in her body, standing before me wrapped tightly in a snug grey skirt which made her curves pop. Her body was perfection: feminine, voluptuous, and enticing. Fuck, I found her gorgeous in jeans and that red jacket, but seeing her dressed in business attire caused my balls to tighten and my mind to flash images of her wearing those red heels, and only those red heels. Her body oozed sexuality, but it was like she was desperate to keep it locked away.

"No, thank you," she answered, and then swung back to face me. An exasperated look swept over her face as she took me in. Eden Rivers was strikingly beautiful; her features complimented each other so perfectly, like rain at the end of a steaming hot day. Her sea-blue eyes came to life as I stared at her and she held my gaze. Seconds passed, but it felt like hours that I was locked in the tranquility of her eyes. Her bottom lip, covered with a thin layer of pink gloss, was tugged between her teeth, and she finally broke our trance.

"I wanted to apologize for rushing out on Josh," she said softly and shot Josh a sweet smile, before turning back to me and the sweet smile disappeared. "And I wanted to ask if you actually want me for this job? Your reaction to seeing me makes me believe you don't."

"Am I speaking with Eden or Kellie?" I asked and stepped toward her.

My blood boiled with lust. Her aggression and the look of complete frustration she thrust at me shot my body to life. The air in my office was thick, and it swirled with an uncontrollable need that only she could bring on. I was losing all sense of reality because she was wearing a tight skirt, heels, and an attitude.

The sound of Josh's soft laughter grabbed my attention. Reluctantly, I pulled my eyes from Eden and shot daggers at him. I was fumbling and losing my shit because of this woman, and Josh loved it.

"I might leave you to it." Josh laughed and raised his eyes brows suggestively. He walked across my office until he stood before Eden, giving her his entire attention. "It was great seeing you again, Eden. You have my number if you ever need me. Call me day or night."

He leaned in and kissed her cheek. *Cocky bastard.*

Josh walked out chuckling as he shut the door behind him. I was alone in my office with Eden. I took a minute to stare at her. She stood by the floor-to-ceiling window, looking out over the city, her shoulders slightly slumped, and the sounds of her deep sighs penetrating the air. I took a moment to get my thoughts into check. My professionalism had flown out the window, and I needed to get a firm hold on it.

Eden turned slowly and faced me. She looked petrified, but with the signs that she was trying desperately to look confident. *Just cut to the chase, Ky.* I took a seat at my desk and motioned to the vacant chair opposite. Without saying a word to me, Eden moved gracefully across my office and sat quietly in the chair I'd offered.

"Why didn't you tell me your name?" she questioned.

"You didn't ask, Eden. Although, I specifically asked what your name was, yet you blatantly lied to my face."

"I'm sorry. It was a shitty thing to do, but for one night I just wanted to be someone else."

"I only want to talk to Eden," I stated harshly. Her eyes widened, and I immediately regretted my tone. "All I want is Eden Rivers." *Fuck!* "All we want is Eden Rivers," I corrected myself quickly.

"Why? I don't understand. You don't even know me, but you're offering the world."

"I'm definitely not offering you the world."

She stood from her chair and walked back to the window. Her hand pressed so delicately against the glass, and I watched as her shoulders rose as she took a deep breath. I took three steps and stood directly behind her. My senses were overcome by her sweet scent. I was standing too close, but I couldn't move away.

"If you're willing to still work with us, then I'd be very happy to have you on board. What do you say, Miss Rivers?"

"Yes," she whispered without hesitating, her words coming out in a husky breath. She turned slowly until there were barely a few inches between us. My gaze grew intense as I stared at this woman standing before me. There was no consideration in her answer, no breath taken, no deliberation flashing within her blue eyes. Tori's words instantly came back to me. She couldn't say no. "I should go. I have to get back to the island." She spoke more confidently, taking a step away from me. An action I didn't miss.

"I will take you," I blurted out. Now I was the one spewing out things without consideration. "I'm about to leave for the day."

I stalked toward my desk without awaiting her answer, packing up my laptop and pulling my keys from the desk drawer while she waited in silence. I knew her eyes were on me. What the hell was I doing? It was four thirty on a Thursday afternoon. I should be staying at work for at least another eight hours. I didn't give her a chance to answer, I pulled my jacket off the back of my chair and put my arms in, finally looking at her. She stared at me wide-eyed and in confusion.

"Ready?" I stood before her. "We should get to know each other, considering we will be working together."

I walked out of my office without another word. My breath held until she fell into step beside me. I didn't think she would follow me. I was expecting her to laugh in my face, tell me to fuck off, and pull out of our deal altogether. She shocked me but confirmed my worst fears. Yes. In silence, we walked to the elevator and made our way to the ground floor. It wasn't unusual to find Josh blatantly flirting with the new receptionist, to be honest, I was shocked that he hadn't already gotten to her.

The look of shock on his face was almost too much to take in. Seeing me packed up for the day so early was confusing for anyone.

"You're leaving?" He gasped, his eyes wide.

I coughed to hide the laugh that filtered out. "Yep, I'm going home."

"Are you sick?" His voice rose high in question.

"No, Josh. I am just leaving for the day."

"But you—Okay, I'll stop by later."

Eden

MY EYES WERE DETERMINED to lock onto the man sitting beside me. He had been a complete gentleman by opening the passenger door for me and making sure I buckled myself in before he walked around the front of the car with confidence exuding from each step. His body folded so perfectly into the leather seat, his hands gripped tightly to the steering wheel, and his strong jaw was locked tight. My eyes roamed vicariously over him, and I had no control to stop it. Seeing him dressed in tailored dress pants and a crisp white shirt was causing my heart to race frantically.

"Where to?" he questioned as he pulled out of the underground garage and into the steady stream of traffic.

"I am staying at Hotel De Luca."

"You are staying at a hotel? I thought your family lived on the island?"

I shot him a curious look. How in the hell did he know about my family? I knew for a fact that I didn't divulge that kind of information the other night. The faintest of smirks graced his lips as he took in my reaction, reading me like an open book.

"Facebook, Eden. You can find out everything on Facebook."

"It seems that I need to change my privacy settings." I chuckled and folded my arms over my chest.

"But if you did that, how could I have possibly found out that you live in San Francisco, you and Tori have a tendency to take a hell of a lot of selfies, and you eat a shitload of pizza."

My mouth dropped open. He had definitely done his research. "Well, aren't you just a modern day Sherlock Holmes."

His deep laughter shot through me, relaxing every inch of my rigid body. I hadn't realized how tense I was. I unclasped my arms from my chest and let my hands fall to my lap as I tried to calm down. Being in a car with a man should have sent me into a wild panic, I should have been overcome with fear, but I wasn't. Nerves swept through me. It was as confusing as fuck.

He shot me a quick look. The conversation was over and the hustle and bustle of New York City traffic was soon behind us. I gripped hold of the door handle and let my head fall against the window as I took in the fading sun. The city was so beautiful this time of year; the colors, the change in scenery, and the falling light so early in the afternoon made it look like true perfection. It was one of the only things I missed about living in this city.

"Just to let you know I am only here until January fifth, and then I'll be flying back to sunny California to continue taking selfies with Tori and eating at Sammy's Pizzeria."

"So that means you'll be my December," he whispered, so delicately that it hit me full force.

We stopped at a red light, and I shifted in my seat to look at him. What did he mean by that? *Be my December?* His eyes glistened with purpose and his face remained completely unreadable. The dimple in his right cheek came to life as the slightest smile took over his lips. I opened my mouth to question what he meant, but the ringing of a cell phone seeped through the speakers. After a couple of clicks, the sound of Josh's deep voice filled the space of the car, instantly taking me away from Ky's absurd statement. Ky shot me a look as Josh started rambling about a problem back at the office. The vibrations of the car hitting the road below caused calm to fleet through my tense body. My eyes fluttered closed under the rumblings, and I felt my body fall into comfortable bliss.

"So are you taking out the lovely Miss Rivers on a date? Are you going to use some of that Ky Crawford charm? Fuck it's been a long time coming."

My eyes shot open and my head fell to the side just in time to watch Ky's shoulders tense and his knuckles turn brutal white as he gripped the steering wheel. The question obviously hit a raw nerve. The atmosphere in the car sped out of control. The air thickened, and I couldn't draw my eyes away from him. I was anticipating his response so desperately. Why? I had absolutely no fucking clue.

"You are on speaker, and Eden is in the car."

"Hi, Eden. I hope my dear brother is driving safely. So what are you two cool kids doing this afternoon? It's not often that my dear brother leaves the office when the sun is still up. Fuck, Eden, you are good for him."

My mind expanded drastically, trying to take in all of Josh Crawford's words. Wasn't this just a ride back to the island? My hands fumbled in my lap and I shifted in my seat so my body was completely facing Ky. He still refused to look at me, and the more his reluctance shone through, the more my confidence roared to life.

"Well, he is ignoring me at the moment, Josh. This afternoon I am going back to my hotel, and then I am catching up with Ashlyn at her apartment."

"So I'll be seeing you then?"

"If your name is Ashlyn, then I guess you will."

I shunted against the leather seat as the car screeched to a brutal stop. I looked up and focused on Ky's unreadable face as he glared at me. What the fuck had I done to deserve that look? For once, I didn't feel fear being this close to a man. I didn't feel the need to run screaming to the confines of my bed. I didn't feel anything.

"Josh, I will call you when I'm home," Ky stated with little emotion.

With a loud click, the call ended without allowing Josh to have another word. Ky's gaze never faltered, and it was only then that I realized we were no longer in traffic. Ky leaned over from the driver's seat, and his eyes, which I was quickly learning had the ability to change right before me, continued to penetrate so deep in my soul that I was afraid he was devouring all of my innermost thoughts. His intrigued gaze danced over every inch of my face; my blue eyes, my button nose, the freckle that sat in the middle of my cheek, and finally landed on my gloss-colored lips. I didn't know what I'd do if he got any closer. I felt the injection of panic flood through my veins. I didn't like being this vulnerable. The feelings of being trapped like a caged animal warped my mind, then my eyes slammed shut and my body completely froze.

"Eden." Ky's soft voice filled my ears, and I finally opened my eyes to find him looking at me completely in shock. "I was just going to get you a card with my number out of the glove box."

It was an innocent move on his part, yet I took it as a threat. What did I honestly think he was going to do? I unclasped the seat belt, opened the door, and stilled. I turned back to look at him, only to find his eyes still focused solely on me. I grabbed the business card he held out to me and gave him the briefest of smiles.

"Thanks for the lift. I'll see you when you need me."

Two days later

"You were made to be fucked. I've been watching you for a long time. I've wanted to have a taste of this pussy, and now here we are. Get yourself on that bed and open up wide, because my

tongue wants your sweet juices."

I woke up with a jolt, the sheets below me drenched in my sweat. My body shook in terror, and my breathing was rushed and panicked. I repeated over and over again that it was just a dream, but still I turned on my light and jumped out of bed. I thought the nightmares had disappeared, but this one had been so real. I swore I could smell him on my body, latching onto my skin, and claiming ownership once again. I tore my pajamas off in the middle of my room, ripping the fabric that seemed to strangle me until I was naked. I rushed to the shower and turned on the hot water. I needed the feeling of burning skin, to feel like I was erasing him off my body with heat and steam. I scrubbed my body raw, using the whole bottle of my favorite body wash in the process and concentrating on the area between my legs. I needed him gone. My mind couldn't comprehend that it was four years ago, that the dream wasn't real. My body slid down the tile wall until I sat on the floor, and I pulled my knees to my chest—this was so unbelievably real, and here I was, alone.

I sat under the heavy stream of water until it turned ice cold and caused a shiver to run down my spine. Time was lost to me. I climbed out of the shower, wrapped my body in a fluffy white towel, and took a chance at looking in the mirror. The girl staring back at me looked scared, almost as if she was beginning to withdraw from the world. I hated being on my own for so long. I always had Tori just a room away, but here I was in a hotel room, in the town I feared the most, and I didn't have anything to grasp on to.

My cell phone pinged with an incoming text on the side table beside my bed, causing me to look away from the girl I was becoming. It was almost midnight and though I went to bed relatively early so I would be refreshed for my first meeting in the morning, I knew that sleep would now evade me. I looked at the bed and I knew I wouldn't be sleeping there. The sheets were drenched, and I couldn't think of anything worse than being back in that bed. I grabbed my phone and moved to the sitting chair near the glass door that led out to the balcony. I guess that was going to be my refuge for the night.

A shocked smile filtered over my lips as I looked at the screen and saw Ky's name. It had been two days since I fled from his car, and this was the first time I had heard from him.

Ky: You ready for tomorrow?

Me: No! I'm nervous so I can't sleep.

Technically that wasn't a lie.

Ky: Would I have hired you if I didn't think you were the best?

Me: Let's just see what you think after the meeting.

Ky: I'll take that as a challenge.

Me: Who will be there tomorrow?

Ky: What? Am I not good enough?

Oh God!

Me: I didn't mean that. That's fine. I'm sorry.

Ky: I was kidding Eden. Tomorrow you'll be meeting with me and Simon Davenport who now runs the LA office of Anderson Publications.
Me: Crap

I placed my phone on my lap. I was wide awake, and I

knew sleep would continue to elude me. It confused me how a couple of simple texts from Ky had provided me with the sense of calm and peace I needed.

I looked out of the window at the midnight sky and wondered when the nightmares and constant panic would all end. I wanted to forget what happened, but I knew it would be with me always. Somehow I had to find a way to stop the horrible memories from ruling my life.

Being back here definitely wouldn't help.

I had six weeks that I needed to survive and then I was gone.

Forever.

KY

I ROAMED AROUND MY apartment before sunrise. Today was meeting day. Simon Davenport was flying over from Los Angeles to discuss the editorial that Eden would be shooting. The band was expected to be arriving in two weeks. I stumbled to the kitchen in my sleepy state and turned on my coffeemaker, desperate for some strong caffeine to run through my veins and bring me to life. My night hadn't panned out as expected, and I sure as hell hadn't expected to be texting Eden at midnight. I felt like a fucking teenager.

She was getting to me at a fast fucking rate, and it was bringing me close to insanity. I had spent the past two days thinking about her reaction in the car. It shocked me, confused me, and worried me. The most shocking part was the need to protect her that I had felt at Delights had come back at a rapid rate. When I saw her freeze in the car, I wanted nothing more than to wrap my arms around her until the fear that was evident on her face disappeared.

I walked back to my room as the coffee simmered away and grabbed my phone from the nightstand. Immediately, I scrolled through until I got to my messages. I reread the last text I had received from her.

Eden: Crap.

I hadn't replied. The message arrived just after I had finally passed out. The clock on my nightstand showed that it was five thirty in the morning when I finally tapped in a quick text, which I knew she'd get when she woke.

Me: Sorry I passed out. You have no need to be nervous. You will be fine.

I locked my phone, then made my way back through my apartment and poured myself a mug of coffee. The chime of an incoming message shocked me. Who the hell was awake at this time?

Eden: Thanks :)

What the hell was she doing awake?

Me: Why are you awake so early? I thought I was the only crazy one awake at this hour.

Eden: I haven't slept. I couldn't shut off my head.

I read her message over again and sighed loudly. For most of the night, I had the same problem, but it was for entirely different reasons. I tapped the counter as I tried to think of what I could possibly say to her message. A minute passed, then five, and then fuck it!

Me: I'll buy you a Red Bull and bring it to the office.

Nice one, Ky. That was a fucking great comeback. I groaned and mentally punched myself in the gut, then busied myself with cooking breakfast.

"Eden has arrived."

Lauren's head poked around my office door, and she smiled knowingly at me as she announced Eden's arrival. I nodded and looked back at my laptop and saw the time.

She was early.

The sound of her voice resonating as she was thanking Lauren grabbed my attention. I sucked in a deep breath as the sound ceased. She was at my door. Why the fuck was I nervous? The door slowly opened, and Eden's head poked in. Once again, she didn't bother knocking. I liked that.

"Am I okay to come in?" she asked softly.

I watched as Eden took a timid step through my office door. I seized the moment to drown in the sight of her. She wore a simple black dress that hugged her curves so tightly yet so perfectly, showing just enough cleavage to make me focus for a second too long. My eyes skimmed down her body and landed on her heels. Purple, high, and sinfully sexy.

Fuck me.

Her cheeks flushed under the intensity of my dark gaze and my ego soared. I got this reaction out of her, by simply looking at her.

"Why are you looking at me like that?" she asked softly, her eyes dropping for a moment to the floor below. "Is something wrong with what I'm wearing?"

She could not be serious. "You have absolutely no clue, do you?"

"About?" The confusion swimming in her blue eyes captivated me. She was serious. She really had no clue about the effect she had on people.

"What you d—."

The soft knock on the door put a halt to our conversation. It was probably for the best, it stopped me from spilling my thoughts out all over the place. Eden shifted on her heel, turned toward the window, and gazed out at the city. I slammed my eyes shut and sucked in two deep breaths, praying that calm would take over my highly unpredictable body and mind.

"Come in."

Lauren pushed open my office door slowly, and the moment she stepped in, her eyes shifted between me and Eden in what I could only describe as expectation. What did she really think would be happening? She coughed quietly to gain Eden's attention, who then turned around sharply.

"Simon Davenport has arrived." Her cheeks instantly flushed. "He also has someone with him." Lauren turned her attention to Eden, and I did not miss the sparkle in her eye or the small smirk that appeared on her lips. I swore they started communicating without saying a word to each other. I looked between both of them as they did some weird girl-only code. I was confused as fuck.

"Thanks, Lauren. Send them in."

Lauren slipped through the door, leaving Eden and me alone. I began tidying up my desk, and I couldn't help but notice Eden fiddling with her hands as she stood awkwardly in the middle of my office, her eyes downcast to the marble floor below. I crossed the room until I was standing just before her. Her blue eyes rose and looked at me so innocently, so nervous, so intrigued. Grabbing her hands in mine, I felt her stiffen slightly, but she didn't pull away. If anything, I'd swear she moved closer to me.

"You need to calm down. You are brilliant at what you do. Would I have hired you otherwise?" The smallest of smiles swam over her lips, and her hands squeezed mine ever so slightly. I'd take it. "You are going to blitz this meeting, okay?"

She nodded.

I led her to the vacant seat on the opposite side of my desk. She dropped my hand and took a seat, crossing her legs at the knees. Yep, the edge of her dress rose in the process. I reluctantly and painstakingly tore my eyes away from her upper thigh and looked to the door as it crept open.

Simon Davenport stepped in with a presence that deserved respect. He was a crazy Australian, who didn't take shit from anyone. He was famous for being brutal in the boardroom, and he scared the fuck out of me at the best of times, but he was also someone who I definitely enjoyed working alongside. He was a man of few words, but recently every correspondence we had involved him telling me about his grandson Max, Savannah, the beautiful Australian girl with a mouthful of sass that was as close to his daughter as anyone, and his son-in-law Tate, who owned the Red Velvet bars.

Simon greeted me with a firm handshake and a pat on the back. Standing beside him was a guy who looked similar to my age and instantly I recognized him as the front man of the band that would be featured in the upcoming issue.

"You must be Eden Rivers." Simon's accent was still thick, even after living in the states for a few years.

Eden rose from her seat and moved until she was standing beside me. She was exuding confidence, and I fucking loved it. The smile on her face, the way her shoulders were back, and the glint in her eye showed me that she knew exactly what she was doing. This was the Eden Rivers I wanted to see.

"What the fuck?" the tattooed man questioned in astonishment, and the next thing I knew, Eden was in his arms and there was absolutely no fear on her face. She was ecstatic. "Baby doll, what are you doing here?" he continued.

Baby doll?

He cupped her face and dropped his lips to her forehead, and immediately the sweetest of smiles appeared on her face. I was lost. Completely and utterly lost.

"I'm assuming you two know each other."

My statement came out harsher than I intended, and suddenly I was under the scrutiny of everyone in the room. Simon shot me a smirk while the guy who still had his arms around

Eden finally took a step back and his eyes darted between Eden and me suspiciously.

"Blake and I are friends from back home," Eden said with a knowing smile on her face.

"Ky, this is Blake Ryan, front man from The Fallen. They will be the featured band for the shoot. He is also an annoying pain in my ass on most days," Simon said, and Blake held out his hand, which I shook firmly.

"This just made being here so much more worthwhile!" The excitement tainting Eden's voice wasn't missed.

Well, that was a kick in the guts, and I couldn't ignore the twist to the heart and punch to my ego. I couldn't let it show though. I was simply the person who was paying Eden for a job, whereas the guy who she was smiling at was someone who she seemed very friendly with.

I shook off the feeling of defeat and went back into Ky Crawford mode—the Ky Crawford, who worked obscene hours, who didn't let women get to him, and who sure as hell, didn't let jealousy tinge his thoughts.

"Okay, enough of the catching up. Can we all take a seat and sort through the details?"

Eden stepped away from Blake and returned to the seat opposite me. I needed to get my emotions in check, and it was time to get this meeting underway. I finally raised my eyes from my laptop and fell into her blue eyes. She looked back at me with apprehension, and I could see the nerves starting to reappear. I reached over the desk and covered her hand with mine, giving her a quick squeeze of encouragement. Her lips twisted into the perfect smile, and before me I saw her switch on confident Eden Rivers.

"Eden, if you can start by letting us know what you envisage for the shoot and then what you will require from us in order to carry it out," I suggested, and out of the corner of my eye I saw Simon grinning at me like a complete fool.

Eden amazed me. Hearing her talk about her ideas and her vision for the shoot was incredible. She had ideas for all of the shoots she would be doing. She informed us of what her requirements would be, the time frame she would need, and she gave us examples of different techniques and styling she wanted to incorporate. She was in her element.

I finally got involved in the meeting and went into business mode. I gave my directions and expectations, and Eden sat silent with the tiniest of smiles playing on her lips. To be honest, it was a turn on showing her what I did, how I did it, and what I expected. I was in my element. As the meeting came to an end, Blake's phone rang. He rose to his feet and excused himself. It had been decided that the main shoot would occur in two weeks and that Eden would accompany the band to the studio where they were recording their latest album and those shots would also feature.

"If we are done, I think I should be getting back to the hotel to try and get my head around this meeting and start scouting some locations. It was really great to meet you, and thank you again for this opportunity." Eden smiled gratefully at Simon and shook his hand with confidence after she stood.

"The pleasure has been all mine. This guy hasn't stopped raving about you." Simon gestured at me, and I gritted my teeth. She didn't need to know that every recent conversation I'd had with Simon involved her in some way, but it was true, and he was clearly loving every minute of divulging it.

Eden's eyes met mine, and I felt my lips twitch into a subtle smile. "I'll walk you out."

I knew I still had more to discuss with Simon, but I wanted a moment with Eden before she disappeared. Following her out of my office and down the hall toward the elevators, I fell silent. I had a billion things I wanted to ask, and so many things I wanted to suggest, but I seemed to have lost my balls somewhere during that meeting.

"So are you going to tell me ho—" I started to ask.

"Eden! Wait up!"

We both turned at the sound of Blake's voice and watched as he jogged down the hall with a huge smile plastered on his face.

"You, Colby, and I need to do dinner while we are here. He would love to see his girl."

Eden's features softened as she looked at him. "Colby is here?" she asked breathlessly.

Okay, now who the fuck was Colby? And why did the sound of his name make her blush, and more importantly, what the hell was the meaning behind *his girl?*

"Shit, I've got to go, but I'll call you when we are all here and organize something. I am so fucking happy to see you!" Blake leaned in and placed a kiss on her cheek, then gave me a solid nod before he ran down the hall and disappeared into the elevator, leaving Eden blushing and me in somewhat of a confused state.

After she had watched Blake disappear into the elevator, Eden turned to me. With a smile, she lifted her hand to her hair and proceeded to untie her loose braid, then with steady fingertips, she unraveled her hair until loose curls hung over her shoulders. I don't think I breathed the entire time she did it. That simple move shot straight to my cock, who enjoyed it just as much as my eyes. She had absolutely no fucking idea at all.

"Ky, Eden, I just saw that we have all missed one signature on the contract." Simon's thick Australian accent sounded from down the hall. Eden and I headed back to my office with her escape being foiled.

"You've got it bad," Simon mumbled softly as I passed him. I shot him a glare that screamed "piss off" and walked straight to my desk while Eden lingered at the door. Fuck. Did she hear? Her cheeks weren't flushed, so I assumed she was oblivious to Simon's ridiculous statement.

I scribbled my signature on the contract in front of me, and then slid it across the table to Eden.

"I will let myself out. You two kids behave yourselves," Simon suggested with a smirk.

The door clicked behind him, leaving Eden and me alone in my office. Eden had crossed the room and was looking at a piece of artwork I had commissioned by a local up-and-coming artist. My head was screaming at me to leave, to disappear and get myself in check, but my body refused to escape the temptation in front of me.

"I told you that you had nothing to worry about." My voice startled her, and she swung around to face me.

"I was so nervous. I swear I stuttered at one point." Her soft laughter filled my ears.

I pushed away from the desk and crossed my office until I was standing next to her. Her gaze shifted back to the painting, and we remained in silence as we got lost in our thoughts. My mind went back to Blake's comment about Colby, and it sat precariously in my thoughts, dangling and teasing me.

"I didn't know you were someone's girl?"

She turned to face me and her eyes said a thousand words before she finally spoke. "I'm not anyone's girl."

I didn't know what came over me. All sense of reality escaped and suddenly, in my office, I lost control. I took one step toward her, gently tucked her hair behind her ear, and circled her waist with one of my arms. My senses were overcome by her perfume and the scent of her shampoo. Her eyes widened, and the moment they dropped to my lips, I couldn't stop the desire roaring to life. I dipped my face close to hers and tightened my grasp on her waist, then I felt her sharp exhale of breath on my craving lips.

"Don't. No!" she pleaded, her hands lifting to my chest and pushing me away.

I stumbled back, knowing that I had completely and utterly

fucked up.

"Look Eden—"

I didn't get another word in. Within seconds, she was rushing out of my office, leaving me to sink into a pit of confusion and anxiety, all the while I was being swallowed by the raw need for this woman.

Eden

ONE MINUTE I WAS floating on cloud nine while getting lost in the presence of Ky Crawford, and the next I was fleeing the building, gasping for air like I was drowning.

The meeting went better than I could have ever imagined. My confidence ignited the moment I began to speak and both Ky and Simon fell into a silent trance as they absorbed my ideas and visions for the shoot. I couldn't have asked for anything more. Then there was the moment I locked eyes with Blake Ryan, one of my closest friends, who seemed to have forgotten to tell me about this little meeting. I felt like I had slipped into an alternate universe seeing him standing before me, but I couldn't ignore the feeling of calm that swam through me the instant he held me in his arms. Then finding out that Colby was going to be in town, it was almost too much to comprehend.

And then there was Ky.

Confusing yet intriguing Ky Crawford.

I rushed down the sidewalk as quickly as my stupid high heels would allow. My mind kept replaying the feeling of Ky's breath dancing on my lips and the weight of his hand, so delicately yet with so much ownership, on my waist as he pulled me into the firmness of his chest. It was so unexpected, so frightening, yet so exhilarating, and that was what freaked me out.

I said no to him.

I said the one word I promised myself I'd never say. What

was I thinking? No meant consequences and pain, it resulted in torment and ramifications, and it was only a matter of time before they would be unleashed on me. Ky would be coming for me, all because I said no.

The moment the cab pulled in front of the hotel, I realized I had a sea of people in the foyer to get through before I got to the sanctuary of my room. Thankfully my room was on the ground floor, so I wasn't confronted with the awkward elevator ride with strangers while I fell apart. I paid the cab driver, shot out of the cab, and with my head down, I moved through the foyer and down the hall until my gaze finally hit the door that would lead me to safety.

It was only after I locked and deadbolted the door behind me that I finally took a shuddering breath. My exhausted body slid down the back of the polished wood door and fell into a heap on the floor as my safety of solitude arrived. A waterfall of tears slid over my cheeks as I drew my knees to my chest. This was my life. This was what I had been living with. It was those moments of intense panic that gripped me, the confusion and fight of my heart versus head, and the constant battle of whether I would ever be able to have a regular relationship, with normal feelings, with normal reactions to a man. This was the reality that had been forced on me and the fear that adorned my every breath.

Fear was a devastating thing. It gripped you to the point of being completely incapacitated and swallowed every rational thought that was your given right. The most frightening part of fear was that it had the potential to completely destroy you if you let it.

I didn't know how long I sat there. My body locked tight until I was frozen stiff and gasping for any air I could summon. Jeremy decided to appear in my thoughts, and once again, he showed me all that made me who I was today. Every time that nightmare appeared, I relived the pain, the agony, the brutal hurt he delivered to me. I tasted every single disgusting, whiskey-fueled kiss he planted on my mouth, and my body ached as I felt every forced and excruciating entry he took without consent from my body. I slammed my eyes shut, praying for something, anything, to take me away from this.

The familiar ring of an incoming call finally offered me my desired solace, ripping me away from my fear-ridden demise. I dropped my hands from around my knees and pulled myself up from the floor to grab my bag that I had chucked on the bed. I fumbled around for my phone and pulled out the vibrating contraption. Ky's name flashed on the screen. His action had brought me here, but now he was saving me from the nightmare of Jeremy. I looked at his name pulsating before me, and for a moment, I questioned whether I should answer it. I slammed my fingertip down on the reject button, and his name faded away from me.

I put my phone on silent and shoved it deep into the black hole of my bag. It was still early, barely midday, but all I wanted to do was forget. I was stumbling down the familiar path of self-destruction, and the moment my eyes locked with the mini bar, my silent prayers were answered.

Vodka.

Vodka would solve all my problems. My greedy hands pried open the bar fridge and collected six bottles. I cradled them tightly against my chest like they were my prized possessions, and made my way across the room to the uninviting bed, collapsing onto the floral comforter with a sigh.

I threw my head back, and the first entire bottle of vodka disappeared. The burn of the spirit cascading down my throat finally made me feel somewhat normal, it made me feel alive, and in some crazy way, it made me feel in control. This was why I had a dangerous and seductive relationship with vodka. It provided me everything that I needed, and when my thoughts got to be too much, it allowed me to disappear. One bottle became two, and two bottles became three before my head started to get foggy, my eyes began to shadow with drunkenness, and I felt the waves of unconsciousness fill me. My body molded into the uncomfortable mattress, and I hadn't bother to change out of the black dress I had worn to the office. At the exact moment I was about to fall into the pits of a vodka induced coma, Ky popped into my head.

A single tear escaped my eye and trickled over my cheek, as his beautifully handsome face and those captivating eyes swam through my thoughts. I was so confused. For a split second, when his deliciously plump lips moved close to mine, I had imagined what he would taste like, what it would have been like to completely hand myself over to him. I had forgotten who I was. He allowed me to forget everything that was hanging over me.

But I knew I couldn't let him.

Pound, pound, pound.

The moment my eyes pried open, my head began screaming bloody murder at me. Vodka had come out victorious yet again. The twisting knife in my head didn't cease when I slowly sat up in bed and looked outside to see the sun slowly rising on the horizon.

"Eden, please open the door."

Ky's deep voice penetrated through the hotel door. I desperately looked around the room for an escape, but there was nowhere to run. I climbed cautiously out of bed, pulled the hem of the dress that had risen to my hips down over my thighs, and stumbled to the door. I didn't even need to look in the mirror to know that I looked like a tragic hung-over mess. With shaking hands, I unlatched the chain and then unclicked the main lock.

I took a step away from the door, not opening it.

"It's unlocked," I said just loud enough to be heard. It took less than two seconds for the door to fly open and for Ky to rush in. He still wore the same outfit he was wearing the day before, and he looked like he hadn't slept a wink.

I watched him carefully. His eyes searched the room around us, and the moment they landed on the empty bottles of vodka, he sighed and ran his hands over his face. Great, not only did he think I was a crazy woman for fleeing, he now thought I was a drunk.

He took two steps toward me and I backed up, my hand feeling behind me for something to hold onto, and my eyes dropping to the bright blue carpet on the floor below. My hand met the fabric of the chair in the corner, and I was trapped.

"Look at me." His voice came out soothing, not one ounce of force behind it. "Eden, please."

My eyes ran over his body as I lifted them from the floor and they made their way to his face. Sadness, confusion, and wariness met me when I fell into his eyes.

"Why did you run?" he whispered in question.

"I said no. I didn't want you to hurt me for saying no. I shouldn't have said no."

The color immediately drained from his face, and he took a step away from me. I watched him carefully, not knowing what to expect. His presence confused me; he intimidated me, yet he drastically captivated me. The thought of him hurting me left the moment he looked at me with eyes that were bristling with concern, like he was fearful and regretful.

"You thought I was going to hurt you?" His words were barely a whisper, and he stared at me awaiting my answer. "Eden, answer me. Did you think I would hurt you?"

"Yes. I don't know," I choked out, and for one of the first times ever, I was using yes honestly.

His face paled, and he swayed on his feet as if I had just taken the air from his lungs. He dropped to the edge of the bed, and his head fell into his hands. I had no clue what to do, so I remained standing, watching a man who demanded respect and who held such a strong presence crumble before my eyes.

"I would never hurt you, Eden. Never. I should never have thought of kissing you."

"So you didn't want to kiss me?" I spat out before I even had a chance to stop myself. I slammed my eyes shut at the stupidity of my question. Here I was, with the man I fled, but now I couldn't ignore the twinge of disappointment I felt when he said he didn't want to kiss me.

Ky lifted his head from his hands and his eyes darkened as he looked at me. He hesitated for a brief moment before he rose from the bed and took a step until his chest was mere inches from mine. I could feel the heat coming off his body, and I was sure that he could hear my heart pounding in my chest.

"I want nothing more than to taste your lips, but I know I shouldn't. Fuck I want to kiss you Eden, but I also need to learn to behave myself when it comes to you." He crossed his arms over his chest as if he was trying to stop himself from reaching out and touching me. "You interest me, Eden. There is something about you that I want to have. You have this innocence about you, but then I see a glimmer in your eye that tells me that there is a sassy woman locked away who needs to be unleashed, who needs the opportunity for freedom. You grabbed my attention the very first time I saw you, and it hasn't been lost since."

"I never thanked you for what you did," I admitted sheepishly. "For saving me from that guy."

"You never have to thank me for protecting you. I should have done it earlier, and I will forever regret that." His voice faltered at his words, and he shook his head slightly. "I should go."

Ky moved across the room with confident strides and stalled when he reached for the door handle. He looked at me over his shoulder, and his eyes pleaded with me. "Never be fearful of saying no to me, Eden. I know there will be a time when I'll need you to say no."

KY

SHE THOUGHT I WAS going to hurt her.

She thought I had the potential to fucking hurt *her.*

I rushed out of the room moments before the twisted hands of anger took hold of me. Everything she admitted sat with me like a tormenting reminder of how fucked up life could be. I had crossed a very hazy line yesterday when I went to kiss her. What the fuck was I thinking? I wasn't thinking, and that was the fucking problem. Eden Rivers was quickly making me lose all sense of reality.

Leaving her in that hotel room was the smartest thing I could have done. If I had stayed one more minute, I would have asked her to kiss me. And with Tori's words taunting me, *"she can't say no,"* I knew that it was only a matter of time before I broke.

With frustration seeping from every pore, I sped back to my apartment. I needed a distraction, I needed to satisfy and put to good use the endorphins running rampant through my body. I couldn't stop thinking about her, and my mind continually taunted me with memories of her face as she admitted her fear.

I threw my keys on the kitchen island, then forcefully ripped my phone from my pocket and dialed Josh's number. After two rings, he picked up, and I didn't give him a chance to speak.

"Josh I need to work out," I roared into the phone as I stepped into my bedroom and headed for my dresser.

"And hello to you too, big brother."

"Are you working out with me or not?" I had no time for his smart-ass remarks.

"I'll meet you at your place in ten."

I didn't bother replying. I hung up the phone, threw it on my bed, and watched it bounce off the mattress and drop to the floor. My head tilted to the ceiling, and a deep sigh erupted from my chest as my emotions bubbled over. I couldn't fathom her fear of me. It was beyond unjustifiable. It was unwarranted and uncalled for. One thing she didn't know about me was that I was a stubborn prick, and now I was more determined than ever to get inside her head, to twist my way into her thoughts, her fears, her seemingly dangerous habit of saying yes to everything. I would make her say no to me and mean it, and see that there was no fear to have.

"Where's the cranky bastard?" Josh questioned from the living room.

"Bedroom."

Moments later, he filled the doorway and gave me an inquisitive look. "So what's crawled up your ass and died?"

"Let's just go to the gym."

Two hours later, I had punched, run, rowed and kicked every ounce of frustration out of my body. Sweat dripped from me, and my lungs ached as they craved air that had been stolen. Finally, calm filled me. Josh watched me, waiting for me to open up about what had caused my sudden pissed-off mood. We both grabbed a shower and then headed to the closest bar we could find.

"So spit it out," he demanded, sitting beside me at the bar after ordering both of us a beer.

One thing about my brother was that he would never give up on finding out what was bothering me. Throughout everything, he knew just what to say or do to get me to open up, even if it was in the most brutal way. He was there during my darkest of days, when regret tore through me, when I believed that I didn't deserve the life I was given, and he had talked me off the ledge more times than I'd like to admit.

"I almost kissed Eden yesterday, and she completely freaked out. So I went to see her earlier today and she was so scared, like terrified of me. She thought I'd hurt her because she said no to me."

"What the fuck?" he exclaimed with wide eyes.

"She is doing things to me, man. I thought I could resist her. Fuck, I need to resist her, but ever since that first night I just need to have her in my sight. I am drawn to her like a fucking moth to a flame."

"Does she know?" he questioned softly.

I turned to Josh and sighed. "She knows nothing."

"You are treading in dangerous waters, brother."

I knew he was right.

Two days had passed since I had seen Eden. I hadn't contacted her, and she hadn't contacted me. Our conversation and everything that had happened still filled my thoughts. It was so fucked up because the longer I was away from her, the more I thought about her. I dived into work, I worked from sunup until way after sundown, yet everything still reminded me of her. I saw her name pop up in emails, I heard that she had come in to pick up things from Josh or Lauren, and I swore I even smelled her perfume in the elevator once. I was completely and utterly screwed.

The door of my office swung open and Ashlyn strutted in like she was a woman on a mission. I raised my eyes from my laptop as she made herself at home on the corner of my desk. It was close to five p.m., so I knew I still had a long night ahead of me.

"You're leaving," she stated matter-of-fact.

"And why would I do that?" I huffed in response.

"Because I'm sick of seeing you in this fucking rut you've wedged yourself into. You are coming to my place for beer and Chinese."

"I'm not in a rut."

"Whatever you say, Ky. Get your ass up and out of this office. I'm parked out front, be there in five minutes."

I collapsed onto Ashlyn's couch and threw my head back against the plush cushions. She had won. I left the office. My eyes closed, and I felt the first waves of exhaustion crash within me.

"You look like shit."

I pried open my eyes at the sound of Ashlyn's voice and watched her sink down on the couch beside me. I grabbed the beer she held out to me and I almost devoured it in one gulp.

"Have you spoken to Eden lately?" I asked without thinking.

So much for subtleness, Ky.

Ashlyn's eyes widened, a reaction I didn't miss. She turned to face me and threw back the bottle of beer as I awaited her response. The longer she took, the more frustrated I got. I clearly wasn't a patient man.

"Yep, I had breakfast with her this morning, and then we worked on some ideas for her first shoot."

Ashlyn fell back against the couch and focused squarely on me, in such a way that I felt incredibly on edge. She was notorious for being able to read me like I was the world's most open book. I didn't have to say shit, and she knew what I was thinking. This wasn't good. I had seen this look before. She was taking everything in, she was sorting through my thoughts, my words, my concerns, my fears, and she would ultimately come to a realization.

"She is getting to you," she whispered. "No wait! She has

already gotten to you. Ky, this is doing a number on you. You have to stop. Step back."

"I don't know how."

Somewhere between sitting on Ashlyn's couch and flipping my phone over in my hand for the hundredth time, I had an epiphany. I couldn't ignore that Eden was getting to me any longer. Hell, I knew that she got to me that very first night when I decided to ride in like a knight in shining fucking armor. This was where the problem lay. Women never got to me, because I never allowed it. I shut down. I put up my walls. I was sometimes an asshole. But now Eden was getting to me. I had allowed her to get to me. There was no chance that this would end well because it had the potential to destroy both of us.

I needed to find a distraction, and I knew who would have a solution.

I scrolled to Josh's name in my phone and my knee bounced as I tapped at the screen.

Me: I need to go out tonight.

Josh: Hang on a minute. Is this really Ky Crawford?

Me: You're an asshole.

Josh: What's got into you or should I say who has got to you?

Me: No one.

Josh: Cough Eden Cough. Come to my place at nine.

Me: See you then.

My idea to go out was squashed when I arrived at Josh's apartment to find that he clearly had no plans to go anywhere. I heard the music the moment I stepped out of the elevators, and when I opened his front door I was swamped by blaring guitars and drums that mixed with the sounds of laughter and chatter. Josh lifted his chin to greet me from across his apartment. I said hello to a couple of people I knew, skimmed over who was here and then went straight to the fridge and grabbed a beer.

"I heard a rumor you'd be turning up tonight."

I twisted around to find Anna, a girl who seemed destined to get into my pants since college. Her eyes were ablaze with want, and her tits were spilling out of her incredibly tight dress. Did she not know that it was fucking winter outside?

"Yep. Here to get drunk. That's it." I dismissed her and stepped out of the kitchen. My escape halted when her hand grabbed hold of my arm. I turned to face her, only to find her putting on puppy dog eyes and pouting her lips. "Anna, it's not going to happen."

"So you're rejecting me. Again." Her voice was breathless, and her face thundered with anger like she couldn't believe it was happening. It wasn't the first time, so it shouldn't come as a surprise.

I groaned and ripped my arm away from hers. "It's not rejection, Anna, it's avoidance."

I left her standing—mouth agape, hands on hips, fury flooding her face—and moved to the couch.

Soon enough, I was opening my fifth beer and a buzz was swimming through my veins. Thankfully Anna had left me the fuck alone, and I was enjoying the peace and quiet. I twisted my body as the couch dipped beside me, and with the bottle to my lips and through hazy eyes, I found Eden staring at me with a shy grin.

"Are you ignoring me?" she asked innocently, her brow rising in the process.

She looked fucking phenomenal in her tight jeans and black top that clung to her body, and her hair flowed over her shoulders in an "I just got laid" look. I was in trouble. The beer had dissolved my resistance, and now there wasn't a chance that my dick and my brain would communicate because my cock twitched just at the sight of her.

I downed the rest of my beer, watching her over the bottle. Her face was passive and unreadable, but I loved the pink tinge sweeping over her cheeks. The party swirled around me, but right there on the couch it could have only just been me and Eden and I wouldn't have cared for a second. She pulled her leg up so it was under her and leaned back, her face resting in her hand, her cheek against her palm as she continued to watch me. It was like we were reading each other, awaiting the other's next move. I lowered the empty bottle from my lips and let it fall to the ground below me.

"I didn't know you were here, so I couldn't be ignoring you." Her face fell and instantly I felt like an asshole. "You should have said something to me when you saw me," I offered with a smile.

"You had a girl with you. I didn't want to interrupt your date again. I've already done that once," she stated, her comment throwing me back to our meeting at Delights when she accused me of being on a date with one of the local girls there.

I shook my head and smirked. "I've told you before. That girl at Delights wasn't my date, and the girl you saw me talking to tonight wanted a good time. She was blond anyway, and I'm pretty sure I've made it perfectly clear that I am more into brunettes."

"So you discriminate against blondes?" She returned my smirk and her fingertips ran through her hair in an action I couldn't be positive she knew she was doing.

"Well, let's just say if you were to dye your hair blond, I wouldn't discriminate against you."

Fuck! I was flirting with her. Her eyes widened fleetingly under the suggestive words I spat out, and I clearly had absolutely no consideration of whether she'd run for the exit door or stay here. The briefest of smiles touched her lips, which further intensified the inappropriateness of my thoughts. I needed to reel it in. I couldn't flirt with her. She wasn't like any other girl I had met before, and it would be so fucking easy to completely freak her out, just like almost kissing her did.

"So how's all the prep going for the photo shoots? I am looking forward to seeing what you come up with. You definitely have a lot of work ahead of you," I mumbled in a pathetic way of changing the subject. I internally groaned at the stupidity of my question.

She narrowed her eyes and shook her head at my absurd statement. "Um, yeah. It's going great. I have a lot of ideas, and I'm actually working on it pretty solidly next week."

"Pretty girl, your drink is ready!" Josh's voice sounded from across the apartment. Eden turned and the biggest of smiles spread across her lips as she looked back at my brother.

"I guess I'll see you around," she murmured softly as she pulled herself up from the couch. Our eyes locked on one another, and I knew I was getting sucked in. I was losing. Fuck you beers. Why did I think drinking would be a good idea?

Eden took off quickly and crossed the crowded living room. Every guy in the room turned and eye-fucked her as she passed and it was clear as day that they were drinking in the curves of her body and the way her hips swayed with every step she took. I was sure as shit that they were all imagining what was under those purple jeans. She got to Josh's side and his arm fell to her shoulders as he handed her a red colored drink.

It took every bit of strength I had not to rush over and throw myself at her and scream, "It's me." But that was something

I couldn't do. Not now. Not ever. I tore my eyes away from Eden and concentrated on the black screen of the television as my mind started flashing every single scenario I had. This was karma coming back to punch me in the throat and make me remember why I didn't deserve happiness or forgiveness or a second chance. Karma was the little voice that kept me awake late at night, the reminder that sat on my shoulder and whispered words of truth to me and the tiny little stab in my heart when I was starting to feel at ease. But now karma was a roaring bitch that was making herself very known.

"Why are you sitting over here like a social outcast?"

The sound of Ashlyn's voice caused me to crack a smile. My arms shot out and she yelped as I pulled her onto my lap, and she immediately wrapped her arms around my neck and fell into my chest. To an outsider, we would look like a couple simply snuggling on the couch together, but this was just us. The closeness that we shared was what kept us together, it kept the strength of our friendship alive, a friendship that had been built on the heartbreak that we both suffered, and the heartbreak that we helped each other get through.

"I am trying to stay away from Eden," I admitted sheepishly.

"It's not working though?"

"I just told her that I preferred brunettes and that if she dyed her hair blond, I'd make a fucking exception for her." I groaned at the stupidity of my statement.

Ashlyn's laughter spun around us, grabbing everyone's attention. My gaze instantly moved to the kitchen where Josh and Eden both stood watching us. Josh knew all about my friendship with Ashlyn, and merely shook his head dismissively at the scene while Eden continued to watch Ashlyn and me intently.

"I never thought I'd be in this position again," I admitted, still locked on Eden's eyes. She broke contact and turned back toward Josh and his friend, and I turned back to Ashlyn. "It's killing me, Ash. The words are sitting on the tip of my tongue, but I can't risk saying everything I want to because I know what will happen."

Ashlyn's face fell at my words, and she was hit by a storm of her own emotions as she glanced over at Eden. "I fucking hate secrets."

"Me too, Ash. Me too," I replied with all sincerity.

Ashlyn climbed off my lap, kissed my forehead, and disappeared back into the kitchen. I kept to myself, talking to those who came to me but wanting to sit on my own while the party continued around me. Later that night, I stood in the bathroom looking at my reflection in the mirror. I had just escaped the craziness of the party for a couple of minutes of peace, and as I stared back at myself, I tried to think of a scenario that would allow me to disappear back to my apartment.

The door burst open breaking my peace. I shot a furious look into the mirror, directed squarely at the intruder who dared to shatter my solitude. The moment my eyes met Ashlyn's panic-washed face in the mirror, my fury disappeared, only to be replaced with unease. I knew immediately that something wasn't right, and it unleashed panic within me. She rushed into the room completely oblivious to what she could actually be walking into and grabbed my arm, tugging me toward the door in desperation. "Chris just turned up completely uninvited, and he's found Eden."

Hearing his name fall from Ashlyn's lips pissed me off. Why the fuck was he here? Actually, I knew why he was here, and it had everything to do with Eden, and everything to do with fucking with my head. I didn't hesitate for a second. I stormed out of the bathroom with Ashlyn following, and rushed through Josh's apartment in search of Eden.

Chris had her body pinned up against the bar by his, and his hands were cupping her face, forcing her to look at him. Eden's eyes met mine over his shoulder as I sprinted across the room toward her and safety flashed within them. The moment I reached him, my protective instincts took over. I tore at the back of his shirt, ripping his body away from hers. My hand encased his throat as I pushed him violently up against the wall, with such force that one of Josh's pieces of art rattled and fell to the ground below.

"How many fucking times do I have to warn you? Stay the fuck away from her and keep your hands to yourself. When will you understand that she is mine?" I hissed with stern warning, pushing harder against his throat until his face started flaming red and his attempts to breathe were cut off.

The smirk that crossed his face wasn't missed. His eyes glided between me and Eden with such intrigue and intent to shock and destroy. I witnessed the exact moment realization hit him. If wickedness had a face, it was now taunting me and loving every single fucking part of it. "Does she know?" Chris choked out with a spiteful tongue.

My body froze, but the pressure of my hand on his throat didn't diminish. He and I were both aware that he was holding all the power in the palm of his hands, but I refused to give him the opportunity to speak any further.

"Shut your fucking mouth," Josh warned beside me. "Who the fuck invited you here? You are not welcome here or anywhere near me, Ky, Eden, or Ashlyn, do you fucking hear me? Get the fuck out of here before you regret stepping foot into my house."

"Ky," Eden's soft, pleading voice hit my ears full force. I had completely forgotten anyone else was in the room. I tore my eyes from Chris's reddening face and found Eden's apprehensive gaze looking back at me.

I released my grip on his throat, and he gasped for a much-needed breath. My arm found Eden's waist, I pulled her close to my body, and she came willingly. "Come with me," I said, breathing into her ear.

I pulled her away from Chris, who was still spitting insults, and with my arm still firmly placed around her waist, I headed toward the opposite side of Josh's apartment. I knew I had grabbed every single person's attention with my outburst, but right now I didn't give a fuck. My attention was completely on the girl who now stood in front of me, her back up against the wall. Her eyes widened as I stepped into her space and wrapped my arms around her waist, resting my hands on her lower back.

"We are acting, remember. This is chapter two of me being a knight in shining armor."

"Okay." She inhaled sharply and her hands gripped the front of my shirt.

I leaned toward her until my forehead rested against hers. My arms tightened so she fell against my chest, my arms cocooning her tightly. Our breath bounced of each other's lips, and, even though, our lips weren't touching, it was the most intense moment I had shared with someone, and I knew all eyes were on us.

"I never imagined our first kiss would be because we had to pretend," I whispered hoarsely. "There is not going to be anything perfect, spectacular, or spontaneous about this, and I fucking hate that."

She opened her blue eyes and looked directly at me without an ounce of fear. It made me breathe a sigh of relief, but it also unleashed a torrent of confusion.

"This is the second time I've pulled you away like a caveman, stating that you are mine, so I need to make it realistic Eden. You have about ten seconds to say no before I kiss you."

"I. . . . . . yes."

"Come with me," I said for the second time in the space of five minutes. My hands fell from her waist and grabbed her hand. She didn't falter. We fell into silence as I clutched her hand obsessively and headed toward the large sliding door that led to Josh's balcony. It was freezing cold, but I didn't want our first kiss to be up against a wall in my brother's apartment while strangers watched on with gawking eyes. I slid open the door and nodded out onto the tiled floor which housed a BBQ grill, two lounging chairs, and a glass table.

"It's freezing," she hissed, her teeth chattering and her arms going protectively around her waist to try and gain some much-needed warmth as I followed her out and shut the glass door behind us.

I pulled her toward me, and she yelped at the suddenness of my movements. The freezing air was awash with evidence of our harsh intake of breath as we both fought our own internal battles. Her body smashed into mine as she lost balance, and her arms went around my waist on instinct and locked tight. Fuck. I could feel her heart beating rapidly against my chest, and it unleashed the beast inside me. I was doing that to her, and whether it was in fear or excitement I didn't really care. My hands cupped her face, and my thumb traced the length of her bottom lip as her eyes beamed at me, not willing or able to look away.

"When's the last time you kissed a man?" I whispered, knowing that I was officially crossing every single boundary I had been desperate to put up.

"Two years ago." Her breath caressed my thumb as she spoke.

I pushed against her body so she stepped backward until the wall beside the glass door stopped her. The feeling of her curves, her breasts, and her heartbeat against me, as we moved, was something I couldn't explain, but I knew my heart, my head, and my dick were thoroughly enjoying it. "I'm excited to taste you, Eden Rivers."

In the moonlight that was shadowing the balcony, her eyes dropped to my lips and that was all the encouragement I needed. My mouth fell to hers and my heart stammered in my chest. If only she knew what this actually meant. I felt the sharp intake of air she took under the sensation of us colliding as one and my breath became hers and her fears became mine.

The moment Eden let herself completely go, she fell into the kiss and her body went limp. My needy hands wrapped tightly around her waist, taking her full weight. The urge to touch her skin overwhelmed me, and I couldn't resist. My fingertips glided under her shirt and rested on her lower back just above the waistband of her jeans.

My eager tongue traced her plump bottom lip, sweeping back and forth, tasting her strawberry-flavored lip gloss. She softly moaned against my mouth, as a growl erupted from mine. Could she really be enjoying this as much as me? The thought only deepened my need. My tongue danced into her mouth, colliding with hers so eagerly. With complete blatant want, she matched everything I offered. She tasted of berries and gin, better than I could ever have imagined, and the warmth swirling within her body flooded through mine.

Her zealous hands bunched the side of my shirt, pulling me closer as she unraveled in the intensity of the moment. This wasn't the girl who had fled my office when I first attempted to kiss her, and this certainly wasn't the girl who exuded nervousness just by being in my presence. Eden Rivers was morphing into a vixen before my eyes. Now, as she kissed me, Eden showed me that she knew what she wanted and wasn't holding back. It felt like this was so natural, so unique, and so wanted, and it confused the fuck out of me.

"Um, you two, Chris has left."

Eden gasped against my lips at the sound of Josh's amused voice. I had been so lost in Eden Rivers that I didn't even hear the door open. Her body jerked away slightly, but her grasp didn't lessen on my shirt.

"Shit," I groaned into the air, and I barely heard the door close as Josh left us in a torrent of heavy, ragged breathing. My eyes found hers still swimming with desperate intensity at what we had just unleashed on each other. I smirked as I leaned in, my heated breath hitting the sensitive skin just below her ear. "You certainly don't kiss like a woman who hasn't kissed a man in two years."

Eden's body drew back to mine like a magnetic force beckoned between us. Her body tensed under my words and her breathing halted. The vixen had left and insecure Eden had returned, yet she was still completely destroying me.

"We seem to be good at pretending," she whispered into the night air.

"I wasn't pretending, Eden." My hands cupped her face, and I was desperate to show her the truth in my words. "I could never pretend with you."

"But you said. . . . . ."

"Did anything about that kiss indicate I was pretending?"

Her eyes tore away from mine and dropped to the floor. There was no way I was pretending, and I knew for a fact that she wasn't pretending. The way her body molded against mine, the way the heat from her body hit mine. How could I possibly never want that again? I was an idiot for thinking once would be enough.

The words that swirled in my head, begging to come out, had the potential to destroy everything. It would be the beginning of a test that I hoped we both failed, a test where I wanted her to prove me wrong. I didn't think I could have handled her answer, but the question had been sitting on the tip of my tongue from the moment Tori made the stark admission, and now after the mind-blowing kiss we shared I couldn't stop myself any longer.

I tucked a piece of hair behind her ear and my lips fell back to hers for an intimate kiss, a single brush of my lips against hers.

"You can't say no." I dropped the bombshell, and her eyes widened in such a way that she answered my question without a spoken word. "That's a really fucking dangerous habit to have, Eden. I didn't believe it when Tori told me, but now I see it every time I am around you. Did you just agree to kiss me because you didn't think you had another option?"

"It's not like I can help it. I didn't ask to be like this, Ky," she spat in anger, her eyes darting away from me and her grip on my shirt loosening. "And I don't want to talk about this."

"Did you want to kiss me?" I pushed on, breaking the distance she put between us.

"You said we were pretending, that you wanted Chris to get away from me."

"Did you want to kiss me?" I repeated.

Her eyes darted away from mine and her face went like a stone. I could literally see her walls shooting up. "Yes," she finally said.

"And suddenly, I don't believe you."

"What do you want me to say? I'm not like other girls, Ky. I don't go around making out with random guys, and I sure as hell don't let anyone hold me like you just did. I don't let myself get into positions like this, and it's scaring the fuck out of me that I actually did want to kiss you. So yes, I wanted to kiss you, and now that it's done, you are making me regret it."

Her honesty was refreshing. I was finally seeing Eden Rivers and not just her false persona.

"I just have one question for you, Eden."

What the fuck was I doing! *Stop Ky, shut your mouth.* Eden looked at me expectantly, her eyes still flashing with signs of anger. I was losing control at a fast fucking rate and spiraling into a world I wouldn't be able to claw myself out of. Was this my penance being delivered on a platter? A platter that I would have to give back after a month? I wanted to test her, to put to rest Tori's fucked-up statement for good.

I wanted her to say no.

I needed her to say no.

"Give me December, be mine for one month. Believe me when I say you won't regret a second of it. Your yes and your no will be mine, and for the right reasons for once."

Her eyes slammed shut under my question.

"I will make you realize that saying no is your given right and that saying yes can still be a beautiful thing."

I was expecting her to shout at me. I was expecting her to say no and tell me I was an asshole. But she just remained silent. Finally, her eyes opened and she looked at me with the most amazingly bright eyes I'd ever seen. I felt my breath hitch as I took her in.

My hand cupped her cheek and my thumb swept over her soft skin as our gaze danced together. "Think about what I've asked, Eden."

I dropped my hand and quickly moved toward the door. I didn't want her answer then, to be honest, I wasn't sure I'd be able to handle her saying either yes or no.

Eden

THE SMELL OF GREASY, comfort food welcomed me as I stepped into the diner that I had visited with Ky, the very same place where his aunt worked and where I just realized my cousin's best friend worked. What were the odds? Tommy looked up at me in recognition the moment I stepped through the door, and soon enough, his arms had engulfed me in a tight hug. I hadn't seen him since he was fourteen and beginning to notice girls, but now he was tall, handsome, and pimple free. He and my cousin Andy had been so protective of me when they were growing up, even though I was six years older. I never had siblings, so they were like my little brothers. They regularly visited me when I was in the hospital after the rape. Even though I didn't want anyone seeing me like that, their stubborn asses wouldn't listen to me. They brought my favorite chocolate milk and trashy magazines, kept me company when I couldn't sleep, and didn't leave the room when the police updated me on what was happening with the case. While my parents were crumbling at the news that their baby girl had been tainted for life, my honorary little brothers were stepping up, and for that reason I would be forever grateful to those two.

"Eden?" Tommy's low voice questioned incredulously.

"Hey, Tommy." I sighed in happiness.

"I cannot believe you are back! Andy didn't even tell me, the asshole,"

"I don't think he even knows, he is too busy traveling

around Europe to worry about his favorite cousin being back in town."

I pulled out one of the stools at the counter and spent fifteen minutes catching up with Tommy. He spoke excitedly about college, his single life, his continued love for surfing, and then—for good measure—he dropped the sly "I'm still waiting for you to accept my marriage proposal." My shoulders shook with laughter. The conversation suddenly took a serious turn and all laughter ceased as he leaned over the counter and began firing questions about what I was doing back here and what I've been up to. But I knew he was skating around asking me how I was.

"I'm okay, Tommy," I admitted quietly, answering his unasked question. He nodded and grabbed hold of my hand, giving it a friendly squeeze. Worried, unsure eyes darted over my face in an attempt to believe what I was saying, and all I could do was give him an encouraging smile—it was all I could muster. When he was satisfied with my response, Tommy turned away and served a waiting customer.

It was beyond amazing to see a familiar face in the place I despised. I tapped on the counter and hummed along to the music flooding the air from the surround sound speakers, and my mind automatically crossed to the night before.

I had barely slept a wink.

My lips were still alight from the sensation of Ky's lips on mine. I couldn't stop touching them, and even now my fingertips ran over my swollen pout. He had kissed me, devoured me, and wholly owned me in those few moments.

Did I regret it? *No.*

Did that fact frighten me? *Yes.*

Not only was I dealing with the thought of kissing a guy who was signing off on my paychecks for the next six weeks, but I was also now dealing with Ky's question and his unrealistic suggestion. His words—*give me December, be mine for one month*—had continued to swirl around my head and left me in a complete puddle of emotions, and I hadn't heard from him since.

"You are currently getting eye-fucked," Tommy announced.

I choked on the Coke that he had just placed in front of me and looked at him with wide eyes. Nice to see his subtleness hadn't developed over the years. He watched me with amusement plastered all over his face, then his eyes left mine and glanced over my shoulder. I didn't even want to know. I shook my head and concentrated on the glass in front of me, but now the feeling of being watched swamped me. Damn you, Tommy. How I could be getting eye-fucked, as Tommy called it, made me question this person's desperation. I had left the hotel in my oldest jeans, the hoodie I usually wore to bed, with my hair covered in one of my favorite beanies, and my face free of any makeup.

"He is coming over," Tommy warned, and I stiffened in my seat. Tommy saw the anxiety greet my face, and he remained standing in front of me behind the counter.

The intoxicating scent of sandalwood and musk hit me like a warm summer breeze. I gripped hold of my glass, raised it to my lips, and took a long comforting drink.

"Tommy, I'm ready to order." Ky's voice hit my ears like silk touching skin. Smooth, enticing, and dangerously flirtatious. "I'll also pay for what Eden wants." His words grabbed my attention, and I swung back around to look at him. He looked back at me expectedly, with inquisitive eyes and stubble gracing his strong jaw.

"I'm happy to pay for mine," I stuttered in response.

I saw his mind tick over, and then the smallest of frowns swept over his face.

"Put it on my bill," he directed Tommy with a growl in his voice, and then he turned to me. "Come sit with me when you are done."

He didn't give me a chance to respond; he turned and crossed the diner without another word. It would seem that Mr. Alpha was visiting for the day.

"How the hell do you know Ky Crawford, A.K.A Mr. Eye-Fuck Eden?"

I chose to ignore his ridiculous statement. "I am doing a photo shoot for the magazine he works at."

"He is seriously into you."

Tommy's admission shocked me. I shook my head at the absurd statement and dropped my eyes to the counter. I couldn't even fathom that. I was in a whirlwind of uncertainty when it came to Ky Crawford, and Tommy's comment was unbelievable. I was here to do a job and then I would be back on a plane, headed to my comfortable, stable life in San Francisco, and I wouldn't have to think of this place again. I wasn't the type of girl who gave out signals that I wanted a guy to *want* me. I couldn't, I would never.

Fear, intrigue, and confusion all swam wildly within me as I tried to desperately get a grip. These were the moments when I got furious with what happened. Not only did Jeremy Davis steal my innocence, my pride, and my right as a woman, but he also damaged me for the rest of my life. He took away my opportunity for a normal, healthy relationship—the experience of feeling butterflies in my stomach when a guy like Ky Crawford would look at me, that feeling of completeness of a first kiss and the overwhelming excitement of sex. He took away my right to be a typical woman in her twenties, and I hated him for that. I despised him for that.

"Eden!"

I snapped out of my trance and looked at Tommy, whose brow furrowed with worry. I found the biggest smile I could muster and shook all thoughts out of my head.

"Are you okay?" He asked with a voice laced with concern;

apparently didn't buy my attempt at covering up my thoughts.

"I'm good, Tommy." I shot a look back at where Ky sat and grabbed my glass from the counter. "I'll see you soon."

I pushed away from the counter and silently gave myself a pep talk, but my eyes never left Ky as I crossed the diner. How could I possibly sit across from him while his absurd proposition continued to plague my thoughts and his kiss still sent shockwaves through my body? He was burning down my walls of resolve terrifyingly quick, and I was stumbling into unknown territory, that for some strange reason made me feel alive again.

I slid into the booth opposite him, and the familiar feeling of being under Ky's watchful gaze immediately hit me. My hands fumbled as I quickly attacked the brass buckles of my bright pink laptop satchel and grabbed my Mac. The thought of using my laptop screen as a shield was a welcome relief, and I had planned on spending the morning working on my ideas for the shoot and searching for locations.

"Thanks for joining me." His deep voice spoke with a certainty, a promise, and an intention that felt surprisingly welcomed but made me so damn nervous. I retracted from my internal battle of refusing to grace my eyes with the pleasure of looking at his face and lifted my gaze to meet his.

Big mistake.

"Mr. Crawford," I acknowledged with a stern nod.

A delicious smirk took over his lips, and I swear I saw a twinkle in his eyes. "So we are using formalities now? Well, in that case, thank you Miss Rivers."

My name fell from his mouth with such ease, and the smile tugging at his lips encouraged a matching smile to flash over mine. The idea of flirting with this man was dangerous; it was temperamental and had the ingredients to be beautifully devastating. But the more I was around him, the more I realized I was beginning to feel and imagine things I never knew I wanted.

I dropped my eyes from his and opened Photoshop, wanting the distraction to end the awkwardness filling the table; awkwardness laced with a confusing need, which made me consider things I shouldn't. It didn't work. I blankly stared at the screen, not being able to concentrate on anything but the man sitting across from me.

"So are we going to pussyfoot around my question?"

"I'm not pussyfooting around anything, *Ky.*" I slammed my laptop shut and glared at him. He could not be serious. "Tori had no right to mention anything about me before she left town. I don't care how drunk she was. I barely know you. You are simply the guy who is paying me to photograph the cover."

"Yep, I'm simply *that* guy." His voice dropped devastatingly low, and he tore his eyes from mine.

"That's not what I meant. I am grateful for what you are doing, but come on, you can't be serious? A month is a long time. Your idea is twisted."

"What's twisted about it?" He laughed. "I've already kissed you, and you were very involved in that kiss, so you cannot say it doesn't intrigue you. It's not as crazy as it sounds. It will simply be two people spending time together. You're only just back in town, I don't get out much, and we obviously have some things in common. If I'm being completely honest, which I always seem to be around you, you are insanely sexy, so as a fully-functioning man, I'd be crazy, not to want to have you in my life, even if it is just for a month, four measly weeks, thirty-one days even."

He could not be serious.

"So what? Are you one of those guys who would use the month to live out some sick fantasy? Is this a crazy way of attempting to get in my pants?" I swallowed hard as my heartbeat increased to the point of pain. I couldn't do this. There was no way.

"Why do you do that?" His eyes narrowed, the frustration in his voice not missed.

"Do what?"

"Pretend to be this person that you clearly aren't. You can be yourself around me. That's what I want. I want the Eden, who I know is in there. Not the Eden that you hide behind. I want the Eden who I met last night on the balcony, the same girl who kissed me within a breath of her life, the Eden who grabbed hold of me like she never wanted me to leave, the Eden, who I know, hasn't stopped thinking about that kiss."

"You know absolutely nothing about me, so don't sit there and pretend like you do."

"Fine, I'll be the mature one who's honest, shall I? There is nothing sick and twisted about this." His voice dripped with sexuality and tinged with promise. "And I won't be attempting to fuck you, so I definitely won't be going anywhere near your pants. That's a promise."

"You just called me, and I quote, *insanely sexy,* yet you don't want to touch me. You are all kinds of messed up." I rolled my eyes before staring at him. I had no clue what kind of game he was playing, but it was a game that I was slowly yet surely being dragged into.

"I said I won't be fucking you, but that doesn't mean I won't constantly be thinking about fucking you."

Hearing those words allowed the breath I was holding to leave my body. One month. Who was I trying to fool? I knew the decision had already been made the moment he asked the question. He had given me no choice. I couldn't deny that Ky Crawford's ability to captivate me ignited that very first time I met him, and that was what was dangerous. He was dangerous to everything I had desperately tried to become in the last four years, but more terrifyingly, he was dangerous to everything I didn't want to remember.

"What would this month entail?" Regret filled me the moment the words tumbled from my mouth, but my attentiveness to hear his response made me lean in closer.

Ky's lips curved dangerously, and a knowing smirk took over his handsome face. I witnessed the exact moment he realized he had me. What the hell was I doing? His body pressed back against the seat, and he sat in complete silence, observing me like I was some kind of sick prize.

"Don't look at me like that," I spat, averting my eyes from his. I couldn't stay here. Why the fuck couldn't I just say no? Really, was it that hard? It was a simple word, but here I was at twenty-four years of age, and I couldn't say it.

"Like what?"

"Like I'm a prize. That's not me, Ky, and I am not going to be a toy you can play with when you desire. That will never be me." I shoved my laptop into my satchel, then slid my body along the leather booth desperate for a reprieve. I needed to leave.

"Eden, wait." Ky shot up from his seat so fast that I never had a chance to escape. His fingers wrapped firmly around my forearm just below my elbow, instantly ceasing my escape plan. My gaze fell to his hand as my breath caught in my throat. Our gazes collided, and everything around me disappeared into a vortex of silence and calm. A mixture of fear and anxiety swept over his face as he watched me so intently. It confused me. What could he possibly have to fear when it came to me? "You are definitely not a toy, Eden. You would be the greatest prize. I know you can't say no, and I am a bastard for using that against you, but I promise you it's for your own good. It's time you started saying yes for the right reasons, and if I need to demand this time I will. So Eden, I'll ask you this question one last time, will you be my December?"

"I am going back to San Fran in January." The words fell from my lips without a single thought.

"I don't care. I am not looking for a relationship with you, Eden; I am looking for nothing but your time for the next four weeks. I will ask you things that will make you uncomfortable,

I will do things that may make you anxious, and I plan on taking you out of this comfort zone that you believe is reality."

With his pleading eyes staring at me, I took everything I knew of Ky Crawford in. I couldn't understand his reasoning behind this, but I couldn't deny the rumblings within my dormant body. Why would this guy want to spend time with someone he barely knew? What was so enticing about me? How could a man with a face like his and a body that oozed sex appeal want someone like me?

But I didn't really have a choice, did I?

"Yes," I whispered.

KY

EDEN RIVERS WAS SECONDS away from saying yes to my absurd request, seconds away from handing over her mind, her body, her everything on a fucking platter for me to feast on. What the hell had I done? My mind bounced through the conversation and landed on my asshole question. I never thought she'd agree to this. I thought Tori had been fucking around with me. Eden shouldn't have agreed to this. Why *did* she agree to this?

I slid back into the booth and fell against the leather of the bucket seat. My eyes traced her steps as she walked through the diner and out the door. She stopped on the sidewalk and turned back, gazing into the diner. The moment her eyes connected with mine, I felt something shift. I might have proposed the fucked-up month idea, but she had cemented something within me. She had created unease within me. How in the hell was I meant to keep my hands and mouth off her for a month?

My urge to spend time with her was too much. Why couldn't I just do what a sane person would do? I was featuring her work for God's sake, it wasn't like I wouldn't be seeing her. I was pissed that she assumed this was a game. I would never do that to her. I had my own secrets when it came to Eden Rivers, so I needed to be careful with how I played this out. It would just be a few outings, maybe some dinners. I wanted to show her that not all men's primary goals in life were to get their dicks in her pussy. I wouldn't be anywhere near her pussy. I couldn't. I promised.

I doubt she realized she had me gripped by the balls and now I was locked in. What was happening to me? Since when had I not been at work as the sun was rising? Since when had I purposely come to the diner that I now knew she visited?

"Be careful with her."

I broke my eye contact with Eden and turned to face Tommy. He stood beside the table, desperately trying to look threatening. I leaned back, folded my hands behind my head, and waited for him to continue. I had seen him watching Eden and me from the minute she slid in across from me.

"She isn't like other girls around here. She is special. Don't fuck with her head, okay?"

"And how do you know that I am going to fuck with her head? How did you become such an expert on Eden?"

"I am her cousin's best friend. I know a lot about her. She doesn't need a cocky self-obsessed asshole from the city screwing her over."

Who the fuck did this kid think he was?

"Just because you see me come in here doesn't mean you know jack shit about me. So why don't you run along and leave me be."

His eyes turned to slits and his mouth opened and closed numerous times as if he wanted to say something to me, but he quickly twisted around and stalked back to the counter, only to disappear into the storage room. Fuck me. I didn't need some pissed off eighteen-year-old telling me what I already knew.

I pulled my phone out of my jean pocket and opened up a blank text message. I needed to speak with Ashlyn and fast. She would make me see some sense. Either that or she'd rip my balls clean off my body. That would probably be the best thing to happen at the moment.

Me: Ash, where are you working today?

Within seconds, Ashlyn's name flashed before me.

Ashlyn: Pier 63, on-set job. What's up?

Me: I did something.

Ashlyn: I don't even want to know. Come down, I'll take a break.

I looked at my watch and realized that I had already missed a scheduled meeting. First time for everything, I guess. Josh would have a field day with this. I closed my laptop and stood from the booth. It would only take me ten minutes to get to Pier sixty-three, ten minutes until Ashlyn would tell me how much of a dickhead I really was.

The pier was a fanfare of models, photographers, and stylists. Why they had decided to have an outdoor shoot as the temperature dropped rapidly was anyone's guess. I shoved my hands in my pockets in desperate search of some warmth and headed down the beach toward the photographer I knew as Alessandra. The moment she saw me, a welcoming grin spread across her face, and she announced for everyone to take five. Alessandra and I went way back; she was a regular photographer for the magazine, and we had developed a close friendship. I had actually attended her and her girlfriend's wedding just this past summer.

"Sweetie, you are looking as handsome as ever. Why are you not at work? This isn't the Ky Crawford I know and love." She leaned in and kissed both cheeks and stepped away, looking at me suspiciously.

"This new Ky is because of a girl." Ashlyn stood beside me, pushed her hip into mine, and raised her eyebrow as if to say *you know I'm right.*

"You have a girl!" Alessandra's screech brought the attention of everyone within a ten-mile radius of us.

"I do not have a girl, Less. Ashlyn is just being premature."

"Let's hope you aren't premature when it comes to Eden."

My best friend's ability to say whatever was on her mind never ceased to amaze me. She spoke first and thought second. The smile and twinkle in her eye was a clear indication that she loved this tormenting a bit too much.

"Ashlyn, seriously, are we really talking about my coming abilities in the middle of a packed beach? You and I both know that I have some killer stories."

"Jesus, Ky, time and place."

"You brought this on yourself." I turned back to Alessandra, who looked at Ashlyn and I like we were sickos. "Do you mind if I steal your stylist for a few minutes?"

"Of course, sweetie. We will break for coffee. Take your time."

Ashlyn linked her arm with mine, and we headed away from the crowd and down the sand of the abandoned beach. I knew Ashlyn too well. I knew she was desperate to break the silence, but was waiting impatiently for me to make the first move. I would let her stew for a while. Fuck, I could be an asshole when I wanted to be, but it was all for my amusement.

"What did you do? Besides kiss her last night."

Ahh, there she went.

"I asked her to spend December with me."

Ashlyn's face darkened and her eyes narrowed in on me. "So you went against everything I advised?"

"So it seems."

"Do you know what you are doing?"

"Nope, I have no fucking clue. It just happened. I kissed the shit out of her last night, and completely got lost in the moment. I've lost every bit of control, and I never lose control, Ashlyn. Never."

"How was she?"

I fell silent, focusing back on the moment she said yes. The small smile that filtered over her lips, the intrigue that set in her eyes, and the change of her body language was something I couldn't ignore.

"She was fine. She can't say no, Ashlyn, and me being a fucking prick, used that against her for my own personal gain. What kind of fucked-up person am I? I couldn't stop. I knew what I was doing, I knew what I was asking, and I knew she would say yes."

"Just promise me you won't hurt her."

"That's one thing I can certainly promise you."

The office buzzed with excitement when I finally arrived for the day. Over the past three years, this was the first time that I hadn't been here to open up. Lauren looked at me with questioning eyes as I strolled past her and made my way to my office. I knew it was only a matter of time before my arrival hit Josh's office.

I opened my laptop and started the task of going through countless emails and looking at the meetings that Lauren had thankfully rescheduled.

A loud knock sounded from my door, and I was soon joined in my office by a smirking Josh. I was ready for his assault of questions. He closed the door behind him and moved toward my desk, taking a seat opposite me.

"Where have you been?"

"Out."

"With who?"

"Ashlyn."

"Bull-fucking-shit."

"Fine, I had breakfast at the diner, saw Eden, and then went to the pier to speak with Ashlyn." I stretched out behind my desk and waited for his opinions to hit me.

"Cool."

Cool!

"Seriously? Cool?" I narrowed my eyes at my brother and awaited his assault, but it never came. "What have you done with my opinionated asshole of a brother? I am still waiting for the taunt about me kissing her last night?"

Josh leaned back and clasped his hands behind his head, and continued watching me. To be honest, he was making me uncomfortable. I hadn't spoken to him since I left his apartment last night, and I knew I had a million and one things I wanted to talk to him about, but how could I really start the conversation? I had been hoping he would have.

Finally, he spoke. "It doesn't surprise me that you kissed her. I knew it was only a matter of time, and who am I to say anything about it. The only thing I'll ask is, was it everything you thought it would be? Was it worth it?"

I didn't even have to consider my response. "Yep, and now I don't know how I'm not going to want it again. A girl has never gotten to me like her, Josh. It's going to seem sudden to people, and they're not going to understand my reaction to her, but you and I both know that this has been a long time coming."

Josh nodded and worry washed over his face for a brief moment. I knew this could blow up, and so did he. He knew my deepest fears, my biggest concerns, but never did I ever think I'd be in this position again, and I didn't know when I'd get the opportunity again.

"I've set Eden up in the corner office. You should see her in there. This massive room, and it's just her and her laptop. She looks tiny." Josh chuckled.

"She's here?" I asked in shock.

"Yep, she called about thirty minutes ago asking if there was somewhere she could work for the day."

Okay, well, that was interesting. Why the hell didn't she call me? Instead, she called my brother. "Um, thanks for doing that. I'll sort through my emails and calendar, and then I'll go and see her. You know, make sure she is okay in there."

He pushed back from the seat and stood. "Be careful," he warned, then turned and left my office, giving me one last knowing look before he disappeared.

For three hours, I was completely distracted by emails and scheduling. I had issues in the L.A. office, I had a conference call with Simon, and then Roger decided that we should have lunch. Three hours passed, and every now and then the thought that Eden was only a couple of offices away would hit me. Finally, when I had a moment to breathe, I walked down the hall toward the far corner office. I opened the door slowly and was greeted by Eden tapping away at her laptop, earplugs in, and her softly humming along to whatever she was listening to. I took a moment to watch her, to drink her in. My eyes dropped to her mouth, and my brain went into overdrive. My desperation to kiss her again was raging within me. I wanted to taste her again, and I wanted her to completely own our kiss again. Fuck, I wanted to do whatever she would let me do. I shook the thoughts out of my head and watched as she twisted a piece of her hair around her finger and her eyes bounced over whatever she was reading on the screen.

"Shit!" she shrieked when she finally realized I was there.

I moved into the room, closing the door behind me. Her eyes followed my every movement as I walked around the office, my fingertip running along the top of the desk that swallowed her laptop.

Josh was right; she looked tiny in here.

"I didn't know you had come in," I stated as I collapsed into the cream leather club chair situated on the other side of the desk and folded my arms over my chest. The sassy girl who greeted me in the diner only hours earlier had bolted, and now a nervous Eden sat opposite me, continuing to twist a length of her hair as her eyes darted away from me.

"The diner was too noisy when I went back, so I called Josh and he said I could work here."

"Why didn't you call me?"

She shrugged her shoulders in reply.

"Tell me," I probed, wanting to find out why she thought she couldn't approach me about something as trivial as finding somewhere to work.

"Because you confuse and intrigue me. You cloud my judgment, and I just don't know who I am when I'm with you." Her words were rushed, and her eyes swam with indecision. I hated that she used the word *frightened* when she spoke of me.

"That could be a good thing," I muttered under my breath.

"Or it could totally destroy me."

We fell into an intense silence as we looked at each other, both falling into our own thoughts and indecision about what we were about to begin. The tension in the room could be sliced with a knife; it was palpable; it was real.

I rose from the chair and made my way toward the door, knowing that it was necessary for me to leave. I needed to escape before I said things I had locked away for so long. I turned back to her, gave her one last smile, and said the words that I knew would rattle her to the core.

"Well, we have December to find out, don't we?"

Eden

Ky: I'm picking you up at 8 a.m.

THE SATURDAY MORNING SUNSHINE beamed through the drapes covering the hotel window, but I knew it was offering fake warmth. It was December first, the first day of winter, and the temperature had dropped at a staggering rate. Stretching beneath the warmth of my comforter, I read over Ky's message and sighed. Today it began. A month with Ky Crawford. I still didn't understand the whole concept, and I was trying with everything I was to ignore the glint of anticipation that shot through me when I received his message. But the excitement was extinguished the moment a bitch called self-doubt roared to life, destroying everything in her path.

I stumbled out of bed and headed to the tiny bathroom. If I had learned anything about Ky since I arrived, it was that he never joked about plans. If he said he would be here at eight, then I should expect him before eight. I turned on the shower as hot as I could, stood under the stream of water, and thought about the next month. I knew the rumblings cascading through my body were the beginnings of messed-up excitement. This was reckless. This was me losing control. Usually I would have regretted the decision, I would have hated myself for saying yes, but for once, it was kind of refreshing, it was intriguing, it was confusing as hell—but it was only for one month.

I wrapped a towel around my clean and moisturized body, walked into my room and gathered my clothing. Where would we be going? What should I wear? Why did the feeling of a hidden agenda suddenly slap me in the face? Shaking my head to diminish the absurd thoughts, I headed back into the bathroom and dressed for the day in skinny jeans, knee-high boots, and a cream sweater with my favorite red jacket.

After drying my hair and allowing the natural waves to fall over my shoulders, I added a touch of mascara to my lashes and gloss on my lips and finished my morning routine with a spray of my favorite Vera Wang perfume. I headed toward the bed to find my cell and bag, while my mind went into overdrive at thoughts of what the day could bring. A sharp knock at the door stopped me.

I twisted my hands together to try and cease the shaking before I took a deep breath. With a silent prayer for confidence, I pulled the door open, and there he stood. He was dressed in dark denim jeans, a black hoodie, thick woolen scarf, and a beanie that covered his chocolate brown hair, but it was the perfect stubble grazing his jaw that grabbed my attention.

"It's lonely out here, Eden," Ky spoke in a deep voice, laced with amusement.

"Sorry, come in."

I stepped away from the door, opening it wider for Ky to step through. He strode past me, and I didn't miss the wink he shot me as he unwound the scarf and threw it down on my bed.

"How do you feel about today?" he asked softly.

How was I feeling? Nervous, anxious, fearful, excited, intrigued—mix them together and that was me. He watched me attentively as he waited for my response. How could I answer without letting my real thoughts show? Being under his watchful gaze was something unique; it was like the pulse my body had needed for so many years; it was a yearning that I never imagined; it was a breath in my lungs that I had been waiting for; it was pure and utter confusion.

"You're wearing the red jacket," he continued, dismissing his initial question. He took two steps until he was standing in front of me. "The girl in the red jacket."

"That was you," I whispered, completely taken aback that it was him that Ashlyn had told me about. "Ashlyn said someone—"

"Yep, that was me, so I am very pleased to see you wearing it today." Slowly, he wrapped the scarf back around his neck, his eyes never leaving my face. "You ready to go?"

I nodded and grabbed my purse off my bed. "Where are we going?"

He didn't hesitate with his response. "Someplace I've wanted to take you since I met you."

We sat in silence as we left the island and headed across the river. I had no clue where he was taking me, but I couldn't ignore my excitement.

The moment the cab pulled up near Central Park, I turned in my seat and looked at him in wonderment. What were we doing here? A smirk played on his lips as he pulled open the door and exited the cab, only to walk around the back and pull open my door. I climbed out eagerly and my eyes roamed around the space, taking in the crowds and reminiscing in one of my favorite places. The moment Ky put his hand on the small of my back to lead me away, I jumped.

"You like photography, right?" The sensation of his warm breath just below my ear caused a shudder to cascade down my back.

"Please do not tell me that's a serious question!" I shrieked and whipped around to face him.

His laughter swirled through me, and I realized it was the first time I had actually heard him laugh. It was warm, throaty, and dominant. I couldn't help but like it. My stare narrowed on his arm that was suspiciously behind his back. His brow rose and a smirk engulfed his lips. Like it was in slow motion, he brought his arm into sight and I gasped at what he revealed. He held my camera bag in his hand, and a grin the size of Everest took over his face.

What? How? When?

"How? When? I don't—" I stuttered in disbelief.

"You shouldn't ask," he suggested with a stern tone. "Let's go for a walk. You lead the way."

I stood staring at him in complete fascination. He continually surprised me; it was like opening a Christmas present when it came to Ky Crawford. You never knew what you were going to get.

I shot back to reality, and we took off along the winding path that led to the glistening lake. I might have been gone for the last four years, but it all came flooding back to me. The smell of freshly baked pretzels, the chattering of thousands of people, and the evidence of a New York winter lingering in the air were burned in my memories forever. I had spent so much time here while I was in college. The hustle and bustle calmed me, and when I made the decision to flee to the other side of the country, this was the place I ran to, the place I needed to say goodbye to.

But now here I was, reconnecting, all because of Ky Crawford.

"Thank you for this." I swallowed hard, finally meeting his intense stare. "You really didn't have to do this."

"Yes I did," he said softly, his eyes briefly losing their intensity as they flickered with honesty.

He walked beside me quietly as I took in everything around me. Ten minutes after we left the warmth of his car, we stood by the frozen lake that was overrun by excited children ice skating.

"It's been so long since I've been here," I admitted softly

as emotions overcame me. "This right here is what I miss."

He didn't say a word, but he didn't need to say anything. I placed my camera bag on a vacant table and wrapped my arms around myself. Winter chill was rolling in at an aggressive rate, but I didn't care. I would stay here until he forced me to leave—rain, snow, hail, or shine. I heard the crunch of the ground below as Ky walked toward a vacant table, but I remained statue like. I just needed to enjoy this moment. I needed to bask in the innocence and beauty before me.

During college, this was the place I would escape to when I needed to study, or when I needed solitude from the dorm. It was a bit of a hike, but when I found it, I felt immediately connected. I didn't know how long I stood there. It was only when I heard the familiar click of a photo being taken that I was drawn from my trance. I turned toward Ky just as he clicked another. He dropped my camera from covering his face, and his expression was completely unreadable. My insecurities plagued me as we stood staring at each other like there was nothing going on around us.

"You are spectacular to look at, Eden Rivers."

My cheeks engulfed into a flame of red under his words. I dropped my gaze to the ground to avoid my emotions spilling out of me.

"You are going to hear me say that a lot over the next month, so I'd suggest you get used to it."

Ky packed up my camera, placing it back in the bag, and then slung the bag over his shoulder. He moved around the table toward me, but his eyes were mesmerized by the lake. As if he knew I was watching him, he shifted his gaze and looked directly at me. His lips tweaked and a sexy smirk shot back at me, then the damn butterflies reappeared. I didn't want butterflies. He held out his hand and I froze, and it wasn't because of the chill in the air. Like the noise was taken from the air and jammed inside an airtight box, everything fell silent around me.

I wanted to grab his hand, I wanted his large hand to swallow mine, but why? He didn't move his hand. He took a step toward me breaking the distance. I didn't think I could handle this. His confidence was encouraging mine to soar.

"You should hold my hand." His eyes dropped to the hand he was holding out to me in silent indication and then moved back up to meet my eyes. "One month, Eden. It's time to get you out of your comfort zone, and I am the guy to do it."

"Why don't you have a girlfriend? I don't understand why someone like you is single?" I blurted out. *What the fuck is wrong with me?*

"Someone like me?" His voice dripped with amusement.

May as well just put it out there, Eden! "You are successful, confident, have that damn dimple, and you are easy on the eyes. I don't understand why you are choosing to spend time with me when there would be a billion women out there who would want you."

"I don't want a billion women, Eden."

I chose to ignore the insinuation in his tone. "So why?" I pushed.

He drew in a deep breath while he considered his answer.

"Because the woman I wanted left a long time ago, and there isn't anyone else who's got my attention like her."

"Oh." I breathed out, dropping my eyes to the dirt below. Suddenly the urge to comfort this man, who spoke with such heartbreak for this woman, took over any hesitation I had. Without a second thought, I lifted my hand slowly and entwined my fingers with his and tried my hardest to give him any strength I could find.

KY

I DIDN'T WANT TO talk about my past with Eden. She didn't need to know a thing about it. The second I opened my damn mouth and spoke, I regretted it. I didn't need questions asked, I didn't want assumptions to be made, and I sure as hell didn't want her looking at me like she was now.

Pity was one thing I hated. Why pity someone for something you had no clue about? It was one of those things that people thought you wanted, but it was something I never needed. I didn't want it, I didn't warrant it, and I sure as shit didn't deserve it from Eden Rivers.

I reeled in my thoughts and concentrated only on the way Eden's hand fit in mine. My eyes dropped to take in the sight of our fingers entwined together, fitting like a perfect glove, like the promise of comfort.

What the hell was I doing?

"Are we going to stand here and be all awkward?" Her voice sang with a smile, and it intrigued me that she was going out of her way to put on Miss Confident just for me.

"Who said anything about it being awkward?"

The laughter that floated from her body distracted me momentarily, and for a flash, I forgot everything that was actually happening. I knew I needed to pull it in, but the comfort of being next to her was so unknown to me; it was like walking on a tightrope and just waiting to fall, it was like losing your sight in the blackest hours of the night and feeling for your footing with anxious steps. It was nervousness, it was unpredictable, it was exhilarating, and definitely not what I planned.

One month was all I had. A month to make it worth her while, to show her the kind of life she refused to live. I was a stubborn asshole at the best of times, and my intentions were clear, but I also knew the risks. If I pushed too far there was the potential to shatter, and if I got lost in the attraction of Eden Rivers I'd lose my fucking mind, and I couldn't allow that to happen. This month wasn't about me, and I had to focus on that. Josh's words continued to echo in my head, as well as Ashlyn's warning, like a record on repeat making sure I was well aware of what I was doing. But that was the thing, was I doing this for my own sick needs? Did I even have Eden as a consideration?

For the next two hours, an ecstatic Eden pulled me around the park. Her face never dropped, and the smile plastered on her face was infectious. I was smiling; a genuine make-my-face-ache kind of smile, one that I had locked away for so many years; one that was brought out by someone who seemed to always be fighting her own private demons. Her smile was fucking incredible; it took over her face and made the blue of her eyes pop and twinkle in delight and unadulterated happiness.

Our hands remained linked together as we made our way all over the park. Occasionally she would halt and take a photo of something that she believed was artistic, but all I saw as I watched her do her thing was a bench, a tree or a child playing. It was only as she focused on the photo and hid her face behind the camera that we lost the connection of our hands. I felt the loss immediately, and the moment she was done, I was back by her side, and she didn't flinch once when I grabbed for her hand.

It was almost becoming a test to see how far I could push before she got completely freaked out. My mind still jumped to the fear on her face when I first attempted to kiss her. I never wanted to see that look again, but I was still willing to test the boundaries. I craved to have my mouth and body on hers. I was a man for Christ's sake, and I'd be lying if I said I didn't. But there was an enormous difference between craving and acting on, and I knew I wouldn't touch her. I couldn't. I shouldn't. I promised. But fuck if I didn't keep thinking about that kiss we shared.

A loud ding sounded around us, and she dropped her hand from mine to grab her phone from deep within her bag. I tucked my hands in my pockets, deciding that it was time to stop touching her while I still had an ounce of control. I watched her close. Her eyes narrowed and then an amused smile took over her face. Her eyes lifted from the screen to look at me.

"Why is your brother sending me inappropriate messages?"

I groaned as soon as the words left her mouth. Josh fucking Crawford struck again. My brother's ability to weasel his way into my life at the worst possible time was what legends were made of. Yes, he was my little brother, but he was also my best friend, my confidant, my annoyance, my brutal honesty, and my exasperation. Eden concentrated on her phone and tapped in a response wearing a smile on her face.

"So, what next?" she asked after placing the phone back in her bag and completely ignoring the look I was giving her. She stared back at me and I returned her gaze. Her brow shot up in question. "Ky?"

My eyes narrowed. "Are you honestly not going to tell me what Josh messaged you?"

Eden chuckled in response. "Apparently I am going to a movie with Josh tonight."

"I'm coming too," I confirmed before I could stop myself.

"I thought you'd say that."

The afternoon chill swept through the air and encased the park in winter delight. During the cab ride, Eden clicked through the photos she'd taken, showing me her favorite shots and talking in photography lingo that I had no clue about, so I just nodded as if I understood. I enjoyed hearing her speak with so much enthusiasm. She was unbelievably talented, yet any time I told her that, she would blush and tear her eyes away from me. It was devastatingly cute.

When we reached the island, Eden was dropped off at the hotel and I was taken straight to my apartment. The day had panned out better than I expected, but I needed to get my emotions in check before I saw her again tonight. Holding her hand today had been too intimate. That simple touch crossed the line; it made me uneasy and fearful that I was stumbling into an abyss where I would no longer stay in control. Fuck, I had no clue what I was trying to achieve. I needed to create boundaries. I couldn't fuck up like that again. My mind went crazy trying to come up with something that I could use. I knew she couldn't say no, but then again, I needed to be able to tell when she was saying yes because she wanted to and not because she thought she had to. This whole idea was fucked up, and it was doing my head in already. Why the fuck couldn't I have just let it be? Why couldn't I have just faded into the scenery and simply been the guy from the office? Nope, I had to go and do something like ask her to spend the month with me.

Idiot.

The idea of sitting on my couch, having a beer, and watching some of the game for a few hours sounded like the perfect plan. The moment I unlocked my door and entered my apartment, the sound of the television greeted me. *What the hell?* I dropped my keys on the glass table in the foyer and walked into my living room to find Josh sitting on my couch, beer in hand, and feet up on the coffee table.

"My cable is out so I'm using yours," he stated, gesturing toward the television before looking back at me expectedly. "How'd your date go?"

I ran my hand through my hair and groaned in frustration. Not even five seconds and he dove right in with questions about Eden.

"First, how the fuck did you get in here, and second, it wasn't a date."

"First, you gave me a key, and second, you picked her up. It was a date," he hit back.

I didn't bother retaliating. I tore toward the kitchen and pulled out a beer, hoping that alcohol would offer much-needed relief to my highly strung self. I chugged back half a bottle before moving to the living room and collapsing beside Josh, who was still looking at me expectantly.

"It wasn't a date," I repeated with more determination in my voice. "By the way, I'm coming to the movie tonight."

"Of course you are." He said with a laugh before we both got lost in watching the game without another word spoken about Eden or our so-called date.

I couldn't remember the last time I stepped foot in Garden City Cinema, but the moment I hit the foyer, I realized it could have easily been yesterday. The interior hadn't changed at all, it was still decorated with framed posters of classic movies and the life-size cardboard cutouts of the original Rat Pack and Marilyn Monroe stood on proud display beside the candy counter.

I heard Eden's laughter before I saw her.

My eyes sifted through the mass of over-eager moviegoers until I found her. Eden stood beside Josh, so casually and so lightheartedly as she laughed at something he had said. I basked in the sight. It was a side of Eden that I was quickly realizing was rarely on display, and I couldn't ignore the feeling of ease that shot through me. I shamelessly took a moment to take her completely in. As if she felt my eyes on her, she scoured through the crowd until our gaze connected. I felt my mouth curve into a smile, and my hand rose in an acknowledging wave.

I crossed the foyer and lifted my chin in greeting at Josh, and leaned in to give Ashlyn a kiss on her cheek. I smiled at Eden. My ego soared as her eyes embarrassingly darted away from mine. Ashlyn grabbed hold of Eden's hand and pulled her to the ticket booth, and my eyes followed their every step.

"They are picking the movie. God only knows what we are in for." Josh huffed beside me.

"Good night for a chick flick?" I laughed in response.

"We should have brought some damn beers," he groaned and ran his hands through his hair.

"This was your idea."

Thirty minutes later, I was sitting beside Eden in the crowded cinema. We had barely said two words to each other since I arrived, and now being in this close proximity, I was overcome by the familiarity of her perfume. I slammed my eyes shut and my head fell back against the red velvet of the seat as I took a moment with my thoughts. The lights faded above, and the four of us settled back in as the movie began. My eyes kept drifting to the side to take in Eden. She was transfixed on the movie playing before us, but I honestly couldn't give a shit what was playing.

I shifted in my seat and leaned over until my mouth hovered over her ear. "You look great tonight."

The light from the large screen allowed me to work out her face in the shadows of the cinema when she turned to face me. Her eyes gleamed at me and she pulled her bottom lip between her teeth as shyness invaded her.

"Thank you," she whispered after she leaned into me, and the moment her breath skidded over my ear, I felt a swelling in my pants. "I like your shirt."

I gave a tight smile, removed my eyes from her, and turned back to the movie. If anyone asked me what it was about, the answer would be the girl beside me because that was the only thing I was concentrating on. The moment she grabbed my forearm during a suspense scene, I knew there was no way I would handle the full movie. Skin to skin contact was fucking dangerous. Her hand stayed on my bare arm, continuing to send a burning sensation through my already-on-edge body, and every so often she would squeeze it just to remind me. I wasn't actually sure she knew what she was doing.

Josh's chuckle from beside me drew my attention, and I narrowed my eyes in on him.

"You look a bit tense there, brother?" he taunted quietly.

I simply flipped him off.

The moment the credits rolled at the end of the movie, we all rose from our seats and walked back into the main foyer. Ashlyn and Eden started talking about how hot the lead actor was, as Josh and I stood by.

"What are you up to tomorrow?" Josh asked.

"I've got some work to do, so I'll either head to the office or just work at home."

"You seeing Eden?"

"Not sure," I replied honestly. "She might be working or something."

He nodded and gave me a knowing look.

Ashlyn and Eden eventually stopped swooning, her words, not mine, and they both turned to Josh and me expectantly.

"I could completely destroy a piece of pie right now," Ashlyn announced excitedly.

My eyes fell to Eden, and for a split second she tensed up, but then put on a façade of comfort. She nodded in silent response after Josh loudly agreed. We all took off to the coffee house on the corner that was in our sights. Eden and I fell into silent step beside each other. One thing I noticed was that the longer the night went on, the quieter she got, and the more anxious she appeared.

"Are you okay?" I asked, dropping my voice so only she heard.

She eventually twisted her body toward me and nodded in silent response.

I felt myself tense. "Are you really okay? Don't just say yes."

"I'm just a little tired. It's been a long day," she finally admitted.

"I can take you back to the hotel if you want. You don't have to come."

"I want cake," she replied with a smile. "Although I'm not sure if it could live up to the cake you bought me for my birthday. That was the best cake I've ever eaten."

"I'll be sure to tell Aunt Carole next time I see her." I chuckled lightly.

The warmth of the coffee house provided comfort as the four of us walked through the doors. I felt my body start to thaw after the assault of winter chill. Ashlyn grabbed Eden's hand and took her to a vacant table while Josh and I were on coffee ordering duty.

The moment it was our turn to order, Josh stepped into male slut mode and started trying to get in the barista's pants. I shook my head at my brother's moves, turned back to the main area of the coffee house, and took a deep breath.

My nerves were shot, my emotions were all over the place, and I couldn't decipher whether it was due to lack of sleep, stress at work or the girl who was unraveling me at a ridiculously fast rate. I glanced at the table where Ashlyn and Eden were sitting, and I instantly met Eden's gaze. She didn't hesitate this time. Her wide alert eyes met mine with such strong intensity that it was like she was reading me, deciphering every thought I was having. Fuck, I really hoped she couldn't read me too well. She didn't need to know who I was. I didn't think she could handle knowing me. She had caught me off guard; I wasn't expecting her to be watching me so intently. I shifted and turned back toward the counter, breaking the connection. Knowing I was under her gaze made my usual confident front crumble.

Eden

THE SANCTUARY OF MY hotel room provided me with ultimate relief. The second I closed the door behind me, I burst into a flood of tears. Pretending that everything was fine all day and continuing my charade into the night left me both physically and emotionally exhausted, and I knew that it was just a matter of time before I crumbled. And crumbling was something I didn't want to do in front of Ky.

After sitting in the rustic coffee house that was swallowed by the intense scent of coffee beans for an hour and enjoying hot coffee and cake, Ky had offered to drive me back to the hotel. The trip was a quiet affair, and my thoughts were filled with memories of the day. My hand still tingled with the sensation of his hand holding mine, and my heart ached at the simplicity and perfection of the day, but it was my mind that was a pit of confusion that I couldn't sort through. There was little to no fear, but I felt like I was pretending from the moment he picked me up until the moment he drove off. I didn't know any other way to survive situations like that, and I had to make the decision of whether pretending was what I wanted to do, whether it was time to try and find out who Eden Rivers was, and whether Ky Crawford was the right person to witness everything that I uncovered.

Tears rolled over my cheeks, and I felt my chest tighten under panic. I rubbed my open palm over my chest in desperation for relief. I knew it was a huge mistake coming back here.

I pulled my phone from my bag and placed it on the bed as I fished through my suitcase to find a clean pair of sweats and a hoodie. The thought of falling into bed and sleeping away my exhaustion was welcomed. My phone vibrated on the floral comforter with a new text. It was nearing one a.m. so immediately I thought it would be Tori.

It wasn't.

Unknown: Still in town I see and still looking as beautiful as ever, shame about the company you're keeping.

Who the hell was this? If I ignored it, it had to go away. Right? All day I hadn't felt an ounce of fear. When I held Ky's hand, I felt nothing but exhilaration. All it took was a few words to cause my fear to roar to life. I needed to ignore this. No one knew I was here, no one knew why I was here. Another five weeks and then I was gone.

I just needed to get through the next five weeks and then I could go back to my life in San Francisco and forget it all.

Sunday came and went without any contact from Ky. Did I expect him to text me? Yep. Was I a little disheartened when he didn't? Confusingly yes. I spent the day lazing in bed, eating room service food, and scrolling eBay for things I didn't need. I should have been prepping for the shoots I had booked and researching the bands, but all I wanted was laziness. I didn't receive any further messages, so I desperately crammed the memory of last night's text into the pits of my brain. By the time I crawled into bed, I had spent two hundred dollars on boots, eaten way too much candy and hadn't stopped thinking about the guy with the honey-colored eyes.

I had just finished pulling on my black boots and was heading to the desk that sat by the window to grab my laptop bag and phone when there was a loud knock at the hotel door. It had just clicked over to midday and, after a rough night of sleep and lazy morning, I was getting ready to head to the diner to get some much-needed work done. I hesitantly walked to the door and was thankful there was a peephole. My pulsing heart rate began to slow as I found Josh Crawford standing on the other side, looking at his watch and dressed in a business suit.

"I am happy to hear you are using all the locks," he announced after I unlocked the deadlock and chain and swung open the door to greet him.

My face must have been asking a thousand questions because a deep chuckle left him before he spoke again. "I have been requested by a certain brother of mine to bring you into the office today."

Shyness invaded me, and I dropped my eyes to the ground and nodded. "Okay."

I rushed around and grabbed my laptop, purse, and phone, and turned back to find Josh's gaze fixed on me. Where Ky had warm, emotive hazel eyes, Josh's were an intense chocolate brown. I could definitely see what Tori had been attracted to. Geez, I could see what all girls would be attracted to. Josh held the door open for me, and we left the hotel behind us and headed into the city, with our destination being Anderson Publications. For what, I had no clue.

The craziness of the office hit me the moment we stepped out of the elevator. Monday madness, as Josh called it, was in full swing. I pulled my bright pink laptop tote close to my body and weaved my way through the staff, sticking close to Josh, and headed for a large boardroom in the far corner. I felt people's eyes on me, and I swore I heard hushed voices asking who I was.

Once we walked into the boardroom, Josh said, "I'll go and see if Ky is in his office, so just take a seat here and I'll be back in a few."

"Sure."

Josh disappeared through the door and left me to my own devices. The room was huge with a large gleaming white meeting table taking up the space, with at least twelve high back, expensive-looking executive chairs surrounding it. Pictures of previous covers graced the walls, and my eyes instantly began scanning them, taking in the colors, the layout, the models, and some of my favorite bands. I still couldn't believe—not in my wildest dreams could I ever have imagined—that photos I would take would be gracing the cover of an international magazine.

"Um, excuse me, who are you, and what are you doing in here?"

I turned to the rude intruding voice that I found belonged to a striking redhead who stood with her hands on her tiny hips and a snigger on her lips. If it wasn't for her bitchy attitude, I would say she was one of the most stunning women I had ever seen. Her pointed gaze roamed over my body, taking in my skinny jeans, knee high boots, and simple white blouse in apparent disgust.

"My name is Eden, and I am waiting for Ky," I said quickly, hoping that she would turn around and leave.

Her eyes widened, and with a couple of steps on her impressive looking heels, she was in the boardroom and closing the door behind her.

"You're Eden Rivers?" she spat in clear disapproval. "It's you Ky is rejecting me for?"

Well, hello insecurities! I felt myself pull back as I took in the glamor before me. Ky was rejecting her for me? What the fuck? She looked back at me expectantly and continued to judge me with hateful eyes. Where the hell was Ky or Josh? She didn't speak another word for what seemed like forever, and I had no response.

"I cannot believe that he rejected me yesterday because of you. I'd heard of the infamous Eden Rivers, but by what I heard him say, I was expecting someone a bit more polished. Jesus, I am speechless."

Clearly she wasn't.

She took a step toward me, so she was close enough for her perfume to hit me full force. Her eyes threatened with vindictiveness, and a smirk filled her inflated pout. "He doesn't do relationships; he fucks and runs, and I was happy to give him that. I hope you know his expectations and can live up to them."

"Are you fucking done?"

I jumped at the sound of a very pissed off voice booming from the door. My body swung around to find the intimidating presence of Ky leaning against the doorframe, arms folded across his broad chest, and a scowl taking over his face. He was clad head to toe in business attire; he looked nothing like I'd seen him before. My eyes, with a mind of their own, ran the length of his body, taking in the dark charcoal suit, crisp white shirt that was opened at the top, with the tie he was wearing loosened around his neck.

"I was just introducing myself to Eden," the redhead stuttered as she urgently tried to backtrack her words.

"I heard enough to know that wasn't what you were doing Angela, so fuck off back to your desk. We will discuss this at a later time." Ky hadn't looked at me once since he entered the room; his eyes were glued firmly to the woman I now knew as Angela.

"Are you serious?" Angela questioned, her exasperated tone not missed.

"Do I look like I am joking?"

Finally, Ky looked at me and his eyes softened. I had no clue what was happening. I looked away and dropped my eyes to my laptop bag and fumbled around inside pretending to be looking for something. I heard the mutter of words under breath and then the sound of muffled voices.

I didn't even hear him move through the room, so I nearly jumped out of my skin when I felt the soft touch of a hand on the small of my back. When I finally looked up from the floor and turned to face him, Ky looked back at me tensely, his eyes taking in my features as if he was desperately trying to gauge my reaction, to make sure I was okay. I offered the best smile I could.

"Are you okay?" His voice had lost the aggression and was now soft and calming, yet still so intense and enticing.

"Yes," I responded immediately.

"Fuck Eden, answer me honestly."

"I am fine," I spat between clenched teeth, all the while glaring at him.

His head flew back, and his eyes locked on the ceiling. I couldn't ignore the loud infuriated sigh that escaped his body. "Eden, once again. Are you okay?"

The tension in the room had gone from concern to frustration within a heartbeat. I stayed silent as I tried to decipher my response. Clearly anything I said wouldn't be what he wanted to hear, and it certainly wouldn't be anything I wanted to say. He dropped his head from looking at the ceiling and focused squarely on me, waiting expectantly for my response. Everything was lost when he looked at me like that. It was a look that I was becoming very accustomed to. His eyes had lost the ferociousness that they showed moments ago, and now they were filled with expectation, protection, and maybe even a little anxiousness. Almost like my response was resting squarely on his shoulders.

"I will be fine," I admitted in a soft tone. "I just wasn't expecting to be bombarded by one of your lady friends."

"Lady friends?" he scoffed, and I could tell he was trying to stop himself from laughing.

"I don't want to keep you from the women you are interested in. It was pretty clear that she had you in her sights, and if you want—"

"Just stop before you go any further," Ky barked, shaking his head in the process. "Do you remember what I said on Saturday?"

My thoughts flew back to Saturday and the conversations we had. I knew exactly what he was referring to. The one conversation that made my heart weep for him. The girl that got away, the one girl he didn't want to say goodbye to. I nodded in silent response.

"For the last time, I do not have any lady friends, as you call them, and even if I did, it would certainly not be someone like Angela. As I told you, I have no interest in any women at the moment"—his voice dropped dangerously low—"besides you, Miss Rivers."

My stomach twisted, and my heart rate quickened at his words. I didn't know whether it was the certainty of his voice, the fact that he was wearing a suit or the look of confidence in his gaze, but suddenly it made me forget everything, and for a brief moment, in the middle of the boardroom, I was just a girl who had the attention of a guy who seemed so out of her league.

I suddenly felt something I hadn't felt in years.

Alive.

KY

OPENING THE DOOR AND finding Angela laying into Eden pissed me off. When would this woman realize that I wanted nothing to do with her outside of our professional relationship? Yesterday I came into the office with Josh, and for some reason, Angela was there. She interrupted Josh and me as we were talking about Eden. Well, Josh was trying desperately to get information out of me regarding Eden. I knew by the time I arrived that morning that word would have gotten around the office, but I certainly didn't expect that the two of us would already be the office gossip.

That also pissed me off.

It was a fan-fucking-tastic start to the week.

"Come with me," I grated out and headed toward the door. Of course, she followed without consideration.

We walked side by side through the open office space, her heels clicking against the polished floor, which caused heads to look up. Angela stood by the desk of the biggest gossip in the office, and both of their mouths hung open as Eden and I passed. I shot Angela a glare in silent warning, and she hastily turned away and pretended to be sorting through paperwork.

"Where are we going?" Eden finally spoke.

"My office." My response was too short. I was taking out my mood on the wrong person, and I regretted it immediately.

She remained silent and, once we reached my corner office, I held open my door and she walked through. I closed the door behind us, even though I knew that would only fuel the office gossip more.

"Have a seat," I requested in a monotone voice, motioning to the chair opposite my desk.

"I didn't mean to cause any trouble. I can leave. It would probably be best for me to leave."

"Did I say I wanted you to leave? Sit down, Eden."

She nodded and pulled the chair back. Her eyes glistened as she lowered herself onto the plush leather. I inhaled sharply and rubbed my temples with my fingertips. This could be the perfect time to tell her that my stupid proposition was a mistake and that we could just see each other when required for the job. I could slip back into simply being the guy who signed her paycheck.

This was completely fucking with my mind, and I was a loose cannon at the best of times, but now I was afraid that I would implode, or worse yet explode in front of the wrong person.

Once I opened my eyes, I took a moment to bask in her beauty. After our day at the park and then night at the movies, I had left her and gone back to my apartment and tried to comprehend what had actually happened. I still felt the heat of her hand in mine, the sound of her laughter in my ears, but I also remembered the look that would float over her face at random times during the night. It was almost like the longer she was out, the more uncomfortable she became. I didn't like to think it, but I couldn't shake the feeling that she was pretending the whole time.

It killed me not to speak with her yesterday, but I knew I had to approach this with kid gloves. I couldn't scare her off with my intense motives, and I knew the longer I spent with her, the more I was losing my battle to restrain myself.

"Look, I'm sorry. I'm not pissed off at you, I am pissed off that Angela would say something like that. Whatever we are doing is no one else's business. Fuck, I don't even know what we are doing." I raked my hand through my hair. Frustration was a bitch of a thing, and it was penetrating to my very core. Eden sat frozen to the spot, looking back at me with wide, shocked eyes. I was failing miserably on the whole intense motives factor, so I thought why the hell not, let's just go full balls to the wall and deal with the consequences later. "Did you actually enjoy the other day and night, because I did, and I may have said that I wouldn't fuck you, but Jesus, Eden, it would be a lie if I told you I didn't want to kiss those perfect lips again. That's what I am fighting with at the moment, so no I do not want you to leave. I want you to stick around so you can continue to torment me."

The intensity in the room went from zero to a billion after my little confession. Our eyes connected as I opened my laptop. Eden didn't look frightened. If anything, she seemed intrigued, and the sweetest flush graced her cheeks. I had asked Josh to bring her here to discuss work, but now all I had done was bring our personal life into my professional space.

"We need to discuss where you will be working and sort out a schedule. There is space if you want to work from here, or we can look at somewhere else. You have a lot of work in front of you, and I want to be able to give you what you need."

Fuck me. If that wasn't a sexual innuendo, I didn't know what was.

Her sharp inhale of breath wasn't lost on me; it shot straight through my pants and began massaging my cock. Josh's warnings rang through my ears, and I knew I was treading in dangerous territory. All I had to do was ask one question—make an asshole move then ask her a question she wouldn't be able to refuse. She couldn't refuse. While her bright blue depths stared at me, I got lost under her gaze while scenario after scenario flashed before me.

"You confuse me, Eden."

"I don't know what you mean." Her gaze didn't drop and

she showed confidence that I knew was in there, but which she had hidden away from the world. Could it be true that slowly she was beginning to find the courage to stand up to me?

"You say yes without considering the consequences, which scares the fuck out of me. You do whatever I ask without question. There are times when I see this sassy, confident girl who wants to come to life, but in the next breath she is lost to a girl who is scared at the thought of a guy touching her."

"I can't help who I am, Ky. It's just me."

"Well, I have a month, Eden, and I'm going to find that sassy, confident girl and bring her out because she deserves to be seen. I will touch you, that's as guaranteed as the air you breathe."

"You said you wouldn't fuck me," she said, panic roaring within her words as she stood up and gathered her belongings.

"There is a big difference between fucking and touching, Eden."

And then she left.

It had been two days since my immature outburst with Eden. Two days of working obsessively, two days without sleep, two days of annihilating myself at the gym until I fell into a pit of pure exhaustion.

I had finally been convinced to leave the office, and I was sitting in the diner with Ashlyn and Josh.

"You look like shit," my ever-so-honest brother decided to announce.

"You do realize you're an asshole, right?" I shot a laugh and rolled my eyes.

Aunt Carole rushed toward us with concern flashing over her face, and she directed it squarely on me. Unease confronted me, and I narrowed my eyes awaiting her words.

"Eden is getting harassed by Chris. She is outside."

My body flew out of the booth, and I felt like my feet didn't even touch the ground. When the fuck would he get the point? I didn't want to discern why he was hanging around. I hit the sidewalk, and standing near the entrance was a fearful looking Eden being spoken to by Chris fucking Edwards. I rushed at neck-breaking speed with one thing in mind: Eden's safety.

I gripped hold of the back of his shirt, pulling him away from a trembling Eden, and slammed him against the brick wall.

"Eden, step away," I roared.

Her eyes shot wide, and she didn't hesitate. When she was out of sight, I turned back to a smirking Chris and pushed my forearm against his throat.

"How many fucking times do I have to tell you? Stay away from her." I felt the vein in my neck pulsating under my anger, and the thought of my fist connecting with his smug face almost overcame me.

"Always so protective, Ky, but what happens when you aren't around?" He shrugged out of my hold and took a step forward, getting right in my face. "I hear her pussy is pretty fucking sweet."

"Shut the fuck up," I hissed. "You go anywhere near her and I swear to God I will bring you down, motherfucker. Stay the fuck away from her."

I turned away from him with anger pulsating through my body, desperate to escape, and that was when he spoke again.

"Secrets always come out, Crawford, and I'll be right in the wings ready to swoop."

I didn't bother sticking around to hear any more of the fucked-up words he would taunt me with. I needed to find Eden. My head flung back and forth as I tried to find any sign of her. I finally locked onto her retreating figure as she crossed the road. I started jogging and weaved my way through the traffic with Eden clear in my sights.

"Eden, stop!" I pleaded when I got within reach.

She froze on the spot and spun toward me, her face completely unreadable. I increased my pace until I stopped just before her. I could see the panic falling around her, and it was evident that her walls were rising at an alarming rate.

My hands cupped her face, encouraging her to look at me. Even when she looked petrified, she was still the most beautiful girl. "Did he hurt you?"

Her bottom lip trembled, and she shook her head slightly before speaking. "I'm okay, I just want to get out of here."

"Hey, come here," I whispered and wrapped my arms tightly around her, bringing her firmly against my chest. Her arms circled my waist, and she pulled me closer to her body. I held her as close as I could until she stopped shaking. "Are you okay?"

She lifted her head from my chest and looked at me through glistening eyes. "I don't know. He scares me."

"What can I do?" I asked, desperately wanting to stop the fear taking over her. "Will you come and have dinner with Josh, Ashlyn, and me?"

Her eyes swam with indecisiveness. She tugged her lip between her teeth and nodded slowly. My irritation grew every time I witnessed this, but I refused to let it boil over again. What if I was someone who wasn't just going to take her for dinner? It made me more determined to get her to say no to something, or at least say yes for the right reasons. It ignited a need within me, a need that I shouldn't crave.

"Come on, let's go."

She uncurled herself from my body and I linked my fingers with hers, then we walked silently back to the diner. My eyes bounced around, feverishly searching for any signs of Chris, but like a dirty rat, he had disappeared into the crevices of the city.

The moment we walked through the door and the warmth of the diner circulated around us, my Aunt Carole was in our space and fussing over Eden.

"Sweetie, are you okay? I'm so sorry I didn't notice sooner. You come in here anytime you want. You are safe here."

My heart warmed at my aunt's worry. She was like a second mom to me and Josh, and knowing her motherly ways, I knew that Eden would get the full Aunt Carole treatment. The sweetness of Eden's smile was comforting to the brutal thoughts I was having in regards to Chris.

"Take her to the booth. I'll bring over some drinks and get your order." She turned to Eden and placed an open palm on her cheek. "This one will take care of you, sweetie. He is a good boy."

When we got to the booth, both Ashlyn and Josh rose from their seats and hugged Eden tightly as I stood back protectively. I directed her to slide in and sit against the window so I could protect her from the world around us. It was my caveman tendencies resurfacing; if anyone wanted to get to her, they had to go through me. Her body shook beside me and she was studying the tabletop as she clawed her way back into the shell she protected herself with. I grabbed her hand under the table and entwined my fingers with hers, desperate to provide her with solace. Her grip tightened, and she shifted ever so slightly until her body was flush against mine. My thumb rubbed over her soft skin, and I placed our conjoined hands in my lap where they would remain.

"I won't let anything happen to you." I dropped my voice so only she heard, and my words were complete and utter truth. I would stop at nothing to ensure her safety.

Her eyes lifted to find mine, and it stabbed my heart seeing them clouded with fear. "No one can guarantee that. Not even you, Ky," she admitted in defeat.

"Don't underestimate me, Eden."

Our eyes latched fiercely onto each other's, and I hoped to Christ my silent words were understood.

"What's for dinner tonight, pretty girl?" Josh's soothing voice floated over the table and broke the trance Eden and I had on each other.

"Um, I think I want pasta," she replied softly, and her gaze dropped to the menu on the table.

"Aunt Carole makes the best chicken and mushroom pasta," I suggested.

"Well, I might have to try that then."

Ashlyn sat opposite us, beside Josh, and had barely said a word since Eden walked in. Her eyes latched tightly on Eden, and her face was like stone. I knew this whole situation was killing her, but she refused to acknowledge it. No matter how many times I told her to speak to Eden, she wouldn't.

"Ashlyn, I was wondering if you want to go shopping in the city sometime soon. I want to hit up Victoria's Secret."

Holy fuck me dead.

Instantly, the thought of Eden's sweet body wearing sexy lingerie appeared in my mind, and lust shot straight to my cock. I squeezed her hand so tightly that she gasped beside me, and I apologized under my breath. Josh's roar of laughter from across the table drew me back to reality, and I shot him a look of pure death.

"Oh, pretty girl, you have just set my brother on a course of no return," he teased arrogantly across from us.

I leaned in until my mouth was close to her ear and whispered, "You shop at Victoria's Secret?"

She shifted until her face was barely inches from mine, and her eyes twinkled with amusement. "Yes."

"Fuck me," I growled. "You kill me, Eden Rivers."

I shook the thoughts from my head and looked back at a gleaming Josh and smirking Ashlyn. They pissed me off. I hid my smile behind my glass as I took a drink of my soda, and finally Aunt Carole arrived to take our orders.

The rest of the dinner went well. Conversation flowed perfectly at the table, and eventually I felt Eden relaxing beside me. I loosened my grip on her hand, expecting her to rip her hand from mine, but she didn't, not even when Aunt Carole arrived with our orders. She ate her pasta with one hand, as I struggled to eat my burger with one hand.

"Well kids, I am heading out. I have a hot date with brand new pussy tonight," Josh announced without a care in the world. He slid out of the booth and stood at the end of the table with a smug look sweeping over his face.

Eden choked on her soda at the honesty that Josh liked to hand out to the universe.

"Shit, sorry Eden, I tend to speak before I think," he apologized profusely and looked at me warily.

"No need to apologize. Go and enjoy your, um, pussy," Eden murmured, and I swore to God even her words blushed.

Riotous laughter filled the table, and Ashlyn followed Josh out of the booth after announcing that she was also heading back to her apartment as she had an early morning meeting. Before Josh left, he had invited Eden to his house for dinner later in the week, which she agreed to immediately.

"I cannot believe you just said pussy." I laughed as I moved across the booth and slid into the seat opposite her.

"Really?" She looked at me in amusement, raising a brow in the process.

"You just don't seem like someone who would cuss."

"Guess what? I say fuck, shit, asshole, and cock too."

My laughter gained the attention of Aunt Carole, who glided to the table with two large slices of her famous chocolate cake. Eden's widened glance took in the cake and then she delivered me the sweetest, most excited smile.

"This one told me that you said this was your favorite cake, so here you go, sweetie. Enjoy." Aunt Carole nodded toward me.

I winked at Eden. "I told you I'd tell her."

We dug into our cake and silence fell over the table, well, until Eden started making the most innocent little moans as she enjoyed every bite of the cake. I thought of cats dying to try and stop thinking about the sounds coming from her deliciously-enticing mouth, that was how fucked up this situation was. Nothing helped.

"So when we're finished, I should walk you back to the hotel."

"I want to stay. I want to play twenty questions," she shot out, completely shocking me with her outburst.

"What?" I stammered back at her, confused.

She stuttered in response and started jabbing at the half-eaten piece of cake. "I meant sure, that would be nice. I should probably get some sleep. I have a big day tomorrow."

"You want to play twenty questions with me?" Humor lingered in my question.

Her cheeks flushed, and her eyes dropped from mine.

"Eden, look at me," I demanded and instantly her eyes found mine again. "You want to play twenty questions?"

"Yes," she whispered.

"Why?"

"I want to know you. If I am spending all this time with you, I don't want it to be weird, and I thought if I knew things about you I'd feel more comfortable."

Well, fuck me. I leaned back against the cushion of the booth and locked my hands behind my head. Eden, locked in my gaze, clasped her hands together on the table, but she didn't waver. How did I get myself into this situation? For an outsider, I would expect them to think I was an asshole who was preying on a girl who couldn't say no, but here she was, taking the reins and dragging us closer together.

One month.

"Twenty questions, eh?"

The smile that lit up her face was the only answer I needed.

"I want to go and get a mug of hot chocolate first. Do you want anything?"

"Coffee. Aunt Carole knows how I like it."

I watched her as she weaved her way through the crowd, completely oblivious to the sideways glances she was receiving from every single guy in the room. As she stood at the counter, she gazed back at me over her shoulder. Innocence and sex appeal radiated from her in a terrifyingly intense wave. One minute she seemed like she was flirting, the next she was reserved and hiding behind a wall. She was pure confusion, and I felt like I was getting whiplash trying to keep up with her.

Every single plan I had was completely fucking up, and it was all due to me not being able to rein in my insecurities. I was obsessively attracted to this girl, but mostly she intrigued me. My ultimate fear was that my secret could be her biggest downfall, yet here I was, coming up with stupid ideas and scenarios to try and have her in my life.

Once our order was ready, she floated through the room and slid back into the booth opposite me, sliding my steaming hot cappuccino toward me.

"How do you know Chris?" she asked quietly.

Fuck.

How could I possibly answer this? I hesitated over my response before finally looking at her through concerned eyes.

"He is the cousin of someone I went to college with. He is an asshole, and you don't need to have anything to do with him. Please promise me that if he ever approaches you again you will say no to anything he asks or says to you. I don't think he will, but just in case."

"What did you say to him?"

"I warned him that it would be in his best interest to stay away from you."

"You did it again."

I didn't understand what she was implying. My brow furrowed as I looked at her over my mug. "Did what?" I finally asked.

"You saved me again."

My heart twisted at her words. If only they were true. Those words were the most blatant lie in the world, but she would never know that. I couldn't get into a conversation like this without freaking the fuck out. It was either leave her here for the likes of Chris who I knew would be lurking around somewhere or quickly change where this conversation was headed.

We were here for a reason.

Twenty fucking questions.

"What's your favorite food?"

"Excuse me?"

"Twenty questions, Eden. What's your favorite food?"

"Oh, um, as you have gathered from the Facebook stalking you did, I do love pizza, but also home cooked spaghetti."

Noted.

"How old are you?" she continued with the game.

"I'm twenty-six. Birthday is August fifteenth," I admitted with a smile, and then continued with my next question. "Where are you from?"

"New Jersey. My parents are out of town, though. I don't come back often, so when I said I would be here for six weeks, they already had their trip to Australia booked and couldn't back out."

Her voice dropped low as she spoke. "Do you do this with all the people you hire?"

"What's that?" I questioned, not exactly sure where she was going with this.

"Ask them to spend a month with you, take them out for coffee. It seems by Josh's reaction the other day, you barely leave the office."

"I can hand-on-heart say you are the only woman who I've asked to spend a month with, and it's quite alarming how quickly you are learning things about me."

"I'm just observant." She smiled and lifted her mug to her lips, a perfect sigh escaping as she took a large sip of hot chocolate.

Eden being observant frightened me.

Her eyes lifted from mine and looked over my shoulder. "Why is your aunt staring at us like that? Actually, why are all the staff staring at us?"

I twisted in my seat and, sure enough, Aunt Carole stood behind the counter flanked with two other ladies, all eyes latched onto Eden and me. As soon as they saw that they had been busted, they all of a sudden got busy and rushed off to different corners of the diner.

"You are the first girl I've brought here. You are officially the talk of Joe's Place."

"Do I want to be the talk of Joe's Place?"

"You have no choice, babe."

She lifted the mug back to her lips to hide her smile behind the porcelain. I took a moment to admire her in silence. Her gaze faded away as a distant thought overtook her. It seemed to drag her away from reality right before me. My thoughts battled with each other, and I didn't know whether to pull her back or let her succumb to her memories. Eden Rivers was the most tightly shut book I had ever encountered. I wanted to rip open the cover, disband the spine, and tear the pages of her story into a million pieces. More than anything, I wanted to help her write new words, on perfectly crisp, untouched paper, and to come up with a flawless title, for the perfect story.

Eden

Ky: Will I be seeing you tonight at Josh's?

Me: I'll be the girl in the red jacket.

FOR TWO DAYS, KY and I had been talking nonstop via text message. He was out of town on business, so this was how it had to be. He did warn me that even though he wasn't in town, he was still going to get his month's worth of me. It was now routine to wake to a text and fall asleep after sending him a goodnight text.

Our twenty questions had continued during these text message conversations. In the past two days, I had found out that his favorite color was green, he was a night owl, he didn't like anything pineapple, and he had a strong aversion to horror films.

His text messages were the only thing making me stay. Just today I packed up my suitcase and lifted my phone from the bed to call the airline, all because of a text message that simply read: *Where's your boyfriend now?*

You would think that I'd tell someone, that I'd call the police, but my fucked-up head told me to ignore it because if I ignored it, it wasn't actually happening. Yep, I had officially lost my mind.

Instead, I opened my laptop and worked until my eyes felt like they were falling out of my head. *Distraction.* I set myself up on the bed with the countless photos I had printed out of potential locations for the shoot that I planned to visit in the next couple of days. My work and Ky's text messages were the only things that were making me stay, as confusing as that was.

I was still trying to get my head wrapped around the fact that Ky, who had come into my life so abruptly, was quickly becoming a safety I depended on. He was the one who saved me from the grips of Chris countless times, yet he had asked me for nothing in return. I was choosing to ignore the intrigue that was being ignited within my closed-off body when I thought of Ky Crawford. The spark that would twist and turn within me with a mere touch of his hand was getting harder to ignore. This was so foreign to me.

But now, as I stood in front of the mirror and ran my hands over my body, straightening the non-existent creases in my top, I smiled at the girl looking back at me. It was a real, legitimate smile, and that exhilarated me. I wondered if I'd just flirted with Ky Crawford because I mentioned the red jacket that I knew he liked. I swept subtle pink blush over my cheeks, swiped my lashes with midnight black mascara, and dabbed my lips with red lip gloss, then I found myself ready to head off to dinner at Josh's.

The moment I stepped out of the cab in front of City Towers, my head tilted back and I took in the ten-story apartment building. The vast building glistened with lights that shimmered against the dark, cold night sky. It was spectacular and more than inviting.

When I arrived on the eighth floor, music hit my ears, and it was coming from behind the door of apartment 8A. Loud bass thumping through my body destroyed the thought of a quiet dinner. I had my closed fist up to knock when the door suddenly burst open and Ashlyn stormed out and rushed down the hall, her steps filled with brutal determination as her face twisted in anger. Her sobs hung in the air. As quickly as she appeared, she disappeared into 8C with a slam of the door behind her. I turned back and looked at Josh's apartment just as he rushed out, his head moving back and forth as he looked up and down the empty hall before his eyes finally landed on me.

"Did you see Ashlyn? Where did she go?" Josh questioned as he hurried toward me with worry-filled eyes.

"She went into that apartment." I pointed and he took a hasty step away from me but stopped when my hand shot out and grabbed hold of his arm. "Josh, I don't think she wants to see anyone."

"Fuck it! I knew this was a mistake. I fucked up yet again." He ran his hands through his chocolate brown hair and began pacing the empty hall like he had the weight of the world on his broad shoulders.

"Has Ky arrived?" I asked, desperate to leave this awkward mess in the hall.

Josh stopped and turned back to me. The worry on his face not lost. "Ky arrived, alright. He took one look at Lachlan and started going all caveman."

"What do you mean? Who is Lachlan?"

"Lachlan and Ashlyn have history and Ky doesn't like it. Thank fuck he left before he did something stupid." Suddenly it seemed like everything dawned on him, and he pleaded with me using his pale green eyes. "Can you go and make sure Ashlyn is okay? She won't slam the door in your face."

Everything that Josh just divulged bounced around in my head. Who was Lachlan? Why did Ky care so much? Were Ky and Ashlyn secretly together? The feeling of being in the middle of some screwed-up game flooded me. Was I a pawn in a sick and twisted game? My mind went through every conversation I have had with Ky and Ashlyn, but I couldn't see any clues. Paranoia was a bitch that had become my evil sidekick.

"Please, Eden," Josh begged. "Go and see if she is okay?"

Nodding in agreement, I had no real choice but to say yes. I took a deep breath and made my way toward apartment 8C while all I could think about was Ky. I needed to know what was going on, but I knew that my first concern was Ashlyn. As I stood in front of the bright white wooden door, I hesitated briefly and shot a look back at Josh.

I lifted my fist, knocked softly, and waited.

"Piss off, Josh."

"Babe, it's Eden."

The click of the lock turning filled my ears, and slowly the door swung open and revealed Ashlyn. Her cheeks were streaked with shed tears and her eyes rimmed red. The usually happy and sassy Ashlyn looked completely distraught as she opened the door in silent invitation.

"Are you okay?" I asked softly. What the hell kind of question was 'are you okay'? She clearly wasn't. "That's a stupid question." I shook my head dismissively.

Her smile gave me hope. I followed her into the vast open space of her apartment and hesitated by the couch as she glided into the kitchen. Not surprisingly, she reached into the freezer and pulled out a bottle of vodka before collecting two glasses from the cabinet and pouring the crystal clear liquid. She seemed to have one mission, and that was to forget. As she came toward me, a frown tinged her lips. Accepting the glass, I followed her lead and collapsed onto the black leather couch that took up the majority of space in her living room.

"Men are fucked up," she admitted after she took a large gulp of straight vodka. "If it wasn't for their cocks, I'd become a lesbian."

"You clearly haven't got the right type of vibrator," I shot back with a smirk.

Her laughter was like music to my ears.

"Are you going to tell me who Lachlan is?" I asked softly, deciding not to hold back.

"He is the one who got away." Her response was lightning quick, spoken without a single thought.

"Oh." I took a sip of the vodka and the feeling of the strong liquor floating down my throat excited me. "Do you want to talk about it? I have all night, and you have vodka."

A sheer look of determination flashed over her face, and it was almost like I was witnessing her sass reignite. "I feel like I should go back to Josh's and flaunt the fuck out myself in front of Lachlan. I didn't even know he was back. You'd think after two years together that he'd tell me when he'd be back in town. Obviously Australians have a different understanding of what consideration means. Fucking kangaroo lovers."

My laughter filled the room at Ashlyn's brutal observation of Australians. A knowing smirk flickered over her lips, and then she tipped her head back and the vodka disappeared.

"So Lachlan came on the scene after I left?"

"Yep, the year after I finished college. Met him out one night in the city. It was the accent that shot straight into my panties, and it stayed there for two years before he decided to go back to Australia without a word or even a fucking note."

Ashlyn's face dropped, and the tough exterior she portrayed to the world slightly shattered with the brief quiver of her lip.

"Josh seems to be pretty upset about it," I probed, trying to encourage her to dish out what was going on.

"So he fucking should," she spat in response.

Josh was clearly a touchy subject. We fell into silence, and I swirled the glass and the vodka swished in front of me. I was so tempted to throw back the vodka, but I knew that would be a mistake. For far too long, alcohol was my best friend, my mind and body numbing sanctuary. Thank fuck my parents didn't see me then. I drank so much that all I had the ability to do was drink, pass out, and repeat. The first six months with Tori was spent in my bedroom, shielded by an oversized comforter and a bad relationship with vodka. It worked. I forgot about Jeremy. I forgot the feeling of his breath on my neck as he pounded relentlessly inside me without remorse. I forgot about the feeling of being torn and destroyed at the hands of another. I chose to forget. It was easier that way. I continued to focus on the vodka in front of me as I sunk into the depths of my memories. I was becoming *that* girl again, the girl who I had worked too long to forget. I couldn't let Ashlyn see that girl. I didn't want anyone to know that girl.

"Eden!" Ashlyn's loud voice shattered my haze. I lifted my gaze and found her worried eyes staring back at me. Fuck. I forced a smile and shook my head. "Where did you go?"

"Sorry, got lost for a minute there." I leaned over, placing the glass on the coffee table in front of me. "So, how about it? Let's get you cleaned up and back to Josh's. Go in there and show Lachlan the confident, sassy, don't-give-a-fuck Ashlyn that I know and love. Don't let any man make you feel like this. They don't deserve it. This is why I am single." I winked and stood from the couch, grabbing her empty glass from the table and taking them into the kitchen.

"If Ky has anything to do with it, you won't be single for long," Ashlyn said softly. My head flew up at the sound of her words.

"We are just friends." I nervously laughed.

"With benefits?" Ashlyn teased.

"He was very vocal when he said he wouldn't be touching me."

"I call bullshit."

Twenty minutes later, Ashlyn and I left her apartment and made our way back to Josh's. Ashlyn's confidence was back, roaring like a lioness ready to show Lachlan just who she was now. I knew there was more to their story than she was willing to divulge, but I had no right to push. With a steady hand, Ashlyn opened the door and we stepped in. Who the hell were these people? Wasn't this meant to be a quiet dinner? The first person I saw was Josh, and his eyes smiled when he saw me and Ashlyn. He had a stunning blonde attached to his neck, and he looked like he was enjoying every minute. When he saw Ashlyn, he pushed the girl away and strode across the room with Ashlyn set in his sights. Ashlyn grabbed my hand, pulling me beside her.

"I am so fucking sorry, Ashlyn. I didn't know he would turn up. I thought he would be the bigger person and contact you. I had no fucking clue."

"Where is he?" she asked sternly.

"In the kitchen."

Ashlyn left without another word, taking off on her heel and strutting through the crowd with confidence in every step she took. My eyes traveled with her. She stormed into the kitchen and stood directly in front of a tall, tanned guy with scruffy blond hair, whose body language eased the moment she gave him a reluctant hug. That was my cue to look away.

"So I thought we were having dinner?" I joked, pulling my attention back to Josh. "A girl needs to eat you know."

"You know what? I am going to get rid of all these people, order pizza, and then I'm going to get to know the girl who has made my brother weak in the knees." His smile was so honest, but his words so unimaginable. "Could I be an ass and ask for another favor? Would you go and see Ky? I know he will be in his apartment stewing on this, and I know you'd be the only person who could get through to him."

"Why me?"

"Oh, Eden, you have no idea what you do to him." He grabbed his key chain from the counter, slid off a silver key, and handed it to me, folding my fingers over it to lock it in my palm. "Here is his key. I know he won't answer if you knock because he will be still pissed off that Lachlan is here. His apartment is on the ninth floor. Go and get him."

Josh leaned in and kissed me lightly on the cheek while my head spun. I flipped over the key in my hand and sighed. Could I just go up to Ky's apartment and let myself in?

The butterflies battling around in my stomach told me my answer.

KY

LACHLAN JOHNSON; ONE OF my friends from college, my sidekick, my partner in crime, but also the asshole who broke my best friend's heart into a million pieces. It had been two years since he pissed off back to Australia, and I've been trying to fix Ashlyn ever since. When I walked into Josh's apartment and saw him, I felt every inch of my body scream bloody murder. My fists had clenched at my sides, and the urge to punch the fuck out of him was almost too much. In an instant, he made me forget all about the excitement I had for seeing Eden after being away for two days.

I was fast becoming aware that I was reliant on seeing Eden smile. If she smiled, I knew I was doing something right, and this crazy idea wasn't just some fucked-up plan. Even though she hid behind so many walls, and there were so many layers of Eden Rivers, she still completely grabbed my attention. She didn't care about what she looked like or what people thought of her, or how the simplest of thing like playing twenty questions for two hours straight allowed the prettiest smile to completely take over her face.

For the past two days, I had been stuck in Los Angeles meeting with the board members of Anderson Publications and catching up with Simon Davenport. The majority of my time, however, had been spent thinking of a beautiful brunette on the other side of the country, the same beautiful brunette who had flirted with me by mentioning the red jacket that I loved in the last text she had sent me. If she was there in that jacket, all bets were off.

I buzzed with anticipation on my way to Josh's apartment, but then I was dealt a blow to the balls when I walked in to find Lachlan and Ashlyn embroiled in a screaming match in the middle of his living room.

It sometimes pissed me off just how well Josh could read me, but tonight I was thanking my lucky stars that he could. As soon as he saw my reaction to Ashlyn and Lachlan, he pulled me away before I had a chance to do or say anything that I was sure I would regret. I fled Josh's apartment and sought solace in mine. The thought of what Lachlan had done still ate at me. He up and left without a fucking word. Just left and went back to Australia, pissed off to Kangaroo land and didn't give two shits about the girl he left in his wake. How could someone do that—especially to someone like Ashlyn?

As I stood by the window, it felt like the weight of the world had landed forcefully on my shoulders. Knowing that Ashlyn was hurting, that Lachlan was back, and the confusion of my feelings for Eden took over all my thoughts.

"I thought you'd have the penthouse apartment."

I stiffened at the sound of her voice, tension quickly invading my body. The soft, angelic voice of Eden Rivers filled every inch of me. I slowly turned around to a nervous looking Eden standing by the front door came into view. Fuck me, she was wearing the red jacket. As if she read my mind, she raised her hand and waved the key to me, showing how she got access to my apartment. She placed the key on the bench and then moved effortlessly as she made her way across the living room toward me, her eyes never leaving mine. I stood completely silent, still trying to comprehend having her in my apartment.

"I'm not that big of an asshole. I gave the penthouse apartment to the maintenance guy and his family. He's the one who runs this place," I admitted when I found my voice, my gaze following her until she stood beside me.

I shifted my gaze and took in the city before me. I was in a shit mood, and she didn't deserve to see me like this. Hell, no one deserved to see me like this. What could I possibly say when all I was thinking about doing was punching my friend in the face? We stood in silence, which I knew I wouldn't break.

"I thought we were having dinner tonight?" her soft voice asked.

I turned to her. Her wide blue eyes searched mine for an answer, and a worrying frown framed her beautiful face. She barely wore a trace of makeup, and her natural beauty was refreshing and enticing. If true perfection existed, its form now stood right in front of me.

"I can't be there," I finally answered.

"Why not? Come and have dinner with me, Ashlyn and Josh." Her tiny hand fell to my arm, sending a searing spike of lust and need shooting through my body. My eyes shot up to meet hers. Did she just feel that? An intense stare-off began between us, and the tension that swirled in the air ignited even the darkest of hearts. I tried to tear my gaze from her, but I was completely locked in. My breathing stilled as her eyes dropped to my lips and then back. It was the first time she had looked at me like this. "I want you to be there." Her voice was thick with what I hoped was anticipation.

That was all it took, one simple look, one flutter of her eyelashes, and my reserves slammed down in a burning heap and everything I had promised her faded into ashes. I could no longer resist the urge to touch her. I craved the contact of her bare skin against mine. I needed to taste every inch of her tempting body that I had wanted from the first moment I laid eyes on her. It was like a wild animal had taken residence in my body, and I needed to feast. I needed to own. I needed to prey.

"Eden, I need to touch you. I know I said I wouldn't, but I've never needed anything as much as I need this. My mouth needs to fuck your body, my tongue needs to taste every inch of what I've dreamed of." I stepped closer so I was almost touching her. "You have about five seconds to tell me to fuck off."

The sound of her sharp inhale and the glimmer of hesitation flashing before me were swallowed as pure lust took over her. My hands gripped her hips, pulling her body hastily against mine. I knew she felt my excitement the moment a deep gasp escaped her throat. My face fell to the confines of her neck, my lips touching her skin, and I breathed her in. My memories went into overdrive, and I basked in everything that was Eden Rivers. Soon enough, I was drunk on the scent of the sweet perfume mixed with the coconut shampoo that had become my most favorite scent in the world. Her arms wrapped tightly around my waist, holding me in perfect sync with her body.

As if music flooded the room around us, we began to sway, my face never leaving her neck. With a soft touch, my greedy mouth began its mission. My lips left a trail of kisses along her collarbone, my tongue darting out to take pleasure in the taste of her sweet skin. This was surreal. Her head fell to the side as her hands gripped my shirt, begging for closeness. What I thought would be frightfully intense once I had my first taste, was nothing compared to what was happening now. This was different. This was comfort. This was intrigue. This was patience.

My fingers dipped below the fabric of her tank top, and shots of electricity bolted through my body as my fingertips met the warmth of her skin. She turned her face, and I felt her eyes on me. I pulled my lips away from her neck to face her, and watched as her eyes narrowed in on my lips.

"Why aren't you scared of me Eden?" I whispered as the ability to find my voice was almost non-existent.

"I don't know," she breathed out, "and that's what scares me, not you."

"Do you really want this?" Why the fuck would I ask her something like that?

"There is so much about me you don't know, Ky." Her eyes fell to the floor, and it was at that moment I knew I wouldn't have her tonight—that I had crossed the line—but it was what she said next that shocked me. "But what I know is that I am glad you came up with this crazy idea. Even if it's just for a month, I'll take it. I don't want you to keep being so considerate with me. I want you to tell me what you want. I want to have a month where I forget everything, where I can just be Eden of today and forget about the Eden of yesterday. If you can give me that, I can give you all of me."

"I want Eden of today." I grabbed her chin and made sure she was looking at me. "Do you realize how sexy you are? How much presence you have? You don't give yourself the credit you deserve."

"I don't want to believe that. I don't think of myself as that girl."

"Well, I'll make sure I get you to believe it."

I released her body from my arms and sighed. My cock strained against my pants, but I knew he wouldn't be unleashed tonight.

"So are you going to come to Josh's, or am I going by myself? I am starving, and there was the promise of pizza," Eden asked quietly as she nervously began twisting her hands.

"I need to shower first and I'll think about it. I don't want to see Lachlan," I admitted.

"But you've already showered."

"You might be sexy as fuck, but you are so damn naive. I need to shower because I need to take care of this." I patted my straining pants, not caring about my honesty. I was pretty sure that after tonight, she could handle my newfound brutal honesty.

"Oh." Her lips twisted into a slight smile. "So then you'll come?"

Holy fuck! I completely lost it. My loud laughter engulfed

my apartment. I hadn't felt this carefree in fuck knew how long, and here Eden was, not even realizing what she was saying. Eden stood there watching me wide-eyed, completely oblivious to what she had said or the effect she was having on me.

It was official; this girl was going to destroy me.

Eden

I STOOD IN THE hall, leaning against the closed door of Ky's apartment completely buzzing. What just happened? The skin on my neck tingled from the feeling of Ky's lips devouring me. This was too fast, this wasn't me at all, and as I said to Ky, that was what frightened me, but I wanted it. I pushed off from the door and practically ran to the elevator and went back to the eighth floor.

There was a peaceful silence when I stepped into the hall once the elevator arrived. There was no loud music, no fleeing girl from Josh's apartment, just pure, untainted silence. I stood at Josh's door, knocked softly, and waited. The door swung open quickly and an amused Josh greeted me.

"Please never knock on my front door again. My door is always unlocked for you, pretty girl." His eyes moved and looked over my shoulder. "Ky isn't with you?"

"He's taking a shower, and he said he might come down later."

"What the fuck did you do to him to make him need to shower?" Josh's booming laugh caused my embarrassment to soar. "Come in, pretty girl. Ashlyn and Lachlan are *talking.*"

I followed Josh through the apartment. It was similar to Ky's, but so much more like how I would have expected a bachelor to live. Blacks and red throughout, the biggest television I had ever seen graced the far wall, and a fully-stocked bar took up one corner. Black and white artwork hung from the walls, my eyes instantly drinking the portraits in.

"I ordered dinner. I wasn't sure what you liked, so I ordered a few different pizzas from downstairs. I think it's just going to be you, Ky, and me if that's okay? I'm not sure what Ashlyn and Lachlan are doing."

"It might just be me and you, seeing as your brother probably won't come."

Josh's smirk filled the room. "Oh, he'd come if you let him."

"Joshua, did you just make a come joke?" My question shocked me.

"I did and I am super turned on that you got it."

I shook my head at his honesty and followed him to the bar where I propped myself up on one of the barstools. He had a damn good collection of alcohol on display. Seriously, could he be any more of a bachelor? He turned suddenly and stared at me like I had said the most shocking thing in the world when I actually hadn't said a word. He remained there, staring at me, and immediately I thought I had something on my face or my mascara had run. The way he was looking at me didn't scare me; it didn't make butterflies appear in my stomach like his brother seemed to do; it didn't make feel anything besides safety. What the hell was it with these Crawford brothers? First Ky, and now Josh.

"Drink?" He finally broke and turned his back to me.

"Sure," I choked out. "Um, can I just have a Coke to start with?"

"Of course, pretty girl. Anything you want."

"Stop trying to chat up Eden."

I jumped at the sound of seduction behind me. I didn't even hear the front door open, but the feeling of Ky standing behind me sent shivers down my spine and I was caressed by the smell of his soap and aftershave. He moved so his chest was pressed against my back, and dropped a kiss on the back of my head tenderly. Josh looked between the both of us wide-eyed and in shock before looking back at Ky.

"I don't need to chat up anyone. They flock to me, to us, remember."

"They flock? Really?" I scoffed and swung around on the bar stool so I was facing Ky. Josh moved from behind the bar and handed me my Coke before standing beside Ky. I sighed into my drink as I took in their attractiveness. "Are you telling me that you two have some crazy brother technique you use?"

Near identical smirks greeted me, and I swore I heard a snort from one of them. Josh spoke with such egotistical delight. "It's called tag team, Eden."

"Oh! My! God!" I shrieked loudly. Yes, I might not be experienced with sex, but I had heard enough stories from Tori to know exactly what tag team meant. My eyes bounced between Ky and Josh, who looked at me amusingly. "You two tag teamed girls?"

"It was once, and I sure as hell didn't touch him," Ky scoffed, shooting a stern look of warning at Josh. I watched on amusingly as a silent conversation started between them. I would admit that the thought of Ky and Josh doing that was definitely a good image to keep locked in my head.

"The things you find out," I teased with a raised brow. "That's kind of hot, though."

"Not happening," Ky growled and moved closer toward me, putting his body between Josh and me.

Josh's deep laughter filled my ears. "Rightio Tarzan, I'm not touching your girl. There is no fucking way I'd let you share her anyway."

Hearing Josh call me Ky's girl sent a searing heat through me. So much had changed in such a short amount of time. I wasn't hiding behind a mask anymore, and I wasn't pretending. I didn't know whether it was because I was seeing Ky every day and talking to him just about every hour, or whether it was because he was so damn confident and told me how it was without regard or fear of my reaction.

"When is dinner arriving? A girl is famished." Ashlyn's husky voice rang from the hall and the sound of two sets of footsteps bounced off the tiled floor. She wasn't alone. I felt Ky's body tense against me and immediately I grabbed his hand, interlocking his fingers with mine. Ashlyn and, who I now assumed was Lachlan, appeared from around the corner and stopped dead in their tracks, as both of their eyes landed on a highly unpredictable Ky.

"Stay with me," I whispered, leaning protectively into the side of his rigid body. Ky's grip on my hand burned with strength. Without a second of hesitation, he twisted his body and stood before me with a face of thunder. My legs parted instinctively, and his body was soon flush against mine. My hands fell to his waist and gripped the cotton fabric of his t-shirt, anxious to keep him from running. I didn't care who was in the room, who was watching us with wide eyes, or who was confused by my actions. My only focus was Ky and the torment flashing within his darkened eyes.

"We need to leave. We can't be here." Ky's breath caressed my ear as he whispered so pointedly. "Please," he continued to beg.

"No."

He pulled away so quickly, tearing the soothing warmth of his body from mine. I felt the air leave my lungs the moment his brows pinched together, and his eyes began to scrutinize me. Panic engulfed me, swallowing me whole, leaving my body completely frozen in fear. I did it again. One simple word. *No.* What the hell was I thinking? With complete desperation to flee I pushed back on the stool, but his strong body was like an impenetrable brick wall and I was cornered. I lost all ability to hear, to feel, to breathe—the comfort I had just felt with him disappeared into thin air. All I saw were those eyes and the unreadable look on his face. Like the world was taunting me, time faltered, and then stopped altogether.

Before my eyes, his face transformed, and softness flashed before me. With a delicate caress, his fingertip traced my jawline, then lingered on my bottom lip while his eyes never left mine. The tension in my body floated away as he took a step back to me and this time his arms fell to my waist. "You said no," he uttered effortlessly.

"I'm sorry," I stuttered, the fear that was strangling me slowly easing. "We can go."

"Never apologize for saying no. Never." Ky's voice was so sincere and he was pleading with me to believe.

"Eden?" a strong Australian accent questioned. Ky swung around toward Lachlan, and by the tension in Ky's shoulders, I knew something silent was spoken between them. "Ashlyn was just telling me about her new friend. I am Lachlan, but my friends call me Lachie."

"Hi Lachie, it's nice to meet you." I held out my hand and was greeted by a strong handshake. Ky remained still, silent, and on guard beside me. The tension in the room was palpable. You could slice it with a knife. "Can you teach me Australian?"

The silence was swallowed by riotous laughter. Was what I asked really that amusing?

"Eden, Australian isn't a language. Pretty girl, you crack me up. Ky, please keep her around, purely for my amusement," Josh said through roars of laughter.

"Australian slang, you idiot," I retorted and rolled my eyes.

Once they stopped laughing at my request, we all settled in the living room around the coffee table. Josh had outdone himself with ordering dinner, and we gorged ourselves with pizza. Conversation flowed, but I noticed that Ky was sticking close to my side and barely saying a word.

"Are you going to talk to him or at least speak with Ash and see what's going on?" I asked softly. "I think that's what you need to do."

I tried to read the expression that flashed across his face, but I was at a loss. His eyes beamed of sweet honey, they were alert and taking in everything that was around him. I sucked in a deep breath as his hand softly brushed my thigh under the table, and I awaited his next move.

"You've got an amazing ability to make me see things I never thought I would."

He rose from the space beside me, and everyone's attention fell to him, awaiting his next move.

"Lachlan, kitchen?" His voice showed no hint of emotion. "Josh, you should come too."

"Uh, sure." Lachlan seemed unsure, and I knew he had every reason to be. Ky was highly on edge, so anything was possible.

I watched the three of them leave the living room and head for the kitchen, and I sighed in relief. I felt eyes on me, and I removed my gaze from the three men talking softly in the kitchen to find Ashlyn looking at me with wide inquisitive eyes.

"What?" I laughed nervously.

"I wish you could see what you are doing."

Okay.

How was I meant to reply to that? A million scenarios ran through my head. I wasn't trying to do anything. All I was doing was attempting to bide my time while I was in New York until I could go back to my life on the west coast. This city uncovered memories I wished I never had, and it put me in places I never wanted to revisit. It made me look over my shoulder and question everyone who gave me a second look. And now those stupid text messages were becoming more regular.

"I meant that in a good way, babe." Ashlyn rose from the floor, grabbed my hand, and pulled me to the couch. Thankfully, it provided a view of the kitchen so we could keep an eye on what was happening, not that we could actually do anything if a fight broke out.

My gaze traveled into the kitchen until it found Ky. He stood beside Josh with his arms folded defensively across his chest and his brow etched with a frown as he stared at Lachlan. Lachlan looked animated as he spoke, and time and time again, he would shake his head. My interest flared as I watched the three men. How was Lachlan possibly going to get out of this mess? He would have to have a good reason because Ky's anger was soaring to epic proportions.

Grinding his jaw. . . . . . check. Glare in his eye. . . . . . check. Intimidating stance. . . . . . check. If Ky had "Beyond pissed off" boxes, they'd all be ticked.

"I love my best friend. He is the best guy I know, but I also know his downfalls."

Ashlyn's soft voice pulled me away from looking into the kitchen. I shifted on the couch, turned to Ashlyn, and found her eyes on me with worry etched on her face.

"The Ky I see now. The Ky who isn't staying at work until early hours of the morning, the Ky who is sitting on the floor eating pizza, the Ky who is now standing in the kitchen attempting to make amends with someone who broke his best friend, is different, and it's because of you," she continued in a rush and her words hit me square in the gut.

"I, ah, I'm not really doing anything. I don't have much experience with guys, so I'm probably really awkward and standoffish. I'm actually really nervous around him, around all guys most of the time."

"Have you been with anyone since?" she asked softly, and I knew exactly what she was talking about.

"Just one."

"Was he a boyfriend?"

I thought of Colby and happiness flooded me. Our night together was something I would never forget. For those couple of hours we spent together, he made me feel like I was a goddess who wasn't broken, and that I could actually feel and be loved. He had kissed me and touched me lovingly, and I trusted him with every ounce of me.

"He is my best friend. It was just once, and it meant the world to me. People think he is this scary guy because of his tattoos and what the press says, but he is the sweetest and most kind-hearted guy I have ever met."

"Hold on a second. Tattoos. Press. Best friend. Holy shit."

"Colby," I admitted, and Ashlyn's eyes shot wide.

"As in 'the sex god drummer from The Fallen' Colby?" her voice screeched.

"As in 'my best friend, teddy bear, sweetheart' Colby."

"Fuck me."

"You'll get to meet him at the shoot," I admitted with a smile. "He is a ladies' man so I'm sure he will flirt with a beauty like you."

"God, I'll probably die."

"Please don't die. You are my only girlfriend here."

Laughter sounded from the kitchen and called an abrupt end to my chat with Ashlyn. Leaning against the kitchen island, the three guys laughed and drank beer like they were the best of friends and that it wasn't just moments ago that Ky wanted to physically hurt Lachlan. Ky moved his gaze from Josh and his eyes found mine. I was locked in as he completely dissolved me in one look. He was confusing. The man eyeing me so intensely, so enticingly, wasn't the man who snapped at me in his office just a couple of days ago. The way he was looking at me now sent shivers down my spine; it made the hairs on my arms stand to attention and encouraged my mind to cross to a place that had been closed off for four years. I was dangling precariously on the edge of reality and fantasy.

Once their beers were finished, Ky, Josh, and Lachlan walked into the living room. Their eyes jumped from me to Ashlyn, and then back again.

"What have we missed?" Josh asked as he sat beside me on the couch and his arm fell across my shoulders.

"Just girl talk," I responded with a smile.

"And by girl talk, do you mean talking about boys?" he teased with a wiggle of his eyebrows.

"Joshua Crawford, I feel sorry for the girl who finally sweeps you off your feet."

"Not going to happen, Ashy."

"Ky, your brother has seriously lost his mind." Ashlyn laughed and wrapped her arm around Ky's waist. "Come make me one of those famous Ky Crawford cocktails."

Ashlyn pulled him closer, and they walked toward the bar, chatting quietly amongst themselves. I turned back to Josh and Lachlan, and fell into conversation about Australia. I finally learned some of the Aussie slang that I had asked for, and I soon realized that Australian impersonations really weren't my thing.

The night soon came to an end, exhaustion was hitting me full force, and all I wanted to do was crawl into bed. Tonight was unexpected, and I never thought coming here would result in Ky telling me he wanted to kiss me again, or that I'd have girl talk on the couch with Ashlyn and meet an Australian. It was a crazy whirlwind in my head, and I was still trying to sift through the layers. After saying our goodnights, I walked out with Ky and waited in the warmth of the foyer for a cab to arrive to take me back to the hotel.

I suddenly felt shy under the intensity of his gaze, and his smirk hadn't left since he walked me down. "I have every intention of asking you to stay tonight, but I won't because I'd only want you to say yes for the right reasons, and I know you aren't there yet." His voice was so smooth.

It was about this time that I stopped breathing.

"Don't look panicked. I'm not asking you, Eden." The cab driver hit the horn as he pulled up and Ky pulled me close to the warmth of his body, placing a sweet kiss on my forehead. "I'll talk to you tomorrow. Stay safe."

KY

I WALKED INTO MY darkened apartment, switched on the lights, and the space immediately illuminated. It had just ticked over to midnight, and I couldn't stop thinking about the awkward goodbye I shared with Eden.

So much had changed in such a short amount of time. I was no longer working sixteen-hour days. I wasn't spending more time at work than I was at home. Fuck, I even had food in my fridge these days. That wasn't Ky Crawford. She was getting under my skin at an alarming rate, and I was losing sight of what I had set out to achieve in the first place.

The sound of my phone ringing echoed through the air, and as I looked at the screen, I was shocked to find Eden's name flash.

I pushed the answer button.

"Ky, please come and get me." She didn't even give me a chance to speak.

"Eden, what's wrong?" I asked, rushing back toward the door and grabbing my keys.

"Someone's been in my room." Her voice was so panicked and breathless with fear.

My body went rigid. "Eden, go to the front desk. I'll be there in ten minutes."

I hung up the phone and bolted out of my apartment, determination flooding my veins. I bypassed the elevator because of the time it would take to go down fourteen floors; I couldn't risk stopping at any floors and wasting any more time. Time was not on mine or Eden's side right now. I ran down fourteen flights of stairs to get to the underground garage with only one goal in mind. *Get to Eden.*

I was at Hotel De Luca within eight minutes, having made five traffic violations in the process. As I pulled to the curb, I found Eden standing outside on the sidewalk with her arms wrapped tightly around her body as her eyes darted around feverishly looking for protection and any sign of danger. My car was stationary before I could blink, and I sprinted until I was in front of her. My desperate eyes scanned her face and her body for any signs of injury. She was shaking so violently and the look of pure fear on her face tore at my defenses. I pulled her close to my chest, one arm around her waist and the other around her shoulders, allowing my hand to rest on the back of her head. She fell into my arms, and I felt the rigidness of her body soften against the warmth of my chest. I didn't know how long we stood on the sidewalk, all I knew was that I'd give her what she needed until she pushed me away.

"I should go and see if there is another room available." Her muffled words against my chest startled me.

"Eden, there is no way in hell you are staying here."

Her blue eyes flashed up to mine.

"You are coming back to my place. You can stay in the spare room until we work something out. There is no fucking way you are staying here."

"Can you come with me while I pack up my things?" she asked timidly.

"Eden, I'm not letting you out of my fucking sight. You are going to get sick of the sight of me before this month is over. We will get your things and then head to my place. Are you okay with that?"

"Yes."

She unwrapped herself from my body and attempted to step away. *Like hell.* My hand shot out and grabbed hers, and immediately her fingers laced with mine so tenderly and so needy. We walked in silence through the foyer and toward her room. My mind felt like it was running a marathon and I couldn't see the finish line. Eden hesitated as she slid the card through and the door unlocked.

"I'll go in first." I gave her hand a squeeze in a desperate attempt to offer her protection and comfort.

Her suitcase lay in the middle of the bed in total chaos. Bras and panties were spilling out of it, thrown around and disturbed by some dirty fucking asshole's hands. My body clenched and I felt bile rise from the pit of my stomach and sit precariously in my throat.

"Do you want to stay in the hall and I'll pack everything up?" I asked softly.

"No!" She gasped and shot me a pleading look. The color in her face had drained and her eyes showed nothing but sheer terror. Her hand grabbed hold of my arm for dear life. "Please don't leave me out here."

"Hey, hey, it's okay. I'm not going anywhere. Let's get in here and get your stuff together then get out of here."

I sat on the edge of the bed while Eden packed up her belongings at a rapid speed. My eyes traced her every movement and I couldn't ignore the fact that she was trembling. Her shaking hands caused her to drop everything she picked up.

"Eden," I spoke so softly that she froze and turned to look at me. "Come here."

She crossed the room, fell into my open arms, and unleashed a deep sob into my chest. I felt the cotton of my shirt dampen under her tears and my arms tightened. She was completely falling apart in my arms and I felt at a loss to what I could provide her.

"I'm scared," she admitted when she pulled away and looked up at me. "I'm really scared."

"What can I do to stop you from being scared?" My fingers

tucked the hair that had fallen out of her braid behind her ears and her eyes closed under my touch.

Her voice strained as she responded with, "I don't know, but you being here is helping."

"How about we finish this so we can leave?"

"That would be good."

Eden stepped away from me and went about collecting her laptop and camera gear, and continued shoving her belongings back in her suitcase. Seeing the expensive items not touched confused the fuck out of me. A breaking and entering like this was always for the most expensive items that could be grabbed, but here they still sat, out in the open and begging to be taken. I couldn't shake the feeling that this wasn't just a random act, and it sent shivers soaring down my spine.

One name kept circling in my head: Chris Edwards.

Fifteen minutes later, with Eden's suitcase in my hands, we were walking out of the hotel and toward my car.

"Thank you so much for coming to get me," she said as she watched me load her bags into the trunk of my car.

"I'm glad you called," I said as I slammed the trunk shut and headed for the driver's seat. She fidgeted in the passenger seat as we took the ten-minute drive back to my apartment. The familiar ding of a text message sounded, and as I looked over to her, I noticed that she slammed her eyes shut and didn't make a move to get her phone.

"What's wrong?" I asked hurriedly, my eyes falling to the phone in Eden's hands.

Her eyes flew open and her mouth twisted with nerves. "Nothing. I'm just tired."

"Are you going to check your text?" I asked, not believing a word she said.

"No."

I wanted desperately to probe further and get her to speak, but she was already shutting down and I didn't really want to have her fleeing into the night because I had pushed too much. I bit my tongue and concentrated on the road ahead, while my mind danced through scenarios of who could be texting her to get a reaction like that.

Ten minutes later, my apartment building came into view, twinkling in the night sky. I pulled into the garage, grabbed her suitcase and bags from my trunk, and we made our way silently to the ninth floor. The moment we walked through the entrance and into the warmth of my home, shy Eden decided to appear. She stood just inside of the foyer as I headed to the kitchen. I pulled out a pot from the cabinet beside my stovetop and turned to find her looking around my apartment with a nervous expression plastered on her face.

"Don't look so nervous. You are staying here for as long as you want, so make yourself at home. I'll give you a tour once I make us some hot chocolate to warm up."

"You're making hot chocolate?" she quizzed, the shocked expression on her face was not missed.

"Of course. It's minus a billion degrees outside, and I need something to warm me up. Well, unless you want to hug me all night?" I teased, desperate to break the tension. "So hot chocolate it is. Do you want white or milk chocolate?"

"White please," she whispered.

I felt her eyes on me as I moved around the kitchen preparing our drinks. It felt good. Soon, the delicious aroma of melting chocolate filled the air. Once I was done, we both moved to the large couch that took center stage in my living room and collapsed into its comfort. Eden pulled her legs under her and blew softly on the steaming hot chocolate I had just given her. We drank in silence, and I knew that her head was going crazy analyzing everything that was going on around her. She didn't say a word, and I was okay with that. Knowing that she was here and not in that pathetic excuse of a hotel satisfied me. It allowed me to take care of her and keep her safe, and that was what I wanted. My eyes slammed shut as an unwanted pounding erupted behind them. Memories could fuck off, I didn't want them intruding on this moment, not now.

"Would it be okay if I took a shower?" Her voice ended my flashback, and I opened my eyes to find her gazing in wonderment at me.

"You don't have to ask me, Eden. As long as you are staying here, you can use whatever you like. I'm going to head to bed, it's been a long day. I'll show you to the guest room."

I stood from the couch, and she mimicked my action and then we moved through my apartment and headed down the hall. I opened the door, then stepped in and switched on the light, flooding the room with a harsh glow. Eden moved beside me as she entered the room, holding one of the smaller bags she brought, having left the bigger one in the living room. A king-size bed, large dresser, reading chair, and side tables with iron woven lamps completed the room. Once again, Ashlyn didn't fail in her interior decorating skills.

"It's absolutely beautiful," Eden's whispered voice hit the intensifying air in the room. She laid her bag on the bed and then walked toward the window. My eyes followed her every step with attentiveness. When she reached the window, she crossed her arms over her chest as she took in the lights of the city dancing in the night sky.

"This room is all yours," I stated. "I'll bring in the rest of your things while you take a shower. The bathroom is just across the hall."

I turned and left the guest room, and rushed down the hall to the escape of my room. My body was a battle of emotions, and my thoughts felt like they were running a marathon as I tried to sift through the events of the night. After pulling on some sweats, I headed back to the living room and collected her suitcase, After taking it into the guest room and putting it on the bed, I returned to the living room and collapsed onto the couch and tried desperately to find a sense of calm. Things between Eden and I had changed tonight. My desperation to taste her again was taking over my every rational thought. I told her I wanted to kiss her again, to taste her, and yet she still called me. I was still trying to get my head around everything. I stood from the couch, collected the empty mugs and took them to the sink. Finding myself with a moment of solitude, I grabbed my ipad and started checking emails and messages. I was due back in the Los Angeles office in a few days, so I hoped that Lauren had sent my itinerary.

Eden silently walked into the living room. She coughed to announce her arrival and my eyes lifted and took her in. Loose cotton pants hung from her womanly hips, and the tightest of camisoles fit her body like a second skin. Her face was completely fresh, and her wet hair hung around her shoulders. My dick decided to pay attention to the sight in front of me, and it strained against the cotton of my pants. What made matters worse was that her eyes fell and took in my bare chest.

"I am heading to bed. I'll see you tomorrow," I choked out. "Goodnight."

I shook my head, desperate to force the thoughts I had to erase. I dropped my head and took off through my apartment, toward the escape of my bedroom. I needed solitude, and I needed to get away from Eden's hot little body. Fuck, she was the perfect example of what a woman should be like. Womanly curves, a small waist, delicious enticing tits, hips that she unintentionally swayed when she walked—she was a fucking delight.

Two hours later I was still wide awake. It was closing in on three thirty, but I couldn't switch my brain off. I couldn't tell you how many times I counted the number of stripes that were on my comforter, or the amount of times I watched the videos on my phone. This was becoming a joke. A groan rose from within my chest as I pushed myself up and sat on the edge of my bed. I stood, and quietly moved toward the door, hoping that the one floorboard that creaked would remain silent. I opened the door softly but slammed to a stop. A faint noise came from the kitchen, the sound of water running. I silently made my way down the hall and looked around the corner and into the kitchen.

Eden stood by the sink with a glass of water in her hand. So it wasn't just me who couldn't sleep. I knew I should just turn around, go back to my room, and pretend I didn't see her standing there. I knew I should ignore the need to be in her presence, but of course I didn't. I crossed my arms over my naked chest and walked through the living room toward the kitchen.

Eden's body spun around, and her shocked expression greeted me. "Couldn't sleep?" she asked softly as her eyes dropped to my chest and an embarrassed smile tugged at her lips.

"Nope."

I grabbed a clean glass from the dish rack and poured myself a tall glass of water, then moved through the kitchen and stood on the opposite side of the island.

"Why can't you sleep?" I lifted the glass to my mouth and looked at her over the rim.

"I guess I've got a lot on my mind," she admitted softly.

"I know what you mean."

Her question back was immediate. "What are you thinking about?"

Why did she have to ask me that? I thought of my options. I thought that maybe I could lie and say that I was thinking about work, or maybe I could just shrug it off, but the need to be honest with her overcame me. I already had way too many lies in my life that I was trying to overcome, and I couldn't lie about this.

My response was simple yet brutally honest.

"You."

Her mouth dropped open in the shock of my truth, but her eyes never left mine. I had no expectations about how she would react although I had the strong feeling that she would flee at any moment. A second passed, and then a minute, but she didn't move. If I said I was shocked, that would be an understatement, but being excited was a given.

"Let's go to my room. We can watch a movie until we fall asleep."

Once again, my dick spoke in place of my brain.

I didn't give her a chance to answer. I grabbed her hand and led her down the hall, switching off the lights and darkening the apartment as we passed. We walked into my room and the dim light from the lamp provided perfect shadows to bounce off the walls and crowd us. Nerves sailed off her as she took in my room. Her hand ran along the satin stripes on my comforter, and her eyes scoped out every corner.

"Tell me, what you're thinking?" I questioned, my voice edged with intrigue.

"I don't know what I am thinking."

"If you could say one thing to me right now, what would it be?"

She hesitated over her words, and her eyes darted from mine as she continued to take in my room. A large king-size bed took up the space, draped with a black and silver striped comforter, side tables sat on either side, with oversized lamps, courtesy of Ashlyn and her need to decorate my apartment. A flat screen television hung on the wall opposite, and floor-to-ceiling windows filled another entire wall.

"I'm nervous about being this close to you."

I sat down on the edge of my bed and took in her words. Her honesty surprised me, but it allowed me to understand the stiffness of her body language. I didn't know whether she was nervous about what I could do or whether her nerves were based on her feelings of what she wanted to do. I knew I was coming to the end of my tether. Those moments when her perfume would hit my nose were like an extra stab to the heart, and all I wanted to do was bury my face in her neck and become completely undone. I knew it was only a matter of time before I lost this battle.

"Come here," I hummed in a thick voice.

I swallowed at the sight of her nodding and lowering herself to my bed. I wanted nothing more than for her to say no to me, but then that would mean that she wasn't the girl who could only say yes. All I wanted to do was tell her that she was the first girl to stay in here, that usually I would take girls to the spare room, but I knew that wouldn't sit well. She was already nervous enough. I pulled back the covers, climbed under the comforter, and waited.

"You can say no to me, Eden," I said in a low tone.

She froze and looked over at me. "I can't," was her immediate response.

"You can, but you won't." I sighed in frustration.

"I can't," she pleaded with wide eyes.

"Why. Tell me why in the world you can't say no?"

"Ky, please. Don't make me talk about this. Not now." Her voice cracked with emotion and those perfect blue eyes begged me to stop.

"Okay," I said reluctantly. "Do you want to climb in?"

She reacted straight away, pulling back the covers on the side of the bed that she was sitting on and sliding in. She remained on her back, staring at the ceiling, and it was the most awkward situation I'd ever experienced when it came to being in bed with a woman. After what felt like an eternity, she finally looked over, and I swear to God she smirked at me, her face flooding with mischievous intent.

"Shit, Eden, your feet are fucking freezing!" I gasped as her feet touched mine.

Her muffled laughter filled my ears as she covered her face

with her arm but continued to press her icy feet against me.

"My feet always get cold. They are my secret weapon." She giggled and, before I could say another word, her feet slid down my legs until they touched my feet again, causing me to shriek.

"Want to know what my secret weapon is?" My eyes narrowed in on her and her giggle ceased. Two could play this game. "This!"

I rolled over, pinned her down, and commenced tickling her. She squealed and giggled as her arms and legs kicked around, desperate to stop the assault of my fingers. I couldn't hold in the laughter, and soon my deep laughter mixed with her high pitched giggles filled my bedroom. Our bodies smashed together and our hands touched and prodded each other like it was the most normal thing in the world.

"Stop, Ky! I promise no more cold feet. I'll wear socks!" she choked out between attempts to take a breath and laughter, and her hands fell to my bare chest.

I rolled onto my back in victory and rested my hands behind my head. I tried to concentrate on everything around me, but all I could hear was Eden's heavy breathing as she struggled to get over my attack of tickles. This wasn't the best idea I'd had because now all I was thinking about was hearing her heavy breathing due from an attack of my mouth, fingers, or cock. How had this gone from wanting her to open up to me, to a tickle fight, and now sexual innuendos?

Yep, I was fucked.

"Okay, now that we have that settled, you need to pick a movie," I declared and handed her the remote.

"What do you feel like watching?" she asked and began flicking through channels, much to my amusement.

"Nope, it's totally up to you. I'll watch anything."

Ten minutes later, Eden was curled up on her side, her hair feathered out against the white pillow as she hummed along to the familiar intro of *Dirty Dancing*. This was new. One, I had never watched *Dirty Dancing* in bed with a girl before. Two, I hadn't had a girl in this bed before. Three, Eden almost looked at peace.

"Eden, come here," I blurted out.

Her head turned and looked at me warily.

"If I only have you for a month, I want you in my arms while we watch a movie, especially if it's *Dirty Dancing*."

She moved across the bed and hesitantly rested her head on my chest and her arm over my bare stomach. I hissed, and I knew she heard me because she stopped breathing momentarily. She waited for my reaction. I knew my heart was thundering in my chest, right under her head, and I knew she felt it. She was getting a response from me that she probably would never have imagined.

"I can move," she stuttered and began pulling her body away.

My hand fell down onto her arm, halting her escape. "You are staying right here, Eden. I'm not letting you go."

I wrapped my arm around her back and curled her closer, breaking the distance that she had put between us. Her arm went loose over my stomach, all tension lost, and we fell into an awkward and highly charged silence as the movie played out. Eden hummed along to every single song and quoted most of the movie in a hushed voice. Her tone and the comfort of her in my arms slowly lulled me into sleep, and the last thing I heard was her singing, "I've had the Time of My Life."

The feeling of fingertips sweeping over my skin and goosebumps rising from the sensation woke me. A light pressure was over my stomach, pinning me to the bed. For a brief moment, everything was confusion and a mass of shock. My eyes fluttered open and jumped around the room, trying to work out what was happening. The credits rolled on the television, and the glow from the screen allowed me to make out the sea of dark hair that was on my chest, and it hit me.

Eden.

Eden was touching me.

I shut my eyes and tried to calm my breathing, not wanting her to know that I had woken. Her soft fingertips continued to run along the muscles of my stomach, dipping lower until she was tracing the band of my cotton pants. Her feather-like touch was so enticing, I almost thought I was dreaming. She was still against my heart, and I felt her breath dancing on my highly reactive skin. The most incredible and intriguing thing was that I felt her increased breathing as she got closer to the band of my pants just above my cock. This was all her, this wasn't anything to do with me. Knowing that she was doing this of her own accord set something on a wild course within me. I remained still, concentrating on my breathing so I wouldn't give away that I was completely awake and enjoying every moment.

This was all for her.

Eden

SUNLIGHT CARESSED MY FACE as my eyes fluttered open to a new day. I had finally fallen asleep just before five a.m. The warmth of being cocooned against Ky's body had left me, and now I was in his bed on my own. I pulled the comforter up to my chin and sighed into the pillow. My fingertips still felt like they were tingling at the sensation of touching his body. It had been risky, and how could I have possibly explained it if he knew. I stretched and allowed my body to fully wake before I sat up and put my feet on the floor. I needed to walk out there and act as if nothing had changed. I couldn't allow him to know.

Ky sat on the couch, iPad in his lap, and a frown etched on his face. I stood in the doorway, watching him briefly before he sensed I was there. The laziest of smiles graced his lips as he looked me over. On instinct, I folded my arms over my chest because it was surprisingly cold in the apartment this morning. He was dressed in sweats and a hoodie, and thankfully he had decided not to shave this morning, so his strong jawline was peppered with stubble.

"Do you want some breakfast?" he asked with certainty.

"Yes."

He shook his head, stood from the couch, walked toward me. He stood before me and once again took me in. "Go take a shower and get in your most comfortable clothes. You and I are having a day together, just us."

"What are we doing?" I asked, trying to ignore the bubble of excitement that unleashed inside of me.

"See that couch?" He nodded toward the inviting chaise lounge. "You and I are going to be sitting on that couch all day, watching television, watching movies, talking, whatever you want."

"Okay."

I left the living room and headed straight for the guest room. We hadn't said a thing about the night before, about me sleeping in his arms all night. I didn't know if I could face that conversation because I didn't need this to be any more awkward. I fished through my suitcase, grabbed my clothes and toiletries, and escaped to the confines of the bathroom where I could try and get my emotions in check.

Twenty minutes later, I walked into the living room wearing my comfiest sweat pants and my lay around top, which hung loosely off my shoulder. Soft music floated through the air, and the smell of bacon hit my nose. My stomach grumbled in want, and I headed straight for the kitchen. Ky had his back to me as he stood at the stovetop, and I took a moment to admire him in silence. I still couldn't believe that this guy was so intent on having me in his life without any consequence. He had the looks, the life, and the confidence to have any woman he wanted, yet here I was on a freezing cold Sunday, standing in his apartment getting ready to spend the day on his couch. It was surreal.

"Are you going to come in here?" His question shocked me. He slowly turned around, a smirk on his lips as he took me in. *How did he even know I was there?* "I've become very accustomed to your coconut scented lotion, and I could smell it as soon as you walked in the room."

And there was the return of the butterflies.

Butterflies that shouldn't be there.

"Are you ready for a Ky Crawford breakfast extravaganza?"

I walked into the kitchen and stood on the other side of the island. Jesus, he knew how to put on a breakfast. Fresh juice, coffee, waffles, and eggs were waiting on the counter, and the sound of bacon sizzling in the pan that Ky was tending to complete the meal.

We were soon eating in silence, and I couldn't help the deep sigh that escaped as I dug into the fluffy eggs that he had piled high on my plate. I'd never eaten eggs this good before. He watched in amusement as I filled my plate with more eggs, and under his gaze, my nerves decided to kick into gear.

"How did you sleep?" His voice was spiked with something I couldn't understand. Was it frustration? Intrigue? Suggestion? "I for one had a very enjoyable sleep."

I swallowed the mouthful of eggs and gulped down some juice before looking at him.

"I slept fine, thanks."

He nodded and I swore to God I saw a smirk and a raised brow as he looked down at his food. He couldn't have, could he? I shook the thought out of my head and continued eating breakfast, although the feeling of him giving me looks rushed through me.

We finished up breakfast and moved into the living room. His couch looked like it was going to wrap around me in pure comfort, and I couldn't wait to get lost in it. I watched Ky as he cleaned up the kitchen while I wrapped one of the comforters around my shoulders. The weather outside was horrendous, and the rain pounding on the balcony was creating the perfect atmosphere for a day of pure laziness.

The couch dipped when he sat beside me and handed me the remote. Yet again, it was my choice of what we would watch. I flicked through the list of movies and television shows that were on and settled on *The Walking Dead.* It was one of the shows that I had been meaning to watch, but never got around to it.

"Eden Rivers, you never cease to amaze me."

We sat in silence as *The Walking Dead* started. I sat beside him, completely enthralled by the show. It was all kinds of messed up. I pulled the comforter up to my chin and my eyes stayed glued to the television.

"Shit!" I jumped and scooted closer to the side of his body. He chuckled, then dropped an arm around my shoulder and pulled me close to his body. I felt my body freeze under his touch, but then as his fingertips ran over my bare shoulder, I instantly relaxed against the warmth of his body.

"I lied to you before." Ky's admission startled me.

I stilled beside him, and my mind replayed our conversations as I tried to find where he could have possibly lied to me.

"I slept well until I was awoken to the feeling of you touching me," he continued.

Oh my God. I lifted my head from his shoulder and twisted on the couch so I was facing him. I dropped my eyes to my lap and began fidgeting as embarrassment flushed through me. "I'm so sorry, I thought you were sleeping. I don't know what came over me."

"You don't have to apologize, Eden. Please look at me." His voice came out wickedly soft. I reluctantly raised my eyes to find him looking at me warmly. "I was sleeping, but then I woke up to the most delicate touch imaginable and I liked it."

"You liked it?"

"Uh, fuck yes. But please, can you make sure I'm awake next time."

"Okay."

His deep laughter shocked me. "Babe, that was an open invitation. I am awake now. This right here is your decision though. Touch me, do what you like, but you are the one in control. I have no say. You don't want to, that's also fine. We will go back to watching zombies and nothing will change. If you touch me, then that's your prerogative. However I cannot promise I won't want to touch you. I've wanted to touch you for a long time."

Instantly my fingertips tingled at the thought of touching his smooth skin again. I enjoyed exploring his body while he was asleep, but could I do it while he was awake and watching me? His body captivated me. My hands were shaking, and I inhaled sharply as I moved toward him. His eyes darkened and he licked his lips at my movement.

"I'm really nervous," I admitted sheepishly.

I didn't even have a chance to consider fleeing because Ky suddenly ripped the comforter off and pulled me onto his body. My legs fell to either side of his lap, and I was soon straddling him. He sucked in a tight breath as I settled in his lap, and for a moment, I felt like I was having an out of body experience.

"Please don't be nervous. You are in complete control. This is all you," he whispered, and I felt his hands fall to the small of my back where they rested.

"Can I take off your shirt?" I asked softly.

He nodded in response.

My hands ran up his arms and down his chest. I dropped my eyes and they followed my hands. The fleece of his hoodie provided surrealism at its best. The thought of what was underneath ignited my senses. He remained silent and stilled against me.

The moment my hands touched his warm skin and slid the hoodie from his body I shuddered at the sensation. His eyes slammed shut and his head dropped back against the couch. I took a moment to look at him while my hands rested on his stomach. His eyelashes rested on his cheeks and his lips parted as he took deep breaths. His reaction to my touch was overwhelming at best. My hands left the confines of his sculpted abdomen, and with featherlike fingertips, I ran up over his chest and toward his broad shoulders. His body rippled beneath my touch and finally his eyes opened and rested on mine. Eyes darkened with lust looked back at me, and I felt heat swirling throughout my body. I was doing this to him, and I was beginning to love every moment of it.

Something came over me at that moment.

Need.

Want.

Desire.

"Eden." His voice was hoarse, needy, and desperate.

His arm wrapped around my shoulders and pulled me to his body. We were so close that I could feel his breath on my lips.

"I need to kiss you again. I can't stop thinking about how fucking sweet you taste. My addiction to your lips is in-fuck-ing-sane. Do you want me to kiss you? Can you handle that? This is your chance to say no, Eden."

"Yes," I murmured, and an honesty that shocked me met my words. My body on instinct moved into his, my hips pressing into his, giving him an indication that I was speaking truth.

His mouth crashed into mine, instantly stealing the breath from my lungs. I gasped at the sensation of his lips on mine. My hands slid over his shoulders and wrapped around his body as he pulled me flush against his chest. His tongue licked my bottom lip so delicately, compared to his hands that rushed over my body. The moment I sighed in response, his tongue slipped into my mouth and began an intense dance with mine. My body reacted instantly. I moved on his lap, pushing myself closer to his body, grinding my body against his, and I enjoyed the groan that escaped the confines of his chest. Our breathing combined as I desperately tried to follow his lead. He owned every moment of this kiss. I had never shared a kiss like this with anyone before. His hands rested on my hips, but the moment I felt his warm palm slide up the back of my shirt, I stilled on his lap. He must have felt my sudden change because his hands soon fell back to my hips and the movement of his mouth ceased its infiltrating attack. He pulled away from my mouth and rested his forehead against mine. We were breathing heavily, my body was on fire, and I knew this had affected him just as much as me.

"Fuck," he whispered. "You are perfection, Eden. I love your mouth."

Like a shattering storm coming from nowhere, I felt the tightness in my chest before I felt the first tears spill over my cheeks. My emotions overwhelmed me. My thoughts were contradicting themselves. One minute I loved the feeling of his body pressed against mine, of his mouth owning me, but the next I hated that I allowed my body to be owned, dictated, and used that way. I had spent years hiding myself from this, yet here I was, in the lap of someone so unlike anyone I had met before, kissing him like my life depended on it, and feeling a pleasure I never thought I'd experience. This wasn't me. This was me losing the control that I craved, that I had worked four years to obtain.

The tears flooded my face, and when Ky realized, he pulled back and watched me carefully. I knew he thought this was his fault when in reality it was all me. I cupped his face in my hands and leaned in, kissing his lips lightly before pulling away to find a look of complete confusion taking over his beautiful face.

"This isn't me, Ky. I'm not this girl. I don't do this."

His arms tightened around me and pulled me closer. "You deserve it all; to be kissed, held, caressed, loved, and cherished. That's your given right. Your tears confuse me, they destroy me, and they frustrate me because I know someone has taken this away from you."

He knew.

"I want your thoughts, your fears, and all of your desires. It's time for you to tell me everything, Eden. Right here, right now," Ky continued as his fingers ran through my hair tenderly.

I pulled away from his chest and climbed off his lap until I stood by the couch, desperate for an escape. "I, uh, please don't ask me that. I need to use the bathroom."

I rushed out of the living room and escaped into the bathroom, locking the door behind me. I rubbed my chest as I felt panic rise within me. The thought of opening up, of telling my deepest secrets to Ky, scared me. I knew I wouldn't be able to handle seeing him look at me like I was broken like I was a wounded animal barely hanging on for dear life. That thought alone confused me because if I were to be honest with myself, I had already considered revealing everything to him, and I didn't know why.

I splashed some water on my face and counted to ten, inhaling and exhaling deeply as the panic subsided. If I walked out and pretended none of this had happened, maybe he wouldn't pressure me. I said a silent prayer, then walked out of the bathroom and into the living room, knowing that the longer I hid myself away, the more chance that he would make a big deal of it.

The moment I appeared, he spoke. "Eden, look at me," he demanded in a soft voice that caressed my heart.

I shook my head and stood in front of the couch.

"Look at me." This time his voice wasn't so soft.

I gave in, lifted my gaze from the floor, and looked at him. His eyes swam with compassion, encouragement, and determination. We locked onto each other, neither of us willing to speak.

It hit me.

Suddenly, the urge to tell him everything took over and the doubts I had vanished as his eyes showed me everything he was. They showed warmth I had never witnessed before, and an acceptance I had always wanted. This man before me, who had stormed into my life, screaming in my face when he had the urge to protect me, was becoming a confusing commodity. Maybe I needed to tell my story to someone who had no ties, no connection, and someone I would be leaving in a matter of weeks? Maybe talking about it in the same city it happened in would offer some closure.

"Just let me talk, please don't interrupt me," I whispered before my confidence fled for the hills.

He sat back on the couch, pushing his back against the side. I sat on the other end, folding my legs under myself, and started twisting my hands in my lap.

This was it.

I dropped my eyes and took a deep breath. "Four years ago, I had the world at my feet. I was in college, I had a great bunch of friends, a loving family, and I loved everything about my life and where it was going. It was almost like I was being swallowed by happiness, and I wouldn't have changed that. I remember the day like it was yesterday. My friend asked me to go to the Christmas end-of-semester frat party, and I thought why not. I usually wasn't one to go to parties, it just wasn't my thing, but I thought to myself, 'what's the worst that could happen?'

"I was having a great time—dancing, drinking beer, doing shots, laughing, and general fun with my friends. The feeling of someone watching me never left, and although it made me feel uncomfortable, I didn't think anything of it. The room was jam-packed with people, and it was so hot in there even though it was freezing outside. It got to the point that the air was so thick that you could barely breathe, so I walked outside to get some fresh air. That's where he approached me. He said all the right things. He made me feel comfortable. He made me laugh. He offered me his jacket, and then asked if I could help him get more alcohol for the party. Of course I said I'd help, he gave me no reason to say no, and I didn't think anything of it."

I slammed my eyes shut as I was taken back to that devastating moment. I had been so stupid, so trusting, so innocent. My skin began to crawl as Jeremy Davis seeped back into my thoughts. I couldn't let him win, and I knew talking about this would somehow allow me find some ounce of strength and make me feel like maybe I could finally begin to heal.

"As soon as we left the safety of the house, he changed. He grabbed my arm so rough, so forcefully, that I remember knowing that it would bruise. I wish that had been the least of my worries. He pulled me through the grounds toward the dorms, and he barely said a word to me. I could hardly keep up with his stride, and that's when I began to struggle. I knew I had to fight, but the more I fought, the more violent he got.

"He dragged me into his room, and the moment I said no to him it was like it was his role to punish me. The first time he hit me I was stunned. I think I was shocked more than anything. I couldn't believe that was happening to me. I remember screaming no and scratching at his face, but that was the worst decision in my life because, after that, I watched the humanity leave his body because I had said no. My biggest mistake was saying no because after I did, he raped me. He made it his right to take everything he wanted from me. He took my virginity, my voice, my respect, and my contentment. Everything. I will never forget that feeling. People say that you can't remember pain, but I will never forget it. I tried to take myself away, to escape in my mind to a peaceful place, but every time I closed my eyes, he would hit me and bring me back to that nightmare. I thought I was dying. I remember tasting blood. My eye swelled shut and my jaw felt like it was barely hanging on. Hit after hit he gave me while he raped me over and over again."

By now, tears flooded my face and my chest felt like it was constricting. Ky hadn't said a word. I finally looked at him and found his face void of any emotion, a blank canvas, but his knuckles were screaming bright white from gripping hold of the cushion in his lap. I sobbed loudly, gasping for a desperate breath, and looked at the ceiling, desperate to find some strength to continue.

"I don't know what happened after that. I woke up to the smell of disinfectant and my mom sobbing beside me. I was in the hospital. From that day forward, I was never the same again. I was in the hospital for a week before I discharged myself. I went straight to my parents' house, packed up as much as I could, then I escaped. I couldn't be here. San Francisco was my destination. I stayed in a hotel when I first arrived, until I saw Tori's roommate wanted ad. Within two days of being there, I found a new house, a new friend, and a life where no one knew anything about me. I couldn't be Eden Rivers anymore."

I didn't know what I was expecting to feel. I didn't know what I expected Ky to do. We sat there, not moving, not speaking; the only sound was my quiet sobs as I tried to find the calm in the storm that was rumbling within me. It hurt, every part of me hurt, from reliving that, but I felt like a weight had been lifted from my shoulders being able to tell it to someone who wasn't involved. Ky remained frozen and watched me so closely. It seemed like he was completely shutting down, and his face gave me no clue as to what was going through his thoughts. After what seemed like a lifetime, he uncurled his body and stood from the couch, his eyes never leaving me.

He held both hands out to me and waited. I grabbed his offered hands and was pulled from the couch until I was standing before him. My breath escaped my lungs as Ky pulled me to his chest. His strong arms encased my body, wrapping me with warmth and offering me protection and the soothing beats of his heart.

It was everything I needed.

KY

THERE WAS NOTHING I could have done to prepare myself for what Eden told me. Hearing her relive her torment and watching her face twist as memories ambushed her ripped my heart to shreds. What could I have possibly done or said to ease her pain? A fury that I never knew existed coursed through my veins with every word she spoke, and with every admission of her nightmare I wanted to kill that man with my bare hands.

As I held her in my arms, my thoughts went into overdrive. I believed my protective instinct of her was already bordering on insane, but now it was beyond anything I had experienced before. My mission was now clear. I would do everything in my power to make her see that life could once again be filled with beautiful and life-altering moments, and I planned on helping her create memories that would diminish the nightmares plaguing her life.

My hands ran down her trembling body and I lifted her into my arms. She gave no resistance. Eden curled into my chest, her head resting so tenderly over my heart, allowing me to get lost in the scent of her coconut shampoo and within seconds, and her arms locked tightly around my body. Moving out of the living room, I walked slowly through the apartment until we reached my bedroom. I placed her gently on the foot of the bed. Once she had unlocked herself from my body, she crawled backward until she sat up near the pillows. She pulled her legs to her chest and rested her chin on her knees as if she was protecting herself.

I lowered myself onto the edge of the bed and turned my back to her. My head dropped into my hands, and I breathed deeply as a wildfire of anger roared within me.

"I'm so sorry," I whispered, my voice cracking with emotion as I desperately tried to get the thoughts I had locked away for so many years out of my head. I was sorrier than she could ever know. I wished I had the balls to admit every fucking thing right there, but how could I possibly start that kind of conversation. My life was full of regrets when it came to Eden Rivers, and she didn't have a clue. "I am so fucking sorry."

The feeling of her hand resting on my back caused me to stiffen under her delicate touch. I fought for the last ounce of strength I could muster in my exhausted body and turned to look at her. Her tears had faded, leaving the tiniest streak of mascara on her cheeks, but it was her gaze that destroyed me. This girl had just relived her worst nightmare. She had spoken of so much tragedy, yet here she was, looking at me like she was more concerned about my feelings, whether I was okay instead of her. This was not how I had imagined today. Fuck, we had only been awake for a couple of hours, and now I felt more exhausted than I had in a long time.

"You are so special, Eden. Your strength is beyond anything I've ever witnessed." My hands cupped her cheeks and her eyes connected with mine as we took each other in. "Thank you for trusting me with that."

"Life hasn't been easy for me, Ky. It's torn me apart, ripped me to shreds, and sometimes I've wondered what the point is? But then I dip my toes in the ocean, I feel the wind sweep through my hair, I smell the arrival of rain, and it reminds me that I am alive. I was put on this earth for a reason. I was born strong enough to overcome this, no matter how long it takes me."

I dropped my hands from her face, laced my fingers with

hers, and pulled her up the bed until we reached the pillows. She took my lead and collapsed against the softness of the comforter, then turned toward me to match my body language. Her palm rested against her cheek, and her free hand laid against her chest. Through the windows, the darkness of the clouds matched the intensity swimming through my bedroom, but I couldn't imagine being anywhere else.

We lay silent and watched each other. No words were needed, and, to be honest, I didn't think there were any words that could be said that would make any difference. I encased her hand with mine and brought it up so they rested between us. My thumb swept over the back of her hand and I watched as her gaze dropped to our connected hands.

"I have so much I want to say to you, but I don't know where to start," I whispered into the still air.

"You don't have to say anything."

"One day I will," I promised.

"That sounds perfect," she said, and suddenly her face was shadowed with a sneaky grin that was totally unexpected. "Can I admit something to you?"

"Of course."

"I kind of want to watch *Dirty Dancing* again."

"Really?" I asked with a short laugh.

"Patrick Swayze was my crush growing up. I remember watching it with Mom every weekend when I was younger. Mom loved him, and that's where I got my obsession."

"The things you learn."

"Who was your crush?"

"Sharon Stone," I replied within a heartbeat.

Her laughter was like soothing music to my ears. "Really?"

"Have you seen *Basic Instinct?* It was every teenage boy's fantasy!"

"You crack me up." She laughed and rolled to her stomach, burying her face in the pillow.

An urge to comfort and soothe her, overcame me, and my fingertips fell to the bare skin of her shoulder blade from where her shirt had fallen down. Her head swung around to look at me, but she didn't say a word. Being under her watchful gaze, I continued sweeping across her skin, drawing patterns and swirls and watched as goose bumps rose on her skin. A satisfied smile tugged at her lips, and her hand swept her hair off her neck in silent invitation. My fingers made a trail from her shoulder blade, up her neck, and down to her throat. A low and barely audible sigh escaped from her throat, and I watched as her eyes grew heavy with fatigue.

"You are going to make me fall asleep," she hummed, and her eyes shut.

I continued running my fingers over her skin as I watched her. My mind was still trying to process everything she had told me. Hearing her go into detail had torn me apart, but seeing the strength she didn't realize she had was comforting. It was inspiring, and I knew underneath her torment was a fighter desperate to claw her way to a happiness she deserved.

"I wish I knew if it is okay to touch you," I whispered into the still air as I watched her sleep.

Eden stirred beside me, flipped her body over, and cuddled into my chest. "I like it when you touch me," she said in a sleepy tone.

"Is what happened why you can't say no?"

Her eyes darted away from me, and I knew that my question had opened wounds that she was desperate to heal. I waited patiently. My hands ran down her side in an attempt to offer comfort and encouragement, and gently I lifted the edge of her t-shirt over her lower stomach, exposing her skin. Her eyes dropped to see what I was doing, and she inhaled sharply. With soft movements, my fingertips danced over her stomach like they did her shoulder, and I instantly saw her relax.

"I said no to my attacker, and it made him hurt me more.

214

Because of that, I am so scared to say no because I don't want to be hurt like that again, and that's what I think will happen." Her voice dropped and a single tear slid over her cheek. "For the past four years I have either hidden away or I have been with people who will take me away from getting in situations I can't control. Colby and Tori are usually always with me, but I'm alone here. "

"You have me."

"I know," she muttered as her eyes fluttered shut under my touch. "But only for December."

"Well, for as long as I have you, I am going to make sure you know that you deserve everything in the world. I want you to know you can say no to me, you can say whatever the hell you want to me. I will never hurt you, Eden. My one wish is to make you see how incredible you are."

"But how do you know that?"

"Believe me, I just do."

Eden

MY MIND RACED A million miles an hour.

I felt cocooned in warmth, and the soothing heartbeats that echoed from below me made my sleepiness thick with want. I slowly opened my eyes and took in my surroundings. The glowing numbers on the alarm clock beside me showed that it was almost four a.m.

A heavy arm slouched over my stomach and soft breathing danced on my skin, causing shivers to run down my spine. Ky curled in beside me, our limbs entangled, a small smile gracing his perfectly plump lips while lost in the middle of what seemed like a peaceful sleep. The night before had changed everything it seemed. I never told people my story, but there I was, so open to telling him everything about me.

His arms encased me obsessively, wrapping tightly around my body, locking me in as if he feared that I would escape during the midnight hours. But I needed to escape. My bladder didn't understand the meaning of spooning. I stared at him for too long before I tried as softly and eloquently as possible to remove my body from his grip, but it was pointless.

"Where are you going?" Ky groaned from the confines of my neck, his arms tightening around my waist, locking me into the warmth of his body.

"I need to use the bathroom."

His lips brushed my neck tenderly, and his arms unlocked from around me. He rolled away from me until he was on his back, and the sheet that had been covering our bodies slipped to reveal his sculpted-to-perfection chest. "Make sure you come back."

I slipped out of bed, padded across the bedroom, and disappeared into his pristine bathroom. As I closed the door, I looked into the room and sighed at the sight of Ky sleeping in bed. There was no longer any doubt in my mind that he was completely crumbling every wall I had been desperate to put up. His words, his actions, his touch, and his patience were all sledgehammers that kept pounding against the walls I had built years ago, and with every day, another brick was falling down. I leaned on the glistening white vanity and looked at myself in the mirror. *One month, Eden, just one month.* I shouldn't be standing in the bathroom of the guy who I was spending just one month with. This was bordering on dangerous ground. I felt myself completely losing control, and control was the one thing that I needed to survive. I had already touched him, kissed him, and divulged my deepest secrets. I was afraid of what I would do next.

Once I finished in the bathroom, I tiptoed back into Ky's bedroom and stood at the side of the bed. The thought of escaping to the spare room flashed over me, but then I thought about how sweetly he had asked me to come back and I couldn't say no to that. As if on cue, he rolled over and opened one eye, then looked directly at me.

"Come on, Eden, I'm cold. I need that cute little body beside me." He pouted and lifted up the comforter that was on the side I was sleeping. Within seconds, I was climbing back into his bed and being engulfed by his arms. As he nuzzled back into my neck, I felt myself melting under the intensity.

You want this, bitch. Of course you do. What little slut wouldn't want me? My cock has wanted your pussy since the first time I

saw you, and now I'm going to enjoy every fucking minute.

Why couldn't I open my eyes?

Why couldn't I breathe?

I gasped for breath as the remains of the nightmare thundered within me. Every part of my body ached from being tense and rigid, and an increasingly aggressive headache had taken up residence in my fucked-up head.

When would this stop?

Why the fuck couldn't I open my eyes?

His menacing grin looked back at me, and the snigger on his lips as his body pounded relentlessly into mine didn't leave. Words of pure and utter evil hissed through my thoughts like a tormenting storm.

"Eden!" A distant voice sounded through the torment as if a light was beaming through the darkness. "Come on, wake up!"

I felt my body being jerked, being pushed into the mattress below, and then lifted so sternly. I felt a pressure on my hips. The more I moved, the quicker I was being saved from my torment and brought toward safety.

Finally, my frantic eyes flew open and the air that fiercely entered my lungs caused me to cough at the sensation. I desperately tried to take in my surroundings, and that was when I realized someone was sitting on me, pinning me to the bed. My fists automatically clenched, and I beat the rigid chest in defense. I knew I had woken up, so why was I still in my nightmare?

"Eden, babe! It's me. It's Ky."

His arms wrapped around my back, and he pulled me up until I was sitting and tucked against the nakedness of his chest.

It was Ky.

I fell into his warmth and completely came undone. Tears streamed down my face as I tried to allow my mind to catch up with reality. I was at my weakest. I was falling apart at a fast rate and I was losing control. My mind flew back to my appointments with Doctor. Sheree Evans, the psychologist I was referred to after the rape, and the many times she had told me how to overcome my panic attacks. I grabbed hold of the memory like my life depended on it. One, two, breathe in, one, two, breathe out. I slammed my eyes shut and repeated this over and over in my head until I felt myself swim into a current of calm while my body still shook.

"Please say something." There was his deep panicked voice again. I pulled myself away from the comfort of his chest and shifted my gaze to lock onto his. He brought his hands to cup my face and looked at me with concern.

"I'm okay," I choked out. I slammed my eyes shut momentarily, trying desperately to avoid the look that he was giving me. I hated pity. "Please don't look at me like that."

"Like what?"

"You are looking at me like you pity me."

"I am worried about you, Eden. I don't pity you." His thumbs ran under my eyes, taking away the fresh tears that had fallen. "Tell me what I can do to make you stop shaking."

"I don't know."

I watched as his face shifted to something of thought. All of a sudden, he released my body and climbed out of bed, leaving me completely and utterly confused. I watched him with wide, curious eyes as he walked into his closet, only to return fully dressed in sweatpants and a hoodie, with a scarf wrapped around his neck.

"Get out of bed. I am taking you somewhere. Wear this."

He handed me one of his hoodies and left the room, allowing me to dress. What the hell was happening and where was he taking me? I followed his orders and crawled out of bed, then slipped his hoodie over my shoulders and was instantly cocooned by warmth.

I walked out of his room in search of where he had escaped to. When I found him, I couldn't have ever imagined what

I would find. He stood by the door, holding a blanket, what looked like two travel mugs, and an expectant look on his face.

"You ready?"

I nodded, completely at a loss for words.

We walked down the silent hall of floor fourteen and took the elevator to the roof. The moment we stepped out, I wrapped my arms around my body and tried to take in everything around me.

Beauty to me was the smile of a young child, the smell of rain at the end of a hot day, and seeing an elderly couple walking hand in hand. It was the overwhelming contentment of silence and feeling completely at ease. Right now, beauty was the city lights dancing on the river before me, blanketed against the midnight sky above and the sleeping city below.

I stood in awe. It felt like we were the only two people in the world. He brought me to the roof of the apartment building, and now, as I watched him pull together two lounge chairs, I felt beauty in so many forms. He held out his hand and I walked toward him, grabbing his offered hand.

"This is where I go when my mind won't shut off, when my thoughts get lost between reality and nightmares, and when I need to forget that there is anyone else in the world. This can be your place too."

My heart flipped over in my chest at the enormity of his words. I had nothing that would be a good enough response. He moved us toward the lounge chairs, which he pulled together. After he sat down, I joined him, and soon we were both huddled under the thick blanket and laying in silence as the darkness surrounded us. But this darkness was the brightest I could ever imagine.

"Thank you," I whispered into the night air, rolling my head to the side to find him gazing at the sky above as if he had a million thoughts running through his head. Upon feeling my eyes on him, he shifted until his gaze landed on mine.

"Whenever you need to escape, you just let me know."

I woke early and slipped out of Ky's warmth. After we had come down from the roof, I collapsed into a deep sleep, the kind of sleep I hadn't experienced in years. Today I was heading into the city with Darren from the magazine to look at two locations for the shoot. One was a vacant warehouse in Brooklyn, and the other was an industrial style art gallery. I was excited about the thought of getting the location locked down so I could then concentrate on working more closely with the stylists. I was also excited about keeping busy.

After drinking a cup of coffee, showering, and getting ready for the day, I snuck back into Ky's room to find him sitting up in bed with his iPad in his hands.

"Hey," he said softly as I made my way toward the bed. I sat on the edge near his hip and he immediately grabbed my hand. "How are you this morning?"

My thumb swept over the skin on the back of his hand before I replied, "I'm actually pretty okay. I slept like a baby when we came back from the roof."

"You wrapped yourself around me so tightly last night."

"Sorry."

"I loved it. Never apologize for that," Ky said with a sincere smile. "Where are you off to today?"

"Darren from Production is picking me up at seven. We are going to look at some locations for the main shoot, and then I'm heading to the studio to do some shots of a couple of the artists who are recording today."

"Call me and let me know how it goes," he said just as my phone chimed with a text from Darren.

"I better go, Darren has just arrived."

I paused briefly before I stood from the bed. His eyes took in my face and dropped to my lips, and for a moment the idea of kissing him goodbye fleeted through my thoughts, and I think he realized it, by the smirk that appeared on his lips. I stood in astonishment as he pulled himself out of bed and moved toward me with crazy bed hair and stubble, wearing only cotton pajama pants.

His hands cupped my face and I lost the ability to breathe as his face dropped closer to mine. What was he doing? He leaned in until his mouth was close to my ear and quietly he murmured, "Have a good day. I'll see you tonight."

My body tingled under his closeness and the perfect goodbye was finished with a lingering kiss on my cheek.

KY

I WAS DEEP INTO proofing the latest issue for production when Ashlyn bounded into my office and promptly positioned herself on the edge of my desk. It had been a couple of days since I'd seen her, and I had a feeling it was because a certain Australian had decided to stay in town.

"You seem happy," she stated as if it was the most shocking statement in the world.

My laughter filled my office.

"Why does it sound like the thought of me being happy is surprising to you?"

"Shit, I didn't mean it like that. You just seem calmer, more at ease, and fuck, you aren't here half as much as you usually are."

"I've got more important things to focus on now."

"Like Eden?"

"Yes, like Eden."

"Is everything okay there?"

"I think so. She had a nightmare last night and seeing her like that scared me, Ash. I just couldn't wake her, and then when I did, she just shut down. Her nightmares are so embedded within her. It's like peeling back the most delicate layers because one wrong move will completely destroy everything."

"Have you two spoken?" Ashlyn asked.

"She opened up to me about everything yesterday."

"That's massive."

"I know."

Ashlyn jumped off the desk and moved to my office door, then closed it. She leaned back on the wood and closed her eyes. Oh fuck. I knew that look. I knew exactly what was coming.

"Can I completely change the subject?" She didn't give me a second to reply before she dropped the bombshell. "So I may have had sex."

Why in the world she chose to have, conversations like this with me never ceased to amaze me. I rubbed my hands over my face and sat back in my chair, then put on my best friend hat. Fuck, this girl owed me big time.

"Lachlan is still in town. He has been staying at my place and he kind of stayed in my bed," she continued in a rush.

"So you are saying that his cock kind of fell into you?"

"Well, when you put it like that. What the fuck am I doing, Ky?" She sat on the couch, dropped her face into her hands, and her shoulders sank. I had watched the demise of Ashlyn at the hands of Lachlan, and it was something I never wanted to see again.

"Do you love him?"

She nodded.

"Well, there is your answer. Fight for what you love. Nothing is worth it if you don't have to fight for it."

Advice that I would soon have to live by.

"We are going out tonight. Be ready in an hour," I announced as I walked into the living room after showering and dressing in dark denim jeans and a black collared shirt.

I had arrived home from work to find Eden sitting at the dining room table engrossed in her own work and tapping away furiously at her laptop. Photos of locations were spread out over the glass table top, and she apologized profusely for making a mess, which I in response told her not to worry about it. I knew she had spent the day busily organizing the shoot. Her emails that came through were regular, and she was in complete business mode with any correspondence we had. It was pretty damn sexy.

But now she was in relaxation mode, curled up on the couch with her Kindle and a distant look in her eyes. She was so engrossed that she didn't even hear me talking to her.

"Eden!" I said a little louder.

"Huh?!" she asked finally looking up from her Kindle.

"Good book?"

"Uh, yes, and you just interrupted an epic kissing scene."

"Well, I apologize to the characters for interrupting, but as I was saying, we are going out in an hour, so you need to get ready."

She furrowed her brow before looking back down at her Kindle.

Come on Eden, say it! One simple word, no. Reject me. You can do it.

"Yep, okay."

Fuck!

Rising from the couch, she placed her Kindle in the side pocket and headed down the hall without another word. I stood leaning against the kitchen island and scrolling through my phone when I heard the shower start. I looked outside at the torrential rain that had been falling for the past two days. Winter had officially set in.

"Ky!" Her voice sounded from the hall and I whipped around to find her standing in there, her hair wet and hanging over her shoulders, and her body covered only by a towel. I couldn't control my eyes from running over every inch of her, taking in the curves that were on full display, and enjoying the vision before me.

"Yeah?" I asked, my eyes finally meeting hers.

"What should I wear?"

"You look cute in that towel, but I guess jeans and a sweater will be okay."

She rushed back down the hall and I couldn't help but laugh at her reaction. I was due to leave for Los Angeles again the next morning for meetings with Simon Davenport at the Beautify office. The thought of leaving wasn't as exciting as usual because I would be leaving Eden, especially after her comment about not having anyone here.

I looked at the clock on the far wall of the dining room; it was close to seven and my stomach announced to the silent apartment that it was hungry.

"Eden, are you nearly done?"

"I'm ready." She walked into the living room in skinny jeans, a tight white sweater, and brown boots, then crossed the space until she stood before me looking like she had the world on her shoulders. She had something to say but was hesitating.

"What is it?"

"It's nothing. I'm ready to go."

"Eden, tell me what you are thinking about," I demanded, and crossed my arms over my chest. I could stand like this for hours. Frustration flew over her face and her gaze flashed with hesitation before she sighed deeply.

"I don't know why you are doing this. You know I can't say no, so why do you even ask. Just tell me, don't ask me."

"Are you fucking serious?" I hissed. "Babe, last night you told me everything. It killed me hearing what you went through, but you know what, it's made me more determined. I am not going to tell you to do anything. I will continue to ask, and I will be sure to make you see that you can say no to me, that you can say no to anyone. Do you have any clue how dangerous what you do is? One wrong person, Eden—you know what, I can't even think about that. I'm not an asshole, Eden, but I will do whatever it takes to make you see that you don't have to fear every single person who comes into your life."

For the first time, I witnessed her shift, and as she glared at me, I couldn't help but smile. She stormed through the apartment toward the door and heaved it open.

She whipped around and glared at me. "Are we going out or not?"

I chuckled as I found my keys and wallet and followed her out into the hall.

"Is this our first fight, sweetheart?" I wickedly grinned at her.

"No."

"You just said no."

"Don't call me sweetheart, we aren't that friendly."

"But you let me call you babe." I shot her a wink and watched in amusement as her lips ever-so-slightly curved.

Babe it was.

Thirty minutes later, after dealing with the constant downpour, I pulled up at Antonio's and shut off the engine. Eden hadn't said a word to me during the entire trip, instead choosing to play on her phone.

"You're taking me to have pizza?" she asked as her eyes took in the bright lights beaming from inside of Antonio's.

"No, I am taking you for the best pizza you'll ever have."

I looked out the window at the downpour of rain that was beating down outside, and then I looked back at Eden, and her white sweater that fit like a second skin over her chest.

"You are going to have to make a serious run for it. Your tight white sweater, plus rain, equals a happy Ky, but an embarrassed Eden."

Realization flashed over her face as she took in the insistent rain, and without a word, she shot out of the car and flat-out ran until she was under the awnings and safely dry. I soon joined her and my eyes went straight to her top.

"Well, that was no fun." I winked at her and felt victory as she rolled her eyes.

Antonio's singlehandedly had the best pizza in the world.

The aroma of fresh garlic and tomato hit me the moment we walked into the authentic pizza parlor. It was like stepping into Italy. Dad had been bringing Josh and me here for as long as I could remember, and my memories were filled with laughter, and eating until I was almost sick.

"Ky, this place is incredible." Eden gasped as she took everything in.

"Just wait until you try the pizza."

I led her through the crowd with my hand on the small of her back, and I felt the look she shot me over her shoulder in my cock. I was testing every single boundary I could find tonight. Was it wrong that I wanted to break down her walls? No. Was it wrong the way I planned on doing it? Probably so.

As soon as we slid into my usual booth and began looking at the menus, we were joined by one of my most favorite people in the world.

"Ky Crawford! You come and bring a beautiful girl with you."

"Antonio, this is Eden. Eden, this is Antonio, the best pizza chef in all the lands."

His hands went to his hips and a scowl took over his round face. "Why did I not know you have a girlfriend?"

"Eden isn't my girlfriend, Antonio. We are just friends."

He looked at us curiously. "Are you sure about that?" He tapped his finger on his chin and an all-teeth-showing smile appeared. "You would make the cutest Bambini."

As quickly as he arrived, he disappeared into the kitchen, and I swore I heard him saying our names and the word bambini to the kitchen staff. I shook my head and turned back to Eden, who sat across from me with wide eyes and mouth agape.

"Did he just say we'd make the cutest children?" She gasped.

"Yes, but I told you we wouldn't be having sex, so no Bambini for us. You can close your mouth." I laughed and dropped my eyes back to the menu, all the while knowing that she was still staring at me. "Have you decided what you want?"

"Wine. Lots of wine."

My laughter echoed through the restaurant, and soon enough, her soft chuckle joined mine. We fell into a quiet conversation as we waited for her wine and my Coke, and she seemed to relax as the night went on. I liked this Eden. The carefree, sassy, confident Eden, who didn't even know she existed. The one who gave me back as much as I gave her. The talk of babies was the joke of the night.

"So when I impregnate you, what will we call our first-born?"

"You did not just say that," she sputtered as she choked on her red wine.

"Oh, you know I did."

"No sex means no babies, so you are shit out of luck."

"Fuck, I enjoy this Eden," I gushed and smirked at her.

"And what Eden would that be?"

"Sassy and confident, Eden."

"It's the wine."

"Okay, well then I'll have to stock up on wine."

Antonio interrupted our discussion of our future non-existent children and arrived at the booth carrying two large white pizza boxes and an expectant grin.

"No order means I choose, and I choose best pizza for you two."

"Crap, I'm sorry Antonio, we got caught up talking." I looked around the restaurant and realized we were the only ones left and the staff had started to close up.

"You two lovebirds were too busy with each other. Here, take this, but you make sure you both come back and see me."

Eden slid out of the booth and avoided my gaze.

"And you two make Bambini for Uncle Antonio."

I grabbed both boxes and followed Eden out of Antonio's,

still chuckling at her reaction. As we stood under the awning and the rain continued to fall, I knew I didn't want tonight to be over yet. The lock on my car beeped and we both made a run for it, slipping in just as another massive downfall hit.

I pulled out of the parking lot and headed toward one of my favorite secret places, a place I wanted to introduce to Eden. Captain's Lookout was my favorite place in the world. The view of the city was spectacular during the day and even better in the dead of the night. Due to the weather, there was no one but Eden and me here. Hearing her gasp as I pulled into the parking lot tugged on my emotions.

"Ky, this place is beautiful."

We sat in silence as we looked through the window at the twinkling of the lights through the downpour. Having her here was surreal, but being in my car eating my favorite food from my favorite place was a mind fuck. This was date material, and I would be a liar if I hadn't thought of that when I told her we were going out. I wanted to give her this, the perfect night, where she could have fun with no expectations.

"Climb into the back seat."

"What!"

I was really beginning to get well-acquainted with her high pitched shriek. "Climb into the back seat," I repeated. "It's easier to eat back there."

"Oh."

"What did you think we were going to do? I told you, no Bambini for us." I laughed and caught the roll of her eyes as she handed me the two boxes that were on her lap and shifted her body to climb into the backseat. My eyes latched onto her ass as she climbed over the seat, and my cock twitched in appreciation before I followed her.

We sat side-by-side and ate in silence. Hearing the tiniest of moans she made after every bite was not only distracting but sexy as hell, and I knew I would never look at Antonio's pizza the same way.

"Have you had a good night?" I asked, stuffing the final piece of pizza in my mouth.

"Yes."

"Eden," I said in a warning tone.

"Why are you being such an ass?"

"It was a simple question."

"Just stop."

The door pushed open, and next thing I knew she was standing outside of the car in the pouring down rain. Fuck it. I threw the boxes to the floor and slid out, and the moment I did, the rain hit full force. I grabbed her by the shoulders and twisted her to face me.

"Talk to me," I demanded as rain drops saturated both of us.

"I'm sorry that I am so far from perfect, and that I don't fit into your perfect expectation of who you want to spend this month with, but you know what, this is how I cope. What else was I going to say when I agreed to this month? I wish I could have said no, but I couldn't. This is my way of surviving situations like this. I don't do this. I don't sit in the back of cars with guys. I don't go out for pizza with guys. I don't do any of this because yes, I will get myself into dangerous situations. Don't you think I know that?" she screamed into the night air.

"You should have said no to me. It would have saved you all of this," I yelled back.

"I couldn't."

"You could have," I hissed. Through the light beaming from the lamppost, I made out her features. She looked back at me completely spent, but so vividly beautiful. I cupped her cheek, and she closed her eyes under my touch "You should have."

"There are a lot of things I should have done, but I can't change any of them now."

My need to comfort her, to soothe her, to own her, overtook every reasonable thought I could find. Whether it was being here, seeing her in a whole new light, hearing her fight me, I didn't know, but the thought of dominating those perfectly pouty lips took control. I took a step toward her and she backed up until her back was pressed firmly against the side panel of my car. Her eyes shot open.

"Eden, I'm going to kiss you, and when I say kiss you, I mean I'm going to completely and utterly kiss the fuck out of those perfect lips. I'm going to touch you and show you that you can receive pleasure from a man without fear. I want you to feel exactly what you do to me with just a simple look, a simple word. This right here is you. I'm going to kiss you until I take your breath and until you can feel your heart thundering so hard in your chest that you fear it will stop beating."

She didn't speak, but just nodded.

My hand grasped her waist, forcefully pulling her toward me, breaking any distance between us. Her gasp fueled the fire burning within me, and my mouth fell to hers. My need to kiss her had turned into sheer lust. My eager tongue traced the length of her bottom lip and a primal growl rose from deep within my chest as she opened for me, offering me the playground of her mouth. Our tongues collided feverishly, dancing through a sea of lust, need, want, and confusion. The sensation of kissing this girl while the rain battered down on us was out of this world.

Her arms wrapped around my neck, her fingers tugged on the hair above my neck, and she pressed her body closer, grinding her hips into mine. With one swift movement, my hands cupped her ass, then I lifted her from her feet and moved our bodies to the hood of my car. I broke our kiss, and through heated eyes, I took in the sight before me. Her lips were swollen and her eyes hooded with desire while the white sweater stuck to every perfect curve of her body. She parted her legs and I took the invitation. My hands fell to her hips, pulling her forward until there was no end to our bodies. My cock thickened and ached for relief.

"Can you feel that? That's all you." I ground my cock into her jean covered pussy, and her moan vibrated against my lips. Our chests formed as one, so close that I could feel the thundering of her heart against mine. "Can you feel your heart racing? That's all me."

Eden pulled her lips away from mine and took a deep, ragged breath as I kissed and nibbled her neck. She dropped her face to my shoulder, and we fell into silence as our breathing combined, struggled and rejuvenated together.

"I will never forget that for as long as I am breathing, and I hope to God I take that memory to my next life," I whispered into the darkness.

I had never spoken truer words.

Eden

IT FELT SO STRANGE being in Ky's apartment when he wasn't around. I had been here for four days and was facing each day as calmly as I could. Every waking hour seemed to be spent attached to my laptop as I searched for the perfect locations for the upcoming shoots. *Beats and Bangs* had hired me for six weeks, so they were definitely getting their money out of me as they just booked me for another editorial.

Ky had left this morning for an overnight business meeting in Los Angeles confirming that he would be back at some stage tomorrow. Before he left, he made me promise that I would make myself at home, that I would eat his food, watch his television, and enjoy the comforts of his home. He had hesitated at the door as if he wanted to say something else, but he didn't.

Walking through the empty apartment, I headed to the kitchen to make my morning coffee. Once my coffee was ready, I moved into the vast living room and finally had a chance to really look around. Photos graced the walls, showing a family of four, and it was clear exactly who Ky got his striking looks from. The man who I assumed was his father stood so proud, surrounded by his family with the exact same smirk that I had witnessed on Ky. This place really was gorgeous. I loved the floor to ceiling windows that were in both Ky's bedroom and the living area, and the stainless steel and black kitchen was a chef's dream. The guest room was like staying in the fanciest hotel.

A loud knock on the door startled me. It was barely ten a.m. I left my mug on the glass coffee table, walked toward the door, and who I saw through the peephole shook me to the core.

Douglas Smith.

I felt my body tense as recognition hit me. I hadn't seen this man for over four years. I didn't even want to know why he was here. Against better judgment, I slowly opened the door, and the moment I came face to face with the man who had put Jeremy Davis behind bars, I stiffened. On instinct, my chest tightened and tears spilled out like waterfalls over my cheeks. His arms wrapped around me tightly, and he pulled me against his chest as I sobbed, destroying his shirt in the process.

"Can I come in?" his gruff voice asked.

I reluctantly released my body from his and stepped back into the apartment, closely followed by Douglas. He stood in the middle of the living room, taking in the space before turning back to look at me. I stood in silence, confused and concerned as to why he had suddenly appeared.

"Where is Mr. Crawford?" his calming voice asked as his eyes darted around all corners of the apartment in search of any sign of Ky.

"In Los Angeles for work."

"I wish I was visiting on better terms, Eden." The moment those words left his lips, I fumbled behind me for something to grab hold of to stop me from crumbling to the ground. My brain went into overdrive, but I knew what his visit could only mean. Douglas was in my life because of Jeremy Davis, so this visit wasn't just a general "Hi, how are you doing" type of visit. I braced myself for impact. I thought I was getting stronger while I had been here. I thought being with Ky, and having him treat me like I was the best fucking thing on the planet, had helped erase some of the all-consuming fear. But right now, I felt the weakest I had ever been.

"What is it?" I asked so softly that I wished he hadn't heard me.

With two long strides, he was standing in front of me and his hands fell to my shoulders. This man had seen me at my very worst, and my moment of complete and utter horror. He saw things I wished he had never seen, but now he looked back at me in concern, like he was sitting on the worst news he could deliver.

"Jeremy Davis has been released."

Those five words were like being handed a death sentence. My head shook violently as the ramifications hit me. I couldn't believe this. This couldn't be real.

"I just can't." My words jumbled as I tried to process everything.

Douglas moved me to the couch where I collapsed and pulled my knees to my chest. Suddenly I felt exposed like my world was now on display to the entire world to judge and destroy. Paranoia was a frightening thing. The days of looking over my shoulder had returned with those fucked-up text messages, but now knowing that he was back out there, set me on the course of no return. Douglas walked back into the room, handed me a cup of tea, and sat down beside me.

"Now I am going to tell you everything, so just listen, and I'll answer anything afterward."

I nodded.

"Word was received last week that he was attempting parole. Every single one of us at the precinct thought he wouldn't get it. There was no way in fucking hell that he would get it, not after what he had done. If I said I was beyond shocked and pissed when I received notification about an hour ago, that would be an understatement. The conditions of his parole are that he is not to contact you in any form, so no emails, no text messages, no letters, and no personal visits. He is not to intimidate you, your family or your friends. He is to attend appointments with his parole officer twice a day, and he is on a curfew."

"When does he get out?"

"Tomorrow."

"I've been receiving text messages since I've been back in town," I admitted, knowing that I couldn't hide behind them any longer.

Douglas narrowed his eyes. "Show me."

I rose from the couch and walked into the bedroom to find my phone. Suddenly the urge to have Ky here hit me. I needed his protection, his safety, his ability to provide me with calm. When I reached Douglas, I handed him my phone and his brow scowled as he read through text after text, scrolling through the threats.

"I am going to need to run these through the system. This is classified as stalking, Eden. Whoever this is knows you, and is keeping tabs on your whereabouts and who you are with."

"I need to leave." I shot up from the couch, rushed into the guest room, and threw my suitcase on the bed. I couldn't stay here. It was the biggest mistake coming back here. I should have listened to my head all those weeks ago.

"Eden, fucking stop for a second." My hand froze at the ferociousness of his words. "Sweetie, just hear me out."

I turned to face him as his large, intimidating frame filled the doorway. Defeat hit me, and fresh tears threatened to overflow over my cheeks.

"Don't let him win anymore, Eden. Stay here, stand your ground. You can't hide anymore. Ky will not let anything happen to you."

"How do you know Ky?"

"Do you think I don't check up on you? I know a lot about the people you hang out with, Eden. You and your case have stuck by me. Even after twenty-five years of doing this job, you are the one who I still pray for. I want a life for you, Eden. You deserve a life, and if you keep running, you'll never get that."

I dropped my voice. "What happens if he comes for me?"

"He won't."

"But what if he . . ."

"Eden. He won't."

After Douglas had left, I sank into the depths of my memories and curled up on the couch in the fetal position. The sunlight of the day turned into the dusk of the late afternoon, and I had yet to move. Everything was a whirlwind, and I wasn't sure how I was going to get out of it.

So much for scouting locations for the shoot. Luckily I was professional enough to send Daniel a text saying that I had to postpone.

My phone came to life beside me, and the moment I saw my best friend's name flash on the screen, I was desperate for whatever he had to say.

Colby: I need to see my best friend. Be ready in an hour. Blake and I are coming to pick you up.

A simple message brought me back to

reality and the ache of my empty stomach was a clear reminder that I hadn't eaten all day. Dinner with Colby and Blake sounded comforting. I needed to do it. Douglas's words about not running had been the only thing circulating in my head all day. Every hour the thought of calling the airline and purchasing a ticket had hit me, yet something was keeping me from doing it.

I peeled myself out of the comfort of the couch and stumbled toward the bathroom for a much-needed shower and attempt to appear somewhat human. Once I had scrubbed my body clean and dressed, I put the final touches on my makeup, did my hair in loose curls, and went back out into the living room.

I could do this.

I was still trying to get my head around the fact that Blake and Colby were even here. What were the odds? In what crazy world was I living in where my new safe and precious life was colliding head-on with the life I wished to forget?

Knowing that they were the main band who I would be photographing for the cover helped calm my nerves. I knew they wouldn't let me fail. They were my boys. Photography was my escape. When I was shooting, I could escape into another world and get lost for those precious moments, and knowing that I would be seeing them through the lens put my nerves to rest.

I reached into my purse and grabbed my phone. A new message notification flashed before me, and a swarm of butterflies unleashed in my tummy when I saw the name.

Ky.

Ky: The flight was long, the cab driver got lost, but I'm finally here, and have been in meetings all day. I wish I were back there.

My heart fell. I wished he were here too. I needed everything he could offer.

Me: It's quiet here without you.

Ky: I'll be back before you know it.

I couldn't wait.

I was distracted in the best possible way at the thought of having dinner with Colby and Blake. In all of their crazy rock star ways, they were two of the best guys I knew. The only two guys I trusted. I had met Colby first. He was a San Francisco local and lived in the rundown place beside Tori's. He was the one who directed me to her place when I first turned up with just a suitcase, a couple of hundred dollars, and a shattered heart. I remembered the day so clearly. He frightened me when I first saw him. He had piercing eyes that could destroy you with one glance, and the timid girl I had become had been overcome by a billion different emotions. He had walked down the rickety steps and came straight at me while I stood on the sidewalk frozen stiff. It literally took him five minutes to make me feel comfortable, five minutes to barge into my life, and five minutes to make me feel safe. I couldn't explain it if my life depended on it.

From that moment, he was in my life, even when I tried to shut him out. He wouldn't leave, he was that annoying neighbor who pried, but I loved him for it. I often described him as having muscle on muscle; combine that with the colorful tattoos, and he looked like a walking threat. But I knew the real Colby. When you got beneath the tattoos, the gruff voice, and the intimidating stare, he was a teddy bear who often was my comforter.

A knock on the door interrupted my trip down memory lane. The last time I opened the door, I had been delivered fucked-up news, so my hesitation was warranted. I peeked through the peephole and my heart fluttered to life as I saw Colby and Blake standing just outside. They were here. Within seconds of opening the door, I was in Colby's arms, and he was swinging me around in the air like they did in the movies. My squeals bounced off the empty hall and the sound of Colby's deep chuckle warmed my heart with familiarity. I didn't realize how much I had missed him until I was back in his arms. Warm contentment flooded me.

"Well, look at you, little miss hot shot. I hear you are shooting some pretty fucking awesome rock stars these days," Colby's rough voice teased.

"Really, and who would that be? I haven't met any rock

stars yet," I countered with a smirk.

"Fuck I missed you," he growled in my ear and buried his face in my neck. My eyes slammed shut under the intensity.

An annoyed cough hit my ears. "Are you two done? I was always the third fucking wheel in the Eden and Colby show!"

Colby pulled away from me and turned toward Blake, a glint of humor in his eye. "What? When you weren't screwing Tori?"

"Fuck you, asshole. If you had Eden, I clearly had to go for the best friend," Blake spat.

My laughter roared out of me. I finally felt like myself.

The Watergrill was a sports bar by the water, and according to Blake they have the best steaks in the country, so of course we had to go there. After ordering nachos for myself and the world famous steaks for the guys, we took a seat at one of the corner tables that just happened to be located by one of the largest televisions I'd ever seen. A football game with Blake's favorite team blared through the room. Conversation flowed smoothly and comfortably. I hadn't seen these guys for almost a year, but it was like no time had passed. They told me all about the upcoming tour and filled me in on Colby's bet with Blake—he would abstain from sex for the duration of the tour, a fact that made me laugh so hard that I choked on my Coke. There was no way in hell that he could do it. I knew Colby, and I knew he loved and needed sex like he needed air.

Halfway through the conversation, my phone beeped with an incoming text.

Ky: Why is it that I know you are probably out at dinner, but I still want to text you?

Me: Shouldn't you be out? I'm sure there are plenty

of L.A. girls who would want to spend the night with you.

Ky: Why do you do that? It's pretty fucking clear that you're the only person I'd spend the night with.

"So what's up with you and that Ky guy?"

My head shot up at the sound of Blake's voice. Did he see my text? What did Ky mean? I shoved my phone in my bag and tried my hardest to look calm while my head was spinning and my heart was beating furiously in my chest.

"Nothing's up," I replied in my smoothest voice.

"Oh, baby girl, I love you like a sister, but you are as blind as a fucking bat. The moment I stepped foot into his office I felt the tension between you two. Fuck, the moment I hugged you, I thought he was going to punch me in the face."

"Well, seems like someone's got an admirer." Colby's teasing tone caused my cheeks to flush. "Speaking of admirers, did this one tell you that he is completely pussy whipped?" he asked, shooting a look at Blake.

"Fuck off! I am far from whipped."

"Okay, Eden, you can be the judge of this. So this one"— he motioned toward Blake—"has some chick who gives him attitude and dismisses his advances, yet he still won't jump on any of the groupie pussy that is available because of Violet. Now tell me that isn't being whipped."

My laughter filled the table. This was what I wanted— friends, laughs, distraction, and comfort. This kind of talk was an everyday occurrence with Colby until he moved to Los Angeles a year ago, and I missed it. I missed him.

Blake rose from his seat. "Fuck you, Colby! I am heading to the bar. If we are talking about this, I need booze. What do you want?"

"I'll just have a Coke."

He nodded and left Colby and me alone.

"You look great." Colby's voice dropped and he leaned over the table, then grabbed my hands in his. They looked so delicate against his decorated hands, covered in bright colors and shades of black.

"I'm so scared, Colbs," I whispered through broken breathing.

His face lost color. "What the fuck is going on, Eden?"

"It's hard being back here, I won't deny that. I am scared that I am going to run into someone or freak out at the worst possible time. I keep getting text messages from an unknown number and that's starting to freak me out, and today Douglas turned up at Ky's apartment to tell me that Jeremy has been released."

"Fuck, Eden! Why didn't you call me?"

"I just wanted to ignore the text messages, but now Douglas is investigating them. If I didn't think about them, then I didn't panic, but now with Jeremy somewhere close I can't help it."

"Eden, promise me that you will tell someone. What about Ky? If Blake has told me anything, it's that he seems to have a vested interest in you, so tell him."

"He knows about what happened to me."

"What?"

I looked at him and sighed. As soon as I admitted this, Colby would go into protective mode. I knew what he was like, and I knew he would storm into Ky's office the first opportunity he got, but I couldn't lie to him.

"The other night I went back to the hotel and found someone had broken in. I called Ky and he came and got me, and now I'm staying at his apartment."

"What the fuck, Eden? Has he tried anything? Has Ky fucking tried anything with you?"

"Colby, calm down. We kissed and then I told him everything that had happened. He knows I can't say no, and it pisses him off."

"It pisses me off too."

My eyes glistened with tears, and I blinked furiously trying to cease their escape. I couldn't cry. Not here, not now.

"Give me your phone, Eden."

"Colby, please. What are you doing?" I fished my phone out of my bag and handed it to him with shaking hands. I watched with wide eyes as he pressed on the screen and lifted it up to his ear.

"No, this is Colby, Eden's best friend. Yeah. She is here. Just fucking listen to me. We have a problem. I know she told you. She is getting text messages from an unknown number and now fuckstick Jeremy has been released. Do you think I don't fucking know that? When are you back? Good. Take care of her. This is on you. Sure."

I stared at Colby with wide eyes. He was ripping Ky a new asshole, and I wish I knew exactly what Ky was saying. I had come to learn when Colby was pissed by the way he would shift his jaw, and right now, sitting opposite me, was a man who was way beyond pissed off.

Colby abruptly held out my phone to me and nodded at the screen.

"He wants to talk to you."

I didn't want to talk to Ky.

"Hello," I choked as I held the phone to my ear.

"Why the fuck didn't you tell me? How long have you been getting these messages? What do they say? Fuck!" Ky roared into the phone.

"Ky, please don't yell at me," I whispered as fresh tears formed in my eyes.

"Babe, I'm not yelling at you." He sighed deeply into the line. "You should have told someone. If not me, then Josh, Ashlyn, Colby, Tori! Don't keep this shit to yourself. Was it happening before your hotel room got broken into? What were you told about Jeremy?"

"I got the first message when I was having chocolate cake with you, on my birthday, and all I know is that he got released today. I'm really scared, Ky. I don't know what to do."

"Fuck!" He fell silent, and I dropped my eyes to the table. "I'm coming home early. Please be in my bed when I get there."

He hung up.

KY

EVERYTHING PASSED IN QUICK succession. I hung up the phone after hearing Eden's petrified voice, called Simon and informed him I would be leaving due to an emergency back home, and rushed to LAX to jump on the first plane back to New York.

Knowing that she was on the other side of the country alone and frightened did something to me that I couldn't explain. All I knew was that I needed to get back *home* and sort this mess out to make sure she was okay. Well, as okay as she could be.

The moment my feet landed on New York soil it had just clicked over to five a.m. and I was soon making my way back to my apartment. My leg bounced as the cab driver weaved our way from the airport and back to the island. I didn't think my feet touched the ground from the moment I left the warmth of the cab and stepped into the eerie stillness and chill of the air. I had one goal in mind, and that was getting to Eden.

Once I was in my apartment, I headed straight to my bedroom. Fuck, I hoped she had listened to me. I wanted her in my bed. There would be no further discussion; my bed was hers for the rest of the month.

The moment I pushed open the bedroom door, the world lifted from my shoulders as my eyes landed on perfection curled up on her side, cocooned in the thick comforter. My chest heaved as calmness and relief swamped me. I silently undressed down to my boxers and slipped in beside her. The moment the weight of my body hit the mattress, I wrapped my arms tightly around her, pulling her to the protection I offered.

"Ky?" her sleepy voice called, waking at the sensation of my body against hers.

"I'm here, go back to sleep."

"Okay." Her face fell to the concave of my neck and her calm breath caressed my skin. "But Ky, thank you for being here."

My eyes closed as I rolled into Eden, circling her waist with my arm and pulling her as tightly as possible against my body. The softest of sighs escaped her lips. I lay in the darkness in silence, wide awake, and listened as Eden slept peacefully in my arms. I was physically and mentally exhausted, but my brain wouldn't switch off. Knowing that Jeremy Davis was lurking in the shadows caused a wave of uncertainty to linger over me. Someone like him wouldn't stay quiet, and he wouldn't remain hidden for long.

Soon the morning sunlight teased through the thick blinds as a new day was born, a new day where things would change. The moment Colby told me about the threat to Eden, it was the jolt of confirmation I needed and it made me see clearly that I wanted her in my life beyond December.

"Did you sleep?"

I rolled my head to the side to find Eden's sleepy eyes staring back at me.

"No," I replied honestly.

She untangled her body from mine, a move that instantly made me feel the loss. She pulled herself up and leaned against the headboard. The sheet fell from her body and puddled around her hips. I hissed at the sight of the tight white camisole molded against her body, creating the perfect curve of her breasts, which only enticed my wandering eye. Her nipples hardened under my gaze, peaking and becoming slightly visible through the stretched fabric.

God, I was losing it.

"Are you okay?" I finally asked once I got my thoughts under control. "Actually, tell me how you are feeling." I back-tracked, knowing full well that she would have said yes.

"I knew this day would eventually come, but I just wished it didn't have to be when I was here. I am scared, Ky. I won't lie. I was already looking over my shoulder because of the text messages, but now I have this to deal with. All I can think about is what he will do if he gets to me."

"I won't let anything happen to you," I promised through a voice thick with emotion.

Her sad eyes looked back at me, and she offered the weakest of smiles. "You can't guarantee that, Ky. No one can."

"I've got to go out for a bit. I'll be back in an hour or so," I announced without giving away too much information. I searched for my keys, phone, and wallet, and eventually found them on the dining table where Eden sat with her laptop.

"Sure, no worries." Her eyes never left the screen.

I walked around the table, peering over her shoulder at the screen. "You are looking at recipes?"

She twisted in her seat and gave me a sexy-as-hell smirk, and I swore there was a twinkle in her eye. "Yep, I think cooking will be a great distraction."

The thought of Eden taking over my kitchen and cooking was something that I liked, and my mind suddenly started playing scenarios in my head, causing my dick to instantly swell.

"You are a mystery, Eden Rivers." I kissed the top of her head and rested my hands on her shoulders. My fingers dug into her flesh, and her neck fell to the side as I massaged her tight muscles tenderly. "Will you be okay while I'm gone?"

"Hmmm," she hummed in response.

My ego soared knowing that my fingers turned her to putty, but I also knew the sooner I left, the quicker I could get back to her. I removed my hands from her shoulders, grabbed the back of the chair, and turned her to face me.

"Make sure you call or text me if you need me. I will be no more than an hour, and then I'll be back to watch you work my kitchen."

Her face lit up like never before. "I think I know exactly what I am going to cook, but I'll keep it a surprise. I think you should bring some wine home."

"I can definitely do that." I kissed the back of her head before heading toward the door. I hesitated briefly and looked back to find her in deep thought, scribbling down something on a notepad. "I'm so sorry for everything," I whispered into the space around me.

Detective Douglas Smith of the NYPD was not a stranger to me. He and Dad went to the academy together, and Douglas soon became a firm fixture at summer barbecues and winter football games. Up until three years ago, Dad was a lead detective in the sexual assault unit along with Douglas.

"I knew it was only a matter of time before I got a visit from you." He stood from behind his desk and shook my hand firmly when I stormed through the door of his office. "Take a seat."

"Where is he?" I cut right to the chase.

His heavy sigh fell from his chest. "You are like family, Ky. Don't ask me this."

"Exactly, we are family." I knew it was an asshole move, but right at this moment my only concern was Eden, and if I had to be an asshole to get answers, so be it.

He glared at me from across the desk, and I knew I had hit a raw nerve. "Jeremy is staying with his parents. Do not fucking approach him, Ky. Do you hear me? Let us do our job. All you need to worry about is making sure Eden stays safe."

"Yeah, because I am so fucking good at doing that," I scoffed in response.

"You need to stop with this fucked-up guilt you live with, boy. None of this is your fault."

I wasn't about to get into this conversation. It was a conversation that had been attempted numerous times over the years, and it wasn't going to change today. I stood from the seat and held my hand out for him to shake in departure. "Call me if anything changes. I need to be kept in the loop."

Mental exhaustion was a bitch of a thing. When I left Douglas's office, I drove around for a good hour, going over our conversation and trying to rationalize the information he provided. The temptation to visit Jeremy was bearing down on me. Every scenario crossed my mind—paying him off, threatening him, hurting him—but what would that really gain besides ratting out Douglas for divulging confidential information?

Jeremy's penance would come.

Once my emotions were somewhat in check, I headed back to the apartment. The moment I walked through the front door, the soft hum of music floated from the kitchen. Silently I put my keys and wallet on the foyer table, and moved through the apartment like a lion on the prowl.

Eden swayed her hips along to the music, her body covered in panties, a loose fitting tank top that barely skimmed the middle of her thighs, and fucking knee-high socks. She was completely oblivious that I had returned. She was a walking wet dream. I felt the rumble of a growl coming to life in the depths of my throat. My control had escaped, and all I could see and focus on was the raw, primal need to devour, to own, and to worship her.

"Get your ass up on the kitchen island, Eden."

My demanding tone startled her. Her body twisted and her eyes darted to the four corners of the apartment, desperately trying to seek me out. When her shocked expression met my heated gaze across the room, innocence dancing with intrigue dripped off her, which only fueled the raging fire within me. Her tiny hands tugged on the edge of the tee, desperately trying to hide those perfectly toned curved thighs. Like hell.

"One last time, get up on the kitchen island."

My words hit her full force, and with hips swaying, she effortlessly walked toward the counter. Dusk was imminent, and the fading light pierced through the room, allowing her silhouette to accentuate her curves into a perfect hourglass.

Eden pulled herself up onto the edge and waited for my next move. Her face void of emotion and her lips parted ever-so-slightly. A billion scenarios filled my mind while countless words lingered on the tip of my tongue, begging to be spoken.

I shrugged off my jacket as my mind swam through dangerous territory. Sitting on my kitchen counter, awaiting my next move, was the girl who controlled my every thought.

She couldn't say no.

She would say yes.

But I didn't want that.

When I reached Eden, my hands fell to the bare flesh just above her knees. Her nerves were visible, and I lost all sense of reality. My hands slowly slid up her thighs, pushing the flimsy material up until I saw the first glimmer of the baby blue satin of her panties.

"Do you trust me?" I asked between rushed breaths.

"Yes."

"Now isn't the time to say what you think I want to hear. I want the truth."

"I do trust you."

Her eyes spoke louder than the words she said. They flamed back at me as my hands continued their journey. I was beyond pretending anymore. I couldn't fight the urge to taste her, to give her everything she didn't think a man could give her.

The hem of the tee bunched at her hips, and the satin of her panties teased me. My body pushed between her legs, and she parted them without thought. My body fit like a glove. All I needed was to be as close as fucking possible to her. The innocence that I had witnessed only moments earlier was now replaced by something I couldn't explain. Was it want? Need? Expectation?

My finger ran the length of her satin covered pussy. I would tease until she told me to stop. She whimpered under my touch, and her head dropped to my shoulder as I increased my pace. Her wetness grew, and soon the lightness of the satin had turned a darker shade of blue. The sweetness of her arousal filled the air in pure fucking delight. I pushed her panties to the side, and the moment my finger slid through her folds, her breathy moans filled the air and her head flew up until she gazed at me in wonderment. Fuck I wanted her. I wanted to be deep inside of her and hear her beg. But I knew I couldn't. I had promised.

"I want you to be mine," I whispered, my lips hovering over hers as I spoke. I pushed a finger into her and gently started pumping inside her.

"I thought I already was."

"I mean mine in every sense of the word. Tonight I'm going to make you come so hard that you forget every single bad experience you've had. Are you ready for that?

"Yes."

I added another finger and continued pumping into her. She whimpered into my shoulder, and I fucking loved hearing her breathing increase. "You are going to forget your name the moment you come, Eden."

"Fuck!" she hissed against my shoulder. Her hips rose at the sound of my words, pushing harder against my hand, encouraging my fingers deeper.

Suddenly she froze, her hips dropped to the counter, and her hand fell onto mine, ceasing all movement. I looked at her, taking in her reaction. Her cheeks flushed with the heat circulating her body, but it was the questioning in her eyes that got my attention.

"Make me forget, Ky. Make me forget that he is out. Make me forget the text messages. Make me forget it all. I just want it to be you and me."

"It will always be just you and me," I murmured as my lips fell to hers. She was as delicate as a piece of thousand-year-old silk, and I planned on handling her with patient hands. All I wanted was for her to see that she was the world in my eyes and that the world needed care, love, and protection. The darkened corners of her world needed new light.

My arm threaded around her waist, and I gently lowered her down until she lay before me on the counter. My lips fell away from hers, and I took a moment to relish in the specimen of absolute perfection staring back at me. Eden's deep blue eyes, hooded with desire and not an ounce of hesitation, stared back at me, and the smallest tinge of pink began spreading across her cheeks.

"So beautiful," I hummed as my ability to speak faltered quickly.

My hands disappeared under her t-shirt and ran over the smooth skin of her hips and up her sides. Her breath hitched as I removed the cotton from her heated body. My gaze roamed over her, taking in her heaving chest and the flesh of her breasts.

I licked my lips in anticipation and need, and my mouth dropped to her breast. My tongue teased her nipple, swirling the delectable peak, and her fingers raked through my hair, twisting and tugging as pleasure ignited within her. My fingers trailed over her belly, sweeping along her hips until they found the satin of her panties and her swollen and needy pussy. Two fingers thrust in, and I continued what I had started.

I removed my mouth from her nipple and kissed along her jaw until I reached her ear.

"Do you want to come on my fingers or my tongue? Your choice, baby."

"Your . . . oh fuck . . . fingers. Please."

My fingers pumped deep inside her, and the harder I pushed, the more her moans and pants filled the air. She was fucking beautiful to watch. The innocence that radiated from her was nowhere to be seen; lying before me on my kitchen counter was a vixen, pushing her hips closer and begging me to go deeper. Her lips were parted as she desperately tried to grab any air she could. Her cheeks were flamed pink, and her eyes looked back at me in a complete haze of need and pleasure.

"Come for me, baby."

I felt her walls clench around my fingers before she exploded with a moan of my name. It was the best fucking sound in the world. Her breathing pounded against my shoulder as I pulled her body back to mine and her arms wrapped tightly around me.

"Let's get to bed," I whispered. She nodded without finding any words.

I wrapped my free arm around her waist and lifted her from the counter in one swift movement. Her legs locked around my hips as I carried her through the apartment while my fingers remained deep inside her. With every step I took, she whimpered at the sensation.

Softly I laid her on my bed, and the smile on her face made my heart sing. Regretfully, I pulled my fingers from her, and the frown that covered her face at the loss nearly made me explode in my pants. Our heated eyes watched each other intently, and I wanted nothing more than to bury myself inside her and get lost for days. Her eyes shot wide as I lifted my fingers to my mouth and licked and sucked the taste of her clean off. I crawled over her like a stalking lion and hovered before my lips landed on her needy mouth. Our tongues collided and she moaned against my mouth as she lavishly tasted herself.

"I'm completely lost in you, Eden, and I don't ever want to be found," I whispered against her lips in an honesty I never knew existed.

Eden

"**I** NEED FREE-STANDING LIGHTING there, there, and there." I pointed, giving directions to the assistant that I had been allocated for this shoot. "And the backdrop needs to be crisp black, no creases, and no lint."

The cover shoot for *Beats and Bangs* was happening in an abandoned warehouse downtown. After spending countless days scouring for the perfect location, Daniel and I had stumbled across it by accident. The natural lighting, the open space, and the flutter of sunlight that smashed through the windows would offer a brilliant backdrop for the ideas I had in mind.

I had arrived on set just after sunrise, leaving Ky asleep in bed. Last night had been amazing. We had gone further than I could have ever imagined. Never in my life had anyone looked at me or treated me the way Ky had mere hours ago. He looked at me like I was the only person in the world. The way he held me, caressed me, tended to me, made me feel like a delicate flower and he was afraid to damage my petals. For so many years, intimacy had meant punishment—it was foreign, feared, and unwanted—but now my body tormented me with a need so profound and a craving that seemed to only be satisfied by Ky Crawford.

My skin still tingled from the sensation of his lips sweeping over every inch of my body. He had treated me like I was an unconquered land and explored and delved into places that I had locked away from any man, but in the process, he had opened me up to so many possibilities. Last night was pure pleasure in the most honest form and I'd ever experienced something so amazing and life-altering.

I jumped as my assistant tapped my arm, breaking me from my trip down an erotic memory lane. "Miss Rivers, lights have been set up, I just need you to come and check the drape."

"Please call me Eden." I smiled and took off toward the far corner of the space where I would be taking the photos of The Fallen. Thankfully, the busyness of setting up for the day enabled my rabid thoughts to diminish, and I concentrated solely on the shoot. Noise was my constant companion, something that I requested whenever I worked. Music, and it had to be loud.

"Eden!" Ashlyn's voice sang from behind me. I placed my camera on the table and turned around to greet her with a warm hug. Thankfully Ashlyn was the stylist on the shoot, much to her excitement at the thought of dressing Blake and Colby, so I knew we would get a great set of photos. "Ky isn't here?"

I knew my cheeks flushed red when a knowing look swept over her too-gorgeous-not-to-be-a-model face. "No."

"I sense we have a serious girl chat in our near future. You're coming, right?"

"What's happening tonight?" I questioned, completely oblivious.

"We always go out for drinks to celebrate a cover shoot."

"Okay, I'm sure I'll be there."

The next hour passed in a blur. The rest of the band had arrived, but there was no sign of Blake and Colby. I fiddled with my camera and props, spoke with the stylists, and went into complete organization mode. Finally, just as I was about ready to send out a search party, I heard Colby's laughter from the main entrance. I swung my head around and found him and Blake sauntering in so casually, so effortlessly, but oozing with rock star charisma.

I didn't even know Ashlyn was beside me until I heard her loud sigh. It wasn't just a regular sigh, it was a "fuck me they are too gorgeous for words" sigh. I wrapped my arm around her waist, and we stood there gawking at my two best friends.

"I think I need to introduce you to them," I said breathlessly.

"Oh fuck, do I look okay? Shit! Colby is coming over."

Colby's eyes suggestively ran over Ashlyn's body as he strolled across the room, before focusing on me. He had serious sex appeal, and every single woman in the room knew it. His face lit up with a cheeky grin as he pulled me into a tight hug and kissed the side of my head.

"Fuck, babe! Look at this. This is all your fucking doing. Proud of you!"

"Well, I've got good subjects to shoot."

"I'll be sure to put on my best moves."

Colby shifted his gaze between Ashlyn and me, hinting for an introduction.

"Colby this is Ashlyn, and Ashlyn this is Colby."

"Where have you been hiding this beautiful girl?" he flirted, before kissing her on the cheek and shooting her a wink that I knew meant *'I'll rock your world.'*

I had never seen Ashlyn act so nervous before. She turned into a grinning mess and the seductress came out in full force, but I also knew she was still hung up on Lachlan.

"Gotta go to work, babe," Ashlyn announced and rushed off to the portable dressing room that had been set up at the back of the warehouse.

Colby kissed me sweetly on the cheek before announcing, "And I've got to go and be all kinds of sexy."

The next two hours were pure bliss; it was going so well that I thought I was in an alternate world where no problems or issues

existed. The whole shoot was flawless. The guys were profes-
sionals behind the camera. Yes, they were loud, obnoxious, and
acted like cocky assholes on occasion, but when it came to their
career, they were as professional as they could be. Blake was
born a front man. He had the looks, the personality, and the
charisma to match the best of them. The camera loved him,
and it made my job easy. Just before taking the last few shots,
I handed my camera to my assigned assistant, stepped through
the lighting equipment, and headed to where Blake was leaning
against an exposed brick wall.

"What do you need me to do, boss?" Blake asked with a
flirty side grin.

"Well, you have the sexiness down pat, so just give me
your filthiest 'let me take you home' look, and that should sell
a few thousand copies."

"I am shocked that you are implying that I have not done
this look already?" he questioned with a feigned gasp.

"You have." I winked and stepped closer, raising on my
tiptoes and leaning toward his ear. "I just need a moment to
breathe."

"I am so fucking proud of you."

He wrapped his arms around me and pulled me tightly
against his tattooed-covered bare chest. Oh yes, of course, he
was shirtless for most of the shoot. With a body like that, I
would have been scorned by the women of the world if I didn't
photograph him half naked. I fell into the comfort and for a moment, escaped the rat race of the highly charged shoot.

"Your boyfriend has just arrived," he whispered into my
ear. "And once again, you are in my arms."

My boyfriend? "I don't have a boyfriend."

His deep chuckle caused me to pull away and look up at
him in question. "Okay, well the guy who you are saying isn't
your boyfriend, but who is looking at me like he is, has arrived."

Before I could respond, Blake was called away by his manager, and after giving me a hasty kiss on the cheek, he disappeared into a sea of people. I took the down time between shoots and headed back toward the temporary dressing room where I had set up a temporary office in one of the corners. Blake's outlandish statement swam around my head. He could have only meant one person. As my hand gripped the curtain, I turned and looked through the main space of the warehouse. My eyes darted across everyone's face, but they never landed on Ky. I couldn't ignore the hint of disappointment I felt. I considered that Blake might have mistaken Josh for Ky because, from a distance, they could have passed as twins, but Josh was now standing beside Ashlyn in deep conversation. I sighed in defeat and ducked into my seclusion in the curtained off area.

Boyfriend.

There was no way he was my boyfriend. He couldn't be my boyfriend. I didn't want a boyfriend. Ky was simply the guy who I spent my nights with, the guy who would kiss me until I couldn't breathe, who would touch me until I trembled and who had pushed his way into the darkness of my heart. He was my—

A breeze grazed the back of my neck and, before I had a chance to turn around to see the meaning of the intrusion, strong arms surrounded my waist and pulled me into a firm and very familiar chest.

"Do you realize what a fucking turn on it is to see you owning the place like you are today?" His thick voice sent a shiver down my spine. "Can you be quiet?"

"What do you mean?" I asked breathlessly, my body fitting so perfectly against his.

"I need to touch you, and I need to know if you can be quiet. Last night wasn't enough, and then I woke up this morning and you had disappeared."

I opened my mouth to speak, but was stopped when he placed a finger over my lips. He stood behind me, so close that

I could feel every curve and muscle of his body against my back. The same body I was slowly becoming addicted to, for its warmth, strength, and protection.

"Only say yes if you mean it. If you don't want this, say no to me. You need to be able to say no." His pleading filled the space around me.

His hands lay on my stomach, and his fingertips brushed the bare skin above my jeans, causing a shot of excitement to fire within me. I shuddered, not because of fear, but because of a strong desire.

"I'll ask you once more, but remember what I said." His breath fell to my ear and the moment his tongue swept over the sensitive skin on my neck, my eyes slammed shut. "Can I touch you?"

"Yes," I said, sighing in response.

As soon as the words left my mouth, his lips fell on my neck. They were full and hungry, and attacked my neck with peppered kisses and gentle nips of my skin. I sighed in absolute pleasure. My eyes slammed shut under the intensity of emotions circulating my body. I fell back closer to his body, desperate to erase any space between our bodies, and my sudden movements didn't make him falter. One of his hands that had been resting on my stomach moved down my body, teasingly slow until he suddenly cupped my heat through my jeans. The pressure alone sent a spark through me, and I inhaled sharply. He rubbed up and down, hard, and then so softly that I thought I imagined it. The friction of my jeans and panties rubbing and pressing on my clit caused my skin to heat and tightness to form in my lower belly.

"Ky, please," I strangled out. The feeling within me grew and spiraled into a pleasure I craved. "Yes," I repeated.

"I never realized how fucking sexy it would be to hear you beg."

With precision, the button of my jeans popped open and the

zipper was torn down. The moment Ky's finger slipped through my slick folds, my head fell back on his shoulder, and my arm flew up and wound around the back of his neck for support. His finger ran up and down so torturously slow while my breathing rushed out of my chest. My hips shifted, trying to get the friction I needed. I was beginning to crave the rush of pleasure this man could bring to me. With his free hand, Ky grabbed my chin and pulled my face around to the side so I was facing him.

"Open your eyes," he growled, and I obeyed. His hazel eyes were bright, determined, and desire ridden. "I love when you beg, but I also love seeing your eyes when you come."

His lips fell to mine, swallowing my gasp as he increased his torture, but he still didn't hit the one spot where I craved his touch. Our tongues collided and swirled, then attacked one another in fevered demands. For a moment, I completely lost all sense of what was happening. He groaned against my lips as I rubbed my ass against his hardness, then he quickly bit down on my bottom lip so erotically that I almost came on the spot. The moment he pulled away from my mouth and narrowed his eyes on mine, I knew what was coming. Two fingers entered me, thrusting in and out, taking the air from my lungs while my head tried to process what was actually happening. I didn't have a chance to analyze the situation before his thumb hit my needy clit. Not being able to hold it back any longer, I erupted into a wave of heat as my orgasm ran riot through me, taking every part of me along for the ride. I moaned, but my sound was taken by his mouth as I rode out the sensation that took over my body.

"Remember where you are," he whispered against my swollen lips. "I don't want to share your pleasure with anyone."

Fuck! It was only then, as I opened my eyes, that I realized we were in the curtained off section of the warehouse with colleagues, friends, and family just a couple steps away. Excitement flooded me at the thought of how close we were to being caught. Since when had I been an exhibitionist?

"You are wrecking me, Eden Rivers." His voice was hoarse with honesty.

With quick hands, he pulled up my zipper and did the button of my jeans, then swung me around to face him. It was the first time I really had a chance to look at him, and I drank in his delights. He smirked and shook his head slightly, then took a step away.

"You need to get back to work, and I need to leave before I do something really inappropriate. Getting you off in this tent might not satisfy the craving."

"Ky!" I gasped at his words.

"Honesty, babe."

He winked and then disappeared through the curtain, leaving me completely gobsmacked.

Truth be told, he was the one wrecking me.

Heat swirled around me as I made my way through the crowd at Delights. The fact that the wrap party was being held at the place where it all began wasn't lost on me. Colby and Blake were in their element. The final photo had turned out more amazing than I could have imagined. I loved standing in the shadows and being able to watch my best friends live their dreams—it was the best feeling in the world.

But then there was Ky.

He had barely said two words to me since I arrived with Ashlyn. I knew he was busy and had to work the room, but fuck, a hello would have been nice. I knew his eyes were constantly on me though because my body hummed at the sensation.

I pushed through the crowd with the sanctuary of main bar in sight. Somehow I shifted my body onto the stool, even though the dress I wore hugged me like a second skin. I smiled at the thought that I had worn it for Ky. I crossed my legs at the knee, grabbed the cocktail menu, and skimmed through the high priced alcoholic concoctions. Just what I needed.

"What can I get for you, beautiful?" I allowed my eyes to rise from the menu and I came face to face with the guy who had served Tori and me many weeks ago. Recognition flashed in his eyes, which surprised me. "Oh, I remember you, how could I ever forget a face like yours."

He leaned over the bar and his eyes skimmed over my face. I felt my cheeks flame under the intensity of his gaze.

"Well, I'm glad I wasn't forgettable."

What the fuck was that? Was I flirting?

"You could never be forgotten. Now tell me gorgeous, what will I be serving you tonight? I will be your personal servant for as long as you need me."

There was no mistaking his insinuation.

And I didn't completely shut down.

"Cosmopolitan, and please make it super strong."

"Coming up." He winked before creating the masterpiece before me. I watched him closely, for the first time letting my mind open to the thought of possibilities. All I could think about was Ky, even though a handsome guy was flirting with me. Ky treating me like a goddess last night, and then again today, was the only thought that had embedded itself into the craziness of my mind. So why was he treating me like I didn't exist?

The bartender who finally introduced himself as Damien continued supplying me with cosmopolitans, and his constant flirting made me giggle like a school girl. The more I drank, the more I forgot, and the more I turned into one of my many alter-egos. Mission accomplished.

The stool beside me became occupied, and I felt the heat of the person before I saw them. Through quickening drunken eyes, I turned to find Josh looking at me with a crooked grin on his face as his eyes moved between me and the empty glasses sitting in front of me.

"What are you doing, pretty girl?" he asked softly, placing a hand on the half-empty glass in front of me and pushing it away.

His arrival had caught me off guard, but it was welcomed.

"Your brother is ignoring me." I cringed the moment I spoke.

"He is probably just busy."

The reason, why I refused to get drunk, was on full display when I spoke next. "Josh, look what I am wearing. He hasn't even noticed how tight this dress is. I can barely breathe it's so tight. He hasn't even told me I look nice. Fuck, he hasn't even given me one of those stupid looks from across the room."

"What if I told you how stunning you look? Because pretty girl, you are gorgeous tonight."

"You aren't your brother."

Through the honesty of alcohol, I realized just how much Ky was getting to me. I was admitting the fact that it upset me that he hadn't noticed me. For so long I had done everything in my power, not to be seen by men, but here I was, craving the attention of a man who had basically demanded that I spend every moment with him while I was in town. Well played, Ky fucking Crawford, you have won.

"What are you doing, Eden?" Ky's voice sounded behind me. "I think you've had enough."

"I'll leave you two alone." Josh slid off the stool and disappeared into the crowd, leaving me in close proximity to Ky.

"What do you want, Ky?" My erratic breathing rushed from my lungs while my heart smashed violently hard in my chest as the feeling of his hand gripping my arm burned through my skin.

"You have been waiting for me to tell you how fucking sexy you look tonight?" My eyes dropped from his. "Eden, the thought of you in that dress has caused me to be hard all night. You think I don't find you the most beautiful girl in the room?

I'm sorry that I've been busy, but you and your shoot have caused a lot of excitement, and people are asking about *that girl.* You are that girl, Miss Rivers."

"Oh." Suddenly I felt like a complete idiot.

Being this close to him and hearing those things was dangerous, and every part of me knew it. It confused me how much I wanted this man. I cringed at the way that I would lose all of my strength with a single glance from him. Ky was taking away every mask I wore, every fear I had, every promise I made to myself.

His eyes burned with lust as they met mine before the lust was shattered by a look I was becoming well accustomed to. I saw a look of confusion and remorse. His hand released my arm before grabbing my hand, and his fingers entwining with mine so perfectly. I refused to tear my gaze away from his. I would not break this time. I slid off the stool, and with a firm grip, Ky pulled me toward the vacant VIP section of Delights without a word.

As we stood in the VIP section, almost chest to chest, all I could focus on was my breathing and the man standing before me. Ky's brow furrowed as his eyes searched my face, before dropping to look at my mouth. My tongue licked my lips in anticipation. A low growl had risen from his chest before he placed his open palms on either side of my face, drawing my eyes back to his. With one step, his chest collided with mine, setting off a million bolts of electricity through my body.

"Seeing you sit at the bar, talking with that guy, should have made me happy because I want you to have confidence, but it didn't. It made me feel like a jealous asshole because someone was flirting with my girl."

"But you still don't want to make love to me!" I spat out.

His eyes questioned for a moment, considering my words until realization flashed before me and a heated look spread across his face.

"You think I don't want to make love to you?" He dropped his face dangerously close to mine and the deep breath he exhaled bounced off my lips. If he moved one more inch, I'd be completely under the spell of those lips that destroyed me in so many ways. "Eden, I want to fuck you in every way you could imagine, but this isn't about me. This month is about you."

"What if I want it though? What if I am ready for that? What if that's the only thing I can think of? You touch me, you taste me, you kiss me, but you never go further. I want you Ky, I want you to take me. I've never begged for this before, but with you I am."

"You're drunk, Eden. You have no fucking clue what you are asking."

"I know exactly what I am asking, Ky. I've had three cocktails, that's not enough to get me drunk." My voice was now coming out as a plea.

He brutally shook his head. "I just can't."

He grabbed my chin, turned my face to the side, and placed a lingering kiss on my cheek. When he looked at me, his gaze told me that he had a billion things to say to me, but he didn't. He just gave me one last look before disappearing into the crowd, leaving me completely rejected.

"Are you okay?" Ashlyn grabbed my hand and pulled me out of my zone. I turned to face her. The moment I saw the concern on her face, I felt myself come undone, and I shook my head in response. "Come on, let's go and have a chat."

I followed her through the crowd, and we made our way toward the stairs that led to the top floor, which had the perfect view of the dance floor. As I crossed the crowded floor, I felt his eyes burning into me. I always knew the exact moment when his devastatingly seductive eyes were on me. My breath would hitch, the hairs on my arms would stand, and I would lick my lips in anticipation. I loved being under his gaze—I had come to crave it—but now, I felt uneasy, confused, and most heart crushingly, I felt unwanted.

I increased my pace, and Ashlyn and I made our way up the stairs then took a seat at a vacant table that gave us a view out over the crowd below.

"So what's going on?" Ashlyn didn't hold back, just straight to the point. I was always so hesitant to talk about anything to do with Ky with her because they were best friends. She immediately caught on to my hesitation and grabbed my hand. "Whatever is said between you and me, stays with you and me. He may be my best friend, but we have sister pride and all that bullshit."

"I want to have sex with Ky."

She choked on her drink, and her eyes bugged wide open. Yep, the exact reaction I expected. She placed her glass on the table and took me in. We sat in silence for a few long minutes.

"Are you sure that's what you want?" she finally asked.

"I don't understand why it's such a shock."

"Babe, this is a massive step for both of you. I love you both so much. You need to make sure this is everything you want. I know you might find this hard to hear, but you haven't had the best experiences with sex. You need to have the greatest experience when you decide to take that step, you deserve everything amazing that sex has to offer."

"That's why I want to have sex with Ky. I trust him, I feel safe with him, and I'd like to think that he would treat me right. I know it hasn't been long, but I am beginning to believe that sometimes length of time doesn't mean a thing when something is right. You've got to understand that this is a first for me to feel this way about someone."

"I've never seen him look at a woman the way he looks at you."

"He confuses me. He says things to me that make me believe he wants this. I've fought this for so long, Ashlyn. I never wanted to be close to anyone, but then Ky came into my life and, slowly but surely, he has broken down my reserves and made me believe again. I don't have to pretend to want to be around him any longer. I feel safe with him."

I pushed back further into the seat, my body molding to the concave of the pure leather, and I focused my attention back to the party and space below. Since the first time I saw him, my eyes were drawn to Ky like a moth to a flame, and I couldn't stop the pull. Ky moved through the crowd with confidence and grace that couldn't be matched. There was a determination in his step that begged for acknowledgment. He worked the room like a true professional, but the scowl etched on his perfect face and the severity of his tight jaw was evident even from here.

Ashlyn leaned over the small table and fired a suggestive look my way. "How about we go and talk to this hot band you know. I want a photo with them. Is that too fan girl? Will you make it seem just like a group selfie or something?"

The combination of Blake and Colby struck again.

Ashlyn and I made our way downstairs. Thankfully the effects of one too many cosmopolitans were starting to dissipate from my body and I was left with the realization of what I had done. I was forced to quickly come to terms with the brutal honesty that I had not only divulged to Josh but also to Ky.

I looked around the bar for any signs of Colby and Blake, and the moment I found them, I drew in a deep breath. My wide eyes landed on Ky, who was standing with them in deep conversation. Ashlyn's hand grabbed mine, and we weaved through the crowd on our way toward them. I couldn't ignore the nerves of watching my two worlds colliding right before my eyes.

My step didn't falter as I walked straight into the arms of Colby and curled my body around his as I hugged him for dear life. I didn't care about anything at that moment, and as usual, being in his arms provided me with the comfort that took me away from reality and soothed the soaring emotions ricocheting within me.

"What's going on with you two?" he whispered gently into my ear, tucking a piece of my hair behind my ear. I didn't even need to ask, I knew exactly who he was talking about.

"There is absolutely nothing going on."

Colby took it as a cue to cease conversation about Ky, and they all fell into conversation around me. I stood in silence, taking in the banter of Blake and Colby, feeling a twinge of sadness at not knowing when I would see them again. I would be going back to San Francisco in a little over two weeks, and they would be hitting the road for God only knew how long. Most surprisingly was Ky's interaction with them. The three of them spoke of the West Coast, music, and football. He spoke so fluently like he was catching up with old friends, yet he continued to avoid meeting my gaze.

"Ashlyn, I either need to get completely drunk or dance until I can't stand. What are we looking at?" Four sets of eyes suddenly turned to me, taking in my brash announcement and offering me unwanted looks of concern.

My eyes met with Ky's narrowed gaze, and the slightest shake of his head in dismissal grabbed my attention. I felt the waves of submission crashing within me. Intensity roared around us, and suddenly it felt like everything and everyone disappeared.

"Don't do this," he growled into my ear after he crossed the space between us and pulled me to his chest.

I wanted to fight him. I wanted to push him away. I wanted to run away.

"What am I doing?" I asked meekly and looked up at him, the feeling of fight floating away. I had no clue whether Ashlyn, Colby or Blake were even still standing around us, and at that point I didn't care.

"Don't push me. I am fighting every single fucking day to stop the thoughts of taking you, and just when I think I have it under control, you go and say things like you said tonight. Eden, why do you feel safe with me? How do you know I'm not just a guy who will fuck you and run? I could be the worst thing that has happened to you. I could destroy everything you deserve, and I can't be that guy."

"You will never be that guy," I whispered.

Defeat and rejection were a devastating combination. Like a continuous slap to the face, over and over again, just to make sure you felt the sharpness of every contact to your brutalized skin.

I found his pleading eyes and felt more confused than ever. For the first time in recent memory, I had actually considered wholeheartedly giving myself to a man, but now that was being shattered by words that I didn't believe. But who was I to fight?

"You should have just told me to leave," I whispered and watched as his face dropped.

I didn't await a response.

The bed dipped beside me at some crazy hour of the morning. I had been staring at the ceiling of the guest room for the past three hours, and to say I was surprised that Ky was in here would be an understatement. I had heard the front door open and the sound of keys crashing against the glass table, then heavy footsteps that disappeared into the bathroom.

I held my breath and lay as still as a statue, faking the sleep that had evaded me. The pillow beside me shuddered as weight landed on it. He was getting into the bed. The coolness of the air as he lifted the comforter shimmered against my skin and instinctively my body curled inward to provide itself with the warmth that had been lost.

"This was never meant to happen; I wasn't meant to fall for you," his thick voice whispered into the silence. I remained still and tried to desperately swallow his admission. *Fall for you?*

He swept my body into his strong arms and pulled me against his naked chest. My head rested against the thundering of his heart, and his hand lay so softly on the bareness of my hip.

"I'm sorry for falling for the perfect girl. You've always been the perfect girl."

KY

I REFUSED EDEN.
She had begged me to fuck her, and I refused her. What the hell was wrong with me? After what had been a perfect day and a tremendous success for Eden, I had to go and wreck it because of my fears. The look on her face as I dismissed her wouldn't leave my thoughts. She had told me everything that was running through her head, yet I still didn't grow a set of balls and give in to what she and I both wanted. It was the only thing I wanted.

I had fallen headfirst for this girl and, no matter how hard I tried, I couldn't stop. I didn't want to stop.

Anderson Publications was abuzz with talk of the photo shoot that Eden had done for the next issue of *Bangs and Beats.* Everyone had an opinion on their favorite, and I had heard numerous women discussing which member of the band they wanted to fuck. Seriously, grown women had very filthy mouths when it came to musicians.

I was standing by the copier talking to Derrick when the sound of heels connecting with the tile floor grabbed my attention.

"Fuck she is hot. I'd fuck her till Sunday if I had a chance," Derrick growled beside me.

I followed Derrick's line of sight and my eyes fell on Eden as she walked toward us wearing skinny jeans, a black turtleneck, and the red fucking jacket. Her eyes locked onto mine, and I swallowed hard at the sight of her.

"Crawford!"

"What? Sorry." Derrick's smirk said all that he needed to say, and I shrugged him off. "Got a meeting, Talk to you later."

I didn't listen to his smart ass comment. I needed to speak with her. I followed the sound of her heels, then walked into the boardroom and shut the door behind me. She spun on her heels.

"What are you doing, Ky?" She breathed in defeat, her eyes dropping to the floor.

I didn't have a clue what I was doing. I pulled out the seat across from where she was sitting and took her in. She looked tired, and I knew I was the cause of her restless night. Her blue eyes had lost the spark and her will to communicate had diminished.

The door flew open and Josh, Roger, and the rest of the team moved in and sat around the boardroom table, but my eyes were locked firmly on the girl being engulfed by nerves opposite me.

Roger Anderson ran the weekly meeting with a shit-eating grin on his face, and I knew it was all because of Eden Rivers. She said all the right things and presented the photos that she thought would work best for the cover. She informed the team of what would be next, then dropped the bombshell that she would be finished by December twenty-eighth. My head had flung up when she announced it, and just as I was about to state exactly how I felt about it, Josh's foot kicked mine. The sharp shake of his head ceased my brief moment of insanity.

Once the meeting wrapped up, Roger guided Eden out of the room and she didn't offer me another look at me. I had royally fucked up.

"Where did Eden disappear to last night?" Josh asked as he closed his laptop and turned to face me.

"She went home."

"Okay, let me rephrase the question. Why did she go home?"

"She told me she wanted to be with me?"

"Be with you?" His brow shot up in question. Honestly, sometimes I wondered if my brother had any clue.

"She wanted me to fuck her," I groaned, rubbing my face with my hands. Even saying it out loud caused my cock to ache and tell me what a fucked-up move I'd made.

"And you didn't because?"

"Because I'm an asshole."

He walked toward the door laughing. "You are going to get a major case of blue balls before this month is over."

"I've had blue balls since I first saw her in Delights."

I slipped into my office and collapsed into my chair, my frustrated sigh hitting the air. My mind was everywhere but work, but I knew I had a shitload waiting. My usual work hours had ceased to exist ever since Eden arrived. I was halfway through organizing my next trip to Los Angeles when I heard heels getting louder as they moved down the hall in front of my office. They slowed as they got closer to my door, and they all but stopped. I held my breath and waited for my door to open, but it didn't. The heels took off faster and disappeared. I knew she had escaped into the elevator and out of the office without a word.

I arrived home just after six p.m. to a pitch-black apartment, and emptiness lingered in the air. A storm pounded outside, and the lightning strikes caused flashes of light to jab through the space. I threw my keys, wallet, and phone on the dining room table and turned on lights. There was absolutely no sign of Eden. Her boots weren't by the door, her Kindle wasn't left on the couch, and her favorite coffee mug wasn't on the table. It was like she had never been here.

Panic raced through me as I walked through the empty apartment finding no signs of her. She hadn't answered my calls or my texts after she left the office, and the longer she was away, the more I worried. Jeremy fucking Davis was out there, and the thought alone sent me spiraling into a world of fear and unease.

On the way home, I did my daily check-in with Douglas. I swore he must have been getting sick of my constant bombardment of texts, emails, and calls, but his response today was no different from any other day. Jeremy had been attending his parole appointments, and he wasn't doing anything to warrant worry. Like fuck, I wouldn't worry. The guy who had raped Eden was loitering in the shadows, and I knew he wouldn't stay hidden for long. The messages she had been receiving seemed to have stopped, which concerned me. None of it sat well with me, and it caused my stomach to twist when I thought about it. Jeremy wouldn't be happy with this new development and wouldn't be happy with my involvement. He was a dangerous fucker at the best of times, and serving four years for something he didn't believe was wrong would only mean one thing.

Retaliation.

Eden had her demons that I wished I could destroy in an instant, but that would be my ultimate redemption.

For years, my nightmares had consumed me, twisting and tormenting me with the belief that I didn't deserve an ounce of happiness; it was a nightmare I chose to believe. All it took was the appearance of the girl in the red jacket. The flash of a second beginning. And now I seemed to be living for the first time with the thought that maybe there was hope for my future.

Eden

I AWOKE TO AN empty bed and an empty apartment. My mind had to have been playing tricks on me. Was he really in bed with me last night? Had he really said those words to me? My heart was heavy, and my confidence shattered. I felt like I was being pushed back to the girl who had first arrived. Ky didn't want me. Did I have too much baggage for him? I deserved this, I wanted this, and I needed this.

I had practically begged him to take me last night.

It confused me.

It frightened me.

It set me on fire.

I shook the thoughts from my head and threw back the covers. I had a meeting to attend at Anderson Publications, and then I would be spending some time getting reacquainted with a deliciously sexy girl called Victoria.

Stumbling out into the vast living room, I was less than comforted by the silence that lingered in the air. The room was shadowed by the darkness of the clouds hanging in the sky that penetrated through the windows. Stormy weather to suit a stormy mood it seemed. I searched the room for my purse and found the red leather sitting on the kitchen island. My eyes latched onto the empty coffee mug beside the coffeemaker that was filled with freshly brewed coffee. A note leaned against the white porcelain of the mug that was meant for me.

I poured myself a fresh mug and fiddled with the note, flipping it over in my hands before I finally found the courage to read his words.

Had a couple of things I need to get sorted. Will be back later today. Ky.

I took the note back to my room and sat on the edge of the bed. The feeling of being dismissed hit me, but then something shocking swept through me—determination, courage, and confidence. If he didn't want me, then I needed to move on. That was the plan, and I had to stick with it.

My arms ached from the bags containing the expensive yet deliciously gorgeous lingerie I had purchased, and I was buzzing from the copious amount of coffee I had consumed during my epic shopping marathon. I hadn't spoken to Ky while I was at Anderson Publications, and I had fled the building before he could get to me. Maybe that was why I had spent a fortune shopping. I felt so much better though. There was nothing like buying a skimpy pair of panties that no one will ever see to brighten up your mood. As I stepped up to Ky's door, I fumbled around in my purse for the key but was startled when the door flew open and an anxious Ky took up the entire door frame.

"Where the hell have you been?" His voice was laced with panic as his eyes darted over my face in concern.

"I've been shopping in the city." I stood in the hall. "What's wrong?"

He shook his head and stepped away from the door. "You just can't disappear like that."

"I didn't disappear, I just went shopping. Why are you so worried anyway?"

I moved into the living room and placed my bags next to the couch, then turned back toward him. His eyes burned back at me, they were so dark tonight.

"I just . . . please tell me where you go in the future."

His reaction confused me.

"I don't like the thought of anything happening to you, and with him out there it scares me, okay."

Jeremy.

He turned his back on me and walked through the apartment toward the dining room table where his laptop sat. What the hell was going on? I jumped at the loud crack of thunder that filled the room, and suddenly the lights flickered out and darkness fell throughout the apartment.

"Shit!" Ky hissed, and I froze. "Stay where you are until I find the candles."

"I'm going to pack up my things and go stay with Ashlyn," I announced into the dark space. "I think it would be best."

I stood in the middle of the apartment, robbed of my ability to see. I didn't know whether it was the darkness, the silence or the jabs of lightning that lit up the room that made the intensity soar.

My shriek filled the room as Ky's arms weaved around my waist and pulled me against his chest. I was fully alert to the closeness of his body, and I inhaled violently as his warm breath skimmed the skin near my ear.

"I don't want you to leave." His mouth was so close to my ear and a shiver of want fled down my back.

"After last night—" I whispered causing my head to involuntarily fall to the side, and I was rewarded with the lightest of kisses.

"Last night you begged me to take you. Do you know what that felt like, hearing you ask me to give you everything? I don't want to hurt you, Eden. I couldn't live with myself if I did. I've been thinking about it all day, and then when I got home and you weren't here . . . I freaked out."

I was trembling against his body, not in fear, but in expectation. His words were flooding my ears and the realization of what he was saying was so confusing. Did he or didn't he want me?

"I needed to distract myself so I went shopping."

"What did you buy?" he growled against my neck, his fingers kneading my hips.

"Lingerie."

His body ripped away from mine so quickly, and the sensation of loss was gravely intense. Darkness still swamped the apartment and, for a moment, I thought he had slipped out of the door to leave me on my own. My ears pricked to life when I heard movement to my left, but still I couldn't see him. Finally through the flicker of candlelight dancing on the mantel I made out his features. He moved through the living room and disappeared into the bedrooms, igniting candle after candle until the apartment danced in shadows.

Ky headed to the couch the minute his eyes locked on to the dark pink bags on the floor. My breathing halted as he lifted them and walked back toward me like a man on a mission.

"I want you to try something on," he suggested in a devastatingly seductive tone as he placed the bag on the floor between us. His dimple popped in his cheek as he smirked and lowered his eyes back to the bag. "You bought it, you try it on."

When his eyes met mine, we stared at each other for what seemed like an eternity. I didn't even know if I was breathing. My heart thundered in my chest and my stomach swarmed with excitable butterflies at the thought of standing before this man in my lingerie. I nodded, then dropped my hand to the bag on the floor and picked it up. His hand came to mine, encasing it with hesitation, and stopped me.

"Only do this if you are really sure because if I see you in lingerie, there is no way I will be able to control myself. Say no to me Eden, because I won't be able to stop once I start."

My actions spoke louder than any verbal response I could have given him. I pulled the bag close to my chest and sauntered down the hall that was illuminated by the candlelight escaping through the doors of his bedroom and the guest room.

I was really going to do this. I stepped into the guest room and placed the bag on the bed. I had begged him last night for this, and now he had told me that he would have me tonight.

I gently pulled out everything from within the bag and my eyes fell to my favorite purchase of the day—a dusty pink panty and bra set with a matching silk gown that sat mid-thigh.

Excitement quivered within me as I stepped into the skimpy panties and clasped the bra around my body, the soft tone of the pink complementing the olive tone of my skin. Pulling the gown over my shoulders, I sighed as the lace and silk caressed my body and swam around my thighs. I stepped in front of the mirror and my gaze roamed over my body, illuminated by the candles that Ky had lit. I felt like a goddess ready to present to her God. I swallowed breath after breath and silently chanted to myself *"you can do this Eden."*

With my head held high and my eyes fixed squarely on the candlelight flickering on the walls of the hall, I moved like a silent assassin. I stepped out into the living room and through the room lit only by candles, and I found Ky standing by the window, looking out over the ocean in thought.

"Fuck!" he hissed as his eyes roamed wildly over my body in the reflection of the glass. "Please for the love of God turn around and say no."

My stomach fluttered with a swarm of butterflies. "I don't want to say no. I want to say yes, Ky. Let me say yes."

Within a flash of movement, his arm was around my waist and his hand wrapped around the back of my neck as his mouth pressed furiously against mine. Pulling my bottom lip between his teeth, I whimpered as pain and pleasure took over my body. My heart thundered in my chest with want. His tongue swept into my mouth, tangling passionately with mine in a fire that had been smoldering for weeks. I gripped hold of his shirt, pulling his body as close to mine as I could, frantic to feel the ridges of his chest against the curves of mine. We stumbled through the apartment, using the candlelight as a guide. His hands gripped firmly on my ass, then lifted me from my feet and my legs tightly locked around his waist. The feeling of his growing erection rubbing against my heat caused me to break the kiss, and my head fell to his shoulder as pleasure I craved roared to life within me. My body took over when my mind decided to cease to exist. I started slowly moving my hips, grinding myself against him, begging for release.

My body screamed at me. I craved the feeling of the perfect ache between my thighs. I wanted to lose my breath with a man above me, below me, and behind me. I wanted the feeling of being owned in the way a princess would be owned by her prince, and I wanted Ky Crawford to be that man. I *needed* Ky to be that man. The fear of my past haunted me, it consumed me, it penetrated so deeply into my soul, but here I was, considering the most intimate of things with a man.

"Please, Ky," I groaned into his shoulder and lightly nipped his skin with my teeth.

My body dropped to the comfort of his bed, and his body hovered over mine. His eyes grew dark with lust as he took in my flushed cheeks and swollen lips. "I want to taste you, Eden. I want to get drunk in your scent, but more than anything, I need to be inside you."

My eager hands ran under his shirt, connecting with his heated skin. He stayed silent as I undressed him, and his eyes never left mine. Once his shirt was discarded, he slowly and torturously pushed open my gown and unclasped my bra. With tender hands, he slid the gown and bra off my shoulders until I was left bare in front of him.

"You are beyond perfection Eden, and for every minute I have you, I am going to cherish you like you are my very last breath."

His mouth fell to my nipple, and I gasped as fire rose within me. His tongue swirled and cherished my hardened peak while his hand ran along my thigh and pushed open my legs. The sensation of his mouth devouring mine and his hand sweeping over my body caused my breathing to stop.

"You're so wet." He moaned against my flesh as his hand slipped into the front of my panties and his finger began teasing me so gently. My hips lifted from the bed, pressing harder against his hand, craving for more. Then, with the tiniest scrape of his teeth against my nipple, he took me to all new heights.

"Ky please," I begged through heated words. He hauled his mouth away, and the most deliciously seductive smirk pulled at his lips.

His hands made quick work of my panties, sliding them down my thighs and throwing them to the floor. I was completely on display to his prying eyes, and as they took in all of me, I had never felt more vulnerable yet so completely at ease.

The moment he reached for his pants and then his wallet, I found my voice.

"Stop."

Once the word hit the air, he froze and his face twisted in agony as he looked back at me.

"Fuck! I'm so sorry. I shouldn't have done this," he apologized with words laced with devastation and started pulling away from me and lifting his body from mine.

What the hell was he doing?

I grabbed his arm and stopped his escape. I swallowed hard, desperate to draw in some confidence. "If we are going to do this, I want to experience everything with you. I want to undress you, I want to worship you, and I don't want anything separating us."

"What?" He breathed out as he ran his finger along my jaw and over my lips. His eyes were vibrant and latched fiercely on mine. "Are you saying what I think you're saying?"

My hand wrapped around the back of his head, my fingertips running through the edges of his hair. "Please, let me feel you. I need to feel you inside me. All of you."

Suddenly his face went serious. "Are you on birth control? I'm clean, completely, but we have to be safe."

"I am, never miss a day."

That was all the reassurance he needed.

Ky's lips crashed into mine with wild abandon and took away my deepest insecurities with a lash of his tongue. Kissing him was like having kryptonite pumped into my veins. Pulling me in and ceasing my ability to escape. With one kiss, he could completely own me, mind, body, and soul. I felt myself falling into his body, and his arms encased me tightly before I crashed. His lips left my mouth before kissing my jaw and neck with softness that felt like the caress of cotton along my jawbone and neck as he moved toward my ear. His heated breath on my earlobe caused a deep sigh to escape me.

"Are you sure, because once we start, I won't be able to stop."

"I don't want you to stop."

My hands trembled as they ran over his warm skin, over his shoulders, and down the muscles of his back. My breathing hitched in a mixture of nerves, lust, and anticipation as my fingernails ran the length of his back. His lips peppered along my collarbones, nibbling my sensitive flesh occasionally, and I loved every minute of it. He pulled his mouth away and pushed back to gaze at me. Everything that I wanted to witness on his face looked back at me.

Protectiveness, compassion, lust, and want.

"You are so beautiful," he whispered.

His teeth nibbled my bottom lip, and the moment I opened my lips to gain a desperate breath, his tongue slipped in claiming ownership. His body moved over mine as my hands fumbled between us. I popped open the button of his jeans and slid down the zipper. Ky lifted his hips, allowing me to slide his jeans and boxer briefs down his thighs.

I sighed at the loss of contact when he lifted himself from my body and removed his jeans. My gaze fell to his throbbing cock and desperation flooded me. I want to feel him, to connect with him in every way possible. I felt like a girl about to experience her first time. My body arched into his, pulling him back to my mine. Skin to skin, heat to heat, heart to heart, we became a mass of need, lust, want, and passion.

"Are you ready?" he murmured against my lips.

I nodded, unable to find words.

"We do this however you want."

The head of his cock met my entrance, and I sucked in a sharp breath. He watched me so intently, almost as if waiting for me to break. I nodded, and he inched in slowly, excruciatingly slow.

"Ky, please. You won't hurt me."

All of a sudden, he wrapped his arms around my waist and flipped me over until I was straddling him. He looked up at me through hooded eyes.

"You control this, Eden. Take what you can. I've wanted to be inside of you for so long, so I need you to control that first moment, otherwise I will pound into you so hard that it will hurt."

My hand wrapped around his thick, eager cock. My thumb swept over the head, massaging the pre-come that glistened in front of me. Ky groaned under my touch, and his eyes rolled back in his head. His hand moved between my legs, and I gasped loudly as one finger, and then two, slid inside me. His fingers pumped deep into me and matched my stroke of his cock, and soon I was tethering on the edge of ecstasy. I felt the moisture pooling between my thighs as I shifted until the head of his cock graced my entrance once again. I lowered myself slowly, and the thickness of his shaft stretched my walls to capacity. The feeling that swept through my body was so foreign;

the need, the desire, the want to be owned and worshiped. He slid his hands up my body until he cupped my heavy breasts. The moment his thumbs began their assault on my hardened nipples, I slid down on his cock, completely filling myself with everything he was. My cry at the sensation of being completely echoed through the room, as the sound of pounding rain outside intensified the room.

"Fuck, Eden!" Ky growled, then his hands left my breasts and fell to my hips, holding me in place. I stilled, allowing his thickness and the intensity of the moment to flood through me. "You feel incredible."

In one swift motion I was on my back again, Ky still completely filling me. His mouth fell to mine, and just as his tongue met mine, I felt him move. He slid out and back in, slowly, too slowly.

"I want this, Ky. Fuck me like you want to fuck me. You won't break me. I am pretty sure I begged for this last night." I smirked up at him, and his eyes immediately darkened.

A billion fireworks went off inside my body the moment he thrust into me. He was so deep that I felt him at the very end of me. Frenzy erupted and he gripped my hips, then wrapped one of my legs around him, giving him greater access, which allowed him to go even deeper. Everything around me dissipated into a sea of twinkling stars and bright lights as I quickly entered into a pleasure I could never have imagined. I moaned in delight as he continued to hit my most vulnerable place over and over again. Our breathing echoed together and the sound of our bodies connecting and combining as one filled the air. Ky buried his face in my neck and his heavy breathing bounced off my sweaty skin. My nails dragged down the flesh of his back and grabbed hold of the cheeks of his ass as I desperately tried to get closer to him. He growled against my neck and increased the ferocity of his pounding. My muscles clenched, and I knew that I was close.

I finally felt a freedom I had craved for the last four years.

Ky's lust-fueled growl grabbed hold of my attention. "Babe, I'm close. Are you sure you want this?"

We locked eyes as I spoke. "I want to feel all of you. We are safe."

"Look at me when you come. I need to see you come." His hands cupped my face and we locked into an intense stare-off. At that moment, I knew that I was stepping into unchartered waters.

He slowed his pace but slammed deep, allowing me to raise my hips to grind against him. My chest tightened and my breathing ceased to exist as my muscles clenched aggressively; an explosive orgasm ripped through my body, making me shatter into a million pieces around him. The world as I knew it ceased to exist at that moment.

"Jesus, fuck!" Ky growled and I felt the exact moment he exploded within me, filling me with everything he had. I gasped at the sensation of being completely engrossed by him, at the feeling of connection. I couldn't ignore the feeling of heaviness that lingered over my heart. There were only two weeks left in December, two weeks of being in his company, two weeks of being the new Eden Rivers.

Our breathing filled the air as we both tried desperately to gain control. Ky's mouth dropped to mine in a sweet, engaging kiss, and he wrapped his arms around my body, pulling me close so there was no space between us. I could still feel him deep within me, our connection not yet lost, and I felt myself slipping into an unimaginable state of bliss.

The last thing I heard was Ky's deep voice whispering in my ear.

"You completely own me, Eden Rivers."

Soft, delicate fingertips swept over my still tingling lips, drawing me from my peaceful slumber in the arms of the man who took me places I never dreamed of reaching. My eyes slowly fluttered open, trying to adjust to the darkness of his bedroom. I shifted my head, and through the flicker of candlelight, my eyes found Ky's worry-etched face staring at me. His brow pulled in concentration, and he gnawed on his bottom lip as his eyes searched mine.

"Are you feeling okay?" he asked softly, scooting closer to me so our naked chests collided. My body hummed, and I winced as a deep ache filled me, showing me exactly where he had been.

"I feel amazing."

I dropped my eyes from his intense gaze and rolled onto my back to stretch. I knew I'd be feeling him for days. Sex had been forced into my life—from my very first experience— causing me to fear it, to despise it, to avoid it. I never thought this kind of sex existed, I never wanted to believe that it existed. The thought that this type of sex—the type where I was cherished, protected, loved, and admired—could be mine, was something I never imagined.

"What's going through that beautiful head of yours?"

I rolled to my side and propped up my head with my hand. The man beside me allowed me to switch on my life again and was quickly becoming the person who made me feel like I was becoming myself. But who was I to begin with?

"I never knew it could be like that," I whispered in pure honesty, then I felt his arms tighten around me. "You make me feel so special, Ky. You make me feel free."

KY

PERFECTION WASN'T THE WORD to describe what I had just experienced. I wasn't sure there were any words in the English dictionary that could explain the feelings aligning within my body, the feeling of complete connection with her on every level possible.

"Let's take a bath," I whispered heatedly as my eyes raked over her still naked body. The evidence of my release still lingering between her thighs immediately caused my cock to thicken at the thought of having marked her as mine. My arms wrapped around her waist and I lifted her from the bed and walked toward the bathroom. The shriek that left her glistening lips when I delicately placed her on the marble vanity filled the empty room. I felt her eyes watching my every move as I ran a bath, and I loved the thought of being under her heated gaze. Everything changed tonight. I had fought back the urge to be with her, but everything was lost the moment I saw her in that lingerie. My heart had beaten my head once again.

How was I meant to ever say goodbye to her now?

I shut off the faucet and tested the water and found the perfect temperature. I turned back to face her, moved between her legs, and wrapped my arms around her waist, lifting her in one motion off the vanity before placing her in the bath. Her gasp as her still-tingling body hit the heated water filled my ears. I stood and looked down at her. The bubbles swam around her, and the sated look on her face completely undid me.

"Are you getting in?" Her words shocked me. Her confidence was beginning to come through, and I loved the thought that I had something to do with that.

I nodded and slid in, resting my back against the opposite end of the porcelain bath so I faced her.

"You asked me what I was thinking, but what are you thinking?" The softness of her voice massaged the intensity of my thoughts so tenderly.

I took a deep breath, meeting her inquisitive eyes as they begged for honesty. The tightness in my chest thundered to life as I prepared to give her my every thought. "Sex will never be the same again. You have singlehandedly ruined me for anyone else." My honesty even shocked me, and, by the way, her eyes widened, I knew it shocked her too. "I can still feel myself deep inside of you, deeper than I've ever been before, and I fucking love it. I tried so hard to deny you because I didn't want to hurt you, I didn't want to lose you, but now that I've felt you, that I've had you, that I've come inside you, I don't know what to do."

My words were absolute truth. How was I meant to move on from this? This was exactly why I never wanted to be with her like this. I didn't think I could possibly move on from this.

The splashing of water hitting the tile floor brought me back. Eden slid toward me until her legs were over mine and we were chest to chest, face to face. A thousand unspoken words shifted between us as her shining blue eyes met my hazel ones. The moment her head hit my shoulder and she crawled onto my lap, I closed my eyes as a contentment I chose to ignore for so many years engulfed me. I had fought every single regret for four years, and now what I craved—a life of peace, contentment, love, and redemption—was brought on by the girl who was my biggest regret in the first place.

"Thank you for making the hardest day in my life into something I will never forget."

December sixteenth.

I knew the day all too well.

The lump in my throat disabled my ability to speak, so I held onto her for dear life as the water around us cooled. I held her as I knew her memories were coming in thick and fast. I held her for my memories of a fateful day that had stuck with me as a constant reminder, and I held her for a secret that I knew I had to admit sooner rather than later.

"Are you hungry?" I asked softly against her neck once the water had completely cooled.

"Mmhmm."

"Let's get changed and get some food."

We walked out of the bathroom once we dried off and put on our sweats, then made our way to the kitchen hand in hand.

"I made some spaghetti; it's a recipe that I stole from Mom." I grabbed a spoon and dipped it into the red sauce, giving off the strong aroma of fresh tomatoes and garlic.

"Oh my God, that is delicious," she groaned and licked her lips, savoring the taste. "I'd ask you to cook this every night if it didn't mean that I'd put on a hundred pounds."

I loved playful Eden and it appeared like she was the one who came out after sex.

"I could make it low fat if you were really that desperate."

"Ky Crawford, did you just insinuate that I had a weight problem?"

"Never! I love every single curve of your body."

I grabbed her around the waist and she squealed as I lifted her from her feet and placed her on the counter. The bubbling of the spaghetti matched the bubbling of tension in the kitchen.

"You are crazy," she whispered.

"Maybe a little, but that's what you like about me, isn't it? Or is it the way I kiss you, or maybe it's the way I make love to you?"

I reached behind her and pulled out the pins holding her hair in place, and then I ran steady fingers through her hair, separating the clumps so it fell perfectly over her shoulders.

"Your kind of crazy is what got my attention in the first place, and you know I enjoy your kisses, and well, you know what else."

"You can say it," I whispered and moved in closer. "I want to hear you say it."

"When you"—she inhaled sharply, and I watched as her eyes moistened with emotion—"made love to me."

"We are going to do that again, you know. It's not just a one-time thing. I want you in my bed all the time; I want to fall asleep beside you and wake up with you in my arms. None of this separate room bullshit. I want you for as long as I can have you."

"You don't frighten me anymore," she admitted so softly that I almost missed her confession.

Now it was my time to watch her. This kind of honesty was so unheard of from Eden, and something that I hadn't been lucky enough to witness yet. I never knew how she felt about whatever this was between us because she had locked it away and hidden the key.

"Babe, I've got to admit you frighten the hell out of me," I replied with complete honesty.

She shifted ever so slightly on the counter and leaned forward, dropping her forehead to my shoulder. It was the first time that she had initiated any intimate physical contact between us, and I savored every moment. This was pure contentment, but a frightening reality. My heart was thrusting itself at her to run with it, and she was slowly breaking down her walls and showing herself to me. And while I was savoring every moment, I was well aware that I couldn't believe that anything could come of this. I had asked for one month, and that was all she was giving me.

When she pulled away, her eyes roamed over my face and she placed one solitary kiss on my lips before turning to the pot of spaghetti and giving it a stir.

Twenty minutes later, we had eaten, and Eden had groaned her way through the spaghetti, and every time she did, my cock woke. She was an evil mistress. I watched her with great interest as she washed the dishes. When she was done, she threw the dishcloth on the counter and turned toward the living room. I was busted checking her out. Her lips twisted into that innocent smile that set me alight, and I patted the couch beside me. The way her hips swayed when she walked toward me made even the best supermodels in the world look like amateurs.

"Why are you looking at me like that?"

"Do you want the honest Ky response, or the trying not to make Eden uncomfortable Ky response?"

"Well, I seem to be getting honest Ky these days, so lay it on me."

She took a seat beside me, sitting so her body was in front of mine. Her legs folded beneath her as she looked back expectantly.

"You are sexy, Eden, and I love the fact that you are so oblivious to it. Every time you walk into the room I just want to kiss you and taste you and devour you. You have completely and utterly gotten under my skin, and that was never my intention when I first decided on this crazy agreement."

"Can I be honest with you?"

I nodded.

"I'm still confused about why you actually wanted to do this in the first place. I was never receptive to you; I tried everything to stay away from you, but somehow you were just always there."

I swallowed hard at her question. I had no idea what she was expecting to hear. The longer this went on, the harder it was to remember my intentions when I came up with this crazy scenario. My goal was still dancing in the grey, whereas some would say that it was black and white. Was it selfish? Probably.

Was it an asshole move? It could be seen like that.

"The first time I saw you, all I wanted was to know you. It wasn't about being physical with you when it started. I just wanted you. My urge to protect you and keep you safe could even be considered insane."

I held my breath as I watched her take in my words. I didn't want to deal with any more questions.

"I like the way you protect me."

I couldn't have asked for anything else, and protect I would.

The past couple of days had been horrendous. I worked from sunrise to sunset, and my time with Eden was limited to coffee catch–ups, late dinners, and stolen kisses. No matter how busy I was, my mind was always filled with her.

I couldn't deny my feelings for her any longer. It would be like denying a starving man food. I wanted her, I wanted her in every sense of the word. Eden Rivers was a new beginning, she was a closing door to my own battles and the injection to my heart that made it beat with life again. She was my first thought in the morning and my last goodnight at the end of the day. She was my brutal reminder of a life that could be. Her nightmares had diminished, but I knew exactly when her thoughts became too much, and the exact moment when they would constrict around her, squeezing the life out of her. She would sink into an impenetrable silence and grip hold of my body so hard that I could barely breathe. I never spoke during that time, and all I could do was offer my body for her protection. It was during those times that I felt the weakest.

The more time I spent with her, the more I couldn't imagine not having her around. Every time I was with her something came alive within me. She was the catalyst that lit up the darkest parts of me and for that I would be forever grateful.

I saw a change in her every day. She was becoming stronger and less fearful; she was becoming the person that I knew she wished she could return to. It made this easier, knowing that it was happening and that I was playing a part in this. It somehow made me forget everything that I needed to redeem, and it made me think that maybe this wasn't just helping her but in some fucked-up way it was helping me.

Tonight was my annual end of year drinks with friends, where I would supply them with booze, food, and my place to destroy. It was almost like my apology for being so distant throughout the year, and not accepting invites because of my work schedule. Tonight would be different though—tonight Eden would be here.

Josh walked into my apartment with a six-pack of beer in his hand and an obnoxious grin on his face. His eyes scoped out the living room, and I knew he was looking for Eden.

"She's in the shower," I answered his unasked question, grabbing the beer from him and walking into the kitchen.

"I really like her."

I removed my gaze from inside the fridge and turned to find my brother staring back at me with a look on his face that screamed heart to heart conversation ahead. "I really like her too," I admitted honestly. "Maybe a little too much."

"She's changed you, man," Josh continued. "It's about fucking time that I finally see you this happy."

My lips twisted into a knowing smile. "How can I not be happy, bro? I have the best fucking girl in the world spending her time with me, falling asleep in my arms every night, kissing me good morning when I wake, and making me feel alive. But I also know the reality of this situation, and that's what is freaking me out."

"Talk to her. Open your fucking mouth and tell her exactly how you are feeling. Give her that."

My brother: pussy lover, timeless bachelor, and now my relationship counselor.

The sound of the shower shutting off halted our conversation, and Josh looked at me knowingly before heading to the couch and pulling out his phone. The guests would be arriving within the hour, and I knew I wanted some time alone with Eden before I had to share her with the rest of the world.

I made my way down the hall and stepped into my room. The combination of vanilla and flowers hit me with force, and I breathed in sharply. I wished I could bottle the scent of Eden Rivers because I wasn't sure how long I'd be able to survive without it. I leaned against the door frame for a few moments of silent wonderment. She stood by her suitcase, wrapped in only a towel, her wet hair hanging over her bare shoulders and her skin still flushed from the heat of the shower. She was the most beautiful sight in the world, and she was mine if only for a few more weeks. Thinking of that caused my stomach to drop. I couldn't think of it.

I crossed the room until I stood behind her, and her body reacted the moment she felt the heat of mine. I didn't think I'd ever get enough of her reaction to me.

"You smell good enough to eat." My voice dropped as I stepped closer, until my chest brushed against her back. "And I know exactly how sweet you taste."

"Ky." She sighed wistfully and leaned into me. I buried my face in her neck and wrapped my arms around her waist, my hand resting on her stomach and pulled her even closer.

"Turn around Eden." My voice hummed as my body ignited under the feeling of her skin against mine.

Without hesitating, she twisted around until we were chest to chest. It would only take one quick movement for her to be standing in front of me naked—just a flick of my wrist and a tug on the towel—and her body would be mine to play with. My eyes dropped to the top of the towel, pulled tight against her skin showing off the top of her tits.

"How do you feel about tonight?" I asked softly as my

hand cupped her cheek, allowing my thumb to trace her bottom lip. Her breath halted, and her eyes closed under my light touch.

"I'm nervous," she admitted softly.

"About what?"

"I don't do crowds well."

"If you get anxious, just come and find me."

She nodded her head, and I dropped my lips to hers, taking away her nerves. Her arms slid around my waist as I pulled her body hard against mine, allowing her to fall into the kiss. I ran the tip of my tongue over her bottom lip, causing her to sigh under the sensation. When her mouth opened, I took a chance and slipped my eager tongue through her lips, kissing her with all my might. I didn't think I'd ever not want to kiss this woman. How would I survive not tasting her? Her tongue battled with mine for ownership. I reined in my need to control the kiss and let her explore. Her teeth nipped at my bottom lip before she claimed complete ownership, sweeping her tongue into my mouth, tasting and devouring everything I was. Her sigh against my lips caused my cock to stir, and the moment I pulled her body closer to mine, her sighs turned to alluring moans.

"You are so beautiful," I hummed against her lips. Her hands gripped tightly onto my hair, pulling my mouth back to hers. "How am I ever going to survive without your body and your mouth?"

She pulled her mouth from mine and, with pink-tinged cheeks and broken breath, she looked at me with heated gaze.

"I can't think about that," she whispered.

I didn't want to think about it either. I still had time with her. She was still my December, my only December.

"Ky, leave Eden the fuck alone and get out here. People are arriving!" Josh's amused voice shot through the closed door, and my eyes slammed shut under the intrusion. Seriously, could he be any more frustrating.

"Well, Josh has spoken. I'll let you finish getting dressed.

Come out when you are ready. Don't be nervous, just be yourself. Everyone is going to love you."

My hand left the comfort of her cheek. I stared at her and her eyes fluttered open; her beautiful blues looked back at me, glistening with lust. A simple touch did so much to her body, and I fucking loved it. I traced her jaw with my index finger, and my eyes followed the movement. Her mouth opened and she drew in a quick breath.

I dropped my hand and turned toward the door as I needed to get out there and put on my socializing hat. The moment my hand connected with the handle, I turned back toward her and found her still looking at my retreating self. A wicked thought filled my head.

"By the way, don't wear panties tonight."

Eden

W HAT THE HELL WAS I doing?
I had no clue who the majority of these people were, but that didn't stop me from standing in the middle of Ky's living room wearing no panties and a dress that left nothing to the imagination. Who the hell had I become? I inhaled a deep breath and took off through his apartment, the heels of my boots clicking on the polished floors as I headed toward the kitchen.

Men smiled while women seemed to snarl at me as I passed. I felt so unbelievably out of place. Where the fuck was Josh or Ashlyn when I needed them? And Ky, where had he disappeared to?

"You look cute tonight."

Finally! I spun around at the sound of Ashlyn's voice and her eyes immediately roamed up and down my body, taking in the dress that fit snuggly around my waist and boobs, but skimmed loosely around my knees.

"Where have you been?" I laughed and shot her a 'don't you dare leave me' look.

"I had to take the Australian to the airport. He flies back to Sydney tonight."

I couldn't ignore the sadness evident in her voice. "You okay with that?"

"I don't really have a choice. But enough about me, how are you? You seem, how shall I say it, sated?"

My brief smile was answered by a clap of celebration from Ashlyn. "You two had sex?" she whispered. "This is massive."

"I'm pretty darn happy." I smiled in response.

Ashlyn grabbed my hand and dragged me through the ever-growing crowd of people until we stood amongst a group of guys in the kitchen who were in the midst of an argument about who would win the Super Bowl. I stood silently, sipping on my usual Coke, and listened as Ashlyn got right in the middle of the argument. It was quite amusing to watch.

"You look so fucking sexy, and knowing that you don't have panties on is making my cock ache." Ky's soft breath caressed the skin by my ear, and I momentarily leaned back into his body. I ached all over for him, and the desire pounding between my thighs was increasing by the second. His arms wrapped around my waist, pulling me back against the firmness of his chest. He kissed the side of my neck before whispering, "I'll see you soon."

My eyes trailed after him, following his every step as he walked toward the couch where three guys had taken ownership. Ky sat on the coffee table in front of them and fell into animated conversation.

How was I meant to say goodbye?

The night progressed smoothly. I would sneak quick glances at Ky and, more often than not, I would find him staring back at me, and every time my heart would sing a brand new note. Ashlyn hadn't left my side, and it was great to spend some time with her. The beers flowed, the laughter got louder, and as more time passed, my confidence began to grow.

I left Ashlyn chatting with Josh and walked down the hall to the bathroom. I heard someone at the door and, just as I was about to call out busy, the door handle turned. The door suddenly flew open, and Ky's large frame filled the space. His presence caused a flash of heat to rip through me. He closed the door, and with a click of the lock, he was stalking toward me with lust-filled eyes. The sexiest of smirks played on his lips, but I knew he had no intention of talking.

"Are you having a good time?" Ky questioned, his voice lower than I had ever heard. His body rested against mine, causing my lower back to press against the vanity, and my hands rested on the cold porcelain.

"I am," I hummed in return.

"My urge to kiss you, to touch you, to fuck you, overwhelms me. I crave being near you. I *need* to be near you. You are completely and utterly destroying me, Miss Rivers, and I couldn't be happier about that."

I didn't know what came over me. It was like I was possessed by another being, but I loved it. Freedom swirled through my veins. I hoisted myself up onto the edge of the vanity and, by the leather of his belt, I pulled him forward until his body slammed into mine.

My actions spoke louder than any words I could say. I opened my legs in invitation, and he stepped in, then I felt his erection against my thigh.

His tongue swept across my bottom lip before completely engulfing my mouth with one scorching movement. Nothing but lust, need, and expectation lingered with every swipe of our tongues. Ky's teeth nibbled at my swollen bottom lip, and I groaned at the sensation. Kissing him was like nothing I could have ever imagined. His arms wrapped around my hips, dragging me along the porcelain top of the vanity until his erection was hard against my heat. My hips moved, grinding against him, begging for friction to calm the ache that was growing by the second.

The moment he released my mouth from his, I felt like I was caught in his web. I couldn't breathe, I couldn't speak, I couldn't do anything but stare at him. Every plausible emotion I had smashed together until I had a need greater than anything I could have imagined. I connected with someone in the deepest of levels, and for once it invigorated me.

"Ky, make me yours," I whispered, the double meaning not lost between us.

"I'd love to." Ky's mouth fell into the crook of my neck as his hands slid up my thighs, pushing the thin black fabric of my dress up over my hips, exposing my aching heat. My hands fell to his zipper, and I tugged it down without recourse, then my hands slipped into his jeans, sliding them and his boxer briefs over his slim hips. My hand circled the thickness of his hard cock, and he growled his pleasure into the silent space of the bathroom. That was all it took.

With eyes locked onto mine, Ky pushed into me so slowly, so intensely, watching my every reaction. The feeling of being completely full of him cascaded within me, and my breath left my lungs. At an excruciating slow pace, he pulled out. His hand encased his glistening wet cock as he teased my desperate clit. I moaned into the still air, and I knew that if anyone was in the hall, they would have heard my cries of desperation. I was willing to beg, but he didn't give me a chance. Before my eyes, the smirk that I craved appeared, and he thrust into me without warning in one animalistic, hard movement.

"Ahhh!" I hissed against his shoulder as his relentless pounding overtook me. My teeth bit into his flesh every time he hit that magical spot while his fingertips kneaded into the softness on my hips. My head flew back as he slowed his rhythm, allowing me to roll my hips and take control. Our breathing danced together in a battle and was lost to the intensity of coming together.

"I warned you that I would never get enough of you, Eden."

His hands slid under me and lifted me clean from the vanity. My legs wrapped tightly around his body, locking at the ankles, accentuating the deepness of his cock still embedded within me as he crossed the room. Ky spun us around and I slammed heavily against the back of the door.

"Are you ready to come, baby? I want your pussy to squeeze my cock until I've got nothing left."

I pulled my face away from his shoulder and opened my eyes to watch him. His gaze met mine and his lips twisted into the most devilish of smirks. I knew he loved seeing my face when I came completely undone. His thumb hit my clit in perfect circular motions, and I cried out his name as my body trembled with delight. The growl from Ky that followed as he unloaded his seed deep within me was the most satisfying sound in the world, like waves crashing on a deserted beach.

"Holy shit." He breathed heavily against my sticky skin as I came down from what was probably the most intense orgasm of my life. I remained locked in his arms as our heavy breathing filled the air. My arms wrapped tightly around his shoulders for fear of what I'd lose if I let him go. Ky remained buried deep inside of me, slowly moving in and out, never breaking our connection, and allowing the constant spark of heat to soar through me. I lay my head on his chest, falling into bliss at the rhythmic beats of his heart.

With soft steps, Ky moved us to the other side of the bathroom and placed me back on the top of the vanity. The moment he pulled out, my heart sank and I felt the loss of connection. His penetrating gaze never left mine as he turned the tap on beside me and wet a wash rag. Lips so soft and full landed on mine as he delicately cleaned me up. I liked the softness of this Ky.

Ky's hands cupped my face and the sweetest of smiles appeared. "So beautiful and all mine."

"I like hearing you say that," I admitted honestly through a thick voice. Ky stiffened at my words and dropped his gaze from mine, which confused me.

"I should get back to the party."

"I'll be out soon. I am just going to go to the bedroom for a minute."

"Are you okay?" he asked, tucking a piece of loose hair behind my ear.

I nodded in response. I was better than okay. I was falling way too fast, and there was officially nothing I could do about it.

"Eden, where are you?"

Ky's voice sounded through the apartment when he arrived home from work. I lay in the bath enjoying the warmth and bubbles, as his excited tone shot straight through me. I had spent most of the day locked away in a darkened studio, finalizing shots of an up-and-coming pop star that was getting interviewed for the magazine. The moment the threat of snow arrived, I packed up for the day. I hadn't seen snow in four years, and the thought of seeing the angelic fall of snow through the air was exciting.

"Bathroom," I replied.

He smirked as he stepped through the door, his eyes taking in my bubble-covered body. "I come home from work to this! Be careful, Miss Rivers, I could get used to this."

I shook my head at his honesty and allowed my eyes to take him in. I was becoming a big fan of the days when he would return to the apartment wearing a tailored suit, and today he didn't disappoint.

"Are you ready for tomorrow?" He leaned against the vanity and crossed his arms over his chest. Him being in the bathroom while I lay naked in the bath didn't seem to bother him, but my emotions were running rampant.

"Tomorrow?"

"A little thing called Christmas."

Crap. I had been so distracted that I hadn't even realized Christmas was here, but Christmas was never a big holiday for me. My parents would usually be traveling to some tropical island, and Tori and I would spend our Christmas watching holiday movies and eating way too much food for two.

"I was planning on spending it here while you were with your family. I have a load of books on my Kindle I'd love to read. I was thinking of cooking myself a big batch of my favorite brownies and eating them till I was in a food coma and then passing out. Christmas. Done."

Ky's face dropped as he stared back at me, trying to digest my words like I had just announced the beginning of World War III. His brow pinched and then he said, "We need to leave at eight a.m."

He walked out of the bathroom without another word, and without letting me speak. There was absolutely no way in hell I was spending Christmas with him and his family. My bath was all but forgotten as soon as he uttered those words. I scrambled out and quickly jumped into the shower to rid myself of bubbles. Once I was clean, I ripped the fluffy gown from the back of the door and wrapped it around my body. I stormed out of the bathroom like a woman on a mission but halted as I hit the entry to the living room. Ky lazed on the couch, shirt off, sweatpants on, and a football game playing on the television. *Damn it.*

"You got something to say, Eden?" he asked without turning toward me. What was it with this guy knowing my every move? "We leave at eight a.m."

"Ky, you cannot be serious?" I huffed in defeat.

"Very serious. I don't mess around about Christmas."

"You cannot be serious," I repeated under my breath.

"We should go to the store so you can get the stuff for those brownies." He rose from the couch. His face was full of amusement with a twinkle in his eyes. "You'll be a hit if you bring brownies."

It was then that I wished a hole would open up below me and swallow me. He was being absurd. I couldn't spend Christmas with his family. I just couldn't. I could barely keep my cool being around just him the majority of the time, so the thought of being around strangers just couldn't be imagined.

"Eden, look at me." His hands cupped my face softly and maneuvered my jaw, so I had no choice but to meet his gaze. "Spend Christmas with me? My family will love you."

"I have no choice."

"You always have a choice, Eden."

"Merry Christmas."

I woke to warm breath dancing over my lips and the feeling of Ky's body hovering over me. I opened one eye and noticed the room was still in darkness. I didn't have a chance to complain about the earliness of the wake-up call before Ky's lips stole my breath and gave me the best wake-up kiss I'd ever experienced. My arms wrapped around his shoulders, instinctively pulling his body closer. His knee probed between my knees, pushing my legs wide so his body could collide with mine. As his lips continued to completely devour me, his body tormented me with every intense move and grind sending fireworks through my very awake body. "You are the best present, Eden Rivers."

He could have asked me to do anything at that moment, and I would have.

When Ky finally allowed me out of bed, we were running late. I showered in the guest bedroom while he took the master shower. What in the hell did you wear to Christmas with parents? Seriously, what the hell was I getting myself into? Last night after I had complained for the hundredth time, he had told me that if I wasn't ready, he would lock me out of his apartment and I'd have to spend Christmas in the hall. Why the hell had my parents decided to be out of the country this Christmas?

Once I showered, I entered Ky's bedroom with the towel wrapped firmly around my body and my hair and makeup already done. Simple yet pretty was the look I was going for. I styled my hair in loose curls that hung to the middle of my back, and my makeup consisted of a little blush, mascara, and soft pink gloss. My nerves were shot, and I kept imagining everything that could go wrong. I wasn't a chatty girl at the best of times. Fuck, to outsiders I was sure I came across as a snobby bitch, and now I had to meet Mr. and Mrs. Crawford. Did I call them Mr. and Mrs. Crawford? Would Josh be there? God, I hoped he'd be there. I had absolutely no experience meeting parents, but in a matter of an hour I would be walking into the family home of the guy who I'd been sharing my body with. I was going to be sick. I didn't even know what I was to Ky besides his December. Oh god.

"Eden we have to leave in ten—" Ky stopped in the doorframe and found me sitting on the edge of the bed. He was dressed in dark denim jeans, a charcoal colored sweater, and was wearing a black beanie over his thick brown hair. Why was it so easy for him to get ready?

"What's wrong?" He took two steps until he stood before me and crouched down, resting his hands on my bare knees. When his concerned eyes met mine, my eyes glistened with the enormity of what was about to happen. Tears welled, before spilling over and sliding over my cheeks.

"I'm sorry," I whimpered in pure brutal honesty.

"Hey, come on now. What are you sorry for?" Ky took a seat beside me on the bed and grabbed both of my hands in his. My eyes dropped to our hands entwined, and that set my emotions off once again.

"What am I meant to do today?"

"I don't know what you mean. You've got to give me something here."

"Everything over the past month has just been crazy, and fast, and intense, and now you are taking me to spend Christmas with your parents. That's beyond insane, Ky. I've never met parents before. What happens if I have a flashback? What happens if I suddenly panic? What happens if I stutter the whole time? Fuck! What happens if they don't like me?"

"You are so fucking unbelievably out-of-this-world sexy when you ramble."

My face dropped as another wave of insecurity hit me.

"Eden, listen to me. You are the sweetest, most confusing, most intense, and most beautiful person I have *ever* met. My parents are going to love you. They already know about you. Josh and Aunt Carole will be there, and I won't leave your side. If you need time out, just squeeze my hand and we will escape somewhere. I cannot leave you here on your own on Christmas, and I can't spend Christmas without my family, so you need to come with me." He pulled me to my feet and gently wiped the tears from my cheeks. "Can you please get dressed so we can go?"

All I could do was nod in response.

Ten minutes later I was sitting in his car, dressed in dark skinny jeans, a cream sweater, and a baby pink scarf. It would take about thirty minutes to get to his parents' house. I sat in the passenger seat and let my mind wander back to the moment I first met Ky.

Never would I have imagined visiting his parents' house for Christmas, or that he could take over and rule my thoughts and body. I shifted in my seat so my back pressed against the door and watched him. His eyes focused on the road ahead, and his lips were in a perfect pout as he concentrated on our destination. This man was becoming something so much stronger than just the guy paying for my photos; he was becoming the thief of my thoughts, the owner of my heart, and my utter confusion. I was slowly but surely falling for him and, after all of the internal battles I had, the idea of becoming something with him was now in the forefront.

It was scary.

It was exhilarating.

It was undeniable.

"I like you, Ky," I blurted out the moment he took a right-hand turn and pulled into the driveway of a beautiful two story Victorian-inspired home.

I heard Ky's sharp intake of air the moment my admission hit the space in the car. He turned toward me after he killed the engine and stared at me. His mouth opened and closed like he wanted to speak, but no words came. A loud shriek sounded outside of the car, ceasing our stare off, and we both swung around to look toward the house. A beautiful lady in her early fifties rushed toward the car, arms flailing, with dark brown hair bouncing around her shoulders. Her face was overtaken by the biggest smile I had ever seen.

"It's time," Ky muttered beside me. He opened the door and slipped out, leaving me in a mass of nerves and confusion. I watched with a smile on my face as his mom wrapped her arms around him and his dad lovingly patted him on the back. Three sets of eyes focused on the car, and I realized I was still in the passenger seat with the seatbelt tightly fastened around my body.

With a shaking hand, I removed my seatbelt, opened the door, and before I had a chance to put a foot on the ground, I was being lifted and swung around excitedly in the air.

"You are even prettier than your photos, sweetheart!" His dad's sincere voice hit my ears as he finally let me stand. "This one has spoken about you constantly. Now come inside, it's freezing out here, and I want to get to know the girl who has my son so smitten."

If I said the day was nothing like I could have expected, that would be an understatement. The Crawford family welcomed me with open arms, and at no time did it ever feel like the first time meeting them. They fussed over me, fed me delicious food, and his parents even bought me a Christmas gift, which hung in pride in place around my neck. The moment Sue Crawford handed me the perfectly wrapped gift box, I felt a burst of unpredictable emotions hit me. What had I ever done in my life to deserve this level of kindness? Ky, sensing my impending meltdown, pulled me onto his lap and tightened his arms encouragingly around my waist as my body shook with emotion. As if forgetting we were around his family, a family who had been watching us for any indication of what was happening between us, he placed the most calming kiss on the side of my neck and encouraged me to open the gift. All eyes were on me and my hands shook as I lifted the lid from the box. Inside was a silver chain with an antique looking heart-shaped locket dangling from it. I was at a complete loss for words. My fingers ran over the beautiful inscription on the back that read "*The heart is there to be filled.*"

As soon as I read the inscription, my emotions hit me full force. My heart had been dead, locked up, and the key thrown away. But then somehow Ky had picked the lock and my heart was open to so many possibilities. Ky was filling my heart with words, actions, soft kisses, and quiet moments, and what was once an empty heart, was now threatening to overflow.

As the day turned into night, a ferocious snowstorm battered outside, with lashing winds and heavy snow fall. After dinner, James Crawford had informed us there was no way we were leaving that night, and much to my shock, Ky agreed without a fight. After I ate way too much food and drank my fair share of eggnog, my exhaustion hit at a rapid rate. I curled up on the sofa beside Josh. My head rested on his shoulder and what could have possibly been the most comforting hot chocolate of my life sat in my hands.

"You make him happy," Josh whispered beside me. "Four years has been too long to watch my brother slowly destroy himself."

His words hit me hard.

"Why has he been destroying himself?" I asked, lifting my head from his shoulder and moving to face him.

"It's not my place to say, but what I can say is that you are giving him a second chance without even knowing it. No matter what the future brings, I will always be grateful to you for that, for however long it is."

Josh was such a mystery. He went through women like I went through underwear, but beneath it all, he was the most loving and fragile man I'd ever met. His protection of Ky was paramount, like something I'd never witnessed before. They had the relationship that I would have loved to have if I had siblings; it was the type of relationship I would want for my children if I were to ever have them. He was the little brother, but more often than not, he stood up for Ky like the big brother.

"I'm supposed to leave soon," I admitted through a thick voice.

"Do you want to leave?"

"I can't stay here, Josh; I am scared every time I leave the house, and now that Jeremy is somewhere out there, it just makes it worse."

"What about Ky? It's going to kill him when you leave. Fuck, I've said too much."

"Your brother has made me feel alive again, Josh."

"And you have made him live again."

"Thank you so much for a perfect day," I said later in the night as I stood in the kitchen with Sue cleaning up the last of the dishes. "And thank you for my lovely gift. You really shouldn't have."

"Oh, sweetie, it has been mine and James' pleasure to have you here today. You make my boy happy. He has changed so much, and it's all thanks to you." The smile looking back at me was so honest and identical to the one I often saw on Ky. "He is a good boy. He just has a lot of demons locked up in that head of his, and he won't let anyone get close enough to get rid of them, not even Joshy. But I can see it in the way he looks at you, the way he always needs to be near you, and how he is smiling and laughing more than he has in four years. You are the one for him sweetie. He will let you in, but please just give him a chance to explain everything."

"Mom, are you telling Eden embarrassing stories about me?" Ky's voice echoed as he came waltzing into the kitchen. His mom's words hit me square in the heart, and I had a billion questions to ask. Ky came up behind me and pulled me firmly into his chest. I molded perfectly against his protectiveness.

"No stories tonight, but the photos come out next time. How about you kids head upstairs and get some rest. It's been a big day. I've put extra towels on your bed, sweetie. I will see you both in the morning." Her eyes bounced from Ky to me, and the sweetest of smiles filled her face.

Sue left the kitchen, and as soon as she was out of sight, Ky spun me around to face him, and pushed me against the kitchen island.

"Bed?" Ky questioned against my lips before they gave me a quick sweet kiss. "I need some alone time with you. You've been very popular with my family today, and I'm a little jealous at the lack of Eden time I've had."

"I've had such a great day. I'm glad your bossy ass made me come." My arms squeezed around his middle and my chin rested on his chest as I looked up at him.

Like a thundercloud, his eyes darkened with mischief. "I haven't made you come yet Eden."

"Ky! We are in your parents' home."

His laughter bounced around the empty kitchen, and soon I was dragged out of the kitchen, my hand in his, as we headed up the grand staircase. I hadn't been up there yet, and I was intrigued to see where Ky had spent his childhood. Ky squeezed my hand as we walked down the hall, until we stood before a door that had a bright blue plaque that displayed *Ky* proudly.

"Welcome to my childhood abode," he said with a soft laugh and pushed open the door. With a flick of a switch, light illuminated the room, and I stood in the center, taking it all in. Pale blue walls were graced with posters of sports stars and bands, a double bed sat in the middle of the room, and a chest of drawers lined with trophies sat against the far wall.

It was almost like his parents had made no changes since he left home.

"You did so well today," he whispered as he pulled me into his chest for a tight hug. "You've got to give yourself more credit."

"You are a big reason for the new Eden you see," I admitted unashamedly.

The look of content on his face dropped suddenly, as did his arms from my waist. It was a move I was becoming very well accustomed to. It seemed that any time I said anything positive about him, he would shut down and feign indifference.

"I'll grab you one of my shirts if you want to shower. I'm pretty beat." He stepped away from me, pulled open the drawers, and grabbed a t-shirt to hand to me. I didn't even bother talking, I headed toward the bathroom in defeat and locked the door behind me.

After showering, I tiptoed back into the dark room highlighted only by the television. Ky was motionless in bed. His chest rose like it did when he was in a deep sleep, and I sighed in defeat.

I climbed into bed and the exhaustion I felt earlier quickly left my body as I rolled to my side and looked out the window at the falling snow.

"You're the first girl I've had in this bed," Ky whispered into the darkness, and I jumped at his admission and felt my stomach drop.

I flipped over to face him and propped my head up with my hand. "You never had girlfriends?"

"I did, but my mom and dad never let me have a girl in my room, and definitely not in my bed. I told you that they would like you. They are letting you corrupt their son."

My laughter was muffled as I dropped my mouth to his bare chest at the absurdness of his statement. His arm wrapped around my shoulders and his laughter fell against my hair.

"And I've never had a girl in here who I've liked as much as you."

My heart stammered in my chest.

"I really fucking like you, Eden Rivers."

Through the light drifting in from the street lamp outside, I saw a wicked look sweep over his face, a look I had witnessed so many times before.

"Remember when you were at the photo shoot and I asked you to be quiet. Can you do that again?"

My heart rate increased and instantly my core awoke. "Ky! Really? In your childhood bedroom with your parents down the hall?"

"I'm not going to have sex with you, Eden." He shifted his body over mine until his hot breath danced on my lower stomach as he pushed up my shirt. With strong hands, he lifted my hips from the bed and slid my panties down my thighs until they sat beside me on the bed. "I am going to finally give you the Christmas gift I've wanted to give you all day."

Oh.

Oh!

KY

I RELUCTANTLY LEFT EDEN in bed after the most exhilarating morning sex of my life. Her body responded to my touch like I was the air in her lungs, like she needed it to survive. If I said it didn't stroke my ego, I would be lying. A huge day was ahead of me, a day that would involve back to back meetings, lunch with Josh, and then organizing everything for the night I had planned with Eden.

Eden had officially gotten to me, and there was no way I could deny it any longer. She had squeezed her way so far into my heart that now I would be ruined for anyone else, but I couldn't be happier. What I was quickly learning was that there were no rules when it came to Eden and me, and that was what I cherished the most. We seemed to give each other what we needed, when we needed it.

And what I needed now was for her to stay.

Tonight I would ask her just that.

I needed her in my life—it was as simple as that. I had waited too many years for this moment, and now that it was in my grasp I wasn't letting it go. Tonight I would tell her everything. I would admit my fears, my insecurities, my reasons, and who I really was. Over the past week, I had let myself completely fall for her, something I had tried desperately to avoid. How was I going to be able to watch her leave? There was no way in hell that I would let her walk away from me. I couldn't even begin to comprehend that.

My day progressed like a freight train. Back to back meetings took up every minute of my morning, and it wasn't until Josh walked through my door that I finally looked up from my laptop.

"Lunch!" he announced with certainty. "We are getting out of the office, get your ass up."

"Fuck me. Your panties in a knot, baby brother?" I laughed and logged out, then closed my laptop. I looked down at my phone and immediately opened my inbox.

Me: My asshole of a brother is taking me for lunch. Are you in the city? We are heading to Sami's for burgers if you are.

Eden: I am desperate for a burger, but I'm out scouting some places for the final shoot. Enjoy lunch. I'll see you tonight.

Me: I have big plans for tonight.

Eden: Like what?

Me: It's a surprise, but I'm sure I'll end the night between your thighs.

Eden: You have a wicked tongue.

Me: That's what you said the other night.

"Are you finished having phone sex?" Josh mused from the door. I shot him a "fuck off" look and slammed my phone into my pocket as we finally left the office.

I needed to talk to Josh about my plans. I knew he was the one person who would give me brutal honesty, and that was what I craved. We caught a cab across town toward our favorite burger joint. Sami's had been our go to place for years.

The moment we walked in we were hit.

"The Crawford boys! Where have you been? Sami has missed you!" Sami was a boisterous Greek man who loved nothing more than kissing our cheeks every time we came to his diner, and today was no different. He fussed over us both, ruffling our hair like we were kids, and the fact that we were twenty-four and twenty-six seemed to have been lost. "Go sit down, I'll bring you your usual orders!"

We took our regular table toward the back, and the usual chatter of the packed diner intensified. Sami's was right on the river, and one of those hidden jewels that only regulars and locals knew about. Black and white photos of icons from the fifties graced the off-white walls, which complemented the red, white, and black trim, and a jukebox that hadn't worked for years sat in the far corner. When Josh and I needed downtime from the office, this was where we would have lunch.

Two Cokes were placed in front of us by Angelica, Sami's even more boisterous and touchy-feely wife. She moved beside the table, hands on hips, and looked at Josh and me. *Oh fuck, here it comes.*

"When are you two marrying my girls?"

"Ky's got a girlfriend, and you know me, I can't settle down yet."

Her shriek pierced my ears. "Baby, you've got a girl-friend?"

Oh yes, I should have mentioned my nickname was Baby and Josh's was Toots.

Girlfriend.

Was she my girlfriend? We had everything in our lives that would suggest we were in a relationship. She was living in my apartment, in my bed every night and was the first person I saw in the morning and the last person I saw at night. The fact that I was having the best sex of my life was the icing on the cake.

She took up my every thought, and when I thought of the future, I saw her face.

Girlfriend.

"I think I do, Angie."

Josh whipped around to look at me with surprised eyes as he tried to come to terms with my admission. Fuck, I was still attempting to come to terms with it.

"Well, she better know who she's got, Baby. I'll go put in your regular orders. Double bacon and cheese for you, Toots, and Sami's Special with extra cheese for you, Baby. I've missed you two." Before she turned on her heel and rushed off in a tizzy, Angelica fell into a zone as she gazed over both of us.

"I was going to ask how things were with you and Eden, but fuck me, it seems like you are officially pussy-whipped. Ky *'I'll always be single'* Crawford has a girlfriend."

"Things are as confusing as fuck, but like nothing I could have imagined. I've fallen hard for Eden, and it's scaring the shit out of me."

"Mom is going to be planning your wedding, I hope you know that."

"Jesus, let me ask her to stay first."

After an amazing burger, Josh and I headed back to the office. My mind was filled with thoughts of the upcoming night. After my chat with Josh, I was more determined than ever to make it perfect. I needed her to see that she was protected, that she was adored, and that she was wanted.

I opened up my laptop and groaned as I saw the email icon flashing that I had fifty-four emails awaiting my attention. After scrolling through the spam, the stationary requests, and the proofs that needed approving, my eyes fell on a name and subject that made me stiffen in anger.

Chris Edwards.

My hands shook with rage as I moved the mouse and hovered over the email. When would he fuck off? His constant presence reminded me of everything and everyone I wanted to forget, a period of my life when I was at my worst, a time when the world seemed to stop.

From: ChrisEdwards@ThomasConstruction.com
To: Ky@AndersonPublications.com
Subject: Secrets

Do you know where your sweet ass girlfriend is? Fuck I'd love to pound into her sweet pussy. She is sitting opposite me wearing this sexy pink top and her tits are just begging to be sucked on. Maybe after we have a little chat, I might take her back to my apartment, comfort her, and see what Jeremy saw in her all those years ago. You know, keep it in the family.

Secrets don't stay hidden forever and in about two minutes all of your secrets will be unleashed upon the one person you didn't want to know.

Fuck you Crawford.

No.
NO!
Everything was spinning so far out of control, and I didn't have any ability to stop it. I had left it too late. My fear of the truth had got me into this mess and brought this to her. I knew as I stood in my empty office that the truth was being unraveled without me being there to explain. I couldn't stay here. I couldn't be away from the one person who had captured my thoughts the first time I saw her, four years ago. I had to try. I had to do whatever I could to get to her.

I bolted out of my office and collided chest to chest with Josh. His panicked face showed that he knew what was happening.

"I need to find her," I pleaded as we bolted out of the office, giving no explanation to anyone who asked. "She can't be near him."

"Come on, give me your keys. Aunt Carole just called, she is at the diner," Josh's calm voice demanded as we stepped into the elevator and headed to the underground parking garage.

I shoved my keys toward him, thankful that he was with me. I was quickly crashing over the edge and heading into the pits of my mistakes. It felt like the trip to the parking lot took forever, and every second that passed seemed like a lifetime. I was becoming agitated and anxious. I needed to get to her. My thoughts concentrated on Eden, how this would be frightening the hell out of her, and how I wasn't there to protect her.

I was failing.

Yet again.

Eden

I HAD LOVED THIS place. The diner was my safe place. While I had been here, it had been my unconventional office, but now it was fast becoming the scene of my worst nightmare.

My back was pressed against the wall of the booth as I tried to get as far away as possible. I knew I was locked in, and at any time he could move and I would be caged in like an animal.

When I turned to face him, a cold, vindictive smirk etched over his face while beady eyes narrowed in on me. If hatred had a human form, it was sitting across from me in the form of Chris Edwards. I had absolutely no idea why he hated me so much, why he continued to appear out of nowhere, but when he slid in across from me, I realized he knew everything about me.

"It's about time we had some one on one time." Even his voice sounded like pure evil. "Your boyfriend just wouldn't back off."

"He isn't my boyfriend," I choked out.

"Answer me this. Do you fuck him? Does he eat your pussy? Do you sleep in his bed?" he hissed while his eyes flashed with hatred. "He is your fucking boyfriend."

Ky.

Beautiful, dependable, life-changing, Ky.

"What do you want from me, Chris?" I questioned hesitantly. I watched the flicker of consideration flash in his eyes before they rose and looked over my shoulder, sending a shiver down my spine.

"Someone wants to come and say hi."

The moment the words left his mouth, the intense fear that had disappeared since I'd been with Ky rushed back like flooding water. I didn't need to turn around to know. I felt it in the way my body froze, the way the terror ran down my spine at being so close to him. My dread was soon replaced with anger. Douglas had promised me that I would be safe, that Jeremy wouldn't get to me, that there was no way that I would come face to face with evil but here I was. Jeremy Davis.

"Eden Rivers." My name curled on his tongue. "You are looking fucking delightful. Love seems to be treating you well." He leaned over the table, inching close enough that his breath smacked me in the face. The darkness of his eyes threatened me. "You and Ky are in love, right? Like a modern day fucking Romeo and Juliet."

"What do you want, Jeremy?" I asked, finally finding my voice.

"How 'bout I get straight to the point. Tell me, Eden, do you really know who Ky Crawford is?" His voice was laced with the intent to shock and cause unmeasurable damage. I didn't understand why he was talking about Ky. How did he even know of Ky? My eyes darted away from his as I looked around for an escape. I didn't want Jeremy Davis tainting something that was developing so beautifully with Ky. I couldn't allow that. Ky was quickly becoming my sanctuary, my beginning and existence, and hearing his name spat from the lips of the creature that almost destroyed me stabbed my already fragile heart a million times.

"I am going to take your silence as a no."

What kind of question was that anyway?

After spending every day with Ky over the past month, I assumed I knew him. From the moment he brought me to his apartment, things shifted. He saw me through my nightmares, my insecurities, my fears, and my new beginnings. He saw me at my best, and he still wanted me at my worst. He broke down every barrier I had put up and he completely owned every part of my body. Nothing had been left untouched.

Jeremy kept staring at me, waiting for me to answer. I sensed that I was about to have my idea of Ky shattered into a million pieces and thrown in my face without regard. Jeremy's smirk said a thousand unspoken words.

What did he really have to lose?

Nothing.

Absolutely fucking nothing.

What did I have to lose?

Everything.

"I'd like to think I do," I returned. It came out weaker than I wanted, and it seemed to fuel his desire to torment me even further. "Just get this over and done with, Jeremy."

He leaned in, his elbow sliding along the tabletop until his chin rested in the palm of his hand. He just sat there, staring. Both of them just stared. Chris Edwards and Jeremy Davis. I felt myself quickly becoming unglued, but I wouldn't cry. I couldn't let Jeremy win again. Seeing them side-by-side hit me hard. How hadn't I noticed the similarities?

They both shared shockingly similar physical features— the sharp nose, a strong, well-defined jaw, almost black-colored eyes, and a thin, athletic build. How could I have been so blind? Chris noticed the moment realization hit me and that familiar evil, vindictive smirk filtered over his thin lips. I instantly felt like I was going to be sick.

"Oh, sweetheart, are you only realizing now? I'm Jeremy's baby cousin."

Jeremy didn't care about anything. He just wanted to go on the attack. "You think you know Ky Crawford, do you?" Jeremy hissed and shot a look of delight to Chris.

"This is going to be fun," Chris taunted.

"Your boyfriend was there the night I fucked you. Ky motherfucking Crawford almost wrecked the whole damn thing when he tried to be a hero. Thank fuck he backed off when he did, because I needed to have a taste before he did, and boy did you taste good. He was so whipped over you, the girl from the coffee house. It fucking made me sick. He became this motherfucking wimp when it came to you. Wouldn't say shit to you, didn't have the balls to even ask you out. Ky fucking Crawford became tongue-tied because of a pretty little brunette."

"What?" I choked. The contents of my stomach rose and sat precariously in my throat, ready to explode onto the table that separated us. This couldn't be real. The fact that he was blatantly reliving the whole experience in his head didn't scare me or fill me with fear; it was the admission of Ky and the mere mention of his name.

"You heard me. You precious little boyfriend was there. Did he not tell you that we were best friends or that we had a bet to see who could have you first? Well, my dear, he fucking lost."

No. No. No. This couldn't be real.

There was no way this wasn't a fucked-up nightmare that I hadn't woken from. On instinct, my nails dug into the tender skin of my palms, hoping this wasn't reality. That wasn't the case. Pain hit me as small drops of blood appeared on my broken skin. This was very real. Ky was there. Ky knew everything about me, a fact that he hid from me.

I couldn't believe this.

Not Ky.

"The look on your face tells me you had no clue." His piercing eyes narrowed even further and his voice dropped. "He isn't fucking prince charming now, is he?"

Everything froze.

My head shook in defiance, and I heard myself whispering *no* repeatedly. A gleeful look spread across his face.

He knew he had me.

Again.

"Did you hear me? Your prince fucking charming, the guy who you have been fucking, was there the night I fucked his precious little crush from the coffee house."

My heart thudded in my chest to the point of pain, and my throat constricted, halting my breathing as panic roared to life. My brain couldn't comprehend what he was saying. Ky knew me? He knew everything about me, yet he chose to pretend he didn't have a clue? He comforted me when I told him the story of my past, a story he was already familiar with. He had hidden behind the truth, a truth that was now destroying me with every breath I took. What I couldn't understand was how he could do something so cruel. My world was quickly shifting around me. It was constricting and jamming me into a reality that I didn't want to live in. I suddenly felt like a sideshow freak, a pawn in some sick and twisted game, a game that was now my life.

I slid out of the booth and rushed through the diner, pushing the glass door open with every bit of strength I could muster. The moment I hit the sidewalk, I inhaled sharply, allowing the late December air to hit me full force. Every moment we spent together flashed before me. Meeting him in Delights, realizing he worked at *Bangs and Beats,* staying in his apartment, telling him my fears, the dates, the kisses, the sex, the beginnings of love.

All of it was based on a lie.

"Eden." A faint voice sounded behind me, a voice that I instantly recognized.

I swung around slowly and came face to face with the concerned face of Josh Crawford. I didn't even know if I wanted to see him. His face dropped the moment our eyes connected, and he didn't falter until he had me tucked in against his chest with his arms surrounding me. I fell into the confines of his broad chest as realization flooded me.

"Pretty girl, let it all out," he soothed in my ear, and his hand ran through my hair. I burst into tears right there on the sidewalk in the arms of a man whose brother was slowly yet surely becoming my everything. Tears flowed for my past, for my present, and for my future. I cried for the sudden sense of closure that flooded me. Seeing Jeremy hadn't frightened me—it had shocked me. An offering of closure of my past was handed to me, the closure that I had been so desperate to gain, the closure of everything that was Jeremy Davis. It felt amazing, like the weight of the world was lifted off my shoulders but that lasted a split second because I now had a new gaping wound to contend with, a new weight on my shoulders, and it all revolved around Ky Crawford.

"What can I do?" Josh whispered in my ear.

"I don't know."

"Eden!" Ky's panic voice roared in my ears. "Fuck! Baby!"

He grabbed me from Josh's embrace and twisted me so I stood in front of him. His eyes anxiously took me in. "Get away from me," I hissed, and he froze.

"Baby, please," Ky pleaded, regret dripping from every word.

My heart shattered. "Please don't call me that."

"Ky fucking Crawford misses his chance to save the day yet again!" Jeremy taunted as he stalked through the diner door in a cloud of spite.

Pure hatred covered Ky's face, and he rushed toward Jeremy like a man being swallowed by murderous rage. Ky pinned Jeremy against the brick wall, and his fist connected over and over again with Jeremy's face and body with bone-crushing intensity.

"Why the fuck would you do this?" Ky roared. "She has done nothing to you!"

I never imagined seeing this side of Ky. The anger, the pure rage in his words and actions, were on full display before me.

This wasn't the guy who had spoken so quietly in our moments together, whose gentle touch felt like heaven. It wasn't the guy who I was willing to leave everything for.

Even through his beaten and bloodied face, I still witnessed the evil on Jeremy's features and heard the vindictiveness in his words when he spat, "She put me in jail for four fucking years!"

"You raped her!" Ky hissed into the chilled air.

Hearing those words fall from Ky's lips made everything so real. I didn't want to be here. I started backing away until I hit the wall of Josh. His hand gripped mine tightly, taking away my desire to run.

"And you couldn't fucking stop me," Jeremy yelled before his fist connected with Ky's cheek. Instantly, blood trickled down Ky's face. I gasped, wanting to help him, to protect him, and it confused me.

"Call the police, Aunt Carole," Josh yelled as Jeremy started laying into Ky.

"I can't be here," I whispered. "Josh, take me away."

KY

I HAD BEEN BACK at my apartment for an hour, and I had no fucking clue where Josh or Eden had gone. Jeremy had disappeared the moment the word police hit the air and I knew he'd go underground. My face was bruised and bloodied and my ribs ached, but I didn't give a shit. I needed Eden, I needed a minute to explain, and I needed to finally tell her the truth.

The apartment door crept open at a painstakingly slow rate. Every creak, every second it took to open felt like a thousand painful stabs to my already aching heart. I stared at the space, my heart beating frantically in my chest as I silently prayed that Eden would walk through. I hoped this was all a fucked-up nightmare, one that I was desperate to wake from.

Eden appeared through the door, and my breath jammed in the back of my throat. The urge to run to her and crush her against my body as my arms locked around her was so fucking strong, but the girl who appeared before me wasn't the Eden I had quickly fallen for. Her face was void of emotion, and her body was stiff and rigid as she walked into the apartment. Josh followed closely behind her with a solemn face and tight lips. When he met my gaze, he gave me a knowing nod.

Fuck!

Eden moved through my apartment so forcefully. There was not an ounce of softness in her step. Her eyes latched onto the floorboards below, and she remained silent. I stood like a statue, watching her with hawk-like eyes. She refused to acknowledge my presence. I cringed as she passed the glass top table in the foyer, the same table where she usually dropped her keys and bag when she came home. *Home.* Today she didn't. The moment she disappeared down the hall, I came to life. I rushed two steps at a time and spotted her just as she turned into my bedroom. Josh was close on my heels.

I stepped through the door and my heart died a little at the sight in front of me. Eden's suitcase lay opened on the bed and she was rushing from the bathroom to the bedroom with her toiletries and the remnants of her clothes that I had torn from her body only hours before.

Josh patted me on the shoulder, and I turned to look at him. "I'll give you a minute," he said softly and then walked out of the bedroom, closing the door behind him.

The tension in the room was abundant, and Eden refused to look at me or even acknowledge my existence. I hesitated and lowered myself onto the edge of the bed, where I sat silently and watched her. Even though she was here, standing barely a foot away from me, I knew she wasn't really here. She was in the zone and making it clear that I was not welcome. She rushed around the room like a mad woman, looking for her things and throwing them into the suitcase without a care. Finality was a bitch of a thing.

"Eden, please say something," I pleaded, finally finding my voice. I reached out, my fingertips brushing the skin of her forearm, and she ripped away from me before I could take another breath. She froze, and finally turned and looked at me. The blue eyes that had started to shine with life and freedom now looked like hope had been ripped from deep within her soul, and I was the asshole who was to blame.

"I have absolutely nothing to say to you," she whispered and took a step away from my touch, then moved to the other side of the room. She stood by the window with her arms folded across her chest and a scowl took over her beautiful face.

I stood from the bed and broke the distance between us. "Well, I have a shitload to say to you."

The briefest of smirks graced her gorgeously pouty lips as she narrowed her eyes at me. She took one step toward me until we were chest to chest, heat to heat, and heart to heart. The intensity around us swirled and tormented every emotion running through my veins.

"Really?" she huffed. "So now you want to talk? You've had four fucking years to talk, Ky. Four years to tell me who you were. But no, you didn't. You had to play these fucked-up games."

"Nothing about you is or was ever a game, Eden." I took a chance and slowly raised my hands to cup her face. Her eyes found mine and swam with indecision as she looked at me. "Do you hear me? Nothing is a game!"

"Well, why does it seem like I've been a game since day one? I'm not a toy, Ky. I am not a game. I told you that."

Her voice cracked under the enormity of her words, and my heart twisted ferociously as I watched one solitary tear slide over her cheek. This was my fault; the pain on her face, the anguish in her voice, and the breaking of her heart, it was all me. My thumb swept up the tear, and her eyes closed under my touch.

"I thought I was doing the right thing. All I wanted was to show you the life you deserved, the life that was stolen from you. I've been sitting on this for four years. I'm so sorry."

She took a step away from me and turned back to the bed, the bed that I wanted to be our bed, in the apartment that I wanted to be our apartment. Her shoulders dropped, and I knew at that moment everything we shared was flashing before her eyes.

"What are you sorry for, Ky? Getting caught up in a lie? Hiding something from me that had the potential to destroy me? I can't even look at you right now, and I hate that." Her voice cracked and her head dipped in defeat.

I stood behind her and lifted my gaze to the ceiling, and my mind went crazy with scenarios. I wanted to touch her, to provide her with the comfort my arms could give. I wanted to give her the world, but I knew all I needed to give her was my truth in the rawest possible form and hope to God she listened.

"Eden, do you honestly think I'd ever want to hurt you? I didn't know when I came up with the idea of a month with you that I would completely fall for you and feel something I'd never felt for a woman before." I grabbed hold of her hand and turned her until she faced me, and finally her eyes met mine. "I thought I'd have a month to show you that you could smile, that you could hang out with a guy and have complete control. I wanted to show you that you were able to say no. I can't help that you have taken over my mind, that every single one of my thoughts involves you, and that you have gotten so far into my heart that you'll be there forever. I never wanted to be some-one's prince charming, I never imagined myself having a future with a woman because I didn't think I deserved it. But you, Eden, you have opened my eyes to possibilities—you make me want to be your prince charming, your knight in shining ar-mor, your protector. Fuck, I want to be your everything. You are what I want Eden; now, then, and in the future. I want every single part of you. All of you."

Her cheeks streaked with tears as she took in my brutally honest words. My hands cupped her face and I dropped my mouth softly to hers, leaving the lightest of kisses on her lips.

"I can't do this, Ky," she whispered and pleaded with her eyes for distance. "I'm going to stay with Ashlyn and try and sort all this out. Please just give me time."

"Tell me what to do Eden. I won't give up on you, on us."

"I don't know how I can move past this because now when I look at you I see the one guy who I never wanted to break my heart . . . but in the end, he did."

The moment Eden walked out of my apartment, I collapsed into a heap. It was done. I had lost her because I didn't have the balls to admit who I was the moment she arrived in my life. All I wanted to do was protect her, to cherish her, and make her believe in happiness. I wanted to give that to her and so much more, but what I had done was break her already fragile heart.

Knowing that she was at Ashlyn's provided me with a little comfort. At least I knew she was safe. I paced my apartment, and the thought of rushing to Ashlyn's apartment crossed my mind repeatedly, but I needed to respect Eden's wishes. That night I drank until I couldn't stand, until my blood had turned to scotch, until I couldn't remember who I was or the fucked-up situation that had unraveled around me.

It was three days before I finally started feeling human again. I had finally slept and showered, and now I stood in front of the window and looked out over the city as I had my usual morning cup of coffee. But it wasn't the same because I wasn't sharing morning coffee with her.

"Ky, where are you?" Ashlyn's voice bounced off the walls as she stormed in with a vengeance. She halted when I came into view. "Fuck me! When did you start rocking the hobo chic look?" she taunted, taking in the newly acquired beard taking over my jaw.

"Hi to you too."

"I am almost afraid to kiss you for fear that I'll get lost in your bush."

For the first time since Eden left, I laughed until my insides hurt. She soon joined me by the window and wrapped her arms around me, pulling me in for a tight hug. I fell against her body and breathed in her perfume, but instantly I thought of Eden. I had been thinking of her every minute of every day. I had kept her wish, I hadn't attempted to make contact with her, and it was killing me.

"I fucking miss her," I whispered into the confines of Ashlyn's neck.

"I know you do, but I can't watch you destroy yourself. I can't deal with having two of my favorite people in the world hurting."

She was talking about Eden.

I pulled away from her. "How is she?" I asked hopefully, praying to God that Ashlyn would find it in her heart to tell me.

"She is hurt, Ky. She is really struggling to try and understand all this. She doesn't understand why you didn't just tell her, and she is scared that she doesn't know what the truth is anymore."

"I just need to talk to her, to tell her, to try and make this right. I will understand if she can't forgive me, and I deserve that, but she deserves my truth. She deserved it from day one. I thought I was doing the right thing, Ashlyn. I just wanted to give her everything I couldn't give her four years ago."

"All she wanted was you, Ky."

Eden

I WOKE FOR ANOTHER day of hiding out in Ashlyn's apartment, another day of allowing my thoughts to strangle me. I had barely said anything about what I was now referring to as the "incident." Ashlyn had tried, Josh continually came to visit, and my phone was relentlessly bombarded with messages from Ky. But really, who could I trust? My days were spent editing photos, watching daytime television, and conversing through email when I needed to discuss the project. I had one more photo shoot, and then I was leaving.

I stumbled into the small guest bathroom in Ashlyn's apartment and was slapped in the face by the distinct smell of Ky that lingered in the air. It was the same scent that had the ability to send me over the edge and into an unknown land of bliss within seconds. It had been three days since my past crashed headfirst into my present. Three days since I had run out of his apartment, three days since his lips had been on my body, and three days since I'd had any sleep. I was a narcissist—that was the only way to explain the thoughts zooming through my mind. I wanted his scent to attach itself to my needy body; I wanted to wash in his familiarity; I wanted him to imprint himself so deeply within me that I would never forget the little things. I missed him. I never wanted this vulnerability or this need, and I never wanted these feelings. Confusion swept through me. I needed a distraction; I needed to get him out of my head, and fast.

I pulled my robe around my body and made my way through the apartment to find Ashlyn making a fresh pot of coffee in the kitchen.

"When was Ky here?"

She looked up and greeted me with a wary smile. She was dressed and ready for work while I was getting ready for another day on the couch. "This morning. He came over to use the shower because his bathrooms are getting some work done."

"Oh, okay." I nodded, a shiver running down my spine at the thought that Ky had been so close.

"Can I ask you something?"

"Sure."

"I know you two are in some kind of crazy agreement, but everyone can see that it is beyond that." Ashlyn walked across the room, grabbed both my hands, and pulled me toward the couch. "Please talk to me."

I collapsed on the couch and pulled the comforter around my body. "I don't know what is real with him. The past month has been incredible. I have experienced emotions and feelings I never could have imagined, but how do I know that anything he said was real, or if he was just saying it to make himself feel better. It's obvious that he has this guilt when it comes to me, but he has no reason to feel guilty. He wasn't the one who raped me. He wasn't the one who ripped my innocence away from me."

"I have known Ky a long time. He doesn't do things he doesn't mean and if he said anything to you, it's the truth. He doesn't open up to people or allow himself to get close, and he doesn't just bring a girl into his world. You need to talk to him."

"When did you meet him?"

She closed her eyes briefly and took a deep breath.

"It was just after you left. I went back to school after Christmas break, and I met Josh. Josh and I hooked up, and as I was leaving his bedroom, Ky was in their living room. That was my first introduction to Ky Crawford. I knew who he was from around campus, and we started chatting. He mentioned you and I told him we shared a couple of classes. He wanted to find out where you were and when you were coming back. I'll never forget the sound of his voice. He was so panicked."

"Why wouldn't he have told me?"

"I can't answer that. You have to ask him that."

"Is he working today?"

"He is." She swiveled on the couch and faced me. "What are you thinking?"

What am I thinking?

I missed him.

I couldn't stop thinking about him.

I wanted answers.

"I want to see him."

An hour later, the cab was pulling up in front of the building. The trip from the island was spent going over what I would say to him, how I would react, and what I would do. I had no answers, no plans, and absolutely no expectations. I pulled my trench coat tightly around my body as I stood on the sidewalk. I felt my nerves rushing in and the thought of leaving barreled in.

"Eden?"

I turned at the sound of my name. Josh stood near the entry and looked at me completely flustered. Obviously I wasn't who he expected to see. I smiled and dropped my eyes.

"What are you doing here?" He pulled me into his body and his warmth soothed me. "Are you here to see Ky?"

"I think so."

"You think so?"

"I don't know."

"Come and have a coffee with me. I want to chat with you about something."

A coffee couldn't hurt, and maybe it would help me come up with some game plan for when I faced Ky. If anyone knew what was going on, it would be his brother. I nodded and followed him to the nearest Starbucks. After ordering, we sat at a quiet table at the back of the coffee shop and a nervous silence fell over us.

"How have you been?" he finally spoke.

"I've been okay."

"Have you spoken to Ky?"

"No."

"I don't want to get involved in your business, because it's not my place, but I've been carrying something around with me since this whole thing went down with hope I would see you. Fuck, he is going to hate me for doing this, but I think you need to see this."

He handed me a beaten up looking envelope. It was torn at the edges and had weathered over time. My name was written across the front in the familiar handwriting of Ky Crawford.

"What's this?" I asked with wide eyes. My hands shook as I grabbed the envelope from the table.

"That right there is my brother's inner thoughts to you. He has been sitting on that fucking letter for four years. I found him writing it, completely fucked up on whiskey the week after—" He didn't have to say it, his eyes said it all. "He sent it, but it got returned. He became obsessed with finding out about you. He just wanted to make sure you were okay."

"Josh, I had no clue."

"Please go and talk to him. Let him at least explain. If you are going to run off back to the West Coast, he will need closure."

Closure. That was what I wanted all along. It was what I craved. Ky and I had a reason for this month, I just never knew. I felt stronger than I had in years, and it was thanks to him. I felt like I could once again be in this town and not feel weak and it was all thanks to him. He ignited hunger within me—desire, expectation, need—and it was all him.

I stood from the seat, holding on to the envelope with dear life. I would know Ky's words, but I wanted him to read it. I pushed back from the table and Josh followed. We walked out of Starbucks and back toward the office. If I didn't go and see Ky now, I wasn't sure if I would. We walked in silence, and I was comforted with Josh by my side. God I hoped he was still there. It was closing in on six p.m., and the winter night had fallen over New York City. We stood in the elevator. I paid close attention to the floors, and it felt like it took forever.

"He will be in his office. I'll make sure you have no interruptions."

I walked through the nearly abandoned office, with only a couple of enthusiastic staff still lingering at their desks. The door of Ky's office was closed when I reached it, and no sound seeped through. With a deep breath, I knocked firmly and waited.

"Come in."

His voice hit me square in the heart. Okay, I could do this. My shaking hand grabbed hold of the doorknob and twisted, the door opened, and I stepped in.

He sat at his desk, and the skyline glistened behind him through the windows. He looked so young sitting there. When I didn't say anything, he finally looked up. Shock spread across his face as he took me in.

"Eden?" he asked in shock, clearly not believing I was standing in his office. I closed the door behind me and turned the latch. "What are you—" His eyes dropped to the envelope in my hand.

"I want you to read me this." My voice shook with trepidation. The color drained from his face as he took in my words.

"Eden, please don't make me," Ky begged in a voice that shattered like glass. He started to rise from his desk, and his eyes locked on mine. I shook my head dismissively, and he immediately sat back down in defeat. I tore my eyes away from his, dropping my gaze to the floor, and inhaled deeply. My emotions bounced all over the place as I tried to comprehend everything around me. I had a man that was utterly defeated in front of me, a heart that had finally opened to the idea of love by the same man, and a lie was now clouding my opportunity to begin again. I finally found my confidence, lifted my head and looked at him. His gaze held firm, though he looked completely shattered. I took him in as he was: strong, protective, passionate, and now drowning in reluctance.

I moved across the room until I stood beside the desk. My hands shook with nerves when I held the envelope out.

Ky's eyes darted between me and the letter. "Do you really want me to do this?"

"I need you to do this, Ky."

"For you, I'd do anything," he whispered, and with a nervous hand he took the envelope from me.

He slid his index finger along the seal, slowly opening it and bringing the folded piece of paper out. I held my breath. My anticipation ran rampantly. I had absolutely no idea what to expect or what he would say. His eyes bounced from the piece of paper to me. I could see his hand shaking as he held the paper, then he cleared his throat and began.

Dear Eden,

I don't know what to say or how to even start this letter. I am so fucking sorry. I am beyond fucking sorry. I thought he was my best friend. I thought I could tell my best friend about the girl I had been admiring from afar. I thought it was simply a conversation between two guys in their dorm room. You were who I dreamt about, who I watched from afar. You made my ability to speak disappear, you made my confidence shatter, and I never found the courage to approach you. This will be my biggest regret. You were the girl who was such a beauty but had no clue how beautiful she was. It was a stupid drunken bet. I thought he came up with the bet to encourage me to finally make a move. Fuck, I am so sorry. I feel like this is all my fault. I feel like there should have been something I could have done to stop this.

I don't even know if you will receive this letter.

I am so fucking sorry, Eden.

I will never forgive myself for this, for as long as I am still breathing.

Thinking of you,

Ky Crawford.

He dropped his eyes, and the letter floated from his fingers and hit the desk. His voice was thick with emotion and hitched over his apology. His face was as pale as a ghost. I knew I was crying, I felt the torrent of tears flooding my cheeks and the twist of my heart as I took in the words of his letter. The first sob escaped my body as soon as he said *Dear Eden.*

My shaking hands skimmed down the front of my coat, lingering over the brass buckles. The urge to comfort Ky engulfed me like a riptide. I needed to comfort him, and I needed him to comfort me. He had been sitting on this for four years, slowly killing himself with regret, when there was nothing he needed to be sorry for. Four long, devastating, and horrendous years.

I crossed the room until I stood beside his desk. His eyes finally lifted to meet mine, and all I saw was regret and remorse staring back at me. I stepped toward him, and before I lost confidence, I lifted my leg and straddled his lap.

"Eden, what are you doing?"

I lifted my arms and slid them around his neck. His hands fell to my hips and pulled me closer to his body. We locked gazes, a thousand unspoken words fired between us. I didn't know what I wanted to say to him. I didn't know what I could say to him, but I knew my actions would have to do. My fingertips ran through his thick hair and his face fell into the crook of my neck where his unsteady breathing hit my bare skin.

It didn't take long until his soft lips caressed my neck, sucking, nipping, and licking my sensitive skin. He knew this area was my kryptonite. My head fell to the side, allowing him easier access. My body reacted immediately, and I shifted closer, grinding my heat into his growing erection. A moan fell from his lips, but he didn't stop the assault on my neck. I needed to feel his skin. My fingers left the softness of his hair and fell to the crisp white shirt covering the body that I admired. I popped each button open, my fingertips sweeping across the muscles of his chest torturously slow.

"What are we doing?" he asked breathlessly.

"Please don't stop me, Ky. We need to do this."

He didn't say another word. His hands grasped onto the brass buttons of my coat and, within seconds, he gasped hoarsely. His hungry eyes roamed over my black-lingerie-covered body.

"You left the house in just this?"

"I didn't think your brother would stop me on my way here."

"You are so damn beautiful."

I felt my cheeks darken under his lustful gaze. The smallest of a chuckle had risen from his chest before I slammed my lips to his. This kiss was full of apology, need, desperation and connection. My tongue grazed his bottom lip and instantly he opened and let me in. Our tongues swayed in perfect harmony together, combining as one, soothing the lies that had been said, the games that had been played.

I moaned against his lips as our hands attacked one another. I was desperate to feel connected to him; I needed to know that there was still something that would allow us to overcome this. I gripped onto his pants, undoing the button and fumbling for the zipper. My hand fisted around him tightly. I ran my hand up and down his length, feeling it hardening in my grip. I loved knowing I had the ability to do this to him. He drew in a strong hiss and his head fell to my shoulder. I kept working him. His breath trampled over my increasingly heated skin and as I increased my pace, I knew he was close.

His hand left my hip and slid down my thigh, and I knew what was coming. I couldn't help but let out a small cry. His finger ran along the lace of my panties, teasing and tormenting my throbbing clit. I wanted contact. I wanted to feel him. With one swift movement, my panties were pushed to the side, and he entered me. I moaned loudly, the echo filling the silence in the office. I stilled and adjusted. Finally, our gaze met, and I could see his hesitation looking back at me. Hesitation I didn't want to see.

"I want this," I admitted. "Please, Ky."

That was all it took. I saw the reluctance leave his eyes, and immediately it was replaced with determination. It was at that moment that I knew I was about to get all of Ky Crawford.

Ky's mouth took mine with fierce determination. His tongue tasted every inch of my mouth as he owned me and took me to a place I had missed. With firm hands, he grabbed my hips and lifted me, silently begging me to take control and ride him. I didn't know if it was because we were in his office, that I was been taken in front of a window that showed us off to the city, or that I hadn't spoken to him in three days, but I had never been this turned on before. I rode him like my life depended on it, up and down, deeper and harder. My arms linked tightly around his body, my breasts bounced and collided with his naked chest. The friction of my nipples against the warmth of his skin caused my eyes to shut as my body tried to comprehend every emotion flooding my body.

The intensity, the raw emotion, the closure of a past I never wanted to revisit again hit me all at once. I pulled my mouth from his, buried my face in his neck, and immediately I was overcome with his scent. The first tear escaped from my eyes, and I slammed them shut. I would not cry. I balanced precariously on the edge of ecstasy, lingering between reality and a dream-like state. God, it felt out of this world. With a swift movement, Ky pushed me back against the desk, my elbows resting on the mahogany top. The air hit my naked chest and a shiver ran down my spine. The shift in movement allowed him to thrust deeper, and I knew it would be any moment before I collapsed against his chest in a heap of fireworks and stars.

His lips fell to my exposed nipple while his thumb made contact with my throbbing clit. That was all it took. My body switched on, my thighs tightened around his hips, and my head fell back as an orgasm ripped through my body. I shuddered against him as pleasure rolled through me, roaring through every inch of my body. I fell against his chest, and as the sheath of our sweat combined, I felt his release fill me as a roar left his chest.

I stayed in his arms as our breathing calmed down. I didn't move. He remained deep within me and made no attempt to slide out. I stayed in his arms for what seemed like forever, and what had just happened between us made me forget everything, and that was exactly how I wanted it.

KY

"WILL YOU COME HOME with me?" I asked softly, and her eyes finally found mine.

After I finally released her from my grasp, I gently cleaned up and then she stood and wrapped her body back in the coat she had worn to my office. I sat back in my chair and watched her so closely, trying to memorize everything about her as fear that this could be one of the last times I saw her flooded me. It was a feeling I couldn't shake. I had so many things I needed to say to her. All I wanted was to implore her not to give up on me. Whether I deserved it or not was completely up to the shattered girl standing in my office.

I pushed back from my desk after doing up my pants, and crossed the room until I stood behind her. Her eyes immediately flashed to mine in the reflection of the glass. My arms wrapped around her waist, pulling her back to my chest, and the moment she relaxed into me felt like a moment to cherish. I had nothing to lose, so if she didn't listen to my words, my actions would have to speak for themselves.

"Can I take you home?" I asked, my words muffled against her neck.

She shifted in my arms and twisted her body to face me, her arms linking behind my neck. Her eyes finally locked with mine, and they swam with indecision. We desperately needed to talk. I just hoped she would give me that chance. I would not stop at begging for her to give me that chance. Her lips were still swollen and glistening from my attack, and her hair was ruffled in the perfect way I loved. Standing before me, surrounded by my arms, was the only girl for me, and I would fight until I was blue in the face to make her see that and to make her truly mine forever. Nothing would stop me because I had waited too long for this moment.

"Say something, babe."

Her lips creased briefly into a smile at the sound of *babe,* and she nodded so delicately that I almost missed it.

"I'm ready to go," she whispered so gently.

My hand never left hers as we walked through the near empty office and made our way to the garage. I opened the passenger door and watched as she buckled herself in. I just wanted to get her to my apartment, I wanted to feel comfortable. I wanted her to scream at me, hit me, anything besides this silence. I pulled my car out of the garage and hit the steady Friday evening traffic.

I felt her eyes locked on me before I found them. She had shifted in the seat so her back was flush with the door, and she faced me, staring at me so intently. Her perfect blues were bright, focused, and determined like she was reading me and trying to divulge information without asking. It made me nervous as hell. That was all she did for the entire hour drive back to my apartment.

Without a single fucking word.

The moment I shut off the engine, I finally broke.

"Eden, can you please say something? I can't do silence. I need to know what you are thinking. Whether you could ever forgive me?"

"Inside," was the only word she spoke.

It was only a matter of time. I knew I had to wait until she was ready to talk. I felt the shift the moment we stepped foot into my apartment. She sat on the couch, still silent, still holding her emotions in. Everything that we had fought for seemed to have been all but forgotten.

"Do you want something to eat?" I asked as I took a seat beside her.

"Yep."

Fuck me. "Please don't do this."

"Do what?"

"Become that girl again."

"I'll always be that girl."

I shook my head in frustration and stood from the couch, walking to the kitchen as my anger swirled around me. There was no way in hell that I was letting her become that girl again. Pulling open my fridge, I realized I hadn't shopped. The past three days had been horrendous without her, but I couldn't help but think it was a prologue for what I was about to endure.

"I don't have any food. Let's go to the diner."

"Sure."

That was it.

"Fucking hell. Stop doing that. This isn't you. Don't let my fucked-up decision screw up everything you've become while you were here."

She rose from the couch, stormed into the kitchen, and stood chest to chest with me. "You have no right to tell me what to do, Ky. You lost that right when you lied to me. Why did you do it? Tell me why the fuck you would keep something like that from me? I trusted you. I gave you every single part of me, but still that wasn't enough to gain your honesty. I don't know if anything you've said or done is true. All those words you said to me, were they lies too?"

Finally, she broke.

"Nothing I said to you was a lie. Everything I admitted to you was the truth."

Her eyes fell from mine and her face dropped. "I want to know everything, Ky. You know my story, now I want to hear yours."

This would be it, the moment when I faced my greatest

fears. The moment when I relived my darkest days. I had told no one the depths of my grief, my hatred, my disgust in myself. She looked at me so expectantly, and I knew I needed to give her this. This would be her closure as much as it would be mine. I grabbed her hand and pulled her toward the couch. She fell onto the comfortable cushion and pulled her legs to her chest. I sighed nervously and ran my fingers through my hair. I needed to search and gather every part of my strength to give her this because if I didn't, there would be no chance that I could ever get her back.

"I was best friends with Jeremy Davis from high school through college. He was that guy who everyone at school admired, purely because he came from money and had the stature. He always got what he wanted, when he wanted it, and I never had that and I didn't want that. My family was working class, and I had to work my ass off every single day for everything that was in my life. The thing with Jeremy was that he thought he was entitled to everything and everyone. Girls threw themselves at him, and guys wanted to be him. The moment we started college, I saw him change. He wasn't the biggest guy on campus anymore; there were guys with more money, with more standing, and with a much better reputation and stature than him. He didn't like that, and it fucked with his head."

I took a breath and looked at her. Her eyes were wide, her mouth agape as she took in my words. I threw my head back and demanded a huge breath to fill my lungs. I fell silent.

"Please keep going." Her words were so soft, so innocent, yet so demanding.

I nodded.

"I remember the first time I saw you. It was across the coffee house that was just off campus. You were like a breath of fresh air amongst the stiffness and predictability of college girls. The first thing I noticed about you were those beautiful eyes. I had never seen anything like them. The blue reminded me of the ocean in summer. They were so wide, so inviting, and so entrancing. I was trapped from that moment. I had no issues with approaching girls, but with you, I was fearful. I couldn't have handled rejection, and from what I had found out when I asked around, I was told that you didn't date. I couldn't risk it. I watched you from afar. I knew you loved that coffee house, so it became my regular place to study because I wanted a moment when I could enjoy you."

I stopped the moment I heard her gasp. Her knuckles were white from her grip on the pillow she held on to.

"You asked about me?" she asked meekly.

"Of course I did. Eden, you were the most beautiful girl I had ever seen. God this makes me sound like a fucking stalker." I ran my hands through my hair and groaned. This was making me look like a fucking asshole too, but I knew I couldn't stop. "You were everything that other girls weren't. I remember the first time I saw you in sweats in the coffee house. You looked so comfortable, so confident, so concentrated, while every other girl there was in her way-too-tight jeans, with tit-exposing tops and a face full of makeup. You were refreshing. You were everything I wanted."

She stilled as it dawned on her.

She surprised me when she moved closer to me. I took a chance and pulled her onto my lap. My arm snaked around her waist, and I pulled her against my chest. We sat in silence as my words sunk in. We weren't even close to being done, but I just needed this moment because I was afraid that this could be the last chance I get.

"I need you to keep going."

I took a deep breath and my hand grasped her waist tightly, almost as if I was locking her to my body.

"Jeremy noticed a change in me. My life revolved around studying. I had a dream of what I wanted to become, and I didn't have the luxury of having a family who could pay my way through college. My grades were what kept me there. I made the mistake one day of mentioning you, and from that day forward you were on his radar. He started coming to the coffee house. He tried to get me to approach you, then he started saying fucked-up things about you."

She shuddered against my chest at the sound of his name and his actions. I hated that I was bringing this up. I felt like I was putting her through hell, but I knew I couldn't stop.

"That night, at the end-of-the-year party at the frat house, I had been told you were going, and I decided that I was going to find you and finally ask you out. I knew what I was going to say to you, and I wasn't going to let you say no. I thought I had everything ticked off and planned. It was during the lead up to the party that Jeremy started saying shit. He got in my fucking face, and I was getting pissed off. I remember everything like it was yesterday—the look in his eye, the tone of his voice—but I never thought anything else of it. When he came up with a bet to see who could ask you out first, I thought he was doing it to encourage me to finally grow a set of balls. Fuck Eden, I never knew that he could do this. I should have realized he was fucked-up. I should have gotten to you first. I should have realized he had no intention of doing anything for me."

"It's not your fault."

"Eden, I saw him taking a girl to the dorms. I asked him what he was doing. I should have stopped him. I should have realized. I should have run over and stopped him. Why did he need to get more drinks? The party was stocked. I should have realized it was you. It's my fucking fault. I should have stopped him."

"Ky, listen to me. What happened wasn't your fault."

"I could have stopped him."

"You didn't know what he was going to do."

I dropped my face to her neck and drew her closer to my body. I needed the warmth of her body, the familiarity of her curves, the one thing that had been my savior over this past month. Her arms encased my body, and we connected perfectly, like two pieces of the puzzle. We sat in silence, content in being as one while the sun faded in the distance. There were no words needed at that moment, but I knew my story wasn't over. She needed to know how I came to know of her. My admission had the potential to destroy relationships that she cared so deeply about, but I couldn't hide the truth from her any longer.

"Can we eat?" She lifted her head from my chest and looked at me with those blue eyes I cherished. I nodded and unlocked my arms from around her, and she shifted off my lap and stood from the couch. She was still dressed in just her coat and lingerie. "I'm going to get dressed."

She stopped when she got to the hall. Realization hit her. All of her clothes were at Ashlyn's.

"I'll go and get your suitcase."

I didn't give her a chance to respond. The moment I stepped into the solace of the hall, my body fell against the closed door, and I gasped for air. My emotions were running amuck, and I felt myself drifting into the darkness that had taken over my life for the past four years. I thought unleashing the truth into the world would help, but so far it was slowly crushing me from the inside out.

Once my emotions were under control, I pushed off the door, stumbled to the elevator, and made my way to Ashlyn's apartment. I knocked loudly, and moments later the lock clicked and the door swung open. Ashlyn took me in and immediately wrapped her arms around me. My walls of resolve crumbled. My emotions—fear, hatred, and despise—roared to life within me and spilled out of my body. I sobbed in her arms. I fucking sobbed like a baby, but I didn't give a fuck. I cried for what Eden had lost. I cried for the pain she had been forced to endure because I couldn't protect her. I cried for the four years of hell she had lived and because I finally got the girl, and now I was losing her.

"Hey, what's going on?" Ashlyn's soothing voice fell around me, and she pulled me over to the couch.

I wiped my face with my hands and looked at her with red-rimmed eyes. "What the fuck have I done?"

"Babe, this is what you wanted. This was your plan all along. You wanted her to shine, and now she is shining bright. Look how far she has come. She is smiling, she is laughing, and she has opened her heart to the idea of love and being with a man. That was all because of you. I can't watch you destroy yourself any longer. Nothing that happened four years ago was your fault." Her voice was laced with frustration.

"I'm going to tell her everything," I admitted softly. "I have to."

She nodded in agreement, although she knew the possible ramifications of this. She had been a vital part of my crazy plan, and I was about to admit it all to Eden. I dropped my head into my hands and felt my shoulders sink.

"She is everything to me, Ash, and I will do whatever it takes to show her what she means to me," I stated with determination.

"You need to tell her that. You two are right for each other, perfect even, and I really hope you both know that."

"We are going to get some food and finish chatting. I just came to get her suitcase so she can change."

"Hang on a second, I'll go and grab it for you."

Ashlyn peeled herself off the couch and disappeared down the hall, only to reappear a couple of seconds later with Eden's suitcase.

"Good luck. Show her your heart, Ky, because your heart is a beautiful thing."

I opened the door of my apartment and stepped into the still darkness. My eyes tried to adjust and scope out my surroundings. I quietly wheeled Eden's suitcase in through the living room toward my room.

What I found halted my breath.

Eden lay in the center of my bed, her dark hair feathered out against the white pillowcase. My eyes fell to her body; she was dressed in my hoodie that she told me was her favorite and a pair of my sweatpants. Her breathing was steady and her eyes closed as she huddled into my pillow. The sight of her made my heart ache.

I lowered myself until I sat on the edge of the bed, trying not to disturb my sleeping beauty. My eyes ran over her body, and then like magnets, they were drawn to her hands. A folded up piece of paper sat clutched in her closed palm. The letter. *My letter.* She was tormenting herself, reliving my words and weak apology.

I crawled up the bed and rolled to my side, tucking my hand under my cheek and gazing at her. The smallest of frowns plagued her face and, with a shaking hand, I ran my thumb along the offending crease on her forehead. Her eyes flickered opened and focused on me. Her lips curled and an innocent, brief smile greeted me.

"Do you want to eat?" I whispered into the darkness.

"I don't want to go out," she admitted softly.

"We can order pizza from downstairs if you like." She nodded and I started moving until her hand caught my arm. I turned my head and looked back down at her. "What is it?"

"Can you just stay here for a few minutes?"

"Of course."

I pulled my wallet and phone out of my pocket, then dropped them on the side table and scooted up the bed to lay down beside her. She was now on her side, mimicking my body. I could tell she had been crying, and I knew she could see it in my gaze. We remained silent; the only sound in my room was our ragged breathing. She raised her hand and cupped my cheek, and my eyes slammed shut under her soft touch. She removed her hand after a few seconds and, with one finger, she ran it softly, delicately over my lips, before tracing my jawline while her eyes completely devoured my face. I didn't want to, but I couldn't help but think she was memorizing my face.

"I didn't do this for me," I whispered hoarsely.

"Why did you do it?"

"Because something had been taken from you. It was ripped from you, and you needed this. You needed to know you could live a normal life, a life where you could touch and be touched, where you could say no, where you could let someone in and learn to love. I needed to give you that because I felt like I was the one who ripped it away from you. When my letter was returned, I spiraled out of control. The blame was strangling me, and when I gave the police my statement, I made sure I told them everything and anything I could remember. He needed to burn for what he did, and Douglas, who is my father's best friend, made sure he did."

She moved closer, and I rolled to my back to give her space. The last thing I wanted to do was push her. The moment I did, she shifted closer and laid her head on my chest, just above my heart like she always did. My arms circled her waist and pulled her taunt with my body.

"When the letter was returned, I thought that was it. I thought I'd lost all chance of getting to you. I didn't know what I'd do when I got to you, but I knew I just wanted to make sure you were safe. From the moment I found out about what had happened, it became my obsession. *You* became my obsession."

This wasn't going how I'd planned it.

"And then everything just happened. I met Ashlyn through Josh, and we instantly clicked. She knew who I was because of talk around campus after I made a statement to the police. It was about a year after that when I asked Ashlyn to check in on you, and you two had a mutual friend on Facebook or something like that. Next thing I know, I'm talking to Tori on the phone to make sure you were okay."

"Why?"

"Because I felt responsible. I felt like I needed to make sure the girl who I was meant to take home that night, who I was supposed to take for hot chocolate and have the perfect date with, was okay. If I hadn't agreed to that stupid bet, none of this would have happened. Maybe you would have said yes, maybe you would have said no, and that would have been okay, but we will never know."

"I would have said yes."

"Please don't say that."

"What about the job? Was that all part of this?" she whispered into the darkness.

"Partially yes and partially no. I knew you were a photographer, but I hadn't seen any of your work. One day a package arrived on my desk with photos of potential photographers for the shoot you just did, but there weren't any names. I picked yours out from the selection and that's when I was informed that the work belonged to one Eden Rivers. The moment I realized that, I felt something set off inside of me. I wanted you here and I did everything in my power to get you here. Seeing you at Delights that night was completely random. When I heard you call yourself Kellie and being told the reasons why by Tori—Eden that fucking destroyed me, and it was then that I came up with the crazy need to give you everything back, to give you everything you deserve and so much more."

We fell into silence in my bedroom. I wasn't sure how long we lay there, but she didn't move from my chest, and I didn't let her go. Eden lifted her head so her chin rested on my chest and she looked up at me. Her eyes flashed with a million shots of emotion before me.

"You were meant to be my December, Eden, but you've

become my absolute everything," I whispered. "I can't lose you. Please tell me what I can do to make this up to you."

Her hand touched my jaw and she shifted her body up mine until our faces were barely an inch apart. "I don't want any more secrets, Ky. I don't want you to feel any more guilt, and I don't want the past overshadowing anything anymore. If this is going to work, if you and I have any chance, we cannot have secrets."

"I promise, baby."

"I've given you all of me, Ky, and I need you to give me all of you," she continued and pressed one solitary kiss on my lips.

"You can have everything of me, Eden. I will give you the world."

"I don't want the world Ky, I just want you."

Eden

CONTENTMENT WAS AN INCREDIBLE life-altering experience. It was the feeling of having your favorite blanket wrapped tightly around your shoulders. It was the perfect wake-up kiss in the morning and the tight loving hug before bed. It was knowing someone out there had your best interests at heart, who had your protection and safety in the palm of their hands. It was the feeling of complete and utter devotion that was fired to you with one simple look. Contentment seemed to now be known as Ky Crawford.

My time in New York was quickly coming to an end. Tomorrow was the fifth of January. It was the day I was due to pack up my things and leave to go back to my life in San Francisco. Tomorrow was meant to be the day I would say goodbye to this place and put a lid on the nightmares that still lingered in my dreams. It was supposed to be the end of everything. I would be saying goodbye to Ky, and it had been the day that I had dreamed about since the moment he came up with the preposterous idea of our month together.

But last night as I lay in Ky's protective arms, with his heartbeat taking me to a place of peaceful unconsciousness, he told me he wanted me to stay. He gave me his heart and a reason to consider the unthinkable.

As the warm water of my morning shower trickled over my body that was still deliciously achy from the effects of morning sex with Ky, I couldn't help but think of everything he had admitted to me. My mind was alive with the honesty that latched on to his every word as he delivered the most precious of embrace that was complemented with every treasured caress of his dominating hand. The pits of my stomach rolled alive because tonight a decision would be made and the potential that hearts would be broken was the reality I faced.

Once I had finished my morning bathroom routine, I stumbled into the open space of the living room and finished braiding my hair over my shoulder. Winter sunshine filtered through the apartment and, after being locked away from the world with Ky, I was looking forward to getting out of the apartment.

I felt like everything had shifted between us during those days spent entwined together. It had been just me and him—no interruptions, no distractions, and no expectations. After everything that had happened between us, it was like our solitary time was the stitches we needed to heal our gaping wounds, and it was the glue to stick our shattered pieces back together. We now possessed an honesty that was so deeply embedded within us, and a brilliant truth that twisted around the very core that was Eden and Ky. Our fears and deepest regrets were shared, our promises were caressed in solidarity, and it was the beginning of something that scared me so beautifully.

I shook away the potential of fresh tears as I reminisced about our time together and grabbed my purse, phone, and spare key from the counter and locked the apartment behind.

After I stepped onto the sidewalk, the bitter January air swirled around, and a thick chill forced me to pull my coat tighter.

I rushed down the path with a spring in my step, toward the diner desperately aware that my morning hot chocolate and complimentary chocolate chip muffin that Carole would always give me was only minutes away.

I pulled my phone out of my pocket as the sudden urge to text Ky hit me.

Me: You left without saying goodbye this morning. Not even a good morning kiss?

Ky: You seemed so peaceful that I didn't want to wake you. I definitely kissed you. You even made that cute little noise you make.

Me: I wish I had felt it.

Ky: Have you thought about what I asked last night?

Me: It's the only thing I've been thinking about.

Ky: Stay with me baby. I can't lose you. I've just got you back.

I looked at my watch and debated on whether to go to Anderson Publications. I wanted to talk about this now. It was eating away at both of us. My feelings for him were insurmountable, but could I actually live here?

My internal battle was halted by the vibration of a new text message coming through. My heart rate increased at the thought of what Ky would say now. I loved seeing Ky like this, Ky Crawford in his purest and honest form. The smile left my face the moment I looked at the screen.

Unknown: Ready to go for a ride Eden?

Panic reared within me as every hair on my body rose in fear. My head swung around, back and forth, looking up and down the crowded sidewalk trying to locate the culprit, but I also knew that evil always hid in the shadows.

People surrounded me, going about their day, talking in

calm conversation, completely oblivious to the terror taking over my body.

In the distance, I saw the safety of the diner and something within me told me that I needed to get to the security of those four walls as quickly as I could. My feet began to take me, and my hands shook as I pressed Ky's number into my phone.

I needed my protection.

He picked up after two rings, and I didn't even give him a chance to speak.

With a rushed panic voice, I whispered, "Ky, I got another message. It said did I want to go for a ride. I'm so scared I'm at the—"

My desperate pleas halted the moment my phone was snatched out of my hand. A strong hand gripped the back of my neck, stopping my movements and paralyzing me instantly. I was pulled against a stone like body, and immediately I knew who had me.

"Guess who's about to take your pussy for a ride."

My heart twisted painfully in my chest the moment I heard the voice I wished I'd never hear again.

Jeremy Davis.

The frightening sound of the call ceasing shattered the air, and I knew Ky was gone. The pressure on my neck subsided and Jeremy slithered around until he stood in front of me with an evil smirk dripping with vindictiveness. Fear froze me as my eyes took him in.

My need to escape beat inside me, but my legs wouldn't move.

"Do not move. Do not scream. Do not look at anyone. And I swear to fucking God if you say a word you will never speak again. Do you understand me?" Jeremy hissed into my ear.

I nodded in response.

"We are about to start walking and head toward my car, do you understand?"

Once again, I nodded.

The air suddenly felt thick and wet, and my lungs squeezed tightly in my chest as breathing became a chore. I stumbled, tripping on pebbled stones and the cracks in the uneven sidewalk as Jeremy held me close to his side, locking me in with his arm. His fingers dug viciously into my hip as he forced me away from the safety of society, away from a chance to run, and into a darkened alley that felt like a hallway leading to hell.

We reached a silver Honda, complete with blacked out windows that sat hauntingly at the end of the alley. My brain screamed at me to run, but my legs felt like an endless weight held them down, planting them firmly on the dirty ground below. *This can't be happening.* My veins pulsated with fear, dread, and anger as the winter air swirled around me, stabbing my skin tauntingly, and making me realize this was now my reality.

"You can't do this again," I seethed. My hands came up to his chest and, with all of the strength I could muster, I forcefully pushed myself away from his rigid body. His eyes flickered with fury at my blatant attempt at rebellion. A liberty I should never have taken. The force of his hand connecting with my cheek sent me stumbling. My back slammed into the car door and the edge of the metal pressed violently into my spine. I gasped in agony as a pain-induced haze immediately clouded my vision.

His body pressed against mine, locking me in, and flicks of spit hit my face as he roared, "I will do whatever the fuck I want, now get in the fucking car."

He shoved me into the backseat of the car, and I landed on my hands and knees with a thud, thrown around like I was a piece of trash. I didn't know whether it was his hand or foot that pushed me, until I smacked into the opposite door with my face. I groaned and shifted until my back was against the leather seat. Jeremy slid in beside me, and the clicking noise of the lock sounded through the space. I was locked in with no escape. Confusion swam through my turbulent mind. Why was he in the backseat? I looked toward the front of the car at the same time as the person sitting in the driver's seat twisted around and my eyes met evil.

Chris Edwards sneered back at me.

"Surprise!" he taunted, maliciousness penetrating from his every pore. I sat there frozen, the ability to breathe, to think, to acknowledge escaped me as his eyes narrowed in on me.

The seat dipped beside me, and Jeremy's body was soon hard against mine. Chris's eyes shifted between both of us before he turned around and the roar of the engine startled me. My hands twisted in my lap, my fingers entwining, weaving their way together as I always did when I was nervous.

"Where are you taking me?"

Jeremy twisted to face me and, with his finger and thumb, he pinched my chin and forced me to look at him. I whimpered in pain at the death grip he possessed, and tears pricked in my eyes. The monster looking at me had absolutely no life in his eyes and that was what scared me most.

"We are going to have some long overdue fun."

After a short drive filled with an unnerving silence, Chris pulled into the familiar parking lot of the motel I had stayed in when I first arrived. It was like a devastating case of déjà vu.

"Don't you fucking say a word when we get out of this car. One word comes out of you, and I'll fuck you twice as hard when we get inside. I will rip you to kingdom come."

"You are a monster," I hissed vehemently as I was pulled out of the car.

"Monster is a bit harsh don't you think? I'd prefer to be called your worst nightmare."

Jeremy slipped a threatening arm around my waist as we

stepped through the entry doors of Hotel De Luca. My eyes darted around for someone familiar, but all I found were strangers going about their day. I thought we would head to the elevator. Shock inundated me when we turned to the left and headed down the equally familiar hall toward the room I had stayed in, the very same room that had been broken into.

"Look familiar?" Jeremy spat as he pushed me through the door with a violent hand to my back. I stumbled forward, colliding with the corner of the wall and smashing my face. My cheek throbbed and my eyes watered as pain shot through me. Suddenly, I was jerked back with brutal force, causing me to stumble and fall face first onto the unmade bed.

I flipped over quickly, wanting to keep my eyes on my predators. Chris lingered by the window, his focus on the outside world. Jeremy stood at the end of the bed, his hands clasped behind his head. He appeared as if he was attempting to shove a sense of determination and fear in the air, a determination I refused to allow him to have, and a fear I didn't wish to feel again.

"Chris, tie her up. Hands behind her back," Jeremy instructed.

I tore my gaze from Jeremy and watched Chris stalk toward me. Every step he took was heavy with arrogance and purpose. His hands fell to his belt buckle, and I swallowed the bile rising from the pits of my stomach as he fumbled with the clasp and pulled it so slowly out of the loops. He snapped it violently as he stood beside the bed and smirked at his grand prize.

A grand prize—me.

"Fuck I am going to enjoy this," he hissed brutally into my ear. His unforgiving hands ripped at my wrists and pulled them behind my back. My shoulders screamed at his force. The leather of the belt dug into me, burning the top layer of my skin as I fought the restraints. I shuddered as his tongue speared along the rim of my ear and along my jawline. My eyes remained fixed on the wall-mounted television, all the while chanting to myself, *I will not break, I will not break.*

"Back off, asshole," Jeremy growled from the end of the bed.

Chris pushed off the bed and took his position by the window again.

I didn't know how long the standoff between Jeremy and me lasted. I sat back on my heels glaring at him, and he didn't flinch. He made no attempts to touch me, to speak to me, to engage with me. I could see Chris hovering in the corner of my eye, but at that moment it was Jeremy who was in my sights.

I flicked my wrists behind me, which only intensified the burning on my skin.

"Do your fucking worst, Jeremy," I hissed between clenched teeth, the standoff finally getting to me. The waiting and the anticipation of pain that was coming mixed with the confusion as to why he was pacing the room and preying on me like a rabid infected animal.

I was propped up against the head of the bed like I was some kind of fucking trophy, and the longer he kept me waiting, the quicker delusion set in.

Any fear I had escaped, and now raw anger was seething through my pores. The thought of him touching me couldn't become a reality. Just the thought of it forced me into protective mode, and a will to fight overcame me.

Finally, I had something good happening in my life. I was finally on the path to living again, and I had someone worth fighting for.

"You've gotten a backbone since I last saw you." He stalked toward the bed and I noticed the gleam from the knife he had clasped in his hand. My breathing stilled. The thought that this could be how my life ended finally opened the doors and all of my fears and regrets trampled through.

Every single regret I'd experienced was at the hands of the

man in front of me. That one act, four years ago, had put my life on a path of no return. I didn't live. I was breathing, but I wasn't living. I hadn't been living until Ky came into my life. Just at the thought of him, and I felt my emotions bubbling over. Ky was now my world, and I might not ever get the chance to tell him. He had spent the past four years in a world full of regrets, and this would kill him. Jeremy didn't just have the potential to ruin my life in his hands, but he had the potential to completely destroy Ky.

I needed to stop thinking about Ky.

Thinking about him would only distract me.

Jeremy hovered at the side of the bed where I sat. Suddenly I felt claustrophobic as if the air was being sucked out of the vents and my attempts to breathe were halted. The moment he forced me into the car, I became his possession, yet it was his unpredictability that frightened me the most. I focused entirely on the sharp edge of the knife as Jeremy stalked threateningly toward me. My gasp rang through the room the moment the cold tip hit the skin on my jaw. With slow precision, he ran the knife back and forth along my jaw before it landed on my neck. The slightest of movement from his brutal hands would end my life.

"What do you want from me?" My voice came out weaker than I had anticipated, my façade fading fast. He immediately relished in my fear.

"What do we want from her, cousin?" Jeremy asked, his eyes never leaving me. Immediately my hands struggled for freedom, but it only tightened the belt. Chris now stood in the corner of the room, leaning against the wall closest to the window.

"I want her pussy."

The air in the room suddenly became extinct as Chris's words repeated over and over again in my head. I refused to break eye contact with him. I needed to find any strength I had left in my body as it slowly began to shut down and go into protective mode.

Jeremy took a step away from the bed as he unleashed his request into the room. "Undress her, Chris. Down to the lingerie that I know the little slut is wearing."

I felt my stomach churn.

"I enjoyed the set of your panties that Chris brought me as a gift when I left prison. I am surprised you didn't miss them. I jack off to them every single fucking night. I cannot wait to pay you back for putting me in there. Do you understand what it was like? Four fucking years of my life gone because you couldn't handle my fucking cock."

"You raped me!" I screamed with the full power of my lungs. My body thrashed around the bed as rage pulsated through my veins. Screaming was now my defense mechanism. If I screamed loud enough, someone would have to hear and come and find me. "Somebody! Anybody! Help! Get away from me you asshole!" I begged until my voice was hoarse.

"Shut your fucking mouth." Jeremy's hand pressed tightly around my throat, stealing my ability to breathe. I gagged as I desperately searched for air. My pulse beat frantically and my vision started fading in and out as unconsciousness swam toward me.

As I fell down the final steps to oblivion, Jeremy released my throat and I gasped as air flooded my craving lungs. "Strip and gag her," Jeremy demanded to Chris.

Chris stalked across the room, his hungry eyes locked onto my breasts until he stood at the foot of the bed. My heart pounded urgently and my chest heaved as a constant reminder that I was still alive and that I needed to fight. The moment his clammy hands touched my skin and ran over my bare arms, I roared to life. I couldn't go down like this. Not again. I couldn't be that girl for the second time.

My knee shot out, and with every ounce of my strength I

could muster, the hardness of my knee cap collided between his legs, connecting with his balls with a vicious intensity. Chris collapsed onto the bed, clutching his quickly-bruising balls with his face twisting in agony.

"You fucking bitch," he roared and flung himself at me. His clenched fist came toward my jaw as if it was in slow motion, but I still didn't have time to brace myself for impact. The side of my jaw took the brunt of his attack, and the metallic taste of blood filled my mouth as an aggressive pain shot through me. "You try anything like that again, and I will break you. I will fuck you so hard that you'll be no good to anyone. You hear me, slut? You. Fucking. Hear. Me!"

"Get off her, Chris," Jeremy hissed from the end of the bed. With brute force, he ripped Chris from my body by the back of his shirt. Chris crumbled on the floor and crawled to the chair in the far corner. He glared at me as he cupped his balls, massaging them so sickly that I had no clue whether it was because of his intent to carry through with his promise or because of the pain I had caused.

"Already causing trouble? I've got to admit, I like this new feistiness. It's going to make for some very enjoyable moments between us." Jeremy stalked around the bed until he reached me. His hands slid up my thigh, over my hip, and disappeared under my shirt to rest on my stomach. "Do you remember what I said to you the last time we were in this situation?"

"Fuck you!"

"I told you that you were mine, and that hasn't fucking changed," he roared and spittle hit my face as the vein in his neck thundered with fury. "I'm going to make sure you never forget it again."

I swallowed the lump of fear that had made its way to my throat and awaited his next move. Jeremy's malicious hands grabbed at my jeans, ripping them open and pushing them over my hips. The air swirled around the room and hit my bare stomach as he tore open my shirt and discarded it in one go.

I lay on the bed, dressed only in my red lace panties and bra. With my hands bound, I couldn't even cover myself. His greedy eyes ran over my body. I froze as his hand ran up my thigh and lingered on my hip. Jeremy leaned over my body and his heavy breathing hit my core, the flimsy lace providing no barrier to his evil. He inhaled sharply, taking in my scent, and I cringed as his eyes rolled into the back of his head.

"I can't wait to feast on you." His hand slipped over the lace and he pressed down, rubbing his finger up and down my folds before his thumb pressed down on my covered clit. My eyes slammed shut in anger. "I wonder what your boyfriend would think of this."

At the mere mention of Ky, my eyes flung open in rage. I didn't want Ky tarnished by Jeremy. I had to protect myself, even if it meant getting hurt in the process. Distraction would be my best friend.

"You want to know what my *boyfriend* would think. He'd think that you're a fucking asshole who can't get a chick unless you rape her. You are a pathetic piece of shit, Jeremy Davis, and you will not get away with this again. Ky will be looking for me, and when he finds me, I hope with everything I am he gives you exactly what you deserve."

I felt the snap of my rib as soon as his elbow hit my side at full force. I gasped in pain and my body convulsed under the pressure raising me from the mattress momentarily. My back hit the mattress as warm tears flooded my cheeks. Waves of intense pain rolled through me and finally crashed as my breath came back.

"Don't fucking mention him again," Jeremy hissed. He ripped my discarded shirt clean apart and shoved a piece of the material in my mouth, taking my ability to draw attention to myself and making my chance of rescue quickly fade away.

The pain, the lack of oxygen, and the fear taking over my

body brought on a darkness that I craved. Before I could struggle any longer, I slipped into oblivion with Jeremy and Chris lingering devastatingly close.

KY

THE WORLD AROUND ME felt like it was crushing every single bone in my body. My apartment was in a frenzy of chatter and anxious energy. Desperation lingered in the air. Police officers, my parents, Eden's parents, Ashlyn, and Josh all paced the floor as time slipped away from us. I couldn't even comprehend what was happening. My fists were clenched at my sides, and my head thumped with a tension headache. I swore I heard every single click of the clock on the wall, every single fucked-up second that he had her.

"I need to get out of here. I need to find her." I rushed to the door as I finally cracked.

"Ky wait!" my father's tired voice sounded from the couch. We had been sitting around for hours, waiting for something, anything to happen, and I was absolutely done. "What good is it going to do if you leave? Where do you think you will go?"

"That fucking asshole has my girl," I roared into the tension-filled room.

"Son, he has my girl too," Mike Rivers said in a low voice, his brow pinched as he looked back at me.

Mike and Anna Rivers had arrived alongside the police officers two hours ago. The first thing I noticed about Mike was how tall and broad he was. His face was covered with a dark beard, and he shared the same deep blue eyes as Eden. He was a threatening-looking man, but the moment he shook my hand with a firm grip and looked me square in the eyes I saw that his world had also disappeared. Anna Rivers jumped into my arms as soon as her husband was pulled away by Douglas. Anna's arms circled my waist, and she didn't say a word to me. She just cried into my chest, dampening my shirt with tears for her missing daughter. It shocked me at first, but I wrapped my arms around her shoulders and held her tightly against my chest, offering all the support that I could find.

I had never met these people before. What a fucked-up way of meeting them for the first time. They had arrived back in the United States the day before but didn't get the opportunity to see their daughter, and now she was missing.

"What the hell am I supposed to do?" I groaned into the air. Anger seethed within me, and my hands rubbed furiously over my face as I stormed through my apartment toward my room. *Our* room.

The moment I stepped foot through the doors, I froze as the intense smell of her perfume smothered me, clouding me with the sweet citrus scent that drove me crazy. My emotions bubbled within my tight chest and my eyes glistened as the reality of what happened stabbed at my barely beating heart. I collapsed on the edge of the bed and my face fell into my hands as a painful sob escaped from my chest.

Knowing that Jeremy had her, and knowing what he was capable of, was tearing me apart. Hearing her petrified voice when she called was replaying over and over in my head like a constant reminder that she wasn't safe, that I had failed her again. I had promised I would always protect her.

All I wanted was a moment of peace, but how could I possibly find peace when a war was waging inside my head, my heart, and the world around me. Eden was my world, and my world was now being threatened in a way I didn't even want to comprehend.

I wasn't sure how long I sat there, huddled over, my emotions seeping out of every pore of my body. My mind sorted through every memory I had of her. We had overcome so much.

Fuck, I had asked her to move in with me just last night. I had already given her my heart, and now I wanted to give her my home, my life, and my future, for eternity. She was stronger now, more resilient. She was trusting, and she was finally mine. But now Jeremy motherfucking Davis had her. He had taken her away from my protection, away from the safety that I had been desperate to provide her. He was making me live my worst nightmare all over again. I couldn't save her once, and now here I was, in the exact same position.

My head shot up from my hands as a succession of soft knocks hit the closed bedroom door.

"Son, can I come in?" Mike's worried voice cracked through the thick wood.

"Sure," I replied.

He walked in, closing the door behind him. I had no clue what to say. I didn't know what he knew about me. Fuck, I didn't even know if Eden had mentioned me before. As far as I knew, I was just as much a stranger to him as he was to me.

He took a seat on the bed beside me, and we fell into a thick silence.

"You saved her." He finally spoke so softly that I almost missed it.

I nearly choked on my own breath at his delusional words.

"If I had saved her, she wouldn't be missing," I stated matter-of-factly.

"Do you know that she would call me and her mother every couple of days? Did you also know that she would text her mother every other day? It was all you, Ky. Every single message we received, every single time we heard her sweet voice, we noticed a change and it was all because of you. You made my daughter come alive again. I thought I had lost her four years ago, but now she has finally come back to us, and it's largely because of you."

"Did she tell you who I was?" I shifted my gaze to him, my

eyes narrowing. "That I was best friends with the asshole who has got her again? That I was the one who wanted her all those years ago but didn't have the balls to do a damn thing about it and then he came in and tore her away from all of us? I am *that* guy."

"She has told me enough." He shifted beside me, nervousness falling off him.

"You should hate me."

"Why would I hate the guy who has opened up his house for the police to work out of? Why would I hate the guy who has opened his home to me and my wife when you have never met us before? Why would I hate the guy who has finally brought a smile to my daughter's face?" He stood from the bed and shoved his hands in his pockets. "Ky, I would be a fucking asshole if I hated you."

My lips twitched at his use of profanity. I didn't think to watch my language around him. I didn't know how to act around him; *my girl's* father.

Eden

MY HEAVY EYES FLUTTERED open as daybreak cracked through the blinds. Every movement I attempted to make paralyzed me as pain shot through my body. My ribs screamed at me and my face throbbed, making me aware that bruising was a certainty. I took a risk and gazed around the room. Chris lazed in the chair by the window as he slept. His arms folded across his chest, and a permanent frown was etched on his face. I shifted my gaze to the left and found Jeremy's sleeping form beside me, his hand resting heavily on my hip.

I hated him. I despised every breath he was allowed to take. I wished for his death, and I didn't feel any remorse when I prayed for the heavy hand of karma to fuck him over. I just hoped it was sooner rather than later. I knew my time was quickly running out, and the realization that he would take whatever he wanted from me at any time caused a dreadful shiver of fear to run down my spine.

My shoulders ached from being pulled tightly behind my back all night, and every single bone in my body felt like it was shattering. I was tired, hungry, and desperate for water. He was fucking torturing me.

Thankfully, sometime during the night, I had been able to spit out the gag, and with a husky voice I said, "I need to use the bathroom."

The monster beside me rolled to his side and shifted across

the bed so he was hard up against my rigid body. His arm felt like a weight over my stomach, adding unwanted pressure onto my battered ribs. I hissed at the sensation, grabbing his attention in the process.

"Good morning, princess." His voice, hot and thick with sleep, brutalized the skin of my neck as he nuzzled his face in close to my ear. "What can I do for you?"

"I need to use the bathroom," I repeated with no emotion in my voice.

"Are we going to have a repeat of yesterday? Remember what I said about calling out like a bitch. One word and you know what happens," Jeremy's spiteful tongue warned.

"I just need to use the bathroom."

He retracted himself from my neck and climbed out of bed. I watched him like a hawk, not daring to blink in case I missed any sudden movement. I could not allow myself to drop my guard. I had to fight. His thick, dangerously-imposing body hovered around the edge of the bed until he stood beside me. He pulled me up with one swift movement, causing me to wince in pain as my ribs screamed at me. His chuckle added insult to my injury. I timidly inched my legs over the edge of the bed and rose on shaky legs, legs that I hadn't used in over twenty-four hours.

I looked at him expectantly, waiting for him to untie the leather belt that dug into my bloodied wrists so I could use the bathroom like a normal human being.

Jeremy snickered and shook his head dismissively, and with that one movement, determined my fate. I was nothing but an object to him. A toy he planned on playing with whichever way he so desired. I stumbled over my feet as he pushed me in the back, floundering like a rag doll down the hall in the direction of the bathroom. "There is no way in hell that I am undoing your hands. You need to piss, you do it in front of me."

I didn't even bother arguing. By now I was completely entranced with the thought of protecting myself. Call me weak, call me pathetic, call me a pushover—I didn't give a shit. Jeremy was manic. He lived in a different reality, a reality where he clearly thought this was the norm, and if going to the bathroom in front of him provided me some moments without injury, then so be it.

Once I had finished, Jeremy led me back into the main room and I took the same position on the bed. I was still only dressed in my panties and bra, and I shivered uncontrollably as the chill in the room hit me. My head fell to the side and my eyes followed Jeremy as he moved through the room. He appeared as if he didn't have a care in the world, like this was normality, like I enjoyed being bound and gagged.

What the hell is that noise?

Swipe! Click! Snap!

Curiosity got the better of me and hauled me away from the trance of watching Jeremy in the kitchenette. At the foot of the bed, Chris was hovering, holding a phone up, which I instantly recognized as mine. I sucked in a breath as the noise sounded again, and I realized exactly what he was doing. He was smugly taking photos of me.

My first instinct was to cower and cover myself. The thought of a photo being taken of me in such a submissive state petrified me. I had fought too long and too hard to be shown in this humiliating state. I wasn't weak any longer, I didn't deserve this. I tugged on my wrists for any sign of freedom. The more I struggled, the tighter the belt got, and the pressure on my raw, broken skin intensified.

The ear-splitting sound of what seemed like hundreds of photos being taken tainted the room and infuriated me beyond limits.

"Fuck off!" I spat. "You are a sick fucking bastard. You won't get away with this."

His evil grin sharpened with my empty threats.

Photo after photo of me sprawled out on the bed, barely covered by my panties and bra and with my injuries on full display, were being taken and there was nothing I could do about it.

"Yo, Jeremy, what do you say? Should I send her boyfriend a nice wake-up message?" Chris taunted and continued his assault with my camera.

Hearing them mention Ky sent me into a whirlwind of emotions and a bone-shattering hope soared within me. Ky would save me. He had to save me. He was the only one who could. It was amidst the cruelty of Chris' taunting with the camera that I realized how different this was to four years ago.

Four years ago, in the loneliness and eeriness of Jeremy's dorm room, I lost everything. I was ripped away from a life that I didn't know could exist. I was a nineteen-year-old girl who didn't have anything to fight for and certainly didn't have a future waiting for me on the other side. Most importantly, my heart and body hadn't belonged to someone else—but now it all belonged to Ky.

"Hold up." Jeremy slithered into the room like a poisonous snake getting ready to devour the mouse before him. He slid onto the bed, a knee falling on each side of my hips as he straddled me. The pressure he forced onto my core shot pain through me. My pain register was sky high, and every time I inhaled, my shattered rib made me collide head on with my nightmare.

"You ready to show your boyfriend who owns you?" he murmured as his thumb ran along my bottom lip. His eyes looked glassy and didn't hold any conviction of reality as they glared back at me.

"You will never own me," I spat, refusing to break eye contact.

He pressed down harder onto my core, mercilessly grinding his erection deeper. I couldn't stop the painful whimper that hissed between my clenched teeth. He knew he was punishing me, and he was gleeful in the knowledge. "That fucking mouth of yours is going to get you in trouble, *princess.*"

"I'm not your princess. I'm not your anything."

With a loud snap, his hand connected with my face, sending my head swinging to the side. The moment my eyes opened, I heard the sound of yet another photo being taken. Jeremy ran his hands over my stomach, pressing down where he knew I was hurting. I gasped in pain, and my head swung back and forth, yet I refused to beg for mercy. I clenched my teeth together and gritted on for dear life. His hands cupped my breasts and his thumb rubbed my nipples through the pathetically thin lace. The lingerie I was wearing was Ky's favorite. He loved the way the red fit against the curves of my body, but now it would be forever tainted, and all I wanted was to burn them into a pile of ash.

"Get off me," I shouted.

I thrashed around on the bed as best I could. Jeremy's weight lay unscrupulously hard on top of me, halting my desperation to escape. The more I struggled, the harder he pushed down on me. I didn't care about the pain anymore. It had disappeared into my will to fight. It had ceased to exist the moment Ky pierced into my thoughts.

"Take the fucking photo, Chris! Make sure you get a shot of my tongue down her throat and my cock grinding up against her sweet pussy." His face inched closer to mine and his hideous breath hit my lips. "You ready to put on a show for your boyfriend, princess?"

"Fuck y—" My words were stolen as Jeremy forced his tongue into my unwilling mouth. His brutal lips collided with mine in a kiss that took my breath, but for all the wrong reasons.

Jeremy ground his arousal against me, causing the lace of my panties to rub against my core. A burning sensation swam through me at the roughness of his assault, and tears sprung to the corners of my eyes. His hands slid between our bodies and he grasped my breasts roughly, squeezing so hard that I knew bruises instantly formed. I wanted to be sick. I needed to be sick. I would rather choke on my own vomit than continue with this.

I allowed myself to float to an alternative world, a world where none of this was happening. A place where it was just Ky and me, where laughter was the only thing I heard, freshly baked muffins from the diner was the only thing I smelled, and Ky's kiss was the only thing I tasted.

"Get the fuck off her!"

Time froze and the world stopped and tilted on its axis the moment I heard Ky's panicked voice fill the room.

Jeremy pulled away with a snicker, and I took a moment of reprieve to collect a deep gasp of much-needed air.

"Ky?" I whispered hesitantly, not believing what I was hearing. My head fell to the side in the direction of his voice. My body was quickly overcome with weakness, due to over twenty-four hours with no food or water, and a simple move-ment was torturous. Chris stood beside the bed, holding out my phone, and that was when I saw Ky's beautiful face filling the screen. "Ky!" I shouted as loud as my dehydrated throat would allow.

"Eden, baby, hang on. I will find you."

"You're a fucking weak prick, Crawford. What's this? The second time you've allowed me to get my hands on her. You aren't worthy of this pussy," Jeremy spat toward the phone. My eyes were transfixed on Ky. The pain etched over his face was excruciating to witness as he listened to Jeremy's taunts. This would be killing him. He blamed himself for the first time, and now this. I didn't know if he would get past this.

Ever since I arrived, his protection of me had been para-mount. Ky had been the reason I was the person I was today. He had unleashed the fighter within me. He'd encouraged me to be the girl who refused to be the victim. He'd motivated me to find my voice, and now I refused to remain silent. Now it felt like I had to protect him. I had to give him his voice back, and I had to return everything he gave me.

I mustered every bit of strength I had before I spoke. "Ky owns me, Jeremy. I give myself to Ky and Ky only."

Jeremy growled like a wild animal and hauled me up by my aching shoulder until I was sitting up against the wooden headboard. I screamed at the stabbing pain that seared through my body.

He snatched my phone from Chris, who had remained silent as his cousin completely lost it. "See this little bitch," Jeremy jeered as he thrust the camera into my face. I closed my eyes and looked away. I didn't want Ky seeing me like this. "She is mine, Crawford. See these tits. They are mine. See this sweet delicious pussy. That is mine. She put me away for four fucking years, so now it's my time for payback." As he spat his taunts, his hands ran over my breasts, squeezing them mercilessly, and then he cupped my core roughly. "Answer this, Crawford: do you want to watch me fuck her because I'm going to fuck her right now. Your fucking choice!"

I felt a piece of me die inside as it hit me what was going to happen. Ky couldn't see this. He would never come back from witnessing it. This was my moment to protect him at the risk of my safety. I had to grow the balls that I didn't have four years ago. I had to play the game.

"Jeremy, don't share it with anyone. It was just you and me the first time, so it should be just me and you this time. Do you really want to share me with Ky or Chris?" I swallowed the vomit that sat precariously in my throat, and I just hoped like hell it worked. I looked at him with pleading eyes and pushed my body forward so my chest was against his in an act of submission.

My pleas weren't for me; they were entirely and without hesitation for Ky.

"Eden! What the fuck are you doing? No! Fucking no! Get away from her." I heard Ky's anger spearing through the phone still held near my face, but my gaze didn't fall from Jeremy.

Evilness spread over Jeremy's face, and I knew I had him. It had somehow worked.

"Goodbye, Crawford. I'm going to fuck my girl."

KY

IT WAS OFFICIAL. I was going to kill a man with my bare hands.

I paced my apartment, crossing every inch of the living room with demanding steps, all the while twitching and fuming like a mad man. Anger seethed within me, piercing my very core with murderous thoughts and ways that I would eliminate Jeremy Davis forever. My reaction to the call was immediate, desperate, and frantic. My eyes had witnessed images of Eden that I knew would be tattooed in my memories for life. They would be a knife in my heart that would continue to haunt me for the rest of my living years and into my death. Seeing Jeremy's hands and mouth on her body was like putting acid on open wounds. My girl was hurting—fuck, she was more than my girl, she was my world. And now she was locked away, facing the evil of a ruthless maniac head on. I felt completely and utterly useless.

The living room was abuzz with frantic energy. My ears ached from the constant noise. Douglas was shouting orders to the police officers and the calls were being traced. Mom and Eden's mom huddled together on the couch, quietly sobbing from what they had both witnessed, and Dad and Mike were in quiet conversation in the kitchen.

Jeremy Davis was a dead man fucking walking.

My gorgeous, courageous, strong girl was fighting him. She was fighting the fuckwit that had taken her. The sheer determination on her face and her extreme desire to survive hit me so deep that it knocked the air from my lungs and twisted my heart.

"Ky, get over here," Dad bellowed from the kitchen. I hurried toward him and noticed that Douglas had joined them, along with a man in his early forties who held paperwork in his hands.

Douglas turned his large frame toward me and leaned back on the kitchen island, his arms crossed over his chest. "We know where she is. The motherfucker isn't a smart man, and we were able to trace her cell phone and know the exact location."

"We have to go now," I demanded and stormed out of the kitchen in search of my keys. Hearing that they knew where Eden was like music to my fucking ears. They didn't follow me. "What are you waiting for? We know where she is!"

I couldn't understand why they were standing around looking at me like I had completely lost my mind.

"Ky, we have to ensure that the premises are secure. If we barge in guns pulled and he isn't there, this whole thing will be useless. He could be watching, and what do you think would happen then? He will take off with her, and he will not make contact again," Douglas said, trying to calm my erratic behavior.

"He has my girlfriend. He has my life in his fucking hands, and we have to wait for confirmation?" I breathed out in frustration. I roughly ran my hands over my face and gritted my teeth. "He has my life."

My dad's hand fell on my shoulder, and he gave me a slight nod. A nod that I knew meant that I should listen to what Douglas was saying.

I couldn't stay there. I needed to get away from all of them. How could they just stand there when Eden was going through . . . Fuck, I didn't even want to imagine what was happening to her.

"Ky, would you come and sit with me?" Anna Rivers' soft

voice fell to my ears, halting my escape. I turned to look at Eden's mom, and my heart broke all over again.

Without another thought, I slipped onto the couch beside her, then her hand grabbed mine tightly and her head fell to my shoulder. Her characteristics were so similar to Eden's, and my throat tightened under the realization.

I needed her back.

I had failed her yet again.

"I need my baby girl back. I need to see her happy. I need to see you two together." Anna sobbed against my shoulder. "Bring my baby girl home, Ky."

"We are heading off. We will call when we have news." Douglas' voice shattered the moment I was having with Eden's mom.

I shot up from the couch and stormed toward him. We came face to face. His face was concrete steel and his eyes almost black while his chest was covered with an intimidating bulletproof vest.

"Don't even begin to think that I'm not coming with you. That is my girlfriend he has, and I will die fighting if you try and stop me."

"You are a persistent prick, aren't you?" Douglas' voice was just as intimidating as his stature.

Minutes passed as we entered a vortex of glares, neither of us willing to budge. Douglas knew the extent of my reasons to be there. He had been the one who worked on the case four years ago. He had been the one who I would harass for information on Jeremy, and he was the one who I gave my statement to that helped in Jeremy's conviction.

"Suit him up," Douglas growled. "I want him in a vest. God only fucking knows what kind of ammo this fuckwit has in that room. We go in ready, guys. Take no chances. Our aim is simple: get Eden safely out of that room."

Twenty minutes later, two sleek black SUVs pulled up to the curb in front of Hotel De Luca. I remained silent through the entire trip, as Douglas rattled off instructions to his team and informed them of the procedure that would come into effect. It was simple. Safety. Distraction. Surprise. But I only had one thing on my mind—getting Eden safely into my arms and away from Jeremy.

I jumped out of the car as adrenaline coursed through my veins. Douglas' hand came down on top of my shoulder, halting my movements. "We are going to get her out of here. I am just as invested in this as you. The image of her in that hospital bed has stayed with me for years, and I want to put this motherfuck-er away."

The look in his eyes told me he had unfinished business with Jeremy Davis, a fact that made me smirk in fucking delight. Everything happened quickly around me. We moved into the foyer, and the armed officers had their guns cocked and ready. The bystanders gasped at the sight of them. I ignored everything until my phone buzzed in my pocket.

Eden's name flashed on the screen. I halted and snapped my fingers toward Douglas to get his attention. His hand rose in the air, stopping the other officers from proceeding. He didn't speak, he nodded once at me in silent confirmation to answer the call.

"What?" I roared down the phone.

Jeremy chuckled. "Is that really any way to speak to your oldest and dearest friend?"

"You are a fucking asshole, Jeremy."

"Do you really think you should be talking to me like that, especially when I have Eden in the palm of my hands? Say hi, Eden."

My body froze as Eden's scream filtered down the phone.

Every single rational thought left my body, and I rushed down the hall toward the room I knew they were in. I felt hands on me trying to stop me, but I shrugged them off.

My hand gripped the door handle, and I twisted. It popped open without force. Unlocked and enabling my entrance. The fucker really was an idiot.

All hell broke loose the moment I ran into the room. I wasn't thinking. I was irrational, and I had only one thing on my mind.

Eden's safety.

My breathing faltered as my desperate eyes found exactly who I had come for. Laying on her back, Eden's panties were shredded and barely held against her body. My stomach churned within me. Her hair was a matted mess, swimming around her anguish-ridden face as she glared back at Jeremy, who hovered over her like a stalking animal. My eyes took in every inch of her face: her cheek was bruised black and her eyebrow cut, with fresh blood running from the new wound.

Jeremy's body twisted above Eden, turned toward me, and the evilest of smirks graced his face.

"About time you joined the party." My first and only instinct was to rush toward Eden, but the moment I moved, an arm crossed my chest and another around my neck was crushing my windpipe. "You remember my cousin, don't you?"

I gasped for air as Chris pushed harder. I was momentarily paralyzed. My vision clouded and speckles of blackness appeared as unconsciousness came close.

"Don't make him pass out! I want him to watch this," Jeremy spat.

Chris shifted my body so I was facing the bed. Jeremy lifted his hand, and with all of his weight behind him, he began his attack on Eden. He was like a man possessed. He slapped her repeatedly across the face, before ripping the red leather lace of her bra until her breasts were exposed to the room. Blood ran down her chin and her deep sobs filled the air. I didn't even know if she knew I was here, and my ability to speak was stolen. My anger roared to inhuman status when the sound of lace and satin ripping hit the air as he tore her panties from her body.

Commotion sounded behind me, and then the room became a war zone. Douglas and his crew burst in with their guns drawn. Through the chaos and shouting, Chris loosened his grip as shock hit him, and I shrugged out of his grasp and bolted to the bed. I ripped Jeremy from her limp body by the back of his shirt. My attack startled him. Like he was weightless, I threw him across the room toward the doors of the closet. His back smashed brutally against the mirror and glass shattered to the floor below. Jeremy sprung to life, his eyes glaring at me with intent to kill. He stalked toward me and lunged.

Every single nightmare, pain, regret, remorse, and year lost caused by Jeremy flooded my veins. My fist collided with his face as I pummeled him with every ounce of my anger. My knuckles ached. They smeared with blood, and I didn't know whether it was mine or his.

"I will kill you, Crawford," Jeremy roared from the floor as my foot kicked in his ribs.

"Ky, fucking go and get your girl." Douglas jerked me away, his hands falling to my arms and shaking me roughly to yank me from my trance. My eyes focused on him as my emotions were still fueled by anger. "Go and get your girl." His voice finally registered. His expression was desperate.

"Don't fucking move. Jeremy Davis you are under arrest for the kidnap and assault of Eden Rivers." Douglas' threat faded behind me as I rushed toward Eden, who looked on with wide eyes.

"She is mine, and you are not taking her from me," Jeremy roared.

I scrambled onto the bed, ripping the shirt off my back and covering Eden's naked and trembling body. With desperate hands, I softly untied her bloodied and bruised wrists that were still bound behind her back. The moment the blood rushed through, she groaned in pain and her eyes flooded with tears.

"Baby, look at me," I soothed, desperate to draw her attention away from the scene unfolding before her, but she seemed to be locked in a spell. "Eden, baby. Please, I need you to look at me," I begged as tears flooded my cheeks. Finally, after what seemed like an eternity, her blue eyes found mine. Having me sitting before her finally registered, and relief flooded her battered yet still beautiful face. I cupped her cheek and, with a soft movement, my thumb wiped away her tears as we stared, drinking each other in and sitting in silence. I had no clue what was happening behind us. I didn't care what was happening. I had Eden back. She was here, and she was alive.

Two ear-splitting shots rang out behind me, momentarily stealing my ability to hear. Eden's blood-curdling scream shook me back into action. My arms curled under her body and I pulled her against my chest, sheltering her from the atrocity that was happening in the room. The smell of blood tainted the air, and a painful groan and a gurgling sounded from the floor beside the bed where I was sitting with Eden.

"I said don't fucking move," Douglas roared behind us. I shifted my gaze. Jeremy lay in a pool of crimson as blood seeped from his chest, and Chris hunched over him with a wound to his head. Neither was moving. A gun was in Jeremy's hand and a knife in Chris.'

"Ky," Eden said softly from her hiding place against my chest. Her voice sounded so distant, so foreign, so empty. "Ky, I . . . I can't hang on any longer."

I hated hospitals.

I didn't know whether it was the overwhelming smell, the promise of pain that hung in the air or the uncertain balance between life and death.

But right now I wouldn't be anywhere else.

The nurses had let me stay beside Eden without question. Even if they had tried to force me out, there was no way in hell I'd leave her.

It had now been twenty-four hours since I had seen the crystal clear blue of her eyes. I prayed every minute that she would open her eyes, squeeze my hand, do anything. But she remained still, looking like an angel against the crisp white sheets of the hospital bed as her hair fanned out beneath her.

Once we arrived at the hospital, Eden had been rushed through to be examined by a doctor; that had been the only time I was away from her. I had paced in front of the closed doors and waited. My parents, Eden's parents, Ashlyn, and Josh had tried to get me to leave and shower, but I refused. I was not letting Eden out of my sight. Never fucking again.

Douglas had turned up at the hospital two hours after we first arrived. He entered wearing a dark tailored suit, with his gun holstered back on his belt and a deep scowl on his face. I had known him my whole life, and he still intimidated the fuck out of me. If I were honest, I felt sorry for the people he interrogated.

He sat at the edge of Eden's bed as she lay sleeping, and flicked through her medical information before he informed me of what actually had gone down at the hotel. Douglas had made the call that Jeremy, with the knife he had pulled on me and a gun he had concealed in a suitcase, had the intent to harm his officers, as well as me and Eden. The moment Jeremy had moved toward us with the gun, Douglas fired his weapon without question. In his words, he "saw a direct threat to our lives and he wasn't taking any chances."

His final words, before he left the room, were simple and clear, and would be forever burned into my memories. "I did what needed to be done to give you two the life you deserve.

The kind of life without fear. It's the least I could do. Don't ask questions."

Eden

I SLOWLY ATTEMPTED TO open my eyes, but the throbbing in my left eye caused me to groan in sheer agony. My senses were overcome by the intrusive smell of disinfectant. My eyes finally pried open, and I struggled to gain focus. Everything around me was hazy. My brain switched on and went into overdrive. My eye hurt, a metallic taste still lingered on my tongue, and my body felt broken.

Panic reared to frightful life.

Jeremy! Where the fuck was Jeremy?

My body thrashed around in bed, my arms punching and legs kicking in grief-stricken fear. I needed to run and get away from him. I couldn't survive anything else. I had fought long enough, and I was too weak to continue. My husky throat rasped out a desperate scream which seemed to echo around the room. I just needed someone to hear me.

"Somebody get in here!" A familiar soothing voice laced with panic floated from beside me, allowing a flash of safety to hit me. "Somebody get the fuck in here."

Commotion sounded, and a thump of footsteps came toward me. A familiar thickness lingered in the air, indicating that there were numerous people around me. Fuck! He had a gang of people here. No! I clawed at the hand that grabbed my arm, while fingers laced so delicately with mine, too delicate to be a monster. I was confused. What the hell was happening? The sheet lifted from my aching body, and instantly I kicked my legs, wanting nothing more than to connect with whoever was taunting me.

I whimpered as a sharp jab hit my bare thigh and my body went into an aided bliss. A soothing calm spread through my veins, a calm like I've never felt before. I felt like I was being transported to a world of endless rainbows and beautiful cuddly clouds where everything was in a trippy haze. It was oblivion at its best.

"It's okay baby, I've got you."

That soothing voice again, the last sound I heard before I slipped back into the darkness.

I woke to the same overpowering smell of disinfectant, but this time my head felt lighter and, though my body still ached, it wasn't excruciating like before. My eyes crept open, and I took in the room around me. A drip connected to my arm provided me with the much-needed pain relief that swam through my veins. My fingertips brushed against the gauze on my head, and I realized I was in the safety of a hospital room.

My gaze landed on the mattress beside my hip, and my heart beat frantically in my chest. Perfect chocolate colored hair greeted my sight, and it was then that I realized an arm was lightly lying over my hips.

Ky.

I couldn't resist touching him. I needed to touch him to make sure this was real. I ran my fingertips through the softness of his hair and sighed as familiarity hit me. Ky stirred, and I felt his head shoot up and my hand fall back on the bed.

A moment of silence passed between us, and my stomach knotted. After he had taken in my injuries, his eyes glistened with tears.

"Hey," I said hoarsely and offered the best smile I could muster.

"Baby," he whispered, his voice laced with anxiety. "I thought I'd lost you."

"You won't get rid of me that easily."

"I was so scared," he choked out. My heart broke as a single tear ran over his cheek and dropped on the white linen sheet. His head fell back to the mattress, and he turned his face toward my body so I could still see his features. I lay there paralyzed with love and as his face fell, quiet sobs coming from deep within his chest.

Love.

During the pits of my turmoil at the hands of Jeremy, everything hit me.

I was in love with Ky Crawford.

It was something I never wanted, something I never needed, but now it was the one thing I craved. Ky wanted to give me his complete love; the kind of love that had the ability to erase every painful memory and wrap itself so tightly around my heart that I would never be alone again. His love was the light I would need in my darkest days. It would be the strength I craved when I was in turmoil. It would be the comfort that I required to overcome my new nightmares of Jeremy.

"Thank you for finding me," I uttered in a whisper, my fingertip tracing his jaw tenderly.

"I would have searched every inch of the world for you."

I closed my eyes briefly as the pain medication shot another blast of relief through my bruised body. I needed to know where Jeremy was. All I remember was passing out as craziness erupted around me in the hotel room. I remembered being in Ky's arms and, as soon as I felt safe, it was almost like my body realized it could shut down.

"Where is Jeremy?" I whispered, my stomach churning at the mere mention of his name.

"He's gone baby, he will never hurt you again," Ky spoke so strongly, with so much honesty.

"What?" I choked out breathlessly.

"Both of them were shot and killed on site. Douglas was protecting us."

I couldn't be sure how long we stayed silent. My hand gripped tightly on his arm, and his eyes never left mine. Jeremy was dead. I said those three words over and over in my head as I tried to come to terms with what exactly that would mean. I could live without constant fear. I would be able to walk down the street without looking over my shoulder or looking at the shadows, waiting for evil to appear. It would mean the opportunity to close the door that had been left wide open for four years.

"I'd never wish harm on someone, but knowing that he can never hurt me or you again feels so incredible." My head fell to the side, and for the first time in three long days, I felt my mouth curl ever so slightly into a smile. "I feel free."

The door of my room flung open, and immediately I was surrounded by my parents, Ashlyn, Josh, and Ky's parents. Ky quietly got out of the chair and went to stand by the window. My eyes traced his every step as I watched him shut down.

"Hey, pretty girl," Josh whispered as he kissed my forehead tenderly. "We missed you."

"Baby girl, oh my baby girl." Mom wrapped her arms around me so tightly that I gasped in pain. My dad simply nodded his head at me, and I knew that was his go-to move when his emotions were crippling him. Sue stood with Ashlyn and Josh, and I watched James walk over to his son. Ky fell into his father's arms, and it broke my heart. Dad's eyes traveled to where I was staring.

"How about we leave Eden to get some rest?" his gruff voice announced. Mom pulled her body away from mine, but not before flooding my forehead with kisses.

"I had prepared myself for the worst. I'm so sorry," Ashlyn whispered when she squeezed my hand. Her eyes were rimmed red, and her bottom lip trembled as she spoke.

"Do you really think you will get rid of me that easily? I need someone to go shopping and have drink cocktails with. Please go home with Josh and get some rest. I'll be home before you know it."

She nodded, then grabbed hold of Sue's hand and left the room. My dad and James followed, leaving just me, Josh, and Ky. Ky hovered at the end of the bed with his arms folded across his chest and a crease between his brows. I tore my eyes away from his as Josh stepped up beside me.

He leaned down so his mouth fell to my ear and he whispered, "I'm glad that fucker is dead. I'm glad we have you back, pretty girl. Ky was a fucking mess, it scared me. I thought I'd lost both of you."

"Thank you for taking care of him," I returned just as softly.

With a kiss to the side of my forehead, he moved away from the bed, gave Ky a pat on his back, and left the room, closing the door behind him.

"Is it okay if I hold you?" Ky whispered so tenderly from the foot of the bed.

"The thought of you holding me was the only thing that got me through," I admitted honestly.

Ky climbed onto the bed beside me and held me as closely as he could. Being in his arms again felt like absolute safety. I felt at home and a contented sigh escaped my lips.

"Eden, I need to ask you something, and it kills me that I need to ask this," he whispered into my hair as his face kissed the side of my neck tenderly.

He didn't have to ask. It was the question that had been hovering in the air since I woke. I had seen the question sitting behind his eyes every time he looked at me and it was the question sitting on the edge of his lips every time he spoke.

I turned my face and looked him square in the eye. "My body belongs to you, Ky. I would never have let him do that again. I fought anytime he got close because I only want to be yours. You were there with me the whole time, and you were the one I thought of when I felt like giving up. I fought for us, it's the only thing I could do. I was so scared, though. I didn't know if I would be strong enough."

"I didn't protect you, though." His voice choked with emotion.

"You protect me every single day, and I love you for that." My honesty filled the room and Ky's body finally relaxed beside me. I couldn't hold my feelings back any longer. Was it ridiculously soon? Whose right was it to judge? My love for Ky stemmed from his protection, his need for my safety, his desire to make me happy, to make me believe that I deserved to be loved. He was everything and more that I not only needed but also wanted. He would be my resolution, and I would be his redemption.

"I love you so much, baby. You are everything I want and more."

My tears fell freely at his declaration of love. His arms wrapped around me, pulling me closer to his firm body, the body that I knew would protect me until its last day on Earth. Peace was in my grasp, and it was all because of the man who loved and saved me.

"I want to go home, I don't want to stay here. I hate hospitals."

Within seconds, Ky had untangled his body from mine, slipped off the bed, and walked out the door. The emptiness hit me hard.

Soon enough, he was back in the room, and now had a doctor in white holding a clipboard close to his chest standing beside him. His face was familiar to me, and instantly I remembered him from all those years ago.

"I wish we were meeting again under better circumstances, Eden." Doctor Sully offered a weak smile, and his eyebrows furrowed as his eyes dropped down to the clipboard.

"Mr. Crawford has informed me that you are looking to be discharged?"

I nodded in response.

"Before we can get to that, we need to discuss your injuries. Would you like to discuss this in private?"

"No, I need him here." Ky grabbed my hands in his and sat in the chair beside my bed as we waited. "Please just tell me," I whispered.

His eyes dropped down to the clipboard in his hands. "You have bruising on your ribs, a cracked cheekbone, bruising to your face, and a cut on your forehead which required two stitches. You will have to spend the night here just so we can monitor you, but you should be okay to go home tomorrow morning. I am assuming that you have somewhere safe to go and someone to watch over you?"

"She has me, and she has my place." Ky stiffened in the chair and looked at Doctor Sully square in the eye. When he said the next words, I felt myself stop breathing. "I will take care of her. Always."

My heart trembled at his words. He wanted to take care of me, he was talking about forever. I squeezed his hand, lifted it to my lips, and lightly brushed his knuckles with sweet kisses. How could I ever thank him for everything he had done for me? His eyes met mine, and he looked at me like I was so breakable, but I knew this time I wouldn't break. Nothing could shatter me because I had my strength right beside me.

"You saved me," I whispered.

"Baby," Ky muttered in a thick tone.

"Ky, you saved me. Not just yesterday, but from everything. You made me live again, you made my heart beat again, you made me believe that I could love and be loved."

"You are the one who saved me. You don't realize what you've given me."

A cough sounded from the end of the bed. Doctor Sully looked at us and smiled.

"I am going to make you an appointment to see Doctor Evans while you are here. It will be good to talk to someone who knows your background."

I nodded at his suggestion of seeing the psychologist who helped me so much four years ago.

"But I think with this guy by your side, you are going to get through this okay. Make sure you two take care of each other. I can see something special there." Doctor Sully patted my leg and smiled sweetly, then turned and disappeared through the door.

"I think it would be a good idea to see Doctor Evans," Ky said softly. He stood from the chair he had been occupying for hours and slowly climbed back onto the bed beside me. I moved at a snail's pace and shifted closer to him, my head resting on his chest. My spot.

"I think so too."

"We can make an appointment before I take you home, but now I think you should get some rest," he whispered as he ran his fingers softly through my hair.

"Okay," I murmured as I felt myself slide into a deep slumber.

The day dragged on, and soon night fell as I dozed on and off. Ky stayed with me at all times. When the nurse came in for her afternoon and nightly rounds, I woke. Ky still sat in the chair beside my bed. He was frowning in his sleep, arms folded on his chest with a small pout on his lips.

"Your guy has been here since you came in," the nurse whispered as she checked the dressing on my forehead wound. "He is a modern day knight in shining armor. I've never seen someone as distressed as he was when he carried you in here."

"He is definitely my knight in shining armor." I smiled at the nurse and turned back to watch Ky.

I could and would watch him for the rest of my life.

KY

THE MOMENT I BROUGHT Eden home, I felt a shift between us. Our relationship was lighter, it was free, and it was unbinding. We spent our days on the couch watching movies, in the kitchen cooking, or playing endless games of Monopoly. We had locked ourselves away from the world, and it was everything we needed. We spent our time healing, loving, talking, and sleeping. After being stuck in the dark, my light was finally back, and she was shining like a diamond.

Eden continued to amaze me. For someone who had been to hell, not once but twice, she was living life with a new vigor. For the first time, she was making plans—she spoke of her dreams, her desires, and her needs.

While she was healing, I felt myself slipping.

Eden was the second chance at a life I had always wanted. She was my girl from the coffee house, my girl in the red jacket. She made me a better person, she gave me something to live for, to work for, and to love for.

She was my future.

It was as simple as that.

Yet I felt like I failed her.

I couldn't protect her.

"We really need to stop falling asleep on the couch," Eden groaned beside me. "I am aching everywhere."

I watched as she yawned and rubbed her eyes to life. She was adorable when she first woke up. My eyes traveled to the windows lining the far wall of the living room. It was sometime in the afternoon, and the sun had started to fade. I hadn't looked at the clock once since we got home because time didn't matter to us anymore.

"We have dinner with the parents tonight. I have to start sharing you with the world again." I kissed her neck softly, and her arm fell over my stomach lightly.

"I've loved that it's just been us." She rolled as best she could to face me. "I loved my Ky time."

Eden's bruises had started to fade and her rib was slowly healing, but when she would move too quickly or twist the wrong way, her face would grimace as pain hit her. I hated that I couldn't do anything about it. It made me feel weak.

"I'll go and run you a bath," I suggested and shifted my body off the couch carefully as to not touch her.

When I reached the hall, I turned back to look at her like I did every time I was away from her. It was instinct. I needed to make sure she was always in my sight; my need to make sure she was safe was sky high. Eden pulled herself off the couch and was now in the kitchen, tidying up from lunch. She looked perfect in my kitchen. She looked perfect in my bedroom. She looked perfect in my apartment.

Her soft hums filled the quiet space as she finished fiddling around the kitchen. I could watch her forever. The moment she turned toward the living room, her eyes met mine. The sweetest of smiles hit her lips, and she threw the dishtowel on the counter and made her way toward me. I watched her every step, taking in every sway of her hips. When she reached me, she grabbed my hands and brought them to her lips, placing delicate kisses on my knuckles.

The twinkle in her eyes danced, and she pulled me close so our bodies collided.

"Will you make love to me?" she whispered. "I miss my boyfriend making love to me."

"I don't want to hurt you," I admitted my deepest fears.

The thought of hurting her, of causing her pain, was unimaginable, and something that I didn't want to risk.

Eden pulled on our joined hands, and we made our way down the hall toward our bedroom. The moment we got home from the hospital, I had unpacked her things, and they now blended with mine in the drawers. My bedroom was now hers.

"You would never hurt me, Ky." She lifted the shirt she was wearing from her body and slid her panties down over her hips until she stood before me like a naked goddess. My eyes drank in her curves, the curves that had destroyed me so many times. My fists clenched at my sides as I took in her flawless skin that was still peppered with the bruises caused by Jeremy. My eyes slammed shut at the thought of him, like they did every time I would get a flashback of what I saw. I felt like a weak prick. She was healing and dealing with everything, and if anything, she had come out stronger than I could have ever imagined, but I was the one who was struggling with it. I lowered myself onto the edge of the bed and my head fell into my hands in defeat.

"Ky, look at me," Eden begged, her voice sounding from in front of me.

My eyes moved up her body until I met her desperate gaze. The light flooding the room illuminated her body, allowing her skin to glow like the moon dancing on the ocean in the dead of the night.

"I am yours, Ky. I've been yours since you screamed in my face at Delights and then bought me the best chocolate cake I've ever eaten." Her lips curled into a smile.

"I was half expecting you to tell me to fuck off and call me a caveman."

Eden's hands cupped my face and her thumb ran over my lips. "You saved me that night, Ky. And from that moment on, I've needed you, and I will always need you."

Eden pulled me up from the bed until I was standing before her. With confident hands, she slid her palms under my shirt, pulled it over my head, and threw it to where her discarded shirt was.

"I am beyond in love with you, Ky Crawford," she murmured as her lips fell to my chest, littering the space over my heart with sweet kisses. "I am completely yours. I need you to have me. I need your hands on me. I want your lips on me. I need you to erase everything. Will you do that for me? Will you do that for us?"

"I love you too, baby. I fell in love with you the moment those blue eyes met mine, from the moment you grabbed on to me in Delights, and when you gave yourself entirely to me. I knew then that my life would revolve around you and you only. I don't feel like I'm breathing without you beside me."

I crawled up the bed and collapsed against the cast-iron headboard, awaiting Eden's next move. Her eyes roamed over my bare chest before slowly and carefully following my lead and moving onto the bed. She straddled my hips and sat before me, every inhibition she'd ever shown was now extinguished. Her fingernails ran over my stomach, causing my muscles to clench, and my eyes fluttered shut under the sensation. Confident hands fell to my jeans, and she undid my buttons then slid my jeans over my thighs.

"I'm not Eden without Ky," she whispered into the air heavy with desire. "It's as simple as that. I don't just love you, Ky, it's beyond that. It's unexplainable. You've saved me. You've risked everything for me. You stopped living for me, and I am ready to live. I'm ready to give everything and more to you. You wanted me to learn to say no, but when it's you, every time it will be yes."

The moment she lowered herself onto me, I finally felt free. Her head tilted back at the sensation of us connecting in a way I've never imagined. This was freedom. This was pure and utter contentment. This was a new beginning.

Slowly she raised herself and moved her body so gently.

My hands fell to her hips as hers fell to the tops of my thighs. She would own this. She knew her limits and her desires. We made love in every sense of the word. Our bodies joined as one, and our breathing combined in a perfect slow dance, and we would never be the same again.

"Ky," Eden breathed out as she clenched around me. Pleasure soared through her and she exploded around me as I emptied myself inside her. "Please find peace with me," her breathless voice begged while her eyes pleaded with me.

"The way you are looking at me now, gives me the peace I have been looking for the past four years."

Epilogue

Five Months Later:

"**B**ABE, TOUR IS ALMOST done. Are you ready to go home?" Colby's deep voice probed beside me. My arms locked around his naked waist as the rumblings of the wheels connecting with the road below. The sound led me to a state of unconsciousness.

Home.

Four months on the road with my best friends had been an incredible experience, and I had seen places I'd always wanted to visit. I had the opportunity to meet some of the most wonderful and talented people and my bookings were back to back for the next six months. I was blessed. But being on the road was also a long time when you were completely and utterly in love with someone.

A month after the incident, as I now called it, I had been offered a job opportunity that I couldn't pass up. Four months as the photographer on The Fallen's North America tour. If I said that Ky wasn't excited, it would be an understatement. His protectiveness of me shot sky high, but once he and Colby had a somewhat heated discussion, he finally realized what this would do for my career. But it wasn't without stipulations.

Ky and I had made a promise that we would see each other at least once a month while I was on tour, and it was a promise that was never broken. Every visit was better than the last. It was intense, romantic, sexual, and each visit showed the raw need we had for each other. The best thing was that we had nothing hanging over us anymore. We had no lies, no secrets, no hidden demons, and no one waiting in the wings to destroy us.

I was completely his, and I loved every moment of it.

"Did you ever believe that we would both be here in love? Well, I'm in love, you are just in denial," I whispered against the warmth of Colby.

"Fuck no. Honestly, babe, I thought we were destined to end up together. We both have our demons, and I thought our demons would have won in the end, but I am so fucking happy they didn't."

"I would have been honored to have ended up with you," I whispered into the darkness.

"And I would have treasured the ground you walk on, baby girl." Colby tightened his grip around my waist as we fell into a comfortable silence.

"I love him so much," I admitted quietly as my thoughts instantly traveled to Ky.

"And you need to be with him," he countered.

Four days later, I rushed off the plane at JFK with a mass of excitement and eagerness. The moment my eyes landed on him, I felt my heart beat back to life. I knew I missed him and I knew I loved him, but seeing him standing there waiting for my arrival with a look of pure happiness on his face and a bunch of my favorite yellow roses in his hand was unexplainable.

I felt like I was the star in a romance movie and was running in slow motion as I made my way toward him. He met me halfway, and his strong arms encased my waist and lifted me from my feet, swinging me in the air, and immediately I felt at home.

"You're like my own personal romance movie," I whispered into his neck as I held onto him for dear life, suddenly never wanting to be away from him again.

"Fuck I've missed you!" he groaned before pulling my face to his and giving me a scorching welcome home kiss right in the middle of arrivals, not caring who was around us.

"And I've missed you." I giggled when he pulled away, leaving me completely breathless.

"These beautiful roses are for my beautiful lady," he said so sickly sweet that I knew my grin was huge.

His fingers entwined with mine as we headed out of arrivals. "I've got a surprise for you, but I need you to wear this," he instructed, holding up a blindfold in his free hand and sporting a cheeky grin.

"I've only just got you back, and you want to take away my ability to check you out?" I laughed as we headed toward the baggage claim and found my pink suitcase. As we walked to the exit, I tried quizzing him, but he wouldn't give me any hints. The warm summer sunshine hit me squarely in the face when we stepped out the double doors and headed for his Range Rover.

"There will be plenty of time to check me out, I promise. Now turn around," he demanded, twisting his finger around, motioning me to move.

"Where are you taking me?" I laughed as he secured a blindfold over my eyes and ran a finger along my jaw. It was beyond sensual, and immediately my body ignited with need and desire.

"Just trust me," he breathed huskily into my ear, sending a shiver of anticipation through my body.

For the next forty minutes, I sat beside him, shooting inquisitive questions as I tried to find out where he was taking me. He didn't give me anything, and I knew he loved every minute. His hand rested on my bare thigh as the sun continued to warm around us, his thumb tracing circles on my needy skin. My senses were on high alert, and the moment the speed reduced I knew we were off the freeway. My excitement was increasing by the second, and I was bubbling with eagerness.

"We're here," Ky announced as the car came to a halt.

The door opened and the feeling of being left alone in the car hit me. Time meant nothing, and now that I was blindfolded, I had no clue how long I had been sitting there. When the door beside me opened, I jumped.

"Are you ready?" Ky asked as he grabbed my hands and pulled me out of the seat. My senses went into overdrive as I tried to determine where I was. His hand went around my waist as he led me down what I assumed was a path. "Be careful, we are about to go up some steps."

Steps?

"Welcome home, baby."

The blindfold fell from my eyes and my gasp echoed through the empty room before me. Ky and I stood in a sun-drenched room with high ceilings, a beautiful fireplace, and a stunning view of the beach through a wall of windows. I was rendered speechless. I spun around, trying desperately to allow the magnitude of beauty around me to fill my mind. He linked my fingers with his, and as he pulled me through the rest of the house, I was at a loss for words. Three bedrooms, all with views of the ocean, a kitchen that would be fit for a professional chef, a bathroom with a large freestanding double bath, and two generous living areas greeted us.

"What do you think?" Ky asked as we stood by one of the windows in the spare room looking out over the Atlantic. His face was eager for my reaction.

"I'm at a loss for words. I don't understand," I admitted with shock evident in my voice.

His hands cupped my face, forcing my eyes to his. "I need you in my life, Eden. It's as simple as that. I love you with absolutely everything I am and everything I will ever be. This house is ours if you want it. This is a place where we can start the rest of our lives together, where we can come and spend our first night as man and wife. And this room right here, I thought it could be your studio until it becomes a nursery for our children. We can't live anywhere near the place that saw our worst nightmares so this can be the place to start our forever."

I tried to comprehend the words he spoke as my eyes searched his. I knew I wanted a future with Ky, but this was everything I wanted and more. He was offering the life I always dreamed of, and he wanted exactly what I wanted.

"You want to have babies with me?" I whispered as tears glistened in my eyes.

"Lots of babies."

"This house is for us?"

"Yes."

"You want to marry me?" My tears now fell freely over my cheeks.

"I cannot wait until you are known as Eden Crawford."

A knock on the front door startled me. The smile that flashed over his face made me believe he knew exactly who was there. God, I didn't think I could handle any more surprises. He grabbed my hand and led me back downstairs.

"This is part two of your welcome home."

The front door burst open and Tori came bounding through the house with Josh and Ashlyn following close behind.

"What the hell are you doing here?" I shrieked into my best friend's ear as we fell into each other's arms. Tears streamed down my face as my emotions erupted yet again. Another three sets of arms surrounded us, and there I was, standing in the middle of the foyer in the arms of Ky, Josh, Tori, and Ashlyn, crying my eyes out.

"How in the hell did you think I could live away from you?"

"What?" All sense of comprehension had been lost.

"Okay, I'll say this as simply as I can." She smirked. "Tori.

Moving. Here. To. Be. Near. Eden."

"What!" I shrieked. "You can stay here, we have so much room."

"Hold up, hold up! Eden, I plan on fucking you in every one of these rooms, so we kinda have to be here on our own," Ky's deep voice announced for everyone to hear. My cheeks flushed and the smirk on Tori's face said a thousand words.

"Jesus Christ, Ky. My virgin ears don't have to hear that," Josh taunted from beside me.

"Virgin my ass," Ashlyn muttered, and I couldn't help but notice the frown creasing her brow. What was going on there?

"I have offered Tori my apartment until she finds her own place," Ky announced, his arm falling around my shoulders. He never ceased to amaze me.

"God I love you!" I sighed and kissed him within an inch of my life, and I didn't care that we had an audience.

My afternoon was spent with my favorite people in my new home. Ashlyn and Tori were set on talking about the decorating we would have to do. They suggested colors and when Ky informed them of his idea for a nursery, I thought Tori's head would fly off her shoulders. Josh and Ky had been quietly watching as my two best friends' excitement grew by the second. I let them run with all of the crazy ideas they had. We had no furniture and no electricity, but I couldn't be happier.

Once night fell, Ashlyn, Josh, and Tori left, leaving Ky, me, and a bunch of candles. It was the most romantic scene of my life. I lay in his arms, my body humming from the unbelievable sex we'd had and my life flashed before me.

Then and now.

Before Jeremy and after Jeremy.

With Ky and without Ky.

I slipped out of Ky's arms as the first sign of morning fell into the room. I needed a moment alone to allow everything to sink in. I found his shirt and glided it over my naked body, then silently plodded out of the room.

My life hadn't been easy; there were times when I struggled to remember to breathe. But through tragedy came a new beginning. They say that the toughest things happened to those who the universe believed could handle it. I never imagined I could handle what I was dealt, but I had come to accept it. I had come to live with it, and I had come to survive it.

If I ever felt myself slipping back into my nightmares, I would think of this exact moment.

Right here.

I made my way back to what would be the bedroom I shared with the love of my life and leaned on the doorframe. I relished in the silence and the sight displayed in front of me. Ky lay where I left him with a smile playing on his face and the sheet sitting low on his hips. He was the epitome of perfection, and he was all mine.

Ky Crawford continued to surprise me. He saved me with every breath and provided me with a love I never knew I craved. Every single day he encouraged me to peel back another layer of myself, and he handed me the sledgehammer to destroy the final wall that I had been trapped behind for so many years.

I wasn't living until Ky Crawford came into my life, but now I was flying sky high.

Finally, happiness, contentment, and safety were mine.

I might have been his December.

But we would be each other's forever.

The End

Are you ready to be tempted by Josh Crawford?

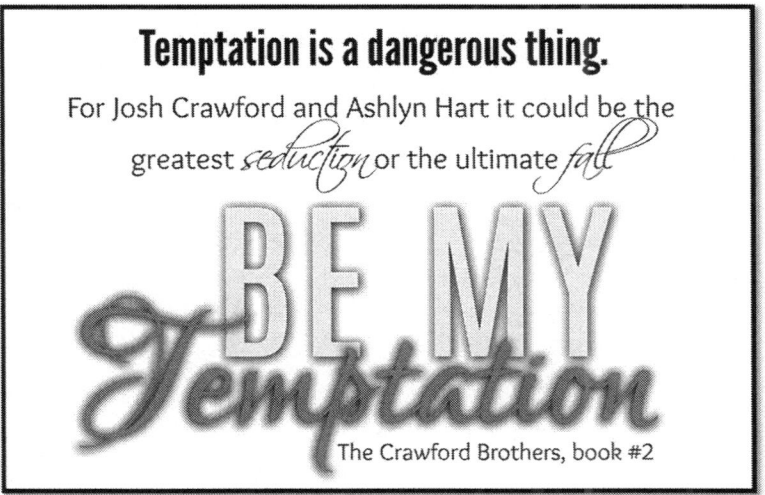

Do you want to be one of the first to know when
Be My Temptation is live?
Sign up here: http://eepurl.com/49BXD

Acknowledgements

Firstly I would like to thank *you*.

Thank you for taking the time to read my words, for your messages and emails, and spreading the word. I wouldn't be sitting here, writing my fourth set of acknowledgements without you. You have enabled me to live my dreams and for that I'm forever indebted to you!

My family for putting up with my crazy writing hours, for listening to me talk about characters like they are real people and for always encouraging me and supporting every decision I've ever made. You are my life.

To the greatest bunch of women I could have met. I am so thankful that this crazy book world has allowed me to meet some of the best friends a girl could ask for! You know who you are! Your support, your words of encouragement and your awesomeness makes every day so much more amazing.

Lyra Parish—Thank you for going through this story with a fine tooth comb and making me 'unclad' it! Your patience, attention to detail and love of Ky and Eden makes my heart swell and I am so happy to call you my friend. Thank you for everything and just so you know it's . . . Victoria's Secret.

Kendall Ryan—I love you. Thank you for your friendship and support. We connected from day one and my love and respect for you knows no bounds. See you in 2015! #Kenchell

The Bombshells—my amazingly awesome reader group. Thank you for the constant support, the laughs, encouragement and the visual inspiration! I could not do this without you all. You make me laugh, you create calm when I am working to deadlines, and you send me photos of Henry Cavill . . . what more could I ask for? #BombshellsForLife.

Jennifer—The editing maestro! Thank you for working

your magic with Ky and Eden. I cannot thank you enough for 'getting' their story and sprinkling your awesomeness all over it.

Jenny—Thank you for giving my words the chance to make sense and sticking with me during this crazy journey. We did it!

Ellie—You rock my world! Thank you for lending me your eyes and making sure Ky and Eden were able to shine bright.

Emma—Thank you for being able to squeeze me into your busy schedule and for giving Ky and Eden the final once over before they went out into the world. They are now ready for their big reveal.

Lauren from Perrywinkle Photography—You brought Ky and Eden to life in a way I could have never imagined and for that, I am forever thankful. Thank you for your friendship, our chats, our laughs and for being so amazing. I cannot wait to see what we come up with in the future.

Robin from Wicked by Designs—What can I say? Thank you for creating an absolutely stunning cover, I cannot thank you enough and I am so looking forward to working with you again.

Stacey from Champagne Formatting—You have made my words beautiful and I cannot wait to hold this book in my hands. Thank you for being you!

To my amazing beta babes; Derna, Wendy, Sam, Kristine, Kellie, and Lydia, thank you for taking Ky and Eden in their roughest form and seeing the story I wanted to share. Your encouragement made the story what it is today and I am so happy that you fell in love with them as much as me.

Finally, to every single blogger, reader and author that has connected with me, shared my links, liked my page, sent me a message or said a simple hello, THANK YOU for everything!!!!

About Rachel Brookes

Rachel Brookes lives on the east coast of Australia where beaches, kangaroos and surfers roam free. Writing angst-ridden love stories with a pinch of craziness, a dash of drama, a cup of romance, a spoonful of sexiness and delicious men to season is what she loves to do. Rachel sometimes forgets to eat, sometimes forgets to sleep and sometimes can't remember the last time she cleaned her apartment, but that's because she is in a long-term relationship with her laptop. When she does step away from her laptop, she spends her time with her amazing family or attached to her Kindle catching up with all of her favorite book boyfriends.

Connect with Rachel Brookes:

Official Website:
www.rachelbrookes.net
Rachel loves hearing from readers, you can find her here:

Facebook
http://www.facebook.com/AuthorRachelBrookes
Twitter
http://www.twitter.com/RachelBrookes_
Goodreads
http://www.goodreads.com/RachelBrookes
Newsletter
http://eepurl.com/49BXD
Instagram
http://www.instagram.com/all_things_rachel
Email: rachelbrookeswrites@gmail.com

Made in the USA
Charleston, SC
12 April 2016